T0146491

The City Beneath

The City Beneath

A Night Blood Novel

Melody Johnson

LYRICAL PRESS
Kensington Publishing Corp.
www.kensingtonbooks.com

LYRICAL PRESS BOOKS are published by

Kensington Publishing Corp.
119 West 40th Street
New York, NY 10018

All Kensington titles, imprints, and distributed lines are available at special quantity discounts for bulk purchases for sales promotion, premiums, fund-raising, educational, or institutional use.

Special book excerpts or customized printings can also be created to fit specific needs. For details, write or phone the office of the Kensington Special Sales Manager: Kensington Publishing Corp., 119 West 40th Street, New York, NY 10018. Attn. Special Sales Department. Phone: 1-800-221-2647.

Lyrical and the L logo are trademarks of Kensington Publishing Corp.

First Electronic Edition: April 2015
eISBN-13: 978-1-60183-421-8
eISBN-10: 1-60183-421-7

First Print Edition: April 2015
ISBN-13: 978-1-60183-422-5
ISBN-10: 1-60183-422-5

Printed in the United States of America

Acknowledgments

Thank you to my friends and family who never stopped believing in me, especially my parents, for always encouraging me toward the next conference; Carli, Stacy, Mere, Erin, Caroline, Katie, Michelle, and Lauren for listening, loving, and knowing how to have a damn good time; and Chrissy, for willingly joining me in over a decade of book talk. Thank you for listening through my earliest attempts at writing about damsels and dragons in high school writing workshop and for sharing the excitement of my romance novel addiction during hundreds of coffee dates. You are my partner in fiction.

Thank you to my teachers and professors who encouraged my progress, especially Miss Doyle and Ms. Ippolito, for igniting an inextinguishable fire inside me; Dr. Beery, Dr. Moses, and Dr. Ciabattari, for the support and immeasurable feedback on my first complete manuscript; and Hawkes, for ripping in when my writing was crap, highlighting when my writing was golden, and most especially, for believing in my vision.

Thank you to everyone I met along my writing journey, especially Jane Friedman, for recommending the most wonderful freelance editor in the world; Nicole Klungle, for being the most wonderful freelance editor in the world; Rita, for gabbing about our work, and more often than not, our hopes and dreams for our work; McCall, for sharing the experience; and thank you to the countless individuals, workshops, and speeches offered by New Jersey and Georgia RWA Conferences. You have immeasurably enriched both my work and my life.

Last, but certainly not least, thank you to the best boyfriend EVER, Derek Bradley, for loving me, and to Esi Sogah, for loving this book.

Vampires Bite in the Big Apple- notes from draft 1
Cassidy DiRocco, Reporter

I didn't need to believe in the paranormal to believe in monsters. I reported murders, rapes, assaults, and robberies every day: men strangling wives, women stabbing lovers, children shooting children. If someone had interviewed me last week—before I was attacked and bitten and manipulated in the pursuit of everyone else's personal and conflicting agendas—I would have said that the world darkened a little more with every sunset and turned a little more bloody and vengeful and uncaring with each passing day. But I'd also have said that after almost ten years in the business, I'm no longer surprised by anything I report.

If someone had interviewed me last week, it wouldn't have mattered how long I'd been in the business; I'd have been dead wrong.

Humans aren't the only murderers and rapists and thieves in this city; the real monsters—vampires and night bloods alike—have hopes and goals and desires just like the humans. But without the limitations of a fragile human body, the vampires achieve every goal and desire without consequence. Who can bring a murderer to justice if the murderer can't be arrested or detained? Who can testify against a rapist when the victim can't remember whether she'd been raped or mugged? Who can stop a crime spree when no one realizes crimes are even being committed?

No one, of course, except for me.

Even after everything this insane week has taught me about the world, this city, and myself, I'm still breathtakingly shocked by everything I've reported—and, most especially, by the one story I couldn't. . . .

Chapter 1

Last Monday

I nearly limped right past him, clouded by my own physical pain and the churning unease in my gut, but the rattling hiss that growled from the alley tripped my interest. I stopped walking.

The night was cool and quiet in the aftermath of sirens and flashing lights. My scalp tingled in response to the noise emanating from the alley, and I thought of all the things I should do: I should return to the main crime scene, I should finish my interviews, I should write my story and submit it to print like a good, reliable, by-the-book reporter. The hiss rattled from the alley again, but as I'd never been one to leave questions unanswered, I slipped a can of pepper spray from my brown leather, cross-body satchel and sidestepped into the alley to find the source of the noise.

What I found was a man, and the rattling hiss was his struggling, gurgling, uneven breathing. His entire body was ravaged by third-degree burns. Tucked into a shadowed alley between two buildings on the corner of Farragut Road and East 40th, he was crouched down as if warding off an attacker—perhaps in his case a flamethrower—and not moving. I cringed, thinking about the injury that was blocking his throat to produce such a horrible rattling. Maybe he was crying. Maybe he was just trying to breathe. I couldn't decipher his expression because his burns were so devastating. His face wasn't really a face anymore beyond the rough distinctions of a lump for a nose and a hole for a mouth. The unease churning in my gut all night bottomed out. I wouldn't have imagined that someone so injured could still breathe.

Trading the pepper spray for my cell phone, I dialed for Detective Greta Wahl.

"Wahl here." She answered on the fifth ring, just before I suspected my call would transfer to voice mail. "I already gave you a statement, DiRocco. Let the other sharks have a bite, will you?"

"I found another victim, G," I said without preamble.

"Alive? Where?" Greta asked, snapping from friend to detective instantly.

"A block up Farragut. He's still breathing, but he's different from the others. No bites." I swallowed the bile that clogged my throat like hot ash. "His entire body is burned to charcoal."

"Is he wearing a necklace, like the ones from last week? They were gold with a wolf pendant."

"I remember," I said. "And no, he's not wearing a necklace. And he's not shot execution-style like those victims, either. He's burned. This is probably a different case altogether."

Greta sighed. "Stay with him. I'll send a paramedic to you ASAP. It might be a few minutes, though. We've still got our seven victims being stabilized here."

"Got it. We'll be waiting." I hesitated a fraction of a second before asking, "Any one of our victims talking yet?"

"The few that still have throats haven't said a word. They're all in shock. It's not pretty down here, DiRocco."

"I know. Keep me posted, and send Nathan to me if you can."

"Will do," Greta said.

I ended the call and sat gingerly on the ground next to the man to offer what comfort I could and to give my arthritic hip the rest it needed. Injuries were supposed to heal with time, but the scar buildup on mine had only increased in the five years since I'd taken a bullet. The first stakeout of my career had set a high standard for my field performance, but it had also left a permanent reminder to listen to my gut. My hip ached on a regular basis, and lately, it would click and grind when put to excess use. After an entire day on my feet, interviewing officers and tracking down witnesses, my activities had apparently escalated way past excess.

Once I settled on the pavement, I held the man's left elbow—one of two visible patches of skin not blackened or blistered—and felt an overwhelming, humbling gratitude, no matter my past injuries or current residual pain, that none of these victims had been me.

According to the brief interview I'd snagged earlier in the night from Detective Wahl, my sometimes informant and longtime friend, seven other victims were still alive at Paerdegat Park out of the twelve or so they'd been able to identify. Most of them were in critical condition. I hoped Greta could send one of the paramedics here soon, and preferably my brother, Nathan, because he wouldn't tip my competition. If the victim's harsh, wheezing gasps were any indication, however, sooner rather than later might not even matter. I'd seen a lot of carnage at varying crime scenes through the years, but I'd never reported a recovery from injuries this severe.

My part-time nemesis and full-time boss, Carter Bellissimo, would chew my ass out for stepping away from the scene to comfort one of the victims. I'd have to race back to the paper, sift through my recorded interviews for quotes, slap the copy together, and make it to press before distribution. We'd be working against the wall, as usual, but I'd always adored the race and the adrenaline of breaking news. Meredith Drake, my photographer and sister (in love if not by blood or in-law), thought I was a little sick to enjoy the taste of only just making the wire. She took pleasure in lazily gazing at the world through her viewfinder. Nights like tonight, when the world was writhing and in pieces, I'd rather feel the pressure to write on deadline than capture a close-up of one of those ragged, bloody bite marks.

The victim next to me made another rattling hiss, the same agonized noise he'd been making with every few breaths. He wasn't visibly bitten like the other victims, but his wounds looked wholly more devastating. The only other body part spared from the burns was the left half of his chin, which, ironically enough, bore an old, healed scar. The scar was thin and pink, and it puckered slightly. It tore through his lower lip in a downward pull, and continued diagonally over his chin where it disappeared into the wreckage of his burned flesh.

A paramedic finally jogged to us from around the block, but I didn't recognize him. He was tall and lanky and very young looking—even younger looking than Nathan, which was hard to accomplish—but thanks to Nathan, I knew all too well that young looking didn't translate to incapable.

As the paramedic approached, he absorbed the scene; his eyes flashed over the victim's body and his surroundings, and eventually, his gaze locked on my hand holding the victim's elbow. I resisted the urge to pull my hand away.

"Detective Wahl said you called in a burn victim." The paramedic snapped on a pair of latex gloves.

I nodded. "Yes, that's what it looks like."

The paramedic knelt next to us, hovered over the victim with his ear over the man's mouth, and trained his eyes on the man's chest. He pressed two fingers on his charred neck. I winced. After about fifteen seconds of concentration, the paramedic straightened and sat back on his haunches.

"What the hell is this?" he asked. He didn't make any moves toward actually opening his equipment case. "We have live victims that need tending at the main crime scene."

I didn't like his tone, and on a normal night, I would react with a blast of attitude. My short-person syndrome wasn't becoming any milder through the years. If anything, turning thirty had completely eliminated my ability to tolerate most people. But this wasn't a normal night, so I played nice and swallowed my temper.

"Yes. Greta did mention that you were busy," I responded civilly. "I appreciate you coming away from the main crime scene to tend to this victim."

The paramedic shook his head. "This man's dead. You've got to return to the police barrier with the rest of the media."

The anger I'd doused flared in a sunburst. I took a deep breath against the words I wanted to say and spoke through clenched teeth, "This man is still breathing, and I'm farther behind the police barrier than any of the other reporters. I think I'll stay where I am."

"You know the drill, Miss . . ."

The paramedic waited for me to finish his sentence, but I just stared right back. Let him finish his own damn sentences.

He cleared his throat. "Look, I'm needed back at the scene, so if this is all you called me here for, I—"

"Are you going to help this man or not?" I finally snapped.

The paramedic stared at me like I was insane. "I told you; this man is dead."

I blinked at him and then down at the man whose elbow I was still holding. After a moment of silence, I heard it—a faint rattling exhale from a man who didn't have a nose to exhale with anymore. I shook my head. "He's been making noises. He's struggling to breathe."

The paramedic crouched to listen again with his ear over the man's mouth. He placed his index and middle fingers over the man's raw neck for a second time, but after another fifteen seconds of concentration, the paramedic shook his head. "The man is dead. He's probably been dead since before you found him."

"No, I've heard the noises. It's like a strained exhale that—"

The paramedic straightened away from the victim and placed his hand on my shoulder. "They do that sometimes."

I narrowed my eyes on his hand, and he pulled away.

"This man does not have a pulse," he said, sounding defensive. "He's dead."

I shifted my glare to the paramedic's face, but the man didn't so much as squirm. "He's dead," I repeated.

The paramedic nodded.

A rattle hissed from the man's chest again, louder than before. He didn't sound dead. He sounded in pain.

"Listen, I've got to get back to the scene, and I suggest you do the same before the police extend their boundaries and catch you tampering with their evidence."

I pursed my lips. "No problem. Where do we take him?"

"We're saving cleanup for the day shift," he said, already walking away. "We've got to get the wounded to medical as fast as possible, which means leaving the bodies for later, once the police finish processing the scene."

"Wonderful," I muttered, not appeased in the least. My story needed to be submitted by midnight; I had less than two hours until the paper was put to bed. It felt wrong to just leave, but deadlines were deadlines. I squeezed the man's elbow gently before letting go. I hoped the paramedic was right. I hoped the man was dead long before I stumbled upon him, and that he'd found a better place than this.

The man's chest rattled.

I stared at the man, hard. He'd been pronounced dead, and I had a story to write. That alone should have been enough to send me on my way, but staring at the scar on his chin, at the proof of a life lived before this burned hell, I couldn't simply leave him the way I'd found him.

I texted Nathan to bring me a backboard, and he appeared around the corner a few minutes later. His thick black hair was straight and identical to mine except for the cut. Where mine hung past my shoulders and was usually yanked back in a high ponytail, Nathan's was close-cropped at the edges and longer toward the top in a faux hawk. His nose ring glinted in the streetlight as he approached.

"That was fast," I commented.

"You've never texted me at a crime scene before, Cass, and I've never seen you walk away before Meredith was done with her shots. Today you did both. You're damn right I came fast." Nathan frowned. "Is it your hip again?"

"No," I said, which wasn't a complete lie. I'd left the scene because of my hip and my attitude, but I'd stayed away because of the man. "How is it down there?"

"Not good. Have you spoken to Detective Wahl?"

"Yeah, Greta and I had a little chat. If she thought an animal attack in the middle of Brooklyn was crazy, she won't have a clue what to make of him," I said, pointing to the man between us.

Nathan whistled. "None of the other victims were burned. Does he have any animal bites?"

"Not that I could tell, but I need you to take a look. The other paramedic wouldn't treat him, and he's still breathing, Nathan."

He frowned. "I thought that Donavan pronounced him dead."

"That's Donavan? Your partner?" I asked. At Nathan's nod, I snorted. "Donavan can't hear a pulse, but I—"

"If he doesn't have a pulse, then he's not breathing," Nathan said flatly.

"I can hear him breathing," I insisted stubbornly.

Nathan stared at me, hard. I knew that look. He was checking my pupils and watching my reaction, calculating the possibility that I was high. I hadn't abused painkillers in four years, and had, in fact, gritted through my hip pain during occasions when a Percocet was probably necessary because I never wanted to slip down that steep spiral again.

I gave him the look right back, annoyed that even after all this time, even after everything I'd accomplished, my brother was the one who still couldn't forget.

Nathan shook his head glumly and laid the board next to the man. "You know what's more ridiculous than checking the respiration of a man without a pulse?"

I shook my head, knowing he'd tell me with or without my encouragement.

"A trial for whoever is responsible for tonight."

I rubbed my eyes, beyond caring if my eyeliner was smudged to hell if I had to listen to Nathan's vigilante speech again. "Everyone deserves a defense. Everyone, no matter what they've done, deserves to tell their side of the story."

"You think there's another side to this story besides insane hate and violence?" Nathan asked, incredulous. "Someone should hunt these psychos down and tear off their limbs. Disembowel them like they tortured these victims." He glanced at the man between us. "Light them on fire."

"Murder does not justify murder."

"The hell it doesn't."

"Killing a monster isn't justice, Nathan. It only makes you a monster, too." I sighed. "Will you please check his pulse a second time? If you're killing anyone right now, it's me."

Nathan rolled his eyes.

"I know you don't believe me, which is why you're stalling, but like you said, I've never texted you at a crime scene before. I'm only asking for this one favor." I locked my gaze on his. "Please."

Nathan sighed heavily, but nevertheless, he squatted next to the man and pressed his ear to his chest. "If I had the opportunity to confront the people responsible for crimes like this, I wouldn't wait for them to confess their side of the story. I'd make damn sure they never—"

The man exhaled in a high, rattling hiss.

Nathan met my gaze, his eyes rounded with shock. "Oh my God."

"You heard it?" I asked, astounded.

Nathan bounded to his feet and unbuckled the backboard straps.

"I told you he was breathing. I told you that—"

"Fuck, don't just stand there. Help me board him!"

I ignored my hip and helped Nathan clip the man onto the backboard. "As much as I hate to say it, I can't help you carry him—"

"Hey!"

I looked up from the backboard straps and groaned. Donavan was jogging toward us, and if the frown creasing his brow was any indication, he had a temper to rival mine.

"What do you think you're doing? The police haven't processed this scene yet. You can't just—"

Nathan stood to face Donavan, and I finished snapping the buckles on my own.

"He's still breathing," Nathan whispered hotly.

Donavan paused, midrant. "What are you playing at?"

"You take his head. If we can get him back to the ambulance, maybe—"

"He's dead," Donavan said, shocked. "Why would we—"

"No, he's not." Nathan said. "We've wasted enough time, time we could've spent treating him. Help me get him back to the ambulance."

Donavan shook his head. "You're crazy. I checked him myself. He's been dead for a while, and I—"

Nathan leaned closer, so I had to strain to hear his next words. "Mistakes happen. Sometimes people notice and sometimes people don't. Cassidy and I noticed, but if you help me get him back to the ambulance, no one else has to."

Donavan stared back at Nathan, shock and anger giving way to fear as he realized that Nathan was serious. He looked down at me. I stared back at him, trying to convey that my mouth was a steel trap, but mostly, I felt wary. He looked back at Nathan, and I knew Nathan's expression as well as my own reflection. Even three years my junior, our shared grief and bitterness could line Nathan's face with an identical aged determination.

"He didn't have a pulse," Donavan whispered, but he bent in front of me and gripped the head of the backboard anyway.

Nathan and Donavan hoisted the man between them, and an ambulance met them curbside just as they turned the corner. I watched as the man was packed into its rear, locked in tight, and transported to the hospital in full lights and sirens. I'd originally wanted to achieve some distance from the gore and death—reminders of my parents that seemed everywhere lately—but as I limped back to the main crime scene, both my hip and my spirits only felt more burdened.

Meredith and I made print with an entire fifteen minutes to spare. The article flew from my fingers in hyperdrive, as was usual when faced with a perilously approaching deadline. I included a statement from Greta about the animalistic savagery of the attack, and Meredith found a shot of what nearly looked like a human bite had it not been so inhumanly wide or deep. The eyeteeth broke through the victim's skin, and blood pooled in the center of each impression.

I was reviewing my article and Meredith's picture when Nathan called with the bad news. The burn victim I'd found in the alley had died. He'd gone into cardiac arrest en route to the hospital and couldn't be revived. Nathan said that they'd brought him directly to the morgue, and I was sure that's where he'd remain until fingerprint analysis or dental records were completed. A next of kin would be contacted to claim him once he was identified, and then he would be their albatross. I rubbed my eyes, but even after five years, I still remembered every detail of the process.

I hadn't expected the man to live. I told as much to Nathan, and he repeated the same back to me, but I stared at the picture of that bite mark for a long while before I could finish editing my article.

With the paper put to bed, I was ready for bed myself, but I had an interview in four hours. As a favor to Greta—I was all for racking up the favors—I'd pitched a humanitarian piece to Carter about her cousin, the owner of a new bakery on Eighth Avenue. The article would certainly counter all the doom and gloom I'd been reporting lately, and frankly, I needed the pick-me-up. Carter hadn't been particularly impressed with my scoop, but he also knew the merits of a favor for Greta when he saw one and let it ride.

Jolene McCall, baker extraordinaire, was extremely excited about being featured in the paper, and even more excited for her grand opening. Her optimism was exhausting, but her miniature cupcakes were darling. She gave Meredith and me two each, and although one had been intended for the road, the little cakes hadn't survived that long. If our samples were any indication, Jolene's Cake Designs would be a finger-licking success, and if Jolene herself was any indication, she would spread joy along with her icing with every cake.

Back at the office, Meredith prepared a jaunty picture of Jolene in her tall, white baker's hat atop her tinsel-streaked, dirty-blond hair. She wore a pink-trimmed apron while balancing plates of cakes and pastries in various colors and patterns. I fluffed up the content with bakery puns to make the article light and sweet like the cupcakes themselves, so people would want to brave the murderous streets I'd depicted the day before for a taste of heaven at Jolene's Cake Designs.

I smiled as I stared at our edited work. I'd have to snag a few extra copies for Greta when it printed. We submitted our copy by five, and

Meredith convinced me that sushi was in order after the night we'd witnessed. I agreed, but that didn't prevent my body from powering down.

Halfway through my second California roll, I tried hiding a yawn behind my palm and nearly poked my eye out with a chopstick.

"Don't you dare cut out early," Meredith warned, waving her own chopsticks at me. "We did great. We deserve this."

"I know. I'm trying to enjoy it," I said, cramming my mouth with another roll before I could yawn again. The roll was tangy and salty from the soy sauce and damn good. Sleep would have been better.

"I *am* enjoying it," Meredith said, stifling her own yawn.

We stared at each other for a long moment, so beat that even sushi couldn't spark our energy. I almost felt like crying, I was so tired. Meredith giggled. I smiled, and she giggled harder, and suddenly we both burst out laughing.

"For the road?" I asked when the heaves had subsided, gesturing to my remaining five rolls.

Meredith nodded, wiping tears from her cheeks. "Jolene really did have the right idea."

"Some girls just know how to do it right," I agreed.

Once our server had boxed the leftovers, Meredith stood, using the table as leverage. "I'll see you bright and early."

"Yeah," I scoffed, ducking under the strap of my shoulder bag so it hung across my body. "I can't wait."

We parted ways outside the Japanese restaurant, still laughing from our moment of sushi insanity. Sunset was creeping later and later as summer approached; eight o'clock and the streets had just plunged into full darkness. The walk to my apartment, however, was only a few blocks and brightly lit from street lamps and storefronts.

I was one block from my apartment, deciding against doing laundry before going to bed but contemplating a glass of cabernet, when a black and glowing blue blur smashed into my ribs and slammed my back into the wall of the alley adjacent to my building. My head snapped back and cracked against the brick exterior. I couldn't move for a moment, dazed from banging my head.

Inexplicably, the first thing I noticed was my take-out box tipped sideways on the sidewalk, my California rolls spewed across the concrete. My awareness slowly pounded into focus like a jackhammer through my skull, and I realized that the blur that had hit me was a man. He was holding me off the ground against the wall by my arms, so we were eye to eye. A strange, rattling hiss vibrated from his chest. I could feel the purr of it against my body.

I couldn't look away. The man wasn't a man. Well, he was the general shape of a man, complete with a body, two legs, two arms, and a head, but something I couldn't quite account for—something crucial—was missing. He stared at me from inches away with icy white eyes ringed by a dark midnight blue. The pupils reflected a strange green tint from the streetlight as he cocked his head, studying me. The motion was almost bird-like.

His skin was flawless, the angles of his cheeks, chin, and jawline sharp, nearly gaunt in their severity. His face was hollow, but his body was unbelievably strong. When he hissed again, the lips sneered away from his teeth. I couldn't look away from the glint of the man's sharp, pointed eyeteeth and the thin, puckered scar pulling at his lower lip. The scar was raised and pink and continued across his jaw-line, stopping near his jugular.

"That was quite an article you wrote this morning, Cassidy DiRocco, although I was mildly disappointed not to have been mentioned."

He spoke, but my brain couldn't wrap itself around the deep, cultured voice that emanated from the man's fanged mouth.

"The police didn't include you in their statement," I replied shakily. "They considered you a separate scene, so I didn't include you in my article about the animal attacks."

"Fortunate for them," he said.

His nostrils flared on another rattling hiss, the same rattle I'd heard from him in the alley last night, and I thought numbly, *I was right. He was breathing.* I eased my hand along my side slowly, attempting to slide the pepper spray from the outside pocket of my leather shoulder bag. I should have carried it in my hand while I was walking. What good was having pepper spray in my bag if I couldn't reach it when I needed it?

Suddenly, he crushed me deeper against the brick, gripping my upper arms a fraction tighter. Talons protruded from his fingers and pierced my skin. I screamed.

"I don't like feeling grateful," he said, and the rattling hiss vibrated inside his chest again as he spoke. "But I wouldn't have survived another day if you'd left me at Paerdegat Park."

I shook my head, nearly panting from the sharp pain tearing

through each shoulder. "I don't . . . understand," I said haltingly. I continued shaking my head, staring with numb awe at the scar on his chin. "You're not possible."

He smiled indulgently. "How so?"

I swallowed. "You died before the ambulance even reached the hospital. They brought you to the morgue."

"Yes, and I thank you for that. You had impeccable timing."

"You were burned beyond recognition. They said you weren't breathing, but I could hear it. You were alive, but you didn't have a pulse," I said, starting to feel a little hysterical.

"No, I don't."

I didn't know how to respond to his lack of circulation, so I stared into his unearthly white and midnight blue eyes, feeling helpless. The sound of my own pulse beating through my ears was deafening.

He leaned in suddenly. I hadn't even seen him move. One moment he was staring back at me, and the next, within the span of a thought, his face was buried in my neck. I could feel his swift inhalation. He held his breath a moment, and his chest rattled as he finally exhaled.

"Your fear smells sharp and poignant, like cinnamon." He traced a slow, wet lick from my collarbone to just over my carotid. His tongue lingered over my pulse before pulling back. "Lovely."

I kicked out frantically, trying to land a blow between his legs, but my struggles were useless. He merely bared his teeth at me again in a sick semblance of a smile.

"Please," I asked. "What do you want?"

"I'll get what I want," the man said. "But I also wanted you to know that I *am* grateful. You saved me, so I shall return the favor."

My anger finally flared over the panic and pain. "I've never been saved before, so I could be mistaken, but I'm pretty certain that this doesn't qualify."

He stared at me a moment before grinning widely. Too widely for a human mouth. "Temerity becomes you," he replied. "Killing you, the photographer, the detective, and the two paramedics would be the easiest method of concealing my existence, but I'll take the time to . . . disarm the five of you instead. That is less efficient, more difficult, and time-consuming, but your life, and theirs, in exchange for having saved mine, is my gift to you."

I kicked out again, my knee in search of his groin. I opened my mouth to scream.

The man pulled me away from the wall before slamming me back against the brick—more ruthlessly than the first time, if that was possible. The breath punched out of my lungs along with my scream.

"Cassidy, look into my eyes."

I felt a sudden pull from the core of my being, desperate to look into the man's eyes. In defiance, I worked to fill my deflated lungs so I could prepare another scream.

"Cassidy DiRocco, you will look into my eyes *now.*"

The man's voice soaked through my resolve and drowned my brain. Unwillingly, I looked into his eyes. The moment his blue-and-ice gaze met mine, the pain and panic and fear leaked away. I felt my body suddenly go limp as it forgot to resist. My head lolled to the side, too heavy to support, and my expression sagged with the release of tension and strain. The physical world narrowed to his penetrating gaze on mine and my willingness to act on the breath of his next word, even as my mind shrieked at me to fight.

"You will write a retraction of the article about the deaths at Paerdegat Park," he stated.

Never! my mind screamed. "I will write a retraction," I murmured. My voice was compliant and monotone and not my own.

"The wounds on the victims were clean slices, from knives perhaps. Not animal bites," he continued.

"The wounds on the victims were probably inflicted by knives," I repeated, internally horrified. "Not animal bites."

"You never saw me burned yesterday, and you never saw me here today. If I ever have need to seek you out again, I will kill you."

My anger skyrocketed, breaking his hold on my mind. The pain and fear and adrenaline spiked through the mental fog, and I shouted, "You sick son of a bitch! If *I* ever see *you* again, I'll stab you through your fu—"

His gaze burned into mine again, and I drooped back into limp numbness. "Cassidy DiRocco, you encountered me neither here nor at the park!"

Fuck! "I never encountered you."

"Someone tried to mug you at knifepoint on your way home from dinner with Meredith. He stabbed you in the shoulder. You used your pepper spray, he stabbed you once more, and then he ran off with nothing more than having spilled your sushi. Your shoulders will heal without medical attention."

"I was mugged, but I don't need medical attention." *Dear God,* I thought, *he knows everyone I know and everywhere I've been.*

"There's a good girl," he growled. "Is anyone in your apartment at the moment? I would hate to leave you wandering the streets with armed muggers on the loose."

Yes, I have a six-foot-four, ex-linebacker husband and a trained, attack rottweiler waiting for me at home. "My apartment is empty," I droned, wanting to tear out my own throat.

He cocked his head slightly, no longer studying me but obviously studying something. He wasn't breathing or moving or even blinking. I realized after a moment that he was listening.

"Most people are eating in," he commented. "Something you should perhaps consider in the future when it's this late. Are you on the first, fourth, or fifth floor?"

"Fifth," I whispered. I couldn't tremble because my body was limp and pliant in his talons, but my heart clenched in a hard, shivering knot of dread. He was going to know where I lived. And I was going to be the one to tell him.

"Does one of your windows face this alley?"

"Yes."

"Perfect," he said, refocusing on me. His eyes bore into mine again when he spoke. "Tell me I may enter your apartment, and you may sleep."

"You may enter my apartment, and I may sleep," I gritted out smartly, and my eyes slammed shut. My body completely sagged, boneless, suspended from the wall only by his talons. My mind, however, remained awake. I felt the man dislodge his fingers from my upper arms and catch me against the front of his body. His claw-like hand pressed firmly at the small of my back, clamping me to him. He crouched forward for a moment. My head lolled back. The rattling hiss in his chest intensified, and I felt his breath move over my throat, the side of my neck, behind my ear. He smelled inexplicably like Christmas, like soft pine next to a hearth. His teeth grazed the slow, calm beat of my pulse. In my mind, I screamed and fought and died with my spirit and dignity intact. In reality, I lay bent back over his arm, immobile and defenseless.

The man suddenly sprang from his crouch. My stomach bottomed out from the movement, and I felt a swift rush of wind against my face as if he'd leapt into the air, but gravity did not pull us back down.

I heard the quick slide of a window opening and smelled the vanilla lime scent of the candles in my fifth-story apartment bedroom. His footsteps tapped on my hardwood floors, and I realized that the man must be wearing dress shoes. How his shoes could ever matter after all this, I didn't know; I just found the thought of him wearing dress shoes, like his voice, at odds with the sheer animal of the man himself.

He laid my body down on the bed. My head dropped at an uncomfortable angle that constricted my breathing. I heard myself wheeze. He cupped the nape of my neck and positioned my head on the pillow at a more natural angle. His fingernail scraped across my hairline to my neck. I felt his thumb caress the skin under my ear as he lingered.

The man's breathing suddenly turned ragged, and his hand disappeared. "Good night, Cassidy DiRocco," he said. I felt the air whoosh around me as he disappeared. The window snapped shut, and my room felt still and silent and peaceful in his absence.

The moment the man was gone, however, my body sprang to life. Everything returned in an overwhelming rush—the fear, pain, panic, adrenaline, and control—and my throat constricted with the aching burn of tears. Trembling and weak, I pulled my leather bag across my chest. I kept my eyes trained on the bedroom window with steady obsession, bracing for his reappearance, but even after what felt like an eternity, he didn't return. I dug the phone from my bag and dialed 911.

The moment that dispatch answered, I whispered shakily, "I need to report an assault. I've just been attacked outside my apartment on 346 East 29th Street. And hurry. He may still be nearby."

Chapter 2

"What the hell is this?" I asked, slamming the door to Carter's office and slapping the morning newspaper on his gleaming wooden desk.

Last night had been excruciating. I'd been out until well past midnight, giving statements at the precinct and waiting in Emergency at the hospital for stitches, X-rays, and antibiotics. Between the sharp ache in my shoulders from the stitches and the constant grind of my hip, it took more willpower than I liked to admit not to pick up the Percocet the ER doctor had prescribed. I took Tylenol instead, pretended it was helping, and lay in bed with my eyes open until my alarm buzzed.

For the first time in the seven years I'd lived in my apartment, I locked every window frame and snapped open every window stop. Five stories high, the only entrance that I'd ever bolted was my front door, but lying in bed with only plastic window locks and snaps between me and my attacker, I couldn't fall asleep. It took less than three minutes to guilt my landlord into buying fortified window locks for my apartment. He'd been expecting my call. The police must have interviewed him, too, because he'd already called the smith and assured me that locks would be installed that afternoon.

With my apartment taken care of, I had fully intended to rest and recover and take care of myself—I swear I would have—until I read the morning paper. A retraction had been printed on *my* headline about the seven deaths at Paerdegat Park, discrediting that the victims had suffered from animal bites. The article stated that an animal attack wasn't even being investigated, that the wounds on the victims were clean slices, likely from knives.

I stared at the paper, shocked. A byline didn't even credit the retraction to anyone. Who would write this garbage, and how did Carter let this bullshit slip past his radar? I called Meredith, but she didn't pick up. Nathan forwarded my call straight to voice mail—the bum—so I tossed my leather bag gently over my shoulder, gripped the pepper spray in my hand as I left the apartment, and caught a taxi to confront Carter himself.

"You don't see them very often, DiRocco, but the rest of us mortals know them as retractions," Carter said dryly.

"This story did not need a retraction," I said, poking the paper on his desk with my index finger. "Every single word of it was true. I saw it firsthand. *Especially* the bite marks."

"You're pushing your luck here. The police are breathing down my neck because of you, so I don't need this bullshit."

"The police gave me that quote! I have a picture of the bite mark. We used it in yesterday's article for heaven's sake, and Meredith took the picture herself. Ask her."

"I did. She wrote the retraction herself."

I pulled back, stunned. "She what?"

"She apologized, said she had no idea what the two of you had been thinking, blamed it on some bad sushi, and printed the retraction this morning."

"We didn't have sushi until afterward. Did you see the picture?"

"I didn't see any damn picture of any damn bite mark."

"Yes, you did. You approved it. Where's your paper from yesterday?" I asked, glancing around the office. "I'll just *show* you."

"There was no picture."

"Prove it. Show me yesterday's paper, and show me that—"

"Are you telling me that I don't know my own paper?"

"No. I'm telling you that there's been a mistake, and it wasn't from me. We printed the picture—"

Carter held up a hand for silence. "There was no picture," he repeated, his voice final. "It's your first retraction in the eight years you've worked for me. I would actually take pleasure in your mistake if it wasn't such a high profile case." He gestured with his hand as if setting a headline, "The great Cassidy DiRocco makes a retractionable error! Stop the damn presses!"

"Carter, I—"

"Don't let it happen again, DiRocco, or you're fired. Get the hell out of my office and rest so you can return tomorrow with something credible to write about!" Carter shouted after me, and he slammed the door firmly shut.

I stared at the closed door, stunned. I'd never been kicked out of Carter's office, not even as an intern. Not that his antics weren't a common occurrence, but they had never been directed at me. I was efficient and ruthless and scrupulous, and my articles did *not* need retractions.

According to Deborah, our administrative assistant, Meredith left for home directly after submitting the retraction, still suffering from the lingering effects of bad sushi, but I had a hunch that her illness was actually the result of an impossibly strong, fanged, ruthless man who seemed hell-bent on coercing retractions from seasoned reporters. I gave up on Carter for the moment and left the office to do what I did best: prove my hunches right.

On my way to Meredith's apartment, I bought a tub of chicken noodle soup and flaky biscuits at the market. If she'd lived through the same night I'd lived through, her body would be aching and sore, too. We needed comfort food.

A taxi dropped me off in front of her apartment. I walked to the entry and pressed the Call button on the intercom, but no one answered. I pressed it six more times.

Meredith finally picked up. "When someone doesn't answer, it usually means they don't want to be bothered," she snapped.

"Nope. It usually means that someone is avoiding my questions."

"I don't feel well, Cass. That sushi—"

"Excuse is bullshit, but I can play nice. I even brought soup."

Meredith paused. "From the market."

"Yep."

"And biscuits."

I smiled. "Of course."

"And you won't ask any questions," Meredith pressed.

"I said that I'd play nice."

"That's not quite the same."

"No, it's not. If I said otherwise, it'd be a lie. Hurry up. Your soup is getting cold."

She buzzed me in.

I tried not to ambush her with questions and accusations the moment I crossed the threshold because, as I'd suspected, she looked as worn and bruised and beaten as I felt. We bundled down on her oversized couch to relax, but once we'd finished the soup, I couldn't contain myself.

"You were attacked last night, too," I said, biting into my second biscuit.

Meredith opened her mouth.

"I can tell. You're mincing around this apartment like you're walking on glass. You're bruised, aren't you?"

"I was just mugged." Meredith nibbled on her biscuit. "Nothing like what you went through."

I bit into my biscuit and shook the remaining half at her as I spoke. "You let that man bully you into writing a retraction, Meredith. How could you? At the very least, you should have talked to me, so I could have talked you out of it."

Meredith blinked, pausing with a flaky chunk of biscuit halfway to her mouth. "What?"

"We need to dig for the significance of the bite marks," I mused. "Maybe he's left behind DNA on one of the victims."

"Cassidy, honey, I don't have a clue what you're talking about. What does the man who mugged me have anything to do with the deaths at Paerdegat Park?"

I trained my hard, alligator eyes on Meredith. "Did the man who attacked you demand that you write the retraction?"

"No, not at all." Meredith said, looking confused. "Why would he? He was interested in my purse, not my profession."

I frowned. "What *did* he say, then?"

Meredith laughed. "He didn't say anything! He mugged me, Cassidy. He sidled behind me on the sidewalk, knocked me to the ground, took my purse, and ran off. He wasn't very verbose."

"Then why did you write a retraction?" I asked point-blank.

"I wrote a retraction because we were wrong. You would have left the lead about the bite marks in the article knowing there were no bites?" Meredith asked, shocked. "The wounds on the victims were clean slices, probably from knives."

"That lead isn't wrong! There *were* bite marks on the victims! Who told you they were knife wounds? The man who mugged you?"

"No," Meredith insisted. "Detective Wahl called me this morning. She didn't want to disturb you after you were attacked, but she's pissed. She has no idea why you quoted her about the bite marks because there aren't any. She asked me to write the retraction."

"That's impossible. We have pictures of the bite marks. You took them, for Christ's sake!" I narrowed my eyes on Meredith as what she said fully processed. "Why did Greta feel like she could disturb you after you were attacked, but not me?"

Meredith took a slow, deliberate bite of her biscuit.

I slammed my spoon down on the end table, disgusted. "You didn't report the mugging."

"He didn't even take anything! It wasn't worth the bother or the paperwork," she said.

"I thought he took your purse," I countered.

"I, well." Meredith frowned as she stammered, looking confused. She turned her head, and I followed her gaze to her black, cloth and glossy leather Coach handbag sitting on the counter. "He tried to take it," she said finally, turning to face me. "I was a little shaken, but really, it's not a big deal," she said.

I covered my face with my hands. "I can't believe I'm hearing this from you right now. We see this nearly every day! Women beaten. Women mugged. Women assaulted. They don't report it because they're scared, which is why you wrote the retraction. He bullied you into writing the retraction, just like he bullied you into not reporting his assault. Admit it."

Meredith pursed her lips. "I just told you, my mugging has absolutely nothing to do with the retraction I wrote."

"It's all right to be scared," I said gently. "I'm scared, too, but you can't just give in. You can't just let this ride. He's a murderer. He could be a cannibal, considering the bite marks!"

"I'm not giving in to anything," Meredith said, exasperated. "And there were no bite marks. Why won't you believe me?"

I sighed. "Do you have yesterday's paper?"

"Of course." She stood, shuffled to the kitchen to retrieve yesterday's paper, and eased herself back on the couch.

"This is why I don't believe you," I said, pointing to the zoomed, color photograph on the front page. "There were bite marks on the bodies. We were there. We saw them ourselves with our own eyes. I wrote about them, and you shot pictures of them. Greta gave me a statement, which I have on record about them." I shoved the paper into Meredith's hands. "The bite marks were real. What's unreal is how everyone suddenly doesn't remember them. Carter approved the pictures and carries the paper on him like a minister does a Bible, but he doesn't remember them, either. He wouldn't even check yesterday's paper to prove himself right."

Meredith gaped at the photo, fisting the edges of the paper in her hand as she studied the undeniable truth of those bloody imprints.

I crossed my arms. "You tell me what I should believe."

"Greta called me. She said there were no bite marks, that we got it wrong," Meredith squeaked, still staring at the paper.

"When do we ever get a story that wrong, Meredith? Why didn't you check yesterday's paper? Why didn't you look at the photo?" I asked, tapping the paper for emphasis.

She shook her head. "I don't know. I didn't even think to check the paper."

"You took the photograph yourself!"

"I don't remember taking this photo. Why wouldn't I remember that?" she whispered.

"I don't know, but the man who attacked me didn't want me to remember him, either. He didn't want me to remember the bite marks, and he wanted me to retract the article, too."

Meredith finally looked up, stricken. "What does that mean, that he didn't *want* you to remember?"

I opened my mouth, so angry about the retraction and at Meredith for writing the retraction and at the man for threatening Meredith that I almost blurted out everything that had happened the night before. I thought of how the man had controlled my mind, and it made me want to scream. I remembered how his fingers had transformed into talons and pierced my shoulders. I remembered the sharp threat of his fangs. I could still see his strange, icy eyes boring into mine, forcing me to say and do exactly as he commanded. I remembered everything despite the fact that he'd told me to forget, and I realized that he'd likely done the same to Meredith. The only difference was, she *had* forgotten. She would never believe me if I told her everything, and I'd only put her in grave danger if she did. I snapped my lips shut.

"I don't know," I whispered. "He was just adamant that I write that damn retraction."

"But you didn't," Meredith whispered. "I did."

I placed my hand on her knee. "What did your mugger look like?"

"I'm not sure. I didn't get a very good look," Meredith said, sounding strained.

"Well, what color eyes and hair did he have? How tall was he?" I asked.

"I don't remember."

"You don't even remember how tall he was?" I asked, incredulous.

Meredith shook her head. "Carter said that my memory might have been paralyzed by shock. I'm honestly not clear on any of the details about what happened. Everything seems vague and hazy. I'm just not sure, Cassidy." She sighed. "What did your mugger look like?"

"He's over six feet tall with styled black hair, longer at the top and faded at the sides," I said, hoping to jog her memory. "His pale blue eyes were even paler than mine, almost white except for the deep blue ring around his irises. He had pale skin with a scar across his lower lip. And he had, well," I hesitated to admit, "he had fangs."

Meredith raised her eyebrows. "He had *fangs?*"

"I don't know for sure if they were real or filed," I said hastily, "but my gut is telling me things about him that can't possibly be true."

"Your gut is never wrong, Cassidy."

"I know, which means that I'm either going crazy or the world is."

Meredith scoffed. "If it's you against the world, you win every time."

I remembered the man flying through the air to my fifth-story apartment window as I lay helpless and immobile in his arms from drowning in his gaze. I shook my head reluctantly. "I wouldn't place your bets just yet."

Leaving Meredith's apartment with more questions than answers, I decided to take said questions and yesterday's paper to the root of the retraction, Detective Greta Wahl. As unbelievable as it seemed for Meredith to write the retraction, it seemed even less likely that Greta would request one. I stepped into the precinct and was struck by the usual pungency of coffee and sweat. The overhead fans were spinning off their screws, but until the air-conditioning kicked in, their efforts were just moving hot air.

I recognized most of the officers from taking statements about cases, and a few of them had responded to my call last night. Two of them nodded their heads at me, and I mustered a smile in return, feeling an awkward combination of gratitude and embarrassment. I requested a short meeting with Detective Wahl, and one of the officers I recognized from last night encouraged me to take a seat.

A man was waiting in the lobby, as well. His legs looked unnaturally long as they bent to accommodate his large, lean frame in the short-legged wooden chairs. He wore a tightly fitted black T-shirt over faded jeans tucked into cowboy boots. The boots were faded from wear. Water and mud had stained the edges a darker brown than the rest of the boots, but the detailing along the shaft was impressive. The man's curly blond hair was springy, like doll hair, and bobbed slightly on his head as he glanced up from his magazine at my approach. His velvet brown eyes were kind and discerning. He smiled, and a dimple charmed his left cheek.

I raised my eyebrows to acknowledge his smile, sat in the row across from him, and crossed my arms. The stitches in my shoulder throbbed from the movement. I uncrossed them to relieve the pressure and slipped yesterday's newspaper from my leather shoulder bag to keep my hands busy.

The man set his magazine back on the table. "It really turned out to be a beautiful day outside. Finally, after all this rain, we could use a bit of sunshine."

I ignored him and his charming drawl, hoping someone else in the waiting room would respond. I shifted in my seat, and my hip fired a sharp burst of pain down my leg.

The man leaned forward. "You all right, ma'am?"

Even without attention, he wasn't giving up. Reluctantly, I met the man's concerned gaze. "Fine, thanks." I shook open the newspaper and pretended to read Carter's article on price-gouging gas stations.

"You read the front page article?" the man asked.

I peeked over my paper and nodded.

"What did you make of it?"

I shrugged. "Not much, considering the press can't decide whether the attack was animal or human. Today's retraction seems strange, though, after yesterday's photo of the bites," I said offhand, waiting for him to respond like Carter and Meredith had responded, and say *what photo?*

The man whistled. "That photo was somethin'. Animal attacks are rare in these parts. I was lookin' forward to gettin' a closer look at those bites, but if there's any credit to this mornin's retraction, it seems as though I made this trip into the city for nothin'."

I let the paper drop to my lap. "You saw the front page photograph in yesterday's newspaper?"

The man nodded.

"And you remember the animal bite?"

"Of course. That's a very vivid photo. How could anyone forget?" the man asked, but his gaze sharpened on me, as if the question wasn't rhetorical.

"How indeed?" I refolded the paper and tucked it back into my shoulder bag. "And what did you say your name was?"

The man smiled broadly, and his dimple deepened. "Ian Walker, environmental science expert, at your service, ma'am. Call me Walker. Everybody does. And you?"

I took his proffered hand, and his fingers enveloped my entire palm in a gentle but firm shake. His hand was callused, dry, and gigantic, but everyone's hands were gigantic compared to mine. Not everyone shook mine like they weren't. "Cassidy DiRocco, reporter for the *Sun Accord*: Shining light on Brooklyn's darkest secrets." I winked.

"That's not your slogan," Walker said, laughing.

"No, and it shouldn't be, not after that retraction," I said, pointing to his paper.

Walker's smile froze, and then he pointed at me in recognition. "You wrote that very article."

"Guilty as charged," I admitted.

"But not the retraction."

"Not the retraction," I said flatly.

Walker leaned toward me, resting his elbows on his knees. "You think there's still hope they'll need my expertise? Detective Wahl called me in as an expert witness last night, but this mornin', she called me off the case."

I forgot my stitches and shrugged. Holding back a wince of pain was impossible. "You'll determine what or who ate from the bodies by examining the bites?"

"If there are bites on the bodies, I sure will, and if it's an animal, I'll find the critter and relocate it. Are you sure you're all ri—"

"There are bites on the bodies," I said dryly. "Without a doubt."

"Accordin' to the paper's retraction and Greta's phone call, there's doubt."

"Then why did you come?"

"There's certainly somethin' interesting about bodies havin' animal bites one day and not havin' them the next. The way I figure it, the good detective can fire me face-to-face. She'll have a bit of explainin' to do about how the images she sent me for review are no longer the wounds on the victims." Walker rubbed his bottom lip with his thumb. "You saw the bites yourself?" he asked.

I nodded. "Yes."

"Then why did someone write the retraction?"

"There's been a"—I bit my lip, attempting to find a delicate phrasing—"a miscommunication between departments. That retraction was a mistake and should never have been printed."

"A miscommunication that you intend to correct?" Walker asked, his lips twitching in a smirk.

I grinned. "You know me so well, so soon. And you came all the way here from . . ."

"The southern tier. Erin, New York, to be specific, ma'am."

"Welcome to New York City. And you can quit the *ma'am*s. If I'm calling you Walker, you're calling me DiRocco. Everybody does," I said, smiling.

Walker nodded. "DiRocco it is."

I leaned forward. "I'll tell you what: You let me speak to Detective Wahl first, and I can guarantee that you'll be examining the bites on those bodies by this time tomorrow."

Walker flashed a little dimple. "What makes you so certain that you can change Detective Wahl's mind? Either there's bite marks on the bodies or there ain't, and the last I heard from Detective Wahl, there ain't."

"Detective Wahl has been misinformed. If you'll be able to identify the bites—"

"I certainly will."

"— then we certainly need you. Let me take care of Detective Wahl."

Walker sat back with an amused expression on his face. "By all means."

When the desk clerk told Walker that Detective Greta Wahl would see him, Walker let me go in his stead. Greta was a curvy woman, but she looked bulky from the secondhand blazers she wore. Her wavy brown hair was slicked back in a tight bun at the back of her head, her usual updo while on duty. I'd felt ashamed the first time I saw her off duty and realized how pretty she really was, all soft curves and curls. I'd mentioned it once, and she had responded that gender neutrality was the point. If she wanted to be a hard-ass cop, she had to look the part; hard-ass cops didn't have curves and curls.

When Greta saw me and not Walker coming toward her, she grinned. "It's not like you to charm anyone, but it *is* just like you to get your way. I don't know why I'm surprised."

"Me, not a charmer?" I smiled back. "I'm offended."

She passed me a steaming cup o' joe and let me take her seat while she sat on the corner of her desk. "How are you feeling?" she asked.

I sipped the coffee. "Not great."

"Are you seeing a specialist about that hip again?"

"What do you know about my hip?"

"I know that you're limping on it," Greta pointed out.

I sighed. "I've had a rough night. Look, G, I need to tell you something that you're not going to like, that you won't even believe until you see all the evidence. Hear me out before you kick me out of the precinct, will you?"

Greta raised her eyebrows. "When you put it like that, how could I refuse? What do you have for me?"

I slapped yesterday's newspaper on the desk in front of her and pointed at the picture. I'd only just opened my mouth when she started shaking her head.

"Now, Cassidy—"

"Detective Wahl, you just promised to hear me out."

"*Detective Wahl?*" she asked, grinning.

"You had that tone. Your 'please escort her out of the building' tone," I said.

Greta gave a megawatt smile. "Cassidy DiRocco will never get kicked out of this building, I promise you that, no matter what kind of paper she slaps on my desk. We have your picture by the water-cooler, so the rookies know who to give statements to."

I shook my head. "Infamy will only carry me so far. This story may be that breaking point."

Greta glared at me. "There is no breaking point when you save a uniform. You had our back, and we'll always have yours."

"I'll remind you of that in a minute," I warned.

"Quit the foreplay, and make a move already."

I nodded. "Look at the picture."

"Uh-huh," Greta said, looking.

"What do you see?"

Greta sighed. "I don't know where you got this picture, but there were no—"

"This picture, along with dozens of shots, were taken by Meredith at Paerdegat Park Monday night," I stated.

"There was not an animal attack at Paerdegat Park. The slices were clean, like knife wounds."

"The pictures—"

Greta shook her head, looking regretful but determined. "I don't need to see the pictures, DiRocco. We have our own photographer on staff. I was there myself, and there were no bite marks on the victims."

"What if I told you that you told me yourself, in person on Monday night, that there were bite marks on the victims?" I asked, tapping the newspaper with my nail.

"I would ask you to show me proof," Greta said.

"Exhibit A, my recorder," I answered, whipping out the recorder from my shoulder bag.

Greta blinked, and for a fraction of a second, she looked worried. "Then I would say that we were all going crazy, because I know beyond a doubt that I never confirmed bite marks on those bodies. I saw the bodies myself, and they were slashed by knives. I never would have called for a retraction if I knew otherwise."

I hit Play on the recorder. The husky rasp of my voice catalogued the date, time, and location before I asked a few of my standard questions about the case. Greta's warm, honeyed tone flowed from the speaker, answering each one in turn.

Eventually, I asked, "Have you ever seen a case like this, Detective? Should people expect more of these crimes in the future, or do you suspect this slaughter is a onetime occurrence?"

Greta's rich, alto voice unmistakably answered, "That's hard to predict, DiRocco. We haven't experienced a case like this since I've been on the force. I'd suspect an animal attack if we weren't smack in the center of Brooklyn. We'll have to confirm with the local zoos before we can determine anything further, but without an animal to blame, we may be looking at human bites. An environmental science expert will be consulted to confirm the bite origin, and at that time, we'll be able to take precautionary measures either way. Locals should be aware of their surroundings, especially at night. Keep to well-lit areas, and stay in groups."

My voice came on again, asking further questions, but I stopped the recorder.

"I never said any of that," Greta denied, looking pale. "I wouldn't have spoken about animal bites, and I certainly never intended to confirm 'bite origin'."

"I believe the environmental science expert in your waiting room would say otherwise."

"DiRocco, what the hell is going on?"

"That's what I'm trying to find out." I sighed, knowing that she would never believe the truth about the man from last night and his strange ability to control people's minds. Hell, I couldn't quite believe it myself, but maybe if we dug just a little deeper, we could find the source of the animal attacks and prevent another massacre.

"Have any of the autopsies been completed yet?" I asked.

Greta nodded. "Only two of them. No bites were recorded."

"Have a different medical examiner redo the autopsies. And if I were you, I'd read the report as soon as it's completed, before another witness is compromised," I suggested.

Greta shook her head, her gaze fixed on my recorder. "But no one threatened *me* to change *my* story. I saw the victims myself, and they were clean slices from knives, not animal bites."

"Just do me this one favor, G," I pleaded. "Have the autopsies repeated, look at the results as soon as they're complete, and if I'm wrong—if the second autopsies reveal knife wounds—I'll let the whole thing go."

Greta narrowed her eyes. "And if you're right?"

"If I'm right, then you will allow the polite and well-mannered Ian Walker to do his job the best he knows how. And you'll let me do mine, without demanding any more retractions. Deal?" I asked, offering my hand.

"You met Walker, I take it?" Greta asked. "He came anyway, despite my voice mail?"

I nodded.

"Maybe Walker was the one who did the charming," Greta commented.

I wiggled the fingers of my outstretched hand.

Greta hesitated as she mulled it over. Finally, she wrenched her gaze from my recorder and took my hand. "It's a deal."

On my way out of the station, I locked eyes with Walker. I gave him a thumbs-up. He nodded back, his dimple deep and distracting. Just as I would have passed his chair, however, he stood and side-stepped in front of me.

I raised my eyebrows. All his height was in his legs. Standing so closely, I had to crane backward to meet his gaze.

"Are you intendin' to walk home?" he asked.

I blinked. "Is that your business?"

"The animal who left those bites on the victims is still wandering the streets. If home isn't nearby, I'd recommend taking a cab. It's already dark," Walker whispered urgently, his speech decidedly less drawling.

"Whether home is nearby or not, I usually take a cab," I said, keeping my weight on my left leg to relieve some of the pressure on my hip. Scenes from Monday night flickered in my mind, and I shuddered, suddenly grateful all over again for the new, fortified locks on my windows.

"Good. Then I'll see you around," he said, the dimple reappearing.

I smiled back. "You'd better. I'm expecting a statement on those bite marks."

"I don't make a habit of givin' statements to the press," Walker tossed over his shoulder as he walked past me toward Greta's desk.

"You wouldn't be talking to the press," I said to his back. "You'd be talking to me."

The police nearby who overheard our exchange laughed. I pointed my finger at all of them as I left. The officers only laughed harder; the lot of them knew me too well.

Walker hadn't lied. While I'd bartered with Greta, the sun had set, casting the neighboring blocks in shadow. I tried to comfort myself with the knowledge that the street was well lit, but the city lights hadn't dissuaded whoever was responsible for the attacks at Paerdegat Park, nor the man who was responsible for attacking me last night. I slipped my hand into the outer pocket of my shoulder bag and clenched the pepper spray tightly in my right fist. I wouldn't be caught unarmed a second time.

The shouts, curses, and beeps of city traffic muffled the tap of my shoes on the concrete walkway. Businessmen and women dodged between the masses, talking sharply on their cell phones and balancing briefcases, laptop cases, and coffees while closing deals. I picked up my pace. My hip didn't appreciate the extra use, but I ignored its grinding ache and walked briskly down the sidewalk toward Rogers Avenue to hail a cab.

As I neared the corner, a group of tall, leggy women in loose sweaters cut in front of me to hail a cab, as well. They were laughing and talking animatedly.

"Excuse me," I said, trying to cut through their group to reach the street.

One of the women snorted at something her friend was saying, oblivious to me.

Just below the bustle of city life, however, I sensed something that made the back of my neck prickle. I glanced down the street. The businessmen and women I'd just passed were still talking and walking. Horns were still blaring and people were still cursing and shouting. Everything around me was normal, but inside, my heart had tripped and was pounding against my ribs in a hard, frantic fall.

Walker's warning is making me skittish, I told myself. I was not being tracked or followed or watched. The retraction didn't have a byline, so for all anyone knew, I *had* followed the man's orders and written the retraction myself. He had no reason to come back for me. I was a few steps away from hailing a taxi and less than ten blocks from my apartment, and I was *not* going to be attacked two nights in a row.

A low and deep and hauntingly familiar hiss rattled from the alley behind me. I gave up on reason, listened to my gut, and ran.

A clear, bloodcurdling shriek pierced the air behind me. I cursed, thinking of the laughing, excited women who were hailing the cab, but I didn't turn to look. I knew what was hunting. I'd seen his fangs and felt the pull of his icy eyes and remembered the slice of his talons sinking deep into my shoulders.

I ran faster.

My shoulder bag slapped against my side. I tucked one of the straps under my arm to keep it tight and steady against my body as I elbowed past other pedestrians. They glared at me, their expressions annoyed and angry. One looked concerned. Others were looking behind me, and their expressions made me run even harder.

I cut across the street against a red crossing light, dodged around a honking taxi, and sprinted down the next block, trying to put as much space and traffic and turns as possible between me and whatever was hunting. A third scream hadn't sounded, and the avenue to East 29th Street was straight ahead. I gripped my pepper spray tighter against the sparking grind of my hip and just ran.

A black and iridescent green blur suddenly rushed me. Something tore through my forearm. I screamed and triggered the pepper spray, but the blur had already disappeared down an adjacent avenue.

"You're hurt!"

People were running and screaming around me, but a few had frozen in shock. They were staring down the alley where the blur had disappeared. A man was in front of me, pointing at my arm.

I peered down, shaking. Blood poured from a deep, jagged gash across my forearm. The victims from Paerdegat Park had suffered from identical wounds. Meredith's close-up in yesterday's paper could have been my arm. A sudden vision of my body lying eviscerated on the concrete like their bodies burst through my mind.

No, I thought, *I am no one's victim, not ever again.* I covered the wound with my hand, hoping to staunch the bleeding and the pain.

The man stepped forward. "You need a doctor."

"Run," I gasped. My voice was low and rasping and not my own. "Get off the street."

"What was that? Who—"

A rattling hiss growled from the alley.

I didn't wait for the man. I ran. East 29th Street was only a few more blocks, but another black and iridescent blur swooped down from overhead to slash at my legs. I screamed again. I heard people screaming around me. Holding my breath, I shot more pepper spray, but the blur disappeared just as quickly as the first. The spray sizzled like acid against my slashed calves.

Gasping, I stumbled around the corner and dodged left onto East 29th. Several of the nearby apartment buildings had walk-in lobbies.

My apartment was only a block away, but any shelter now was better than this cat-and-mouse bullshit. Resolving to slip into the next open apartment complex, I tucked my chin and pumped my arms and legs as fast as I could despite the pain.

A blur of black, flapping cloak, and glowing violet eyes darted out from a side alley and tore a gash over my stomach.

I faltered midstep, and the pepper spray slipped from my hand. A suspended moment of shock and breathless disbelief washed over me, and I suddenly felt the warm gush of blood pour over my abdomen and drip down my thighs. My knees almost buckled. I caught myself against the side of the building's brick face, struggling for balance.

The familiar, rattling hiss vibrated from the surrounding shadows. There couldn't have been just one or two; there must have been dozens surrounding me in every direction—in front, behind, to the side, and above me—as the dissonant crescendo of hisses overpowered every other city sound.

Another tearing slash cut through my lower back. I fell to the ground from the impact, and my knees pounded hard into the asphalt. I focused on inhaling and exhaling, taking long, deep breaths, but it hurt to breathe. It hurt to remain upright on my knees. The pain didn't recede or ebb, and through its constant, sharpening ache, I became aware of a sparking charge in the air. The air was electric, almost snapping.

I glanced up. The men, creatures—whatever the hell was attacking me—were closing in, and the frequency of their rattling was a tangible, expanding, vibrating swell on the air. Their glowing eyes surrounded me. Luminescent shades of blue, green, and purple were gliding out of the darkness and enclosing me in their ranks. I crawled to the side of the building and leveraged to my feet.

A fire escape hung above me. If I jumped high enough, I might be able to reach it and climb away from the creatures. I might still be able to escape and survive. Gathering what remained of my strength and hope, I bent my knees, held my breath, and leapt to reach the handle of the fire escape. The handle was close, and I stretched as high and long and tall as I could. The tips of my fingers grazed the rough, rusted metal handle.

One of the creatures jumped in front of me, crossing an insurmountable distance in a single bound. He clamped onto my left wrist with his teeth like a rabid, growling animal. We faced one another, eye to eye, in the single instant suspended between jumping and falling. This one had icy violet irises that bled to white toward the pupil. His mouth suddenly re-formed and elongated, like bones were shifting position beneath his skin, into a snarling muzzle. He tore the flesh and muscles and tendons from my wrist.

I jerked back, screaming, and my fingertip slipped from the fire escape. I crumpled to the ground against the building. Blood poured down my arm. At least a dozen more of the creatures peeled from the darkness to surround me. They all resembled the man who wasn't quite a man who had attacked me last night, all flashing the same luminous eyes and bearing a nearly skeleton-like leanness. Although they all had individual facial features, like siblings have differing features, they were all impossibly tall and strong and male. And hunting me.

I eased my hand into my shoulder bag slowly, trying not to trigger their attack. My cell phone was buried amid my recorder, notepad, wallet, and pens. If, like animals, they couldn't reason, maybe they wouldn't know that I was calling for help. If they were anything like the creature from last night, however, they might look like animals, but they could think. They'd know my intent.

I looked at them, one by one, as they surrounded me. The feral hunger and anticipation lighting their eyes convinced me that whether or not they could reason, whether or not I made a sudden move or called for help, they were going to attack anyway.

I swept aside a few pens in my bag, frantic to find my phone.

The man with icy violet eyes broke formation and crouched directly in front of me. "You didn't want us to remain a secret," he hissed. "And neither do we. We plan to show the world exactly who we are, but you can help us do that without writing a single word."

I blinked, thrown by his articulacy. The creature from last night had been well-spoken, too. I'd nearly forgotten his voice, overwhelmed by the lasting impression of his fangs, strength, and ferocity. This violet-eyed version of him had all of those traits, as well. I stared at him and knew that the daily life I'd grown accustomed to living would never be the life I'd live again.

"Nothing to say now, without the anonymity of your paper to stand behind?" the creature growled.

I shook my head. "I, um." I swallowed. "This is about my article?"

The creature stared at me, a slow smile widening his muzzle-like, protruding mouth.

"A retraction was written," I whispered. "I haven't told anyone about your kind, I swear."

The creature cocked his head. "You remember seeing us last night?"

I shook my head. "No," I assured him. "Just one of you. And I did everything he asked."

"Liar," he murmured. He brushed a matted, blood-spattered lock of hair away from my cheek. "Lysander wouldn't have let you live with your memories, yet here you are, and you still remember him."

I narrowed my eyes. "How could I possibly forget?"

The creature cocked his head to the right. "Easily."

One of the other creatures growled behind him. "Lysander's power must be deteriorating faster than we thought if he can't even link his mind to a human."

All of the creatures growled in a sudden, shrieking discord. The sound was uncomfortable, like a squirming pressure against my chest, nuzzling beneath my skin. The back of my neck prickled. I fought not to plug my ears and to keep my hand inside my purse, searching for my phone.

The line of creatures hadn't moved, but they were suddenly noticeably closer.

"Please," I begged. My hand had finally found my phone. I tried to unlock the screen saver without breaking eye contact with the creature. "Whatever you're planning, don't. I—"

Like birds that fly in tandem, they descended on me. My shoulder bag was torn over my head. I reached out to fight for it and my phone, but they bit into my wrists and neck. I fell back onto the pavement, screaming. Another creature shucked my skirt up around my waist and tore into my inner thighs with his fangs. The pain was immediate and unbearable. I shrieked and struggled and tried to buck them off, but their weight and grinding, relentless teeth crushed me in place.

The creature at my left wrist reached bone. He clamped his jaws on it and shook his head like a dog. My skin tore in his mouth. I heard the snap of my wrist, and the shock of the break sang through my shoulder. I shuddered. I didn't have breath left to scream.

There were too many of them for me to have a real chance. I struggled against them anyway, but they held me down and fed on me from all points—neck, arms, wrists, and thighs—and I lay, sprawled and exposed on the sidewalk in the tatters of my pencil skirt, bleeding and broken and dying. Had I known everything was going to hell anyway, I should have taken the damn Percocet last night.

One of the creatures jerked my body sideways and sucked at the cut on my back. I felt it widen as a tongue licked into my spine.

"Help!" I shrieked as long and as loud as I could manage. "Someone help me!"

The creature at my hip was suddenly torn away. I felt him take a chunk of my flesh with him, and I screamed again, although it didn't sound like a scream anymore. It felt like screaming, but the only noise I could produce through my damaged throat was a whimpering squeal.

Another creature, the zealous one at my wrist, was suddenly yanked back, too. His body soared through the air and smashed into the brick side of a building. The building crushed inward, and the creature crumpled to the ground amid broken brick powder.

One by one, each feasting creature was ripped from my body—from the pulsing wound at my right thigh, from the neat punctures at my right wrist, from the flapping flesh at my collarbone—and when the last creature was gone, I saw him. The man from last night, with his strange, glowing midnight eyes and that perpetual sneer scarring his mouth, was struggling with the articulate, violet-eyed creature who had been feeding from my thigh. The man stabbed his bare hand through the creature's chest. He severed something inside the chest cavity with a flick of his wrist, and the creature suddenly dropped, writhing on the ground alongside the dozen others that were strewn across the pavement, incapacitated.

I tried to drag myself away while the man was preoccupied with the others of his kind. Maybe he wouldn't notice my retreat. I squirmed down the sidewalk in a slow struggle, desperate to contain the gasps and wheezing whimpers of my effort, but my back scraped against a few loose stones as I moved. The man's gaze jerked to mine immediately. Our eyes locked, and I froze. I didn't even breathe.

The man swooped over me, wrapped a firm arm around my midsection, and bent low over the ground on one knee. He was still for a moment, with me gathered in his arms. My body trembled against his unnatural, inhuman stillness. He suddenly, slowly, moved his cheek against my cheek.

"Be calm," he murmured. "It's nearly over."

His body tensed and in the next moment, in the space between an inhale and an exhale, we were flying through the air. The rushing wind of our speed whistled across my ears, and its pressure ached through my injuries. I whimpered and keened against the pain—the agonized sounds that remained of my screams.

As quickly as we launched, we landed. For a moment, I thought that the attack or perhaps his flight had damaged my hearing. The cacophony of voices, honking horns, and the bustle of city life and construction was dampened. I turned my face away from the man's chest and gaped at the view. The street noise wasn't dampened, and my hearing wasn't damaged; the street was simply farther away. We'd landed on a flat, brick rooftop, and across the expanse of thousands of buildings to the horizon, the light-scattered city skyline stretched for miles.

The man dropped to his knees and bent over me almost protectively. Last night, he had gouged his talons deep into my shoulders to keep me restrained, but tonight, he cradled me gently in his arms. It took a moment to tear my eyes away from the view and refocus on the nightmare holding me.

"Do you know who I am?" the man asked, visibly shaken.

"Of course." I muttered. "I found you burned in the alley on the corner of Farragut Road and East 40th. Last night, you attacked me behind my own building. You have fangs and talons, and you flew me to my fifth-floor apartment. Believe me, you made an impression."

His hold on me was suffocating. I could feel the pressure increase on my wounds, and I tried to squirm away. His grip only tightened. "Do you remember the bite marks on the victims? Do you remember me demanding that you write the retraction?"

I thought about lying, wondering what more he would do to me if I told the truth, but the blood from the bite on my inner thigh was squirting in little pulses against my other thigh. What more *could* he do to me that hadn't already been irrevocably done? I laughed at the fear pumping through my heart and out of my thigh. I was dying.

The man shook me. "Cassidy DiRocco, what exactly do you remember?"

"Everything," I murmured. "I remember all of it."

"I had more time." The man shook his head. A severe frown wrinkled his brow. "I know I had another month at least before my strength waned completely, but if you still remember, the rebellion must be stronger than I'd ever imagined and quickening the process. I can only hope that I have enough for you now. My final gift."

The man lifted me to him with one hand around my waist and swept my hair aside with the other. He cupped my cheek. I protested weakly against his embrace as it turned suddenly intimate, but the most I could manage was a tiny body jerk, a flinch as I winced away from his nearness.

"No," I whispered. "Please."

He sighed in a throaty moan, seeming to enjoy my fear and struggles. Keeping his hold, he licked the wounds on my neck in long, thorough glides. I squirmed, disgusted. He licked with ardor, becoming more excited the more he licked and the more I pulled away.

Suddenly, I felt a hot, almost burning sensation radiate from my neck. It would have been painful if it didn't feel so right and healing and wonderful. A moment later, the burning faded, and my neck no longer ached from the creatures' bone-deep bites.

"How?" I whispered, trembling. My entire body began to shake, and I couldn't stop.

The man pulled back from my neck slightly, the rattling hiss from his chest vibrating constantly now. He bore his teeth at me in a semblance of a smile. His left fang grazed the side of my cheek as he moved, and I felt a drop of blood lick over my face to my earlobe.

"I need unbitten flesh for this to work. If I still have power enough for it to work."

"For what to work?" I asked.

The man sighed deeply, regretfully this time. "I apologize for your suffering. If times were different, if members of my coven would agree to hunt in secret and anonymity, perhaps our paths would never have crossed, but now you know of our existence. I can't allow you to live with those memories intact, but I am unable to erase those memories. Your very existence now jeopardizes mine," he said gravely. "I'm so sorry."

"No," I managed to say through my chattering. My body's shivering was turning violent. "Please."

"Hush. It'll be all right, Cassidy. It'll be all right."

Suddenly, the man bound me to him with the steel muscle of his arms around my body. I gasped, and his mouth clamped on the meat of my neck. His teeth pierced the skin he'd just healed a moment ago, and I felt the blood pull from my body and into his mouth in a swift jerk of suction.

I came.

Hard.

I gasped again, but for an entirely different reason. The man sucked my blood and my life from my torn and ravaged body, but all I could feel was the spiraling ebb and swell of unbearable, throbbing, electric pleasure. My toes curled, and I ached to press closer, though I could barely move. Physically, I knew I was dying, but as another wave broke through me, I simply could not feel or think beyond the rushing pulse of heat surging through me from his bite.

The man jerked me away from his mouth, dropping me like *I'd* scorched *him*. I fell back onto the hard, scraping brick, too overcome by blood loss and twitching pleasure to move. His muzzle had extended slightly and was drenched scarlet with my blood. I watched with a nearly impartial fascination as his face re-formed to that of a man, except for the anomalies of his eyes and fangs.

"It wasn't me. I'm still at my full strength," he whispered in what I could only interpret as awe. "It's you. I can't control your mind because you're a night blood." As if suddenly seeing me, the man's gaze jerked from my face to scan the ravaged meat of my wrist, my sliced arm and stomach, the gashes over my sides and legs, and the slow pump of blood squirting from my inner thigh. His gaze snapped up to meet mine again.

I didn't have the strength to do more than stare back.

The man's chest rattled. "Fuck!"

He tore his own wrist open with his teeth. Gathering me to him with one hand at the back of my neck, he pressed his pulsing, wounded wrist against my lips. I turned away, gagging. He forced my mouth over the wound with a jerk of my neck.

"Drink," he said.

I shook my head.

He pressed his wrist painfully against my mouth, so my own teeth cut the inside of my lips. "Cassidy DiRocco, look into my eyes," he whispered harshly.

I closed my eyes against the yearning his voice stirred, remembering how my will had evaporated the last time I'd listened to him.

His grip on my neck turned bruising. "Cassidy DiRocco, you will drink from my wrist now!"

I screwed my eyes tighter.

The man changed his hold, so my head was clamped in the crook of his arm while his hands pried my mouth open. I struggled, trying to squirm out of his grip and close my mouth, but my battle was short-lived. He was simply too strong and too fast. I was at his mercy.

I screamed, and the sound tore through my already raw throat. My voice was hoarse and bloody, but I was desperate. I didn't want his hands on me. I didn't want his blood in my mouth. I didn't want a part in whatever the hell he had planned for me, but apparently, my wants were not being considered.

With my mouth finally wedged open, he flexed his wrist over my lips. A rush of blood bathed my tongue. I held it in my mouth; its warm and sticky viscosity made me nauseated. The man hesitated, trying to flex his wrist harder to produce a better flow, and I spat his blood from my mouth. Its spray arced over his shirt and across his face in bright speckles.

He blinked for a moment, looking startled.

"Idiot," he growled, and dropped me back onto the pavement. He doubled over and wedged his head between my thighs.

I screamed and tried to crawl away.

The man clamped his hands on my knees, pried them open, and ducked his head down to lick my thigh. The wound squirted into his mouth. He closed his eyes, shuddering with pleasure.

My stomach rolled.

His grip on my knees turned painful, but he continued to only lick at the wound. The heat started again, like it had at my neck. Sitting up on my elbows, I watched as the blood's squirting flow slowed to a trickle, as the wound clotted and closed, and as the man finally licked away the scar until all that remained was smooth, milky, healthy flesh.

"Impossible," I whispered.

The man turned his head to lick the open fang marks on my other thigh. Within only a few short licks, those punctures were healed, as well, and he moved on to the gaping wound at my left hip. One of the creatures had ripped an entire chunk of flesh away. The man buried his mouth inside of the cut, and I felt the slide of his tongue under my skin. I gagged. The feel of his mouth on me and watching his obvious enjoyment sickened me, but I couldn't argue with the result.

More heat built under the skin of my hip. The cold night breeze against my heated flesh puckered goose bumps across my skin. I shivered, feeling hot and cold and terrified and amazed all in one breathless moment. The man pinched the torn edges of my skin together and licked over the seam to close the wound. The skin fused together as he licked, and I didn't know what to say or think or do beyond simply gape in pure astonishment.

He healed my fresh, bleeding wounds one after another—my right wrist, my left wrist, and the tears on my stomach and forearms. He shifted my body and slid the waist of my skirt down to bare the puncture at the small of my back. He hesitated after healing that particular wound. I glanced over my shoulder, wondering what could give the man pause after all the gore he'd seen and touched and ingested. Nothing was on my back except for healthy, smooth skin.

Even as I thought it, I realized I was wrong. My skin wasn't smooth, although he'd healed it. He was studying the puckered, star-shaped scar on my hip from the bullet I'd taken for Officer Harroway. He traced it with his finger. I held my breath, trying not to feel, but tingling shivers stole up my spine. He lingered there a long moment before adjusting my skirt back into place. Finally, he leaned over my body and licked the twin punctures from his own fangs on my neck. The warmth of their healing and his tongue trailed goose bumps down my shoulder.

"Who are you?" I whispered.

The man pulled away from the healed wounds at my neck and sat on his haunches in front of me. He licked his lips as he regarded my expression. "You may call me Dominic. I am the Master Vampire of New York City."

"Vampire," I said numbly.

Dominic smiled, and my blood glistened in the crevices of his teeth and gums. "The bite marks on the victims *were* from an animal attack, but not from an animal anyone will be able to identify." He sighed. "Thanks to you, I'll have to take care of that, as well."

I shook my head in denial, but I knew I couldn't deny everything I'd just witnessed. I felt the smooth, unmarked skin of my neck with my fingertips. "Unbelievable."

A low, rattling hiss suddenly vibrated from around us. Dominic crouched over me as if shielding my body from whatever was approaching. "Jillian will be here shortly with her guard to arrange the scene, but the rebels are already regenerating. We must return to my coven. Now."

Dominic reached for me, but I scuttled backward, gaping. "I'm not going anywhere with you," I snapped.

The fire escape was only a few yards away. If I could reach the edge of the roof, I would only need to climb one story down and break into an apartment window. Maybe I could—

Dominic bowled into me and smashed me flat on my back. His hand cradled the back of my head, protecting my skull from bouncing against the brick roof. I winced from the impact nonetheless, my back aching. The line of his body pressed against every inch of mine.

"I don't think you understand your current position, Cassidy," Dominic breathed harshly. "I have *allowed* you to live. Since you are a night blood, I will even protect you, but until you are a vampire, you are still food. Food that I want to fuck, but food nonetheless. And everyone, including myself, is very, very hungry. Do you understand?"

The fire escape was only a few feet above my head. If I could just wriggle one arm free and reach up, maybe I could leverage—

Dominic pressed me deeper into the brick with the force of his body, crushing the air from my lungs. "From this moment forward, your will is not your own. Your will is mine, and you are coming with me, Cassidy."

My body suddenly longed for his command. I fought against it, but the pull was amazing and unavoidable. "This is insane," I ground through my teeth.

"Cassidy DiRocco, look into my eyes."

My eyes searched for his, so I shut them before they could meet his gaze. "Just leave me alone!" I screamed, terrified of my own body nearly more than I was terrified of him.

Dominic growled in frustration. I could feel his chest vibrate against mine. "Open your eyes, Cassidy. We don't have time for hysterics."

My eyes peeled open against my will and met his beautiful icy gaze. "No!"

"Cease struggling and shouting," he hissed.

I instantly stilled, my gaze caught and helpless against the lure of his eyes. "Shit," I whispered.

Dominic grazed his fingertips over my brow with a feathery touch. His hand was trembling slightly. I eased away from his touch carefully, so the movement wouldn't be considered struggling but would still separate me from his fingers.

His eyes widened. "You can still reason around my command after you meet my gaze," he murmured. "Extraordinary."

Before I could whisper something scathing, Dominic pulled me roughly away from the brick rooftop, gathered me tightly against his body, and crouched on one knee. I knew what he was doing, having experienced it twice before, but nothing, not even prior experience, could have prepared me for the rush of wind and the boundlessness of his strength as he launched like a soaring missile across the city with me in his arms.

Chapter 3

The coven, as Dominic referred to it, was technically the many vampires under his rule, but the word also referred to their home. For New York City vampires, the coven was a labyrinth of corridors, tunnels, and rooms carved from the city's sewers and subways. An entire city of bloodthirsty predators existed beneath our own city, and, according to Dominic, no one knew.

"Of course no one knows of our existence," he'd assured me once I was secure inside a cage located in what was apparently Dominic's bedroom, none of which was reassuring in the least. "We are but fictional nightmares in movies and literature."

I scoffed, unable to comprehend that not one person, not one government agency, had discovered them before me. The look he returned was chilling. He was certain no one knew of their existence because, as Master of New York, his very purpose was ensuring their secrecy—which I had obviously, and now repeatedly, threatened.

The cage he'd locked me in contained a bed and flushing toilet. Dominic had flown over the city blocks at blurred speed, dove into the subway system through a secluded sidewalk grate, navigated through its depths, and deposited me inside the cage without delay. My only consolation was that he hadn't locked himself inside with me.

"I won't tell anyone about you or your coven. Please, just let me go," I whispered, already planning the hook to my article. "The City Beneath: Vampires Bite in the Big Apple." I still couldn't scream, and I worried how long his command would remain in effect.

Dominic smiled his frightening, fanged, predator smile. "You lie beautifully, Cassidy. The strong acceleration of your heart is delicious." He drew one finger down the squared edge of a metal bar, and a sizzle of smoke drifted from his fingertip. "You'll be safe here while I'm gone. The cage is made of silver, so no one can penetrate these bars without the keys, not even me."

I blinked. "While you're gone?"

"Pining for me already, Cassidy?"

I stared at him, nonplussed.

His smile widened. "I must check on Jillian's handiwork at the scene, but I will return shortly."

"Why are you doing this?" I whispered. "Why did they kill innocent bystanders just to get to me?"

"I'm not doing any of this," Dominic said, no longer smiling. "And no one was killed trying to get to you. Whether or not you were present, my vampires would have hunted last night and slaughtered whomever they chose. They were hungry and prefer to hunt in that manner. Their lack of discretion is a note of contention between many in my coven and myself, but if I survive the Leveling, my coven will once again hunt in secret. Until I regain my full power, however, their hunts will continue and likely escalate in violence and notoriety." Dominic stepped closer to the cage. "I'm not a party to their hunts, Cassidy. I'm trying to contain them."

I shook my head. "Why do you care if humans are slaughtered?"

"I care because hunts that are not contained bring unnecessary and unwanted attention to our existence. We have survived this long in the city because of our anonymity." Dominic sighed deeply, as if this conversation was a topic he was weary of defending. "Speaking of which, I must help Jillian tend to the scene. There are uncountable victims and witnesses we need to address."

I stepped forward, intrigued despite myself. "How do you 'address' something like this? How can you possibly find and convince hundreds of people who witnessed tonight's slaughter that they didn't see anything?"

"I know who witnessed tonight's attack and I know the friends and family they told and I know where they live the way you know your heart is beating and your valves are pumping and your blood is carrying oxygen to your muscles."

"What do you mean?"

"It seems to me that such human bodily functions are a constant and time-consuming activity that would consume your life. They are a matter of life and death, yet do you consider them a priority?"

"Of course not. Bodily functions occur without conscious thought." Dominic smiled.

I blinked. "That's ridiculous. How can you just know those things without conscious thought?"

"Let me explain it this way. Imagine if every bodily function depended upon conscious thought, and you had the capability to control your body and still function throughout your daily life."

"That would be impossible."

Dominic smiled. "Imagine if you could not only control your own body and thoughts, but others' bodies and thoughts, as well. Imagine an entire city's worth of thoughts, feelings, wants, desires, wills, and memories as your own and having to focus to separate everyone else's mind from your own. That is how my mind feels. Some people's minds simply slip into mine, and I need to actually push against them to keep them out. Others' thoughts are more difficult to control."

I narrowed my eyes. "But you can only control my actions. You can't control my thoughts at all."

"No, I can't."

"Why?"

"I thought at first that my powers were severely diminished or your mind was very strong or a combination of both, but I was wrong. Vampires simply can't control night bloods like we can humans."

"But I'm human," I said.

Dominic's smile widened. "We will continue this conversation when I return. I promise."

"But I—"

He was already gone. I was talking to the darkness.

The moment he left, the confining grip his mind had exerted on my will disappeared. I took a deep, gratifying breath, reveling in free will. The moment passed quickly, and panic constricted my throat in a stronger, more deadly hold than even his will. Before I could consider the ramifications, I screamed and pounded against the bars of my cage. *This isn't happening*, I thought, even as I shouted for help and bruised the sides of my fists against the metal bars in desperation. *I am not being held captive within a locked cage by a vampire in a secret tunnel system that no one knows exists below the city and where no one will ever find me*. I rattled the cage door desperately.

"Help! Someone, please, I'm underground! Can anyone hear me? I—"

In the surrounding darkness, pairs of glowing blue, green, and purple eyes stared at me. I couldn't decipher the outlines of their bodies in the pitch-blackness, but if the looks on their faces were any indication, they could see me just fine. Some of them wore expressions pinched with hunger. One had exceptionally purple eyes—almost a shade of plum—shining with the same luminosity as the blues, greens, and violets. All of them were flanking the cage and stalking closer.

I jerked away from the cage's edge and stood in the center where, I hoped, none of the creatures could reach me. I tried to think of them as vampires. Although they were pale and fanged, they certainly weren't romantic or hauntingly lovely. They were gaunt, stoic animals. The only way I'd willingly approach one was if it ordered me with its eyes, like Dominic; even then, I'd be screaming inside.

"How many years has it been since Lysander caught and kept one?" a vampire hissed. He had a severe widow's peak highlighted by hair slicked back into a ponytail. He was one of the few with hair that looked brown—maybe even dirty blond in the light—as opposed to black.

"The Solstice is approaching," the plum-eyed vampire growled. "Maybe he needs the extra strength."

"He didn't need the extra strength for his last Leveling."

"No one has ever challenged him as Master."

"She smells"—a third vampire, the nearest to the cage, released the same rattling hiss I recognized from Dominic and from the vampires who had attacked earlier tonight—"like lightning. Burning. Electric."

His murmured words were hissed between rattling growls. He was so close that I could see a slight vertical scar between his upper lip and nostril, like he'd endured cleft-lip surgery as a child. I stared at that scar, and a slow realization settled in my bones, a realization that should have been obvious but was impossible to accept. These creatures had been born human.

"She's not ours to enjoy," a fourth growled, but it didn't sound very convinced. It crept closer as it reprimanded the others, its nose and mouth transforming into the muzzle I'd witnessed from Dominic.

The cleft-lipped vampire was inches from the bars. "Kaden said that her blood crackled on his tongue."

I fought not to cringe away to the opposite side of the cage. More vampires were closing in from behind.

"Kaden has returned to the coven? How did he regenerate that quickly?" the dirty-blond vampire asked. He looked excited by the prospect of Kaden's regeneration.

"Kaden healed within minutes of Lysander tearing his aorta," the plum-eyed vampire answered tightly. "We should intervene, Sevris. Lysander will need more allies against Kaden."

Sevris grinned, releasing a dangerous, satisfied growl. "Lysander can take care of himself, and if he can't, then he shouldn't be Master."

"I don't want to live in a coven with Kaden as Master."

"Then you should leave before the Solstice."

The cleft-lipped vampire bared his fangs. "Kaden said that her blood spread heat down his throat, like rum."

"You don't remember what rum tastes like," the fourth vampire hissed, his muzzle now fully extended.

"Oh Neil," the cleft-lipped vampire murmured. "We would if we tasted her."

Neil lunged for me. I screamed, anticipating that his strength and momentum would break through the metal bars. He would tear through the cage and then tear out my throat. The vampire hit the bars of the cage in a full body slam, desperate to reach me, to taste and kill me, but instead of the bars breaking like I'd expected, they sank deep into his flesh and began to smoke and sizzle.

I stared in disbelief as Neil's forearms and left cheek melted around the bars. The smoke was like steam as the bars boiled his skin, but it smelled sickeningly foul. Neil shrieked. He tried to jerk away from the cage, but his skin had suctioned in around each bar, like a hot knife through butter, lodging the bars deep in his flesh.

After a few attempts, he finally tore himself from the cage. The melted tissue slopped away from each bar with a wet *pop*. He staggered back, staring in stunned horror at the gaping, blistering wounds on his arms. Like Neil, I couldn't look away, especially from the one wound he couldn't see. The blisters on his cheek were so deep, I could see his cheekbone and teeth through the exposed, raw wound. I tried to breathe deeply against the pitch of my stomach, but the nauseating smell of burnt flesh was thick in the air around me. I pursed my lips against a gag.

A deep, throaty female laugh echoed down the corridor. "Rafe, darling, you know better than to tease our newest vampires."

Rafe, the cleft-lipped vampire, ducked his head, his expression almost sheepish—if an eerily iridescent-eyed, seven-foot-tall, fanged creature could look sheepish. The woman was my height, not an inch over five-two. Rioting, curly blond hair bounced down her back to the curve of her waist. Her eyes were an icy blue, similar to Dominic's, and her fangs seemed extra-long in her petite mouth; she had a slight overbite to accommodate them. She strode up to Rafe, the tight cut of her leather pants hugging the lithe curves of her hips with each step.

Rafe grinned as she approached despite the warning in her gaze.

The woman hissed, and Rafe lost the grin. He dropped to both knees, clasped his hands behind his back, and dipped his head in a dramatic show of contrition. On his knees, he was mere inches shorter than the woman was, standing. The woman rolled her eyes. She leaned over him, sliced a thin cut over his neck with a fang, and walked past him to Neil. Once her back was to him, Rafe looked up at me, extended his jaw into a muzzle, and rubbed his tongue slowly over one fang.

I shifted my gaze from Rafe, who was playing head games with everyone, to the woman in leather, who was half-reprimanding and half-comforting Neil, and finally to the rest of them, who had momentarily reined in their blood-thirst. The vampires might have seemed like rabid savages while they hunted on the streets, but an obvious order was established here in the coven.

The woman growled a deep, vibrating noise from the center of her chest, and the males all took a collective step back from the cage, creating a semicircle around me. Once the men had cleared some space, the woman stepped up to the cage and smiled. She was better at smiling than Dominic. Even with her fangs, her expression seemed genuine, but the rest of the vampires—who had seemed bloodthirsty, ruthless, and crazed—had obeyed her every command immediately and without question despite her being diminutive and female. I glanced between the smiling woman and the pack of ravenous creatures behind her and shivered. Who was more dangerous: the pack or the leader they ceded to?

"I apologize for the commotion. Dominic will return shortly." The woman's voice was soft and airy.

I nodded. "And who are you?"

"You may call me Jillian. I am the Master's Second."

Dominic had worded his introduction in the same manner, introducing me with his first name and rank, but the vampires had referred to Dominic as Lysander. I glanced at the semicircle of vampires around Jillian and pursed my lips. I wondered if Jillian had another name, too.

"Something to say, love?" Jillian asked, her voice growling slightly on the endearment.

I shook my head.

She took a step closer. "I could extract the thought from your mind if I wanted to."

"You could try," I whispered. I slid my eyes to the side, so they were no longer gazing into hers. Looking away felt wrong and weak, but if she was anything like Dominic, I knew what was coming.

Jillian was now inches from the cage. "Cassidy, did you have something to say? What were you thinking just a moment ago?"

Her pull on my mind and will was strong—painfully strong—and it only worsened the more times she spoke my name, but her strength was nothing compared to Dominic's unendurable power. He could whip my mind into cream with just a glance.

"Cassidy DiRocco, tell me what you were thinking when you heard my name."

What is your full vampire name? The words filled my mind and oozed from every pore. My tongue shaped the words inside my mouth and strained against my teeth and lips to speak them; I kept my mouth clenched tightly against their release and against Jillian's will.

"Is something the matter, Jillian darling?" Rafe asked, laughing. "I don't hear her speaking."

Jillian whirled on Rafe. She simply extended her hand, and Rafe was yanked off his feet. He rushed neck first through the air as if she'd hooked him with fishing line. His neck hit her hand, and she pounded him into the ground.

Rafe gasped a gurgling, protesting noise from between his teeth.

"I don't hear *you* speaking now, either," Jillian whispered. She jabbed her sharp, claw-like fingers into his neck, fisted her hand, and tore out his throat.

Rafe fell to the ground on his knees. His eyes were frantic and his mouth opened and closed, but without a throat, he couldn't scream.

Jillian tossed the meat of Rafe's throat on the stone floor, like someone else would discard a wet paper towel.

She slowly turned around to face me again. I focused on her, trying not to stare at the heavy, glistening chunk of blood and tissue strewn across the stone.

"Cassidy," she murmured.

My brain tuned to the timbre of her voice, and I realized that I had met her eyes. "No," I whispered.

"Ah," Jillian sighed. Her exhale trembled. "Lovely. No wonder he wants to claim you."

"Why would he want me at all?" I asked from between my clenched teeth. I remembered what Dominic had said about feeling my thoughts and desires, and I realized that Jillian was likely feeling mine right now.

"Did you prefer the fate my brothers had in store for you?" Jillian spread her arms wide to indicate the semicircle of vampires still lining the room.

I shook my head. "Isn't that what lies in store for me anyway, just delayed?"

Jillian leaned closer. She wasn't even near the cage, and I flinched away from her. "How did it feel when Dominic tasted you?"

I felt the scorch of my blush through to my hairline.

"Death is inevitable; whether Kaden had drained you earlier tonight or young Neil had feasted on you today or time decays your body's ability to sustain life fifty years from now, the end will come for you. Life is a delay of death. The beautiful parting moment of Dominic's bite is what lies in store for you now, and I can guarantee that one last moment with Dominic is more life than years of living could give you."

"What do you know of Dominic's bite?" I snapped, still tingling from the heat of my blush.

"Everything you do." Jillian grinned. "He is ravenous."

"Then you can keep it. I'll take my years of living, thank you very much." I tore my gaze away from hers with the force of my rage. I stared at the slop of Rafe's neck and felt my temper harden. Rafe had healed. His neck was once again smooth and perfect, but the evidence of his former neck still lying on the ground sickened me. "If you're so loyally devoted to your Master, why did you leave Dominic to die?"

Jillian's smile wiped clean off her face. "Excuse me?"

"You left him outside the coven to fry in the sunlight, allowed police to find the remains of your hunt before you could hide the evidence—"

"That was not my hunt," Jillian growled.

"—and you allowed his gasping, dying, crispy body to be found by *me*. A human."

"I didn't know that Dominic had left the coven the night before," Jillian said, shaking. "I didn't realize how weak he was becoming nor how strong the rebellion had grown. I didn't think they would be able to incapacitate him and—"

"*I* found him, Jillian. *I* saved him. Is that why he's checking your work at the crime scene? After you let his fate rest in the hands of a *human*, he doesn't trust you anymore. You didn't have his back when he needed you most, and now he doesn't trust you to cover it."

Jillian's face contorted in anger, and her fangs elongated. "That's not true," she said, her voice grave.

"Where were you when they attacked him? Why didn't he have any warning or help? Why didn't you come to his rescue?"

Jillian was suddenly inches from the cage. I jerked back.

"That silver may keep the younger vampires at bay," Jillian whispered. "But I assure you that it will not deter me."

"I'd rather die under you, knowing I'd struggled and lost, than under Dominic, with his orgasmic bite, knowing I hadn't struggled at all."

Jillian slowly narrowed her eyes on me, and I could feel their weight, like an anchor, settle deep in my mind. She hissed. "That can be arranged."

"But not tonight," Dominic's deep bass vibrated from somewhere within the darkness.

Jillian straightened away from the cage and actually took a step back. All the other vampires in the room shifted in a slow-turning wave to face the side corridor, where presumably they could see Dominic. I couldn't see more than six feet beyond the cage because of

the surrounding darkness, but I could still decipher the glowing lumi-
nescence of the vampires' eyes. Once they turned in the direction of
Dominic's voice, they bowed their heads—some obediently and others grudgingly, but all without question.

Jillian was the only one to bow her head and then straighten to
face Dominic squarely. "Master," she acknowledged.

Dominic stepped out from the corridor's pitch-blackness and into
the room. I could just barely distinguish the shadow of his outline in
the darkness. "Perhaps antagonizing the second most powerful vampire in this coven while surrounded by her allies isn't the wisest
course of action."

I crossed my arms over my chest. He was right, of course, but I
wasn't going to acknowledge that.

"And as for you, Jillian," he continued.

Jillian's face was stoic.

"Your arrangement of the scene was impeccable. Witnesses won't
report the scene until tomorrow afternoon, correct?"

Jillian's expression didn't so much as twitch. She nodded.

"Perfect, as usual. Yet I return, and the coven is a wreck," Dominic
commented blandly.

"You exaggerate, Master," Jillian said tightly.

He tipped his head slightly. "I doubt Neil and Rafe would agree."

"Rafe's punishment was well deserved, as you can see by Neil's appearance," Jillian replied smoothly, indicating Neil's still-smoldering
injuries.

"That's debatable," Rafe grumbled.

Jillian growled softly.

Dominic raised his eyebrows. "Perhaps his lesson could have
been better learned outside my rooms."

"Of course," Jillian replied with a nod.

"You are dismissed."

Jillian bowed her head once more, and all the vampires filed out,
losing most of their formality. She followed their retreat, ignoring my
presence as she passed. Neil hissed at me as he left. His wounds had
stopped bleeding but were still gaping and blistered and grotesque.
Rafe was the last to leave, winking at me as he passed. I frowned at
their retreat, not sure how to compartmentalize the animals who had

attacked me with these creatures who had order, personality, and conversations. I shuddered to think of an encounter with any of them here in the coven without the cage between us.

Rafe's body blended into the inky blackness, leaving me alone with Dominic. He stepped closer to the cage in slow, measured movements. "Neil hasn't learned to control his cravings yet. He's still very young."

My first impulse was to snap that I couldn't care less about Neil's cravings or his age. Dominic was staring at me with a certain look on his cold, angular face, as if he anticipated such a response, but before I could oblige him, my reporter's instinct kicked in. Death was the most likely outcome in this twisted place, but if escape or rescue were even remote possibilities, I'd need to know more about my environment and company.

"Are his wounds permanent?" I asked.

Dominic paused midstep. "No, he'll heal with sleep and blood," he replied, "but his regeneration will take longer than most."

"Why?"

He resumed walking toward me. "He's the youngest of our coven, only two years old."

I bit the inside of my cheek, afraid of the answer to my next question: "How old are you?"

Dominic smiled, the same terrifying flash of fangs that he'd shown me from the beginning, not the more palatable, lying curve of lips that Jillian could express. "I was created approximately five hundred years ago, in 1537."

"You're mocking me," I accused. I don't know why I was offended or how I could feel anything besides loathing and fear in his presence, but his claim to have lived for five hundred years put my teeth on edge. If I died here, I wanted the truth.

Dominic was inches from my cage now. "I am the furthest thing from mocking you. In my coven, here in my rooms, with only me present, I assure you that you will receive my honesty and protection."

Dominic spread his palm across the bars of the cage. I gaped, anticipating the melting and scorching burns I'd witnessed when Neil touched the cage, but nothing happened.

"Patience," Dominic murmured.

After a moment, I smelled it: burning flesh. I leaned closer to Dominic's hand and watched, amazed, as what had happened instantaneously to Neil transpired at a nearly infinitesimal pace with Dominic. Minutes passed, and finally the outer layers of his skin were ravaged by blisters. The skin eventually enveloped the bar like liquid, and began to boil around it.

"Enough," I said, helpless to look away even while the sight of his boiling skin sickened me. "Please stop."

Dominic scraped at the liquefied skin of his hand and yanked free of the bar where it had suctioned into his palm. He held out the wreckage of his palm toward me. I leaned closer again. The same exact wounds I'd witnessed minutes before on Neil healed on Dominic before I could even blink.

"Unbelievable," I whispered.

Dominic smiled, keeping his mouth closed, so the expression was less grotesque. "A testament to my age and accumulated power."

I frowned. "That display was for my benefit, so I'd believe you?"

He laughed again. "It certainly wasn't for mine."

My temper burst in a white-hot backdraft. "Why do you care what I believe? I don't care if a cow enjoyed its time on the pasture. I just enjoy the damn hamburger! You said so yourself that I'm just food to you." I pounded the bars of the cage with the flat of my hand. "So why didn't you just enjoy me? Why are you keeping me here? Why are you answering my questions like they matter?"

"I was wondering where your anger had gone. Never far from the surface, I see," Dominic murmured like he knew me, which chafed because he was right. "Your questions matter because *you* matter. You are food, but unlike most, you aren't *just* food. You are also a night blood, one of the rare humans who possess the blood type that can survive the change."

"I don't, I—" I took a deep breath. "What are you implying?"

"I'm not implying anything," Dominic said succinctly. "I'm telling you that you are a night blood."

"Survive the change," I repeated numbly. "What change? How do you know what I am?"

"Everyone's blood tastes recognizably human, similar to how one hamburger tastes relatively the same as another hamburger to you," Dominic said, smirking, "but just because you can recognize the taste of two hamburgers as being hamburgers, doesn't necessarily mean their quality tastes the same. A fast-food hamburger tastes mediocre compared to a steak-house hamburger. Although they're considered the same food, they're certainly not the same dish.

Night bloods have a scorching, smoky quality to their blood that tingles at the back of my throat when I swallow. The taste is unmistakable, and I've tasted you, Cassidy. You are a rare dish."

I raised an eyebrow. "I'm a steak-house hamburger?"

"With bacon and onions and a signature sauce," Dominic added. "You possess the blood necessary to perform a successful transformation from human to vampire. There aren't many of you left, and there are even fewer who display resistance to mind control—let alone to my level of power—while still human. It's impressive, and I intend to make you my night blood."

I didn't like or quite believe anything he'd just uttered—although I didn't quite believe anything else I was living or witnessing at the moment, either—but one statement in particular disturbed me profoundly. "*Your* night blood?"

"Yes, my night blood. I will serve as your protector and mentor while you serve as an added fuel for my power. Your blood actually weakens vampires when ingested—the opposite of human blood—but you can assist me in many, many other ways," Dominic said, seeming to enjoy the thought. "We'd be what your law enforcement considers partners, for lack of a better word, but the relationship between a vampire and his night blood is extremely intimate—" Dominic grinned broadly. "And I don't share."

I would have laughed if what he was saying wasn't so completely, insanely terrifying, and if he hadn't been so utterly serious. "So you don't intend to keep me locked here as a source of food to sustain you?"

Dominic blinked at me like *I* was insane. "I have an entire city of humans from which to hunt and feed. Why would I need one readily caged?"

I crossed my arms. "Yes, I've witnessed the massacre of your hunt."

"No, you haven't." Dominic sighed. His exhale rasped at the end in that vibrating rattle that pricked the hairs at the back of my neck to attention.

I shivered.

"Neither you nor any human have ever witnessed my hunt. I ensure our coven's secrecy to ensure our safety, as do all coven Masters throughout the world."

My mind spun at his words: *coven Masters throughout the world.*

"But there are vampires within all covens, and a growing minority within my own, who believe that secrecy is no longer essential to our survival," Dominic continued. "It's *their* feedings you have witnessed. It's their hunts you have been victim to, and it's those vampires I must prevent from exposing our kind to the human population. If another Master realizes how close my coven is to exposing us all, they may challenge my rule or report us to the Council. With the Solstice approaching, I'm in no condition for such an attack on the coven."

I shook my head, feeling overwhelmed. "Who are the Council? And why are the vampire attacks escalating so rapidly? I didn't even notice their kills until last night."

"Of course you have," Dominic said mildly. "You've reported about them numerous times. In fact, most of the murders you've written about within the last three weeks have been caused by vampires. The Council is our governing body. If I fail to rein in my coven, the Council's Day Reapers will most certainly intervene."

"That's ridiculous," I sputtered, stuck on his claim that most of the past month's murders were vampire-caused. "None of the other murders had bite marks."

"No, they didn't, not after I arranged the scene and persuaded the witnesses."

"Why didn't you arrange the scene to hide the bite marks at Paerdegat Park?"

Dominic's lips thinned over his teeth, exposing fangs, "I never made it back to the coven Sunday night. The rebels ambushed me before I fed, and they left me to die by sunlight."

I wanted him to continue, and when my silence only met silence, I nudged. "That must have been excruciating. How did you survive?"

"I nearly didn't. The alley I crawled into offered mediocre protection, except from the midday sunlight. Another hour, and I would have been ash. You saw my condition Monday night. I didn't have the strength to arrange a scene, and Jillian didn't realize our predicament until the bodies had already been discovered by human authorities. We never had time to properly prepare it."

I frowned. "You seemed more than capable against the rebels today."

Dominic sighed. "They were unprepared tonight. After drinking from you, they couldn't defend against me. Sunday night, however, I was the one unprepared. The rebels never challenged me before. Our politics may differ, but I thought they were loyal to the coven." Dominic looked weary. "I thought they were loyal to me."

"You were overconfident."

Dominic hissed through his fangs, and I shrank back slightly. "I was betrayed. My power will steadily weaken until I'm near human strength, and the rebels will undoubtedly attempt to overthrow my rule. These feedings—'massacres,' as you've referred to them—are their attempts to amass followers to their new culture. Their final drive to usurp my power will be much, much worse."

"How much worse can it get?" I whispered, thinking of their piranha-like frenzy on the street tonight.

Dominic shrugged. "From experience, I can assure you that this is only the beginning."

I blinked. "This has happened before?"

"Yes, it's known as the Leveling. Like all Masters, my power wanes and regenerates on a seven-year cyclical cycle." Dominic raised his palms in a helpless gesture. "Members of my coven have always wanted to hunt indiscriminately, but until recently, they didn't have a vampire to lead them. Now they not only have a leader, they have a vampire who, for the first time in my rule as Master of New York City, may challenge me on the Leveling and may actually win."

I massaged a pointed, throbbing pressure in my right temple. "How long do you have before your next Leveling?"

"Four weeks, two days, and thirty-four minutes. June 20th, to be exact. The longest day of the year: the summer Solstice. When I rise at sunset after the Leveling without having met the final death, my power will be restored, and I'll reclaim my rightful position as Master of this coven. If I fail to rise, vampires of this coven will no longer remain simply fictional nightmares. They'll become your reality, and they'll kill indiscriminately."

I crossed my arms. "Don't you already?"

Dominic cocked his head. "Don't I already what?"

"Don't all of the vampires already kill indiscriminately? The only difference is that people will know vampires are doing the killing instead of assuming human violence. Maybe if everyone knows that vampires exist, we'll actually have a chance at surviving against you."

"Like the chance you had against me in the alley or the chance you had against Kaden a few hours ago?" Dominic laughed. "Vampires feed on humans, but unless we are newly born, careless, or angry, we rarely kill them. Secrecy is essential to our survival, and those of us who want secrecy are typically more careful with our prey. The humans I feed from return home bruised and weak and confused but otherwise unharmed. Those who no longer care for secrecy, however, no longer hunt to feed. They hunt for the joy of the kill, and feeding is simply a bonus."

I mulled over what he said, not sure if I believed him. "You don't need to drain a human to feed?"

"Do you need to eat an entire cow to feel full?" Dominic countered, obviously amused.

"No," I admitted grudgingly, "but I also don't eat mine while it's still mooing."

"Dietary preferences," Dominic replied, grinning now. "I must retire for the day, but speaking of diet, you will find dry cereals, protein bars, fruit cups, and Twinkies stacked in shelves under the bed along with bottled water. I recommend staying away from the perishables as I haven't stocked the shelves in some time. Otherwise, please help yourself. You need to replenish your blood-cell count."

"Right," I muttered. "Fatten me up again."

Dominic reached out sharply and placed his hand over mine. I'd unthinkingly left my fingers wrapped around the bars after pounding on the cage door, so they were vulnerable to his attack. His strength was breathtaking. Just his hand covering the knuckles of each finger held them crushingly immobile against the bars. I envisioned one horror after the next—Dominic grinding my fingers into dust against the bars, snapping each knuckle backward, ripping each finger from its socket and sucking down my blood from an upturned appendage, like a row of shots. My heart clenched with fear and self-chastisement. I ground my teeth and braced myself.

"Any other vampire would've pulled your arm through the bars to get at your wrist. I can hear your heart accelerating and feel the beat of its healthy pulse against my tongue. It tempts me, but I've learned control. I want to speak with you tomorrow more than I want to rip through the veins at your wrist, but most vampires in this coven would choose the wrist when faced with a similar choice." He grazed one long finger across the tiny veins at my wrist to emphasize his point.

I swallowed. "Lucky for me, then, that you're not any other vampire."

"True, but that isn't to say that I won't indulge." He grinned, and his face began to transform into the creature I was beginning to suspect was his true form. "You have such lovely wrists."

His fingers extended into bony talons. He peeled my fingers from the cage, stabbed the razor-sharp nail of his thumb into my flesh, and sliced across my wrist with a swift, efficient twitch of his finger.

I inhaled sharply at the sudden pain. The cut was deep—disgustingly, alarmingly deep—and overflowed with blood instantly. Dominic knelt and tipped my hand, so the blood poured over my palm and fingertips to his mouth. His tongue lapped the blood from each finger, swiped over and under, from tips to knuckles, savoring each drop. The hissing rattle started to vibrate inside his chest. A moment later, just as his grip tightened and his lapping became more insistent, Dominic tore his mouth away from my hand.

He closed his eyes as he swallowed, seeming to relish the taste. The hand holding my wrist trembled. It pained him to stop feeding. I could see the iron will of his control in the flex of his clamped jaw muscles and the strained set to his shoulders, but he didn't give in to the temptation. His face transformed back into its original, human-like form. His hold on my wrist steadied, and when he opened his eyes a moment later, his expression was once again bland, amused, and confident.

Dominic brought my hand to his lips, but instead of lapping up the flow of blood, he licked into the wound. I felt nauseated, but I couldn't look away. Heat expanded through my wrist and hand and up my arm as his tongue probed into my flesh. Just as the heat began to burn, the cut healed. It clotted and scabbed, and Dominic licked more thoroughly over my skin to eliminate the scar. When he finished, my wrist was as smooth and unharmed as before he drank, although my hand was coated in a sticky glove of half-dried blood.

"I recommend you gain a measure of control over your temper, as well. Many times, control is all that separates us from the monsters."

I nodded quickly, beyond words.

He released my hand and stepped back.

I stepped back immediately, as well, mirroring his movement to bring all my extremities within the cage. Although healed, my wrist ached. I cradled it with my other hand, but both my hands were trembling.

"Rest. I will return at dusk," he murmured, and all that remained of his presence was the scent of soft Christmas pine and the tack of blood and saliva coating my palm.

Chapter 4

As inexplicable as it seemed after the gore I'd just witnessed and experienced, I was hungry. Shelves of foodstuffs and water really were under the bed as promised. Some of the cereals were expired and some of the brands should never be eaten anyway, but one cereal in particular didn't have sugar or marshmallows or frosting. It seemed strange to eat and drink here, like I was a guest instead of a prisoner, but as the immediate danger lay abed for the day, my adrenaline faded, and my stomach growled.

I knelt to retrieve the cereal and water from under the bed, but when I stood, the world twisted out from under me. Suddenly, I was lying flat on my back, dizzy and disoriented. The stone floor felt cool on the backs of my arms, and as the world somersaulted and twirled, I decided to stay put. I ate my cereal while lying on my back next to a perfectly cozy-looking bed. The mattress and bedspread were preferable over a stone floor, but even after I finished eating, I was still dizzy. I closed my eyes against a nauseating loop-de-loop and felt myself slip away.

A warm hand cupped my cheek, and two fingers pressed firmly against the left side of my neck. "No, no, no. Wake up, darlin'."

I knew that voice. I didn't know it well, but something about its timbre reminded me of humid, lazy days spent drinking lemonade. I'd never lived in a house where a person could sit out on a porch, look over an acre of yard, and enjoy the breeze, but that voice had.

The man sighed heavily. The hand at my neck disappeared for a moment and just as quickly returned, assaulting my cheek with little sharp slaps.

"Come on, Cassidy. Can you open your eyes for me, darlin'?"

Every part of my mind and body felt weak, but the man's endearment struck like untuned chords on my nerves. "I'm no one's darling," I whispered.

The man laughed, a deep soft rumble. "Yes, ma'am."

I knew that *ma'am*. "Ian Walker?"

"That's Walker to you," he said, his voice still deep with amusement. "Can you show me those gorgeous eyes of yours? Bat your baby blues for me. *Darlin'*."

I forced my eyelids open despite their weight and sluggishness. Walker's face hovered above me. His expression was pinched and serious despite the lightheartedness of his voice. His head twirled in circles above me, in opposite circles than the cage was twirling, and suddenly I was somersaulting between the two. I groaned and closed my eyes.

"Shh, shh, shh," Walker hushed soothingly. "It's all right, DiRocco. Take it slow and easy. Did he drink from you?"

"Yes," I whispered.

"Did he drink from the artery?"

I nodded stiffly.

"Which one?" Walker asked, but his voice seemed farther away. I heard the long rip of Velcro.

"Every artery," I muttered. "Where didn't they drink?"

"They?" I felt Walker's hands on me. His touch was light and efficient, checking over my body.

"More than half a dozen of them a block from my apartment. Dominic saved me and brought me here."

He grunted. "I knew you'd been attacked, but I didn't realize there had been so many. Did you drink from any of them?"

"No," I whispered. "Dominic tried, but I spit it out."

"How did your bites heal?" Walker asked. His voice sounded cautious. He lifted my left eyelid and a burst of light flashed over my vision. I cringed away, but he flashed a light into the right eye, too. "Sorry."

I heard another tear of Velcro and a light pat. Dancing colors swirled behind my closed lids. I swallowed against the rising nausea, and my throat ached. "He licked my wounds closed." I swallowed again, and it ached even worse, like my throat was clamping on razors. "It sounds insane, but he licked each wound, and they healed."

Walker sighed again, deeper than before. His hands cupped my face, and his palms were warm and steady and calm. "I know. This whole crazy situation is insane, but it's all real. One day you'll wish you were just insane."

"Already there," I whispered.

Walker chuckled lightly. "Here," he said, and a straw was suddenly at my lips. "Drink this."

"What is it?" I asked wearily. I peeked between my lashes and tried to focus past the dizziness.

"Juice box," Walker said kindly.

My eyes finally focused, and I could see a cartoon apple on the side of the square container of juice he was holding for me. I hesitated and met Walker's eyes.

"It's all right," Walker assured me. "The box was sealed. Besides, poison wouldn't be their style, trust me." He looked a little amused by my caution, but a little saddened, too. His jaw muscle flexed and twitched as he clenched his teeth.

I pursed my lips around the straw and drank. Apple juice is a fine juice, but this particular juice, as it passed over my tongue and flowed down my throat, might have been the best, most divine, nourishing, God-given liquid I'd ever tasted. I sucked down the entire box, swallow after swallow, in one long pull. The straw eventually crackled and gurgled empty, and I still wanted more. I closed my eyes again and groaned.

"Thirsty?" Walker asked. He let his hand holding the juice box drop to his side. His jaw had unclenched.

I nodded. "I know it was just apple juice, but it tasted like heaven."

Walker chuckled. "Your body needs sugar and rest to replenish the blood you lost."

"How did you know?" I asked. I opened my eyes, and the world stayed in one place this time. Walker was kneeling next to me. The cowboy boots and jeans were gone, and in their stead he wore black from head to toe. If I wasn't mistaken, he was wearing Kevlar. His brown eyes were kind and gentle, and I felt comforted meeting his gaze. The dimple in his smile disappeared at my question, but despite those big brown eyes trying to convince me that everything was all right, I needed to know. "How did you know that I was here and that

I'd been attacked? How did you know that I would need blood?" I swallowed and forced myself to ask, "How do you know about vampires?"

Walker sighed. "I'll tell you after I get us out of here."

"Tell me now."

"It's a long story, and we've wasted enough time."

I touched his hand still holding the juice box. "You can tell me the long version later. Please. How do you know about any of this?"

Walker looked at my hand touching his. His eyes widened, and I realized I was touching him with the hand that Dominic had fed from. My fingers and palm were crusted with a macabre glove of dried blood. I pulled away from him, embarrassed and disgusted with myself, but Walker took my hand and sandwiched it between both of his. "I'm what the vampires call a night blood."

"A night blood," I repeated, dumbfounded. Part of me had still wanted to believe that Dominic had spewed nothing but lies and bullshit, but hearing those words straight from Walker's lips was unsettling. I had the potential to turn into a vampire.

Walker nodded, his tone and expression dead serious. "If a vampire attempts the change on a typical human, he simply dies from exsanguination. If he lives through the feeding, however, and actually drinks vampire blood, his remaining blood clots, like having a transfusion with the wrong blood type."

"But you're not most humans," I said dryly.

"No, *we're* not. *Our* bodies can sustain life for an extended period of time with very little blood, and *our* blood readily accepts the integration of vampire blood, transforming to match its DNA," Walker said pointedly.

I raised an eyebrow. "Are you implying something?"

"No, ma'am. Just statin' a fact."

"You don't know anything about me," I whispered.

"I spoke with Detective Greta Wahl today, and she likes to brag. I know more than you think I know."

I rolled my eyes. "One good deed never goes unpunished."

Walker grinned. "But I know somethin' about you even she doesn't know."

I shook my head. "I'm not a night blood."

"The vampires wouldn't have kept you here otherwise," Walker said patiently.

"I don't believe in vampires, either," I snapped. I looked past Walker at the silver cage surrounding us and the cave-like room beyond that. The room was still dark as night despite the sun having assumedly risen, but I could discern something splattered and glistening on the stone floor. I squinted at the object until its shape took form in my mind, and I groaned. A chunk of bloody flesh still stained the floor: Rafe's throat. "Fuck," I whispered.

"I know. They're animals. Worse than animals, they're parasites, but they're also stronger, faster, more mercenary, organized, and cunning than any animal alive. In the end, however, it's our decision: death or this eternal life," Walker said, gesturing to the cage and cave surrounding us. "I made my decision years ago."

I looked back at Walker—into his kind, warm eyes—and realized that beneath the velvet was forged steel.

He squeezed my hands. "But no one is making you decide today. Not me, and least of all the fucking vampires."

I squeezed back. "Get me the hell out of here."

"That's precisely what I intend to do, darlin'."

"And stop calling me darling," I snapped, but I smiled when I said it.

"I guess you don't want this then," Walker said on a sigh. He reached behind him and handed me a leather shoulder satchel.

I reached out, gaping. "My bag!"

"You betcha."

I dug inside. My phone cover had cracked, but otherwise, everything was accounted for, even my recorder and writing pad. I played the recorder, and Greta's voice was sweet heaven's harps to my ears. "You're my hero, Walker. You can call me darlin' all night if it makes you happy."

Walker laughed. "Well, it's no fun if you actually like it, DiRocco."

Leaving the coven wasn't the great escape I'd envisioned. Since Walker had already broken into the cage—which was apparently easy for someone who could actually touch silver without his skin boiling off and knew how to pick locks—and the vampires were tucked away for the day, we simply walked out. It seemed highly improbable that Dominic would leave the entire coven vulnerable while it slept, but we didn't encounter one vampire, guard, or creature to prevent us from leaving.

Walker didn't seem surprised by our easy escape. "The vampires are overconfident. They think they're gods, and we're nothing but cattle. Plus, I doubt they even know I'm in town yet," he explained as we turned left down another vampire-made tunnel.

"Would knowing you're in town make a difference?" I asked. "Do they know you?"

Walker ignored my questions and heightened an already grueling pace.

I never would've successfully escaped on my own. Even having tracked me to the coven, Walker spent two hours scavenging the sewage system, and according to his calculations, we still had another hour until we reached human-made drainage pipes. For Dominic to leave the entire coven unprotected based on my inability to escape, however, was ridiculous. How could he keep the coven secret and safe without daytime protection? Maybe I shouldn't look a gift horse in the mouth, as Walker suggested, but our unhindered escape bothered me.

My hip had progressed from grinding to a gnawing, scraping sensation around the second hour of our hike, and I was forced to either accept Walker's assistance or collapse. He offered to carry my bag and eventually me since I started limping, but the little help I had accepted was mortifying enough. I needed to accomplish some tasks on my own, and walking out of the sewers on my own volition after having been attacked and kidnapped by vampires was one of them.

Eventually, we emerged from a manhole in the sewer system and into the warm, glowing Friday morning sun, stinking and exhausted but alive. As I soaked in the clear, crisp breath of freedom and the radiant heat of daylight on my skin, I tried to let the pain and fear and stubborn pride melt away. Vampires couldn't exist in this moment. I was human and alive and home and not sure which to cherish most.

As I blinked back to reality, I realized that Walker was staring at me. His hand was still around my waist as he waited silently and patiently. A knowing twist shaped his lips. I swiped at the tears with the back of my hand, feeling simultaneously embarrassed by my reaction and unbelievably grateful for his assistance.

"Walker, I—"

He squeezed my hand. "I know."

"Thank you."

"What kind of animal tracker would I be if I'd allowed Detective Wahl's only credible witness to disappear?" He winked. "You're very welcome."

Much to his consternation, Walker escorted me home like I'd re-quested instead of to the hospital like he'd insisted. He offered to stay with me in my apartment while I rested, but I adamantly refused. I'd lived on my own for nearly six years since I left Adam. This was my apartment, and I could take care of myself, damn it. Still, letting Walker leave had been unsettlingly difficult. I didn't mind his help—in fact, I very much appreciated everything he'd done—but I didn't want to *need* his help. Gratefully accepting help from others without depending on that assistance was a tightrope walk I'd never learned to negotiate well.

Walker conceded to leaving my apartment only after wringing a promise from me that I'd take Tylenol, ice my hip, and beeline it to my bed. That had been my general plan anyway, so it wasn't much of a concession on my part. Finally alone in my apartment, I tucked my-self into cold sheets, knowing I could have kept Walker in the apart-ment had I wanted. I hated myself for wanting him there, possibly needing him, but more than that, I hated myself for being too stub-born to act on it.

The insistent trill of my cell phone startled me awake. It was one o'clock in the afternoon, but it felt like sunrise. I rolled over, reluc-tant to wake, reluctant to even move, and picked up the damn phone more to shut it up than from an actual desire to communicate with anyone.

"DiRocco here," I croaked.

"Where the hell are you? Are you okay? Did you get my mes-sages? Carter is going to stroke out!"

I winced from the pitch of Meredith's voice and tipped the phone away from my ear. The voice mail icon was indeed activated.

"In bed; I am now; no; and we can only fantasize about such things. We're not that lucky," I answered.

"Ha! We will be if you don't get your ass to this scene," she warned.

"What kind of scene are we talking about?" I asked, feeling my heart quicken.

"Triple homicide, three blocks from your apartment."

I winced. "I hate it when they're close."

"I know. Come see for yourself."

"Yes, ma'am," I said, and winced, thinking of Walker.

I hung up with Meredith and crawled out of bed. My hip gave its normal wake-up twinge, but its aching was substantially improved from last night. Typically, I wouldn't have bothered with a shower, but I hadn't bothered with one before bed, either. I was in critical need of bathing. Half an hour later, I had scrubbed the blood and sewage funk off my body, dressed, dried my hair, and listened to six voice mails—each varying between alarm, panic, and outright rage.

Meredith's hushed voice murmured in the first message, "Where are you, Cassidy? Pick up! We have a staff meeting in five minutes. It's urgent, and I do not want to put up with Crabby Carter on my own. Are you there? I hope not, because you need to be here! Like, now."

The voice mail clicked to the next call, and I let the pillow smother my face as Deborah Rogers, our grumpy, grandmotherly administrative assistant, rasped over the line. "Is this you, Ms. DiRocco? I'm calling on Mr. Bellissimo's behalf. You are late to work, and you are missing the budget meeting. Please call us when you get this message."

The moment Deborah hung up and the machine beeped, Carter's voice blasted from the tiny speakers. "DiRocco! I'm going to assume that you didn't show for this morning's meeting and haven't answered anyone's phone calls because you're already at the scene outside your apartment. I'm assuming this because you're already on my radar from having written an article that needed a retraction. NYPD is on my ass about you! Did you talk to Detective Wahl? Did you ask her for the autopsy report? You are on thin ice, DiRocco, and I am not—"

Carter was cut short by a voice mail miracle, and Meredith's voice whispered over the phone again. "Are you okay? There's a big scene less than five blocks from your apartment. If you get this message, just sneak in. I'm here, and I told Carter you are, too. Don't make me a liar!"

Beep. "—I am not going down with you when all of your sources freeze you out, DiRocco! Meredith assures me that you are with her at the scene, but she refused to put you on the line. You better be taking statements, DiRocco. Pulitzer statements to dig yourself out of the shithole you've dragged us all into. And I better not see so much as one mention of animals, teeth, or bite marks in this article, or so help me, God, I—"

I deleted the rest of the messages until I scrolled to a number that wasn't anyone from the office. The smooth, amber tones of Greta's voice sounded through the speaker, and my gut leapt at her words: "The autopsy reports from Monday night came in. You were right. Call me."

I replayed the message again, and the phone shook against my ear. I closed my eyes to listen. Greta knew the bodies had animal bites. I gnawed on my lip, torn between feeling justified and nauseated. The reporter in me was itching to inform the world about my experience, to enlighten New York City with the truth about the murders, and to be the first to announce the existence of vampires; the human in me, however, hesitated.

First of all, who would actually believe my story? Everyone would think it belonged alongside alien abductions and Elvis sightings, not alongside hard news headlines. Second, even if by some miracle the public did believe me, *all* vampires might then decide to hunt to kill. Without the need to hide their existence, they might forego Dominic's slightly tamer version of feeding in favor of Kaden's version. They'd kill without remorse or hesitation and revel in their new freedom, and the ensuing slaughter would be my fault.

With thoughts of slaughter, blame, and potential Pulitzers weighing heavily on my mind, I buried my face in my pillow and clicked to the next message. My brother's voice whispered breathlessly over the phone. "For shiz, sis, what's the biz? Are you home? Meredith just called, asking where you are. Why aren't you at work, kickin' ass and takin' names?" I heard him sigh heavily over the line, and his voice deepened. "I need to talk to you. It's about the article you wrote for Tuesday's paper, the one that needed a retraction. Call me back ASAP."

I stared at my cell as the voice mail icon bounced closed. Dominic had likely attacked him, like he'd attacked me and Meredith and every witness to wipe our memories of Monday night. I scrubbed my face with my hands. Dread tightened in a knot through my stomach as I called him back.

He answered on the first ring. "Cass?"

"Yo, bro, who else you know?" I heard him sigh over the phone. "I got your message. Are you—"

"You're just getting up now?" he asked. "Meredith said you were at the crime scene."

"Meredith has very high standards for me to live up to."

"This is the second day in one week that you've missed work."

I frowned. "I'm not missing work. I'm using my sick days, which I'm actually entitled to, you know."

"Yeah, I know, but you're not sick. You were attacked."

My argument deflated along with my anger, and I gnawed on the skin around my already torn thumbnail. "Who told you?"

"You're not the only one who has friends at the precinct."

"And you've waited until now to call?" I asked snottily. "Your message mentioned that you wanted to talk about my retracted article. How about we just skip to that conversation?"

Nathan didn't respond. I heard the floorboards of his apartment creak as he paced to fill the silence, so I knew the next words out of his mouth were probably going to be a lie.

"I'm worried about your career. Skipping work after writing that article does not look good. Your reputation is on the line. I covered for you and found you help when you were addicted to percs, but I can't help you this time. You disappeared headfirst down the crap shoot before I even knew you'd jumped this time."

His words twisted through my heart because they were completely, utterly, devastatingly true, but I could still hear him pacing. I'd been clean from percs for four years. He only brought it up now to piss me off enough to trip up and admit something. He was worried, but not about my career.

I let him stew in silence. I held the phone away from my mouth, so he couldn't even hear me breathe.

"And it's not just Carter who's pissed. The police are more shocked than angry at this point, considering your reputation, but your infamy at the precinct will only keep you afloat for so long."

I didn't respond.

"Without their inside connection, you'll be like all the other vultures gnawing the scrap leads for the juiciest morsel of printable news. Next time, Meredith might have to retract her image, and you know how she is about her photography, especially the close-ups. I doubt you want to bring her career down along with yours, so—"

"Funny thing about photography is that you actually can't retract it," I said, pouncing on his slip. He remembered seeing the close-up of the bites. "A retraction is an admission of error, but a photo itself is proof that an error never occurred." I paused, waiting for him to admit it himself, but all I heard was the creak of his pacing. "Do you remember Meredith's photography that matched my original, re-tracted article? Do you remember that particular close-up?"

I heard clear silence from his end. He'd stopped pacing. "Why did you write that retraction?"

"I didn't write it. Meredith wrote it. That article did not need a re-traction," I hedged, needing him to admit it himself because saying it first, even after everything I'd seen and experienced with Dominic, still seemed crazy.

Are you a night blood? Even as I thought the question, my mind wanted to dismiss the possibility, but Nathan was questioning the re-traction. My gut knotted. I'd bet my recorder that he remembered the bite marks, and something else nagged at my memory, something I hadn't thought of until now. Only Nathan and I had been able to hear Dominic's rattling breaths when he'd been burned at the crime scene. Donovan had pronounced him dead and the machines hadn't detected a pulse, but Nathan and I could hear him breathe.

I'd always prided myself on the ability to ask the hard questions at the right moments to get the truth, but I didn't want the truth this time. The one time in my whole life when it probably mattered most, and I choked.

"I didn't think it needed a retraction, either, but no one else re-members Meredith's photography." Nathan's voice was brittle. "No one else remembers the bite marks."

I squeezed my phone and heard the plastic squeak beneath my grip. "How many people have you talked to about this?"

"It's ridiculous!" he snapped suddenly. "Why would Carter force you to write a retraction when you were right? It doesn't make any sense! Who's covering for who? Whose ass got exposed that paid to have it covered back up?"

I closed my eyes briefly and told myself to remember to breathe. "How many people have you told?" I insisted.

"The police are especially suspicious of the retraction. Even though they're convinced that the bites never existed, they know and trust you, and they think you're being blackmailed or bought or some-thing. They think Carter's using the hype about the bites to cover your involvement in this case."

"You sure have been talking to the police a lot lately."

Nathan ignored me. "What's really going on, Cass?"

I licked my lips. "What do you think's going on?"

I could hear his sigh over the phone, and the helplessness in its tone melted the iron-plated backbone that I'd forged throughout most of my life.

"You wouldn't believe me if I told you. You wouldn't believe me even if the truth bit you in the jugular." He laughed and the noise was bitter and grating and very unlike Nathan.

I bit my lip and finally hedged at the hard question. "Would the truth only be able to bite me after sunset?"

Nathan didn't say anything. The floorboards didn't even creak from his pacing.

I forced myself to laugh. "It's an expression."

"No, it's not."

"You don't get out much," I said, feeling unfathomably disappointed. I covered my eyes with one of my hands and dug the heel of my palm over my face.

"I won't anymore," Nathan said, gravely serious. "Like you said, not after sunset."

I stopped breathing. *He knows about vampires*, I thought.

I swallowed and cleared my throat before speaking. "We need to talk. In person. Before the sun sets again. Tonight."

"Yes," Nathan said, and that single word poured through the phone like an unbearable mound of ice had melted from his shoulders.

"I need to catch up with Meredith at the crime scene, but we can meet after work."

"Yes." I could hear his smile.

"I'll come to your apartment, and we—"

"No," he said suddenly. "I'll come to your apartment, and—"

"No," I said, thinking of Dominic. Nathan and I needed to settle somewhere safe after sunset. I'd given Dominic permission to enter my apartment, and now that I believed in vampires—I groaned to myself—I doubted my fancy new locks would deter him in the least. "I need you to trust me. We need to stay in and stick together tonight, and it can't be at my apartment."

"I agree, but it can't be at my apartment, either."

"Why don't you want me to stay at your apartment?" I asked, and I couldn't hide the pain in my voice. There had only ever been one time that I wasn't allowed in his apartment. The feelings I'd buried where they belonged seeped between the cracks in my anger. My breath hitched.

"Cass, it's not like that. You know I trust you, but I—"

"I need to come over to your apartment tonight. We need to stick together, and we need to lock ourselves in at sunset," I said in a rambling, blurted rush. "Please. Nathan, I—" My throat was tight and aching from trying to dance around the truth. I swallowed down the tears and choked. "I'm scared."

Nathan sighed, and it sounded as horrible as I felt. It was a long moment before he spoke. "I'll figure something out."

"Okay," I said, wanting him to say more.

"I'll see you at seven," he said.

"All right," I said, knowing something wasn't right at all. "You know that I wouldn't ask if it wasn't—" I began, but he'd already hung up.

Chapter 5

This crime scene, like the majority of the cases I'd covered through the years, was an obnoxious, disrespectful audience on the outside—media trying to shine spotlights, snapshots, and squeeze statements—and an efficient, well-rehearsed play on the inside. Every officer had a part to play. Every media member, on the other hand, was vying for the same role, and everyone wanted the lead.

Meredith was shooting angles of one of the three victims. This particular victim was male and on his belly, as if he'd been crawling away. He had endured multiple stab wounds to the back and calves. Other photographers surrounded him, too, attempting to snap the same angle Meredith was shooting, so I bided my time until she finished.

A few officers who walked the beat near my block made it to the scene. They were on the other side of the street, behind the tape with, presumably, the other two victims. I nodded at them when our eyes met, and they nodded back. Another officer from Greta's precinct was standing with them. He turned to see whom the others were acknowledging, and I recognized him and his salacious grin as Officer Harroway. He waved me over.

Wonderful, I thought with a groan. I ducked under the police tape toward the officers, glad to have been summoned but wishing it had been by any other officer. Harroway had a knack for flirting while simultaneously twisting the knife on our shared history that I found uncomfortable. Although my temper usually dissuaded unwanted attention, my snappy attitude only made Harroway try harder. The more he tried to sweep me off my feet, the more I walked away unswept. The more I remained unswept, the more he flirted. He was handsome in a block-jawed, solid, manly-man kind of way that most women found attractive (and I loved), but he came with the matching personality (which I hated).

I think my biggest problem was knowing that when a situation got hairy, he would freeze. He would cover his own ass instead of watching my six, which was how my hip took a bullet. Maybe his instincts and attitude had changed since then, but he still walked a beat while Greta had advanced to detective. The department had a long memory, and so did I.

"Cassidy DiRocco," he said, enunciating the consonants in my name so he sounded like a sports announcer. "What brings you here on this fine Friday afternoon? 'Shining light on Brooklyn's darkest secrets,' as usual?"

"Well, it's certainly not the company that keeps me around, Officer Harroway," I jibed.

Harroway winked. "Lies do not become you."

I grinned. "If you know so damn much, why don't you tell me why I'm here?"

"The truth *bites*, DiRocco," Harroway said innocently. "I'm not sure you can handle it."

The knife slid between my ribs, cold and swift, as usual. I couldn't even stab back because Greta obviously hadn't made the autopsy report public. For all intents and purposes, I was still the crazy who'd reported animal bites. I narrowed my eyes and did what I did best when I couldn't win; I got angry.

"You call me over just to jerk my dick, you're wasting both our time," I snapped.

Harroway laughed. "Got your panties twisted tighter than usual this afternoon, I see."

"Keep dreaming about things you'll never see, Harroway." I stepped aside in the hope that Meredith had finished her shots.

"Aw, come on, DiRocco, loosen up. It's a Friday, for fuck's sake."

"You sure know how to sweet-talk a girl," I threw over my shoulder.

"It's another local gang fight, fourth so far this month," he said, pitching his voice lower, so I'd have to turn back. "How sweet does that sound?"

I stopped walking, stared at Meredith ahead of me still taking shots, and cursed under my breath. I should have known I'd never escape from Harroway that easily. I turned around and stomped back toward him and his smug grin.

"The same gang?" I asked.

Harroway nodded.

"How do you know?"

"Would I steer you wrong?" Harroway asked, looking wounded.

I pinned him with my hard, alligator-grim gaze. "How do you know it's the same gang?"

Harroway cleared his throat. "Technically, we won't know until the medical examiner compares the wounds, but it's the same pattern as all the others."

"I'll hold out for the medical examiner."

"I'm telling you, DiRocco, all the victims have bullets to the head, execution-like. Someone is either new on the block and needs to prove themselves, or someone old on the block feels threatened."

"That doesn't prove they're from the same gang."

"The victims also have gold necklaces with a pendant that matches necklaces on victims from three previous scenes," Harroway confided, finally serious. His face relaxed, and he gave great eye contact when he kept it real. "The cases are gang related, and it's the same gang."

My breath caught from his sincerity. "What kind of pendant?" I asked, remembering a couple of scenes I'd covered last week.

His face screwed up into another grin. "A wolf."

I nodded. I'd definitely covered those cases. "Is that so?"

"Yep, you know, something native to Brooklyn that *bites*."

I felt my cheeks burn and resisted the urge to strangle the man. Meredith was walking toward me, finally, so I jabbed my finger in his chest. "Sounds like you're describing someone we both know." I snapped my teeth together with an audible *clack*. "So watch it."

Meredith met me outside the police tape, which was a healthy twenty yards from Officer Harroway, and I could still hear the grate of his gut-deep laugh at my expense. She looked over my shoulder, presumably at Harroway and the unnecessary ruckus he was making. She shook her head.

"That man has it bad," she said.

I scoffed. "Whatever he has, it's not manners."

"You saved that man's life, and he'll never forget. He just has a peculiar way of showing it."

"If by 'never forget' you mean 'never forgive,' then I agree with you," I snapped. "He hands me so much shit, I don't know what do to with all the excess after I've thrown some back at him."

"He also gives you, and only you, the best leads," Meredith pointed out.

"True," I agreed grudgingly. "Although I wouldn't say they were the *best*."

Meredith smiled. "What did he give you this time?"

I smiled back. "Mediocre. This scene is apparently the fourth in a series of gang-related cases, and police have evidence to support that the victims in all four cases are from the same gang. All the victims in all the cases including this one are killed execution-style and are wearing matching gold necklaces. If I'm not mistaken, we covered the previous two scenes in last week's paper, but we covered them as separate cases."

"Mediocre?" Meredith scoffed. "Ask how many officers spilled their guts to the *Post* or *Times*. Face it; he's wrapped around your middle finger."

I raised my eyebrows. "I think you mean little finger."

"Nah, for you, it's the middle one."

I rolled my eyes. "What did you get?"

"Black and white and Pulitzer all over."

"What did you really get?" I asked, smiling.

She sighed. "Something real. It's disturbing, and it should be."

"Sounds like my cup of tea," I assured her.

Meredith smiled wanly. "Where were you this morning? Anything that nearly gives Carter a coronary is usually okay in my book, but you've never missed a budget meeting, let alone two in one week."

"Well," I said, stretching out the word to stall. I certainly couldn't tell her that I'd been kidnapped by vampires, but what else besides being kidnapped would make me miss a scoop? I shrugged. "It's been a rough week."

"Every week's a rough week," Meredith scoffed.

I nodded.

When I didn't elaborate, Meredith stared at me expectantly. "It's about those bites again, isn't it?"

"Just let it go," I hissed.

"I can't, Cass," Meredith said, her expression pained. The strain in her voice made my heart ache for her. "I stare at that photograph that

I shot, that we published in *my* paper, and I cannot for the life of me just *let it go*."

"Keep it down." I looked around warily as Meredith's voice rose and hitched, but no one was paying much attention to us when there were bodies to snapshot and witnesses to interview.

I scrubbed my hand down my face, torn between protecting her from the truth and letting ignorance rot between us.

"Cassidy," she whispered, and I forced myself to meet her gaze. The pain there shredded my resolve. "Please."

I sighed. "Greta left a message on my machine last night."

"She called you about the bites?"

"Yeah, she wants me to talk to the medical examiner. They brought in an environmental scientist, and he, um"—I sighed again—"he tracks animals."

"Detective Wahl called in an environmental science expert to track an animal here in New York?" Meredith squeaked.

I nodded.

"And you're talking to the medical examiner today?"

I nodded again.

Meredith covered her face with both hands. "What the fuck is wrong with me? Why can't I remember?"

Damn Dominic, I thought. "I'm sure that it's just shock from being mugged, like Carter said."

"If you're agreeing with something Carter said, I know something's wrong with me." Meredith let her hands drop down to her sides. She shook her head, frustrated. "I never should have written that retraction."

"No sorrys needed," I assured her. "I would have written the retraction myself if Greta had called to bitch at me."

"No, you wouldn't have. You would've done exactly what you did do. You would've gone to the station, showed her the picture, played your tape, and confused the hell out of her until she saw bites even where there weren't any."

"There are bites," I insisted.

"I know," Meredith whispered, unable to meet my gaze.

"But I wouldn't spread that around if I were you."

She met my eyes then, her expression somber. "I know."

* * *

Twenty minutes later, I walked into the lobby of the Kings County Hospital Center, which included the morgue. A tall woman with thick black bifocals sat behind the counter. I smiled as I approached, but she just stared back, blank-faced. I glued on my smile despite her frost.

"Cassidy DiRocco, here to see Detective Greta Wahl and the chief medical examiner," I ground out pleasantly.

Someone behind me let out a high catcall. I turned, about to blast the man's head off, but my temper fizzled to steam when the man's deep, velvet brown gaze met mine. My smile was swift and genuine, not something I was accustomed to. My reaction to him took me aback, but considering the man had rescued me, I decided not to overanalyze my feelings.

"Stalking me, Walker?" I asked.

The pleasure and warmth in his eyes at seeing me was unmistakable, but something had obviously set him on edge, as well. A muscle in his jaw ticked. "I believe I was here first, so if anyone's stalking anyone, sugar, it's you."

I turned back to the stoic woman at the desk. "Are Greta and the good doctor ready to see me?" I asked, smile in place, but my tone was creeping toward sarcastic.

"Detective Wahl and Dr. Chunn will be with you in a moment, if you could take a seat," the woman said, indicating the few empty chairs behind me.

I looked behind me to where Walker was seated, and he smirked.

"Fabulous." I walked to the chairs and sat across from Walker, my back to the receptionist. "We've got to stop meeting like this," I said, matching his smirk. "People will think we're in love."

Walker laughed. "Who knew reception areas were so ripe with datin' potential. To think, all the time I've wasted at the bar and on-line."

He stood suddenly and switched chairs to sit next to me, putting his back to the receptionist, as well. The smell of fresh mint wafted from his movement.

He slouched and spoke directly into my ear. "You should have called out sick today."

"I'm not sick," I whispered back.

"We just got home this morning. A nap is not long enough for your body to regenerate its cell count after losing the amount of blood that you lost. You were attacked, injured, and kidnapped. You could barely walk this morning. You're not well, and in order to get well, you should have called out."

I stared at him a moment, stunned by his sharp tone. He simply stared back. "You're serious," I murmured, trying to douse the flame under my temper.

"Of course. You're putting yourself at risk."

"As you can see, I'm walking just fine. Besides, the vampires won't rise again until sunset. I'm safer now than I will be at dusk," I snapped. "Mind your business."

"Should I have minded my business last night?" Walker asked coolly.

I bit the inside of my cheek and took my time before answering, so I didn't snap again. "I'm very grateful, Walker, that you did not mind your business last night. Thank you," I said, meeting his eyes. His own eyes widened in surprise, but I continued before he could respond. "But I still have a life and a career and a reputation, and not one of those things allows taking a sick day." Walker opened his mouth and I interjected, "Especially the career."

He pursed his lips, obviously not appeased. "They'll know you haven't fully recuperated. You're the injured antelope to their predator's sense."

"I understand, but—"

"No, you obviously don't understand, because if you did, you would have called out sick, despite your career. You were already prey, but now you're prey with a flashing target on your back."

I rolled my eyes. "The target was going to flash at full strength whether or not I called out from work. I'm supposed to be in that cage when Dominic rises at sunset. When he wakes tonight and realizes that I'm gone, do you really think staying in bed all day would make a difference? I doubt that my aching hip or low cell count will be the focus of his attention. He'll find me tonight either way, and he's not going to be happy when he does."

Walker leaned back in the chair and crossed his arms. "Well, the low cell count certainly won't help," he groused.

"Can't even give an inch," I chided.

He shrugged. "Not when I know I'm right."

A sudden burst of anger nearly short-circuited my brain, but then I noticed the dimple in his left cheek deepen as he smirked. He was half-kidding. My anger fizzled out again.

I bumped his shoulder with mine. "Arrogance isn't attractive."

"Neither is stubbornness, but I had the good manners not to point it out."

"Just keepin' it real," I said.

Walker elbowed me back. "I don't suppose it's a coincidence that our paths have crossed again."

I shook my head. "And with you here, I think it's safe to assume what the medical examiner found."

He nodded. "They got sloppy, that's for sure."

"What do you mean?" I asked.

"Vampires are discreet. They rarely leave a fresh kill out for display. After decades of practice, they've developed quite a knack for not getting caught," he said bitterly. "Frankly, I'm taken aback that they've exposed themselves on such a large scale. I thought they had a ruling class or government of sorts that killed vampires who risked their survival."

I nodded. "They do. Dominic called their government council members Day Reapers, but he also said that a growing sect of his vampires are rebelling. They don't want to remain a secret, like he does, and despite the threat of punishment from the Day Reapers, they are challenging Dominic as their Master. He loses strength every seven years on the Solstice, but this is the first year that his status as Master is being challenged."

Walker frowned. "Get to the point, DiRocco."

"My point is that you think the vampires just got sloppy."

Walker nodded slowly. "Yes, ma'am, that's my theory. It's not consistent with their normal behavior, but that's the most likely situation."

"Well, I'm proposing a different situation in which this wasn't just a sloppy mistake. I think the rebels are growing stronger as Dominic's powers weaken, and the rebels are taking full advantage of the situation to enjoy their hunt. Dominic said that—"

Walker suddenly reached out and covered my hand with his own. "Anything Dominic said is a lie to get what he wants from you. He's older than we can imagine, and in that time, I'm sure he's learned a thing or two about persuasion. Since he can't mind-fuck you like he can everyone else, he'll use whatever mind games necessary to convince you that he's more than what he really seems."

"And what's that?" I asked, sliding my hand away from his to cross my arms.

"A dangerous predator who wants to attack you, drain you, and turn you, if he doesn't kill you first."

"Why would he lie about this?" I snapped. "He doesn't have anything to gain by lying about an uprising."

"He's taking the blame of the vampire attacks off himself, so you see him like a victim instead of a predator. And it's working. You're already sympathizing with his situation," Walker explained patiently. I could tell he was deliberately keeping his temper in check to prevent mine from exploding.

"I don't think he wants to kill me," I confessed. "If that was his ultimate goal, he would have done that already. Instead, he saved me. I would've been killed by the other vampires last night if it wasn't for him."

Walker shook his head, disgusted. "There are other ways to steal your life besides killing you. The Master of a coven near my hometown does the same for me. She saves me from other vampire attacks and protects me while I'm tracking large game. Dominic doesn't protect you because he cares about you, like a human feels compassion toward another human."

Walker met my eyes, and I could read his unspoken implication: *Like I feel toward you.*

"He protects you because he's invested," Walker continued. "He wants you in every way he can't have you. He wants your mind, your body, and eventually your humanity, but you only truly matter to him as a night blood, nothing more. If you were a human, he wouldn't have thought twice about drinking from you, killing you, and continuing on his way."

I mulled over his explanation, part of me shocked that he'd experienced the same from the Master of his local coven back home. The other part of me was annoyingly disappointed. "How many night bloods are out there?" I asked.

"At least seventy of us exist in the United States, maybe only a hundred total in North America. It's difficult to know for sure. Many humans don't even know what a night blood is, let alone whether they are one," Walker said, tilting his head at me. "In my life, I've only spoken to one other night blood besides you, my partner from home. I don't know of any others who live nearby."

Partner. I thought of Dominic's explanation of the near intimate relationship between vampires and their night bloods, and I wondered if Walker's relationship with his night blood "partner" was any different. Although the dynamics between a night blood and a vampire compared to two night bloods were obviously different, I couldn't help but think of the tension that existed between Walker and me and how easily the high stakes of being a night blood and the danger of interacting with vampires could turn the tension of any relationship more intimate. A sharp twinge I'd rather not identify nagged through my gut.

"Is night blood hereditary?" I asked instead, thinking of my conversation with Nathan.

Walker shrugged. "It must be a recessive gene, but it hasn't been studied."

"In all these years—a couple thousand years of genetic science—it hasn't been studied by anyone?" I asked, incredulous.

"We're lucky to discover who we are and survive, let alone find other night bloods. I doubt anyone found the time or had the opportunity to perform scientific research."

"Dominic said something similar about us being rare," I mused.

Walker's eyes darkened. His accent thickened as he became more frustrated with me. "I just warned you; anythin' that creature tells you is suspect. The best lies are submerged in truth, and everythin' out of his mouth is nothin' but—"

I raised both my hands in surrender. "Back down, hoss. I'm just mulling the possibilities."

"Mulling is not allowed," Walker griped, but the corners of his lips tipped up again, revealing that hidden dimple.

I smiled back, helpless not to, and something clicked between us. His eyes were so brown and beautiful, and he smelled fresh, like mint. Suddenly, I was very aware of how close his lips were to mine. I should have turned my head or pulled away or done absolutely anything except nothing, but I couldn't bring myself to move. I knew he felt it, too, because his smile tipped and turned serious. He stared back into my eyes, unblinking and motionless except for the slow rise and fall of his Adam's apple as he swallowed.

He eased closer, and I opened my mouth to say something—God knows what—when the woman at the desk buzzed her microphone.

"The medical examiner will see you now, Ms. DiRocco, Mr. Walker," she said, her metallic, monotone, machine-like voice cut through the PA system. "Through the double doors and second examination room on the right."

I jumped away from Walker's lips and from the precipice of insanity. What the hell was I thinking? We were waiting outside a morgue, preparing to examine a body, for heaven's sake. I heard him clear his throat, and when I glanced over, his eyebrows were raised.

"We're being summoned." I stood, relieved to end the tension and gain a little distance before my skin singed from the heat between us. I snatched my leather satchel from the chair, the same satchel that he'd saved along with my life. I groaned to myself. "Do you have a usual protocol for this kind of thing?"

Walker looped the strap of a black briefcase over his head and stood. The woman buzzed us through, and he strode in step with me out of the waiting room. The tap of the briefcase was rhythmic against his hip. "Protocol for what thing?"

I locked my eyes on his. "Well, you're not going to inform Dr. Chunn and Detective Wahl that, in your expert opinion, this victim suffered from vampire bites."

"Of course not."

"Exactly. So what's the usual protocol?"

Walker laughed. "Nothing about this is usual, darlin'."

"I told you, I'm not your dar—"

"You've made the assumption that because I'm a night blood, I've been in this situation before, but like I said, vampires don't leave evidence. I've never had to examine a vampire victim in an official investigative setting."

"And it just keeps getting better and better," I grumbled. "How the hell did Greta pick you out of all the environmental science experts in the state? What are the chances she'd hire a night blood?"

Walker cut me a sharp look. "Just one of many questions, darlin', that probably won't get answered today."

Nine gurneys filled the examination room, eight of which had sheets covering bodies I assumed were the victims from Paerdegat Park. The sheets on the ninth gurney covered something that had the shape of a human head and chest, but the sheet dropped against the bed where it should have flattened over the abdomen. A metal basin had been placed on a table next to that bed. I would be examining both in a moment, and the inevitability of looking into that basin made my heart pound harder.

Greta and Dr. Chunn glanced up from their conversation when we entered. Dr. Chunn was my height. I liked her a little more knowing I wasn't the only five-foot flat woman in the room. She was very slender. Her thick-framed, black glasses seemed severe on her delicate, heart-shaped face, and her hair was cut pixie short. She styled it with the top a little longer than the sides, the closest she could get to being punk and still wear a lab coat.

"Always good to see you, G, despite the circumstances," I said, forcing a mask of cocky bravado over my anxiety with a smirk. "Thanks for the call."

Greta frowned at me, but the corners of her lips twitched. "No one likes a smug reporter."

"No one likes a reporter, smug or not, but when you're right, you're right."

She sighed. "I hate that you were right."

"I know. Me, too."

"No, you're not," Greta said. "The two of you are obviously well acquainted by now," she said, gesturing at Walker and me.

Walker nodded. "Yes, ma'am, lobby conversation is becoming quite the pastime."

I tried not to blush and failed. I could feel the heat flame over my cheeks.

Greta looked from me to Walker and back to me again. She raised an eyebrow. "Dr. Susanna Chunn, I'd like you to meet Ian Walker, environmental science expert, and Cassidy DiRocco, reporter for the *Sun Accord* and my personal friend."

"Pleasure to meet you, ma'am," Walker said, shaking hands.

I shook Dr. Chunn's hand and asked, "Why are there nine bodies? I thought we only recovered five from the scene."

"Four of the seven live victims from the scene died at the hospital," Dr. Chunn answered.

I groaned. "How are the survivors doing? Has anyone spoken to them?"

Greta nodded. "Of the remaining three, one hasn't regained consciousness, but she's expected to make a full recovery. The other two can't recall a single detail of the attack. The woman only incurred minor lacerations, but her memory is just as compromised as the other victim, who suffered moderate head trauma. The doctors claim that her memory loss could be triggered by shock. Other than Paerdegat Park, her record is spotless, so fortunately for her, but unfortunately for this case, I agree with the doctors. She wasn't involved. In any event, both conscious victims have given us zip in terms of leads, which leaves us with nothing but bodies."

Sudden and complete memory loss is becoming a common calling card, I thought. *Damn Dominic.* "Well, maybe the bodies will help."

"We can only hope," Dr. Chunn stated. "But, honestly, the evidence here only makes this case more confusing."

"I'm guessing that's where I come in," Walker interjected.

"Astute, as usual, Mr. Walker. We can begin with this one, if you'd like," Greta said, pulling back the sheet on the nearest bed.

"Of course," Dr. Chunn began, "Stephan Mathews, age thirty-six, died of cardiac arrest from blood loss."

I'd seen my share of bodies at crime scenes and at the morgue, but seeing a dead body was gut churning every time. Five years had passed since I'd identified the bodies of my parents. Nothing could compare to the blow of seeing them white and still and somehow unreal, but seeing others in the same state on the same white sheets always brought back the roiling nausea, grief, and bone-deep anger.

I pushed back the memories and buried them beneath the anger, as usual, to focus on the present body. "Are the bites at his carotid the bites that killed him?" I asked, pointing at his neck.

"No," Dr. Chunn said, her voice hardening. She pulled the sheet down farther. The man's arteries weren't the only part of him bitten. He was ravaged everywhere, worse than I'd been bitten. The vampires had feasted on him. His neck, arms, torso, stomach, and thighs had all been chewed raw.

This would have been my fate if Dominic hadn't found me in time last night. I pushed back another wave of emotion.

"The bite to his carotid was one of the first to occur, but one of the bites to his chest actually punctured the aorta. He died relatively quickly after that injury, if not immediately," Dr. Chunn stated.

Walker pulled a large, black DSLR camera case from his briefcase along with a ruler, legal pad, several forms, and a pen. He slid the pen over his ear and unzipped the camera case. "May I?" he asked, stepping closer to the body.

Dr. Chunn waved him forward. "By all means. You have access to my reports and photos, as well." She handed him a pair of latex gloves. "And we have the materials to make casts if you're still interested. My assistant said that you called ahead."

"I did. She was extremely helpful. I'm most obliged to use your materials, ma'am." He snapped on the gloves and measured the bites meticulously, noting the location and size of each on his forms. He placed the ruler on different places over the body while he took a variety of shots, but there were so many bites that the ruler often laid across one wound while he photographed another. I imagined him placing the ruler back in his briefcase and took a shallow breath against the nausea.

"Have you ever seen bites like these in a city?" Greta asked. "Could it be something as simple as someone's loose dog?"

"Or something exotic, like from one of the borough zoos?" Dr. Chunn added.

Greta shook her head. "We've checked the zoos. According to their records, all animals are accounted for."

"I need to analyze these patterns for consistency before narrowing the possible species, but—"

"Consistency in what?" Greta interrupted.

"In bite radius."

Greta's eyes widened. "You think there could be more than one animal loose in this city?"

Dr. Chunn blew the bangs out of her eyes. "It's difficult to accept that even *one* animal is out there, let alone a pack."

"Where there's one, there could easily be more, and with this many victims, it's certainly possible," Walker said grimly.

There certainly are *more than one*, I thought miserably.

"See here? The animal appears to have exceptionally long canines." Walker pointed to a particularly gnarly bite on the man's upper chest. "See the deep grooves there and there?"

Greta and Dr. Chunn nodded.

"In this bite, however," Walker continued, pointing to a different wound, "the long canines are also present, but they're positioned differently in the mouth. They're closer together, implying smaller or narrower incisors, and therefore, a different animal. Just by a cursory examination, I can tell we're dealing with two animals, at the least."

"Wonderful," Greta whispered.

When Walker finished examining Stephan Mathews, we moved on to the next body and then the next in the long line of victims. Carl Rogers, fifty-two; Lillian Grat, seventeen; Ronald Ramirez, forty-five; Victor Jones, forty-three; Hanna West, thirty-nine; Frank Holand, twenty-two; Terrance Holand, twenty; and Jill Darby, fifty-one, had all died from either cardiac arrest or exsanguination. No connection could be found between any of the victims. They were from different neighborhoods, backgrounds, ethnicities, careers, and social circles. Vampires apparently don't discriminate against who they attack. Walker measured each victim's bites, notating page after page of descriptions and measurements.

Hanna West's bites were particularly difficult for Walker to measure. Her bites had more tearing and evidence of frenzied gnawing compared to the other victims. Walker worked with what he could measure on her neck and torso before folding the sheet down to examine her thighs.

Dr. Chunn turned from her conversation with Greta. "That victim doesn't have—" she began, but Walker had already pulled the sheet clear of her torso.

Hanna West didn't have legs. The pelvic bone socket was exposed. The skin where her hip should have dipped into her thigh was ragged; long, jagged pulls of flesh dangled over the wound and rested on the gurney, and between those strips of flesh was red, shiny muscle. I looked away quickly. My eyes caught on the basin next to Hanna's gurney.

"What parts of her legs did you find?" I asked carefully, trying to keep my voice modulated and my eyes focused on the basin.

Greta's voice was clipped and deliberately modulated, as well. "Not much. A few toes. The instep of her left foot. Her entire right foot. One of her knees." She shook her head. "Not nearly enough."

I nodded. "Why are her injuries so much more devastating than the others?"

"That hasn't been determined," Dr. Chunn replied.

"If the other victims were already being eaten by larger members of their pack, assuming this was a pack attack, two predators of the same size will fight over food. This could result in a tug-of-war-style fight until one wins the prize," Walker offered.

"Or until they each tear away a part for themselves," I murmured.

"What pack of predators would be roaming Brooklyn?" Greta asked, perplexed.

Walker shook his head. "Hard to say, but I'm doin' my best to find out."

When Walker was finished and the bodies were once again covered, Greta offered Walker copies of the police files, which included images taken at the scene. Walker met my eyes. I opened my mouth, but Walker shook his head. I'd snatch the files from him in private anyway, so I closed my mouth.

"Thank you very much, ma'am," Walker said, sounding genuine, but the tone in his voice was more strained than usual.

I cleared my throat. "Yeah, thanks, G. I appreciate you calling me in."

Dr. Chunn shook my hand. "It was a pleasure meeting both of you."

"Thank you for allowing me to observe."

"Of course. This was your call, Ms. DiRocco. Detective Wahl wouldn't have had it any other way," she said.

I glanced at Greta and winked. "Always happy to oblige local law enforcement. You know my motto: shining light on Brooklyn's darkest secrets."

"Yes," Greta said, having heard my joke on several occasions. "I know your motto."

I grinned and turned to follow Walker out of the room.

"DiRocco," Greta called. "Can I talk to you for a moment in private before you leave?"

Walker glanced back at me, smirking like he'd gotten away with something that I hadn't. I ignored his look, turned on my heel, and followed Greta, feeling suddenly like a student following her teacher to the principal.

We walked into one of the other empty examination rooms down the hall, and she shut the door behind us.

"Why do I suddenly feel like I'm about to be interrogated?"

"Because you have goddamn good instincts," Greta said, facing me squarely. "How the fuck did we miss the bites on these victims when we wrote the report on this case?"

I raised my eyebrows.

Greta sighed. "*We* as in my team."

"I don't know who took point on your end," I said, cringing inside for throwing her team under the bus, but who would believe the truth? "All I know is that when I wrote the article, the facts were clear and obvious. I had photos and recordings as proof. You know that I never supported that retraction."

She narrowed her eyes and took a step forward. "And you don't know anything more about these bites? You can't confirm if it was an animal attack?"

"I wasn't at the scene during the attack, G," I said, keeping my voice dry and sarcastic to cover my quickening heart. "How *would* I know?"

"You tell me." Greta crossed her arms and waited.

I cocked my head to the side. "I arrived at the scene with everyone else. I wrote my article based on facts that you gave me. I don't know why you, your department, and even Meredith changed your minds, but I never did. I'm the only one who stood her ground and was right, so why am I the one getting squeezed right now?"

"I'm not giving you the squeeze, for heaven's sake, DiRocco. I'm just trying to understand."

"If you want a clearer understanding about why the bites were missing from the report, maybe you should talk to the officer who wrote the report," I suggested, feeling miserable. I'd been indignant about my article and the retraction, but if I'd known the endless pile of shit imbedded beneath the rubble, I never would've started turning up stones. When Dominic woke later that evening, most of the local law enforcement would once again know about the bites. He hadn't wanted to kill me before I started undoing all his handiwork, but he'd surely want to kill me now.

"Believe me, I intend to." Greta swiped a hand down her face. "Let me know if your digging unearths anything. Stay in touch with me on this one, all right?"

"Yes, ma'am," I said in my best Walker twang.

Greta grunted. "Get out of here."

Walker was waiting in the lobby for me, and when the reception-ist buzzed me through the locked double doors, he stood and walked me outside.

"You didn't have to wait up, but I appreciate the gesture," I said, reaching for the police reports.

He held them out of reach. "Hands off."

"I just want to see how the vampires altered the pictures," I said, still reaching.

"They didn't alter the pictures. They altered everyone's mind, so their brains couldn't see the truth in the picture." He pushed me back. "These are confidential. I need them for my research."

"Yes, I'm sure researching the bites will be a lot of hard work for you," I grumbled.

"It will, actually," Walker said, falling into step beside me. "Even if *we* already know the cause, I still need to report something plausible to the authorities, and I need to find something that another expert, if called in, can verify."

"That doesn't sound easy," I admitted.

"More like impossible. So, like I said, I still have to do the research."

I puffed out a long breath. "Jesus. Everything is so screwed up."

He nodded. "What did G want with you?"

"She doesn't like that she and her officers missed the bites, not that I blame her. And, of course, she knows that I know more than I'm telling her."

Walker took hold of my upper arm and stopped walking. His grip was gentle but firm, so I had to stop in the middle of the sidewalk to face him. "What did you tell her?"

I raised my eyebrows and glared at the hand holding my arm, but he didn't budge. "I stalled and blamed her team for missing obvious evidence, but that's not enough to satisfy Greta. She's going to ask more questions when you give your report. Impossible questions to which we unfortunately know the answers." I shook my head. "How long can we possibly play dumb?"

"Forever. Remember, we're just as dumbfounded by the evidence as everyone else."

"That might go over fine for you, but I blew my cover from the start by requesting that autopsy," I griped. "Greta's already questioning why I know so much about this case when she and her department know so little."

"What are you trying to say? That you want to tell her the truth?"

I shook my head. "I don't know what I'm trying to say. No one would believe the truth. And if they did, the vampires would mesmerize them and wipe their memories anyway. Unless we find a defense against the vampires and undeniable proof of their existence, telling anyone the truth is an exercise in futility."

"Agreed." Walker stroked his thumb over my skin while still holding my arm. "What are you doing tonight?"

I frowned. "That's none of your business."

"I'm certainly making it my business. You're the only other night blood in New York," he said, grinning.

I sighed heavily and finally admitted out loud what I'd been too scared to admit over the phone with Nathan. "That's not entirely true. I think my brother might be a night blood, too."

Walker's hand stilled on my arm. "You think or you know? Did you talk to him about it?"

"Not really. How do I begin a conversation about vampires without sounding insane?" I shook my head. "I'm still figuring that one out."

"You can practice on me. I'm free tonight." His hand resumed stroking my wrist.

I felt my cheeks flame, and as my embarrassment escalated, so did my temper. "I already have plans. Let go of my arm."

Walker shifted his eyes to my arm, and his thumb stilled as he realized he was stroking my skin. He hesitated a moment before loosening his grip, but then his eyes met mine. He held his ground.

"Do you know how the change occurs from human to vampire, exactly how it's done, why their blood is addicting, and how to protect a home that they've already entered?" he asked. "There's so much I can teach you, and I'm more than willing to help."

I opened my mouth and closed it again, unwilling to admit my complete and utter ignorance. How could I know *why* their blood was addicting if I didn't even know that it *was* addicting? How could I hope to protect myself when I knew next to nothing about vampires or about myself? I shook my head.

"Do you want to know?"

I narrowed my eyes. "How dare you use this situation against me? You *ma'am* this and *ma'am* that with your slow drawl and you think that makes you a gentleman, but gentlemen don't blackmail."

"I'm not blackmailing you. I'm simply reminding you of the fact that I'm your friend and fellow night blood. Don't push me away, DiRocco. I need to talk to you in private, and I'm the only person who can answer all your vampire and night blood questions."

I bit my lip, hating my indecision and knowing he was right. I had uncountable questions. "I have my own research and work at the *Sun*, and I'm staying with my brother tonight. I really don't have time to—"

"Perfect. We'll meet at your brother's apartment, and I'll educate the both of you." Walker smiled, and his beauty blindsided me. His teeth were luminescent surrounded by his golden five o'clock shadow. The dimple on his cheek made him look boyishly charming even if the glint in his eyes indicated that he had something else entirely in mind than boyish intent.

"All right," I grumbled and gave him Nathan's address despite my grudging reservations. "I'll need help with my brother anyway."

"I'll bring Chinese. Do you have any recommendations?"

"I prefer sushi," I muttered stubbornly.

His smile widened. "Sushi it is, then." He brushed his hand down my arm as he pulled away, and a trailing, burning path of goose bumps cropped over my arm from the whisper of his touch. "I'll look forward to it."

"Me, too, assuming you bring a California roll."

Walker laughed. "You're incorrigible."

I shrugged, and then took it as the compliment it was and smiled. "Did you want to share a cab?"

He jerked his thumb at the chrome and matte black Harley-Davidson curbed behind him.

"Guess that's a no." I stepped back and started off toward the street to hail a cab.

"Did you want to share my ride? I've got a spare helmet and jacket."

I shook my head. "See you tonight, Walker."

As much as I attempted to feel neutral toward Walker and his *ma'am*s and dimples and unflagging charm, I could still feel the warmth and strength of his fingers and the scratch of his calluses against my forearm long after I'd hailed a cab. His lean figure disappeared around the corner as the cabbie turned onto New York Avenue. I kept my head buried in my phone and ignored his wave as we left him behind. I wasn't sure how I felt about sushi after my last sushi experience with Meredith, and in particular, how I felt about looking forward to sushi with him.

Chapter 6

The slant of the sun's rays were just starting to narrow through my office window as I finished my piece on gang violence. It had come together easily, and I'd submitted it for print without the typical crunch to meet deadline. In my previous gang violence articles this month, I'd blamed society for our youth's corruption, so for this article, I decided to focus on the recent upswing in gang violence. I quoted Harroway and described how today's crime scene was likely connected to last week's murders. Meredith used a montage of different photos she'd collected from each scene: a boy with multiple stab wounds—his arm outstretched for his gun in death—close-ups of broken bodies, landscapes of fallen victims, bullet holes, stab wounds, and the gold wolf pendant.

I'd taken my time and crafted a piece I was proud to print, but writing that article was cake—just one of Jolene's mini-cupcakes I could munch on the road—compared to the article that was slowly cooking inside of me about vampires. Instead of going out with Meredith like I'd normally do after an early submission, I decided to stay for a little extra research on the history of Brooklyn's gang activity. I'd need more material for hooks if these crimes continued, and maybe I could convince Carter to allot some of the budget toward a retrospective piece on our police department's solved cases. Greta would love that, and I was nothing if not loyal to my sources.

According to the *Sun*'s record, this year wasn't the first time that multiple articles on gang violence were written. Gang violence was a serious problem seven years ago in May of 2005. Looking further back, another wave of homicides was pinned on gang-related activity in May of 1998. I bit my lip. Spikes in gang violence occurred every seven years. I searched further back in our records, and sure enough,

May of 1991 hit a record wave of two hundred fifty gang-related murders, beating the previous record of two hundred seven deaths during an especially bloody May in 1977.

Within the first week of May this year, we'd already experienced fifteen deaths. If this pattern continued, it looked as if we were headed toward another record. My stomach pitched, and I struggled not to scream as the truth was laid out, as undeniable and unavoidable as death. Brooklyn wasn't experiencing spikes in gang violence every seven years. We were experiencing spikes in vampire attacks made to look like gang violence, and those spikes coincided with Dominic's Leveling—just like he'd said.

I thought of today's crime scene—the knife wounds and execution-like bullet holes and gold wolf pendant—and a sick, curious part of me couldn't help but respect Dominic's resourcefulness. That scene had been the vampire attack from last night. Those victims were the people Kaden and his rebels had killed while chasing me, and Jillian and Dominic planted that evidence to fool everyone. I'd witnessed the real attack myself last night—hell, I'd known their plan to cover it up—and they'd even fooled me. Who could have guessed that the torn, ravaged bites from the vampire attack would be healed to look like knife wounds and gunshots? I'd just submitted another article to add to the hundreds of archived articles on gang violence in Brooklyn, and they were all false, every one of them. Even mine. Especially mine.

My cell phone vibrated inside my jacket pocket. I snapped out of my reverie and groaned at the time. It was already six thirty. I fumbled for my phone, wondering exactly when reality had unraveled so completely or if it had ever really been solidly beneath me at all.

Nathan's picture flashed on the screen in time with my phone's vibrations.

"Yo, bro," I said, and I didn't have to fake the enthusiasm I felt at the thought of seeing him tonight. "A friend of mine is picking up sushi for us. Well, he thinks it's Chinese, so I'm really not sure what we're getting. Either way it'll be questionable because he doesn't—"

"You're staying with Greta tonight."

"—live in the city," I finished flatly. "What?"

"I thought about calling Meredith, but Greta will undoubtedly be better equipped should something occur, you know, after sunset."

I squeezed the arm of my chair, and it shook under the pressure of my grip. "What are you talking about? I'm staying with you."

"She'll protect you better than I can, at least for tonight," he said.

"Guns won't protect us from what we're up against."

"Someone who knows what we're up against needs to do something, Cass. Someone needs to bring these psychos to justice, and you know well enough that they're beyond the system." Nathan's voice grew hoarse. "If no one remembers who's committing these murders, who else will fight back?"

A shiver of creeping dread crawled over me. "There are other people like us who remember. We can figure this out together. We can do something *together.*"

"Together or separate, it doesn't matter. We're no match for them. We need to even the playing field."

"What are you talking about, Nathan? We can't—"

"Give yourself enough time to stop at your apartment," he said, ignoring me. "Greta might have guns, but you have a ton of Mom's silver jewelry."

"Where are you right now?" I snapped.

"My silver cuff links weren't really effective, but your crucifix is pretty sharp. You'll be able to do some damage."

"Nothing can do damage to the creatures we're up against. It doesn't matter if we have guns and silver jewelry or cuff links. If they decide to kill us, we're dead. There is no 'even playing field.'"

"Not yet there isn't." Nathan was silent for a moment. One of the old floorboards in his apartment creaked in the background. He was pacing.

"What's that supposed to mean? Nathan, don't—"

"Keep safe tonight, and I'll see you tomorrow," he said finally.

I shrugged on my jacket, snatched my leather satchel from under my desk, and sprinted out of the office. "Yeah, I'll see you tomorrow."

By the time I caught a taxi and reached Nathan's apartment, he was already gone. I tossed his spare key into my shoulder bag and paced the creaking living room floor in his footsteps, hoping to divine where he might have bolted, but my pacing only confirmed that his apartment needed new floorboards.

My phone rang, and I yanked it from my leather bag, thinking Nathan had seen the light and changed his mind, but Greta's picture flashed on the screen. I groaned. Greta would be able to hear if something was wrong, so I took a deep breath, pounded the Answer button, and forced a measure of pep into my voice.

"DiRocco here."

"How are you feeling?"

"I've been better, but I've been worse. You?"

"Oh, you know they only grow daisies and butterflies here at the precinct," Greta said. "So I hear you need a ride from work?"

I pinched the bridge of my nose. "Don't worry about it. Nathan just feels guilty for bailing on me."

"At least he feels guilty. Brothers rarely do," Greta said, laughing. "How late are you staying at work? I get off shift at eight."

"You don't have to pick me up at the office." I forced a laugh to match hers. "I actually submitted my work early today." *And the sun would undoubtedly set before eight*, I thought. I needed to hide for the night before sunset.

"Miracles do occur."

"Once in a while. So if you want to meet at your apartment, maybe around seven, I could—"

"I don't get off until eight," Greta said. "Nathan was pretty specific about picking you up from work."

I could hear Harroway's big, bellowing voice in the background, teasing someone about something he probably shouldn't, as usual. I froze, realizing that if I could hear Harroway in the background, she might hear the creak of my pacing Nathan's apartment.

"Honestly, I'd just prefer not to walk after dark," I admitted. "If you have a spare key, I could wait for you in your apartment."

"I don't have a spare. If I pick you up at the office, you won't be walking home in the dark. You'll be driving home with me."

I gritted my teeth. "That's true."

"Why don't you want me picking you up from work, DiRocco?" Greta asked. An edge sharpened her voice.

The phone shook against my ear. "My office isn't exactly on your way home, G. Nathan's just overreacting, as usual, and putting you out."

"No, he's not, and no one is putting me out," Greta said. Her voice softened. "Don't worry about the drive. I got you."

"All right." *Fuck.*

"I'll pick you up at the *Sun Accord* at eight."

"Yeah, I'll see you then." I swallowed and forced out the next words. "Thank you, Greta."

"No problem."

Greta hung up. I stared at my phone as the call ended, trying to think how I was going to meet Greta at the office at eight without us being caught out past sunset on our way back to her apartment. My cell phone case creaked under the increasing pressure of my grip, so I tossed it back into my satchel before I tossed it across the room.

If I didn't show at the office when Greta arrived to pick me up, I'd lose another notch of credibility, and I didn't have many left to lose. But if I waited for Greta until after sunset, I'd risk Kaden or Dominic picking me up instead. I covered my eyes with my hand, undoubtedly smearing my already smeared eyeliner. The certainty of losing credibility versus the risk of bodily harm was a contest I'd wagered and won before, and I had no doubt that by the time this case was through, it was a contest I'd have to wager on again.

My hip ached as I jogged down the stairs of Nathan's apartment and caught a taxi back to the *Sun Accord*.

I watched the digital clock in the corner of my computer screen flick to 8:07 p.m. and tore another nail with my teeth. The sun had just slipped below the horizon. An hour and a half after Greta's phone call, and I was still staring at the blinking cursor on my monitor, attempting to pass the time with another Pulitzer-winning masterpiece.

I'd written the title, "The City Beneath: Vampires Bite in the Big Apple," and the cursor hadn't progressed down the page since.

I gnawed on the next nail, mercenary in my serial attack. I only had three more left before all ten were bitten, ripped, and nibbled to the quick.

My desk phone buzzed. I snatched the phone from its charging cradle and pounded the Talk button savagely.

"DiRocco here."

"A man is here to see you, Ms. DiRocco," the administrative assistant said, her voice uncommonly pleasant. Deborah's tone usually rasped from seventy years of smoking and disapproval. "He says it's urgent, that you had a meeting scheduled this evening that you missed."

"Shit, I left Walker waiting at Nathan's apartment." I checked my phone, and sure enough, I'd missed three calls in the last hour.

"I wasn't aware that you had a meeting today, Ms. DiRocco," she said dreamily.

I gritted my teeth on a particularly stubborn cuticle and took pleasure in ripping it from the nail. "It's personal. You can let him in."

"Of course," Deborah breathed, sounding wistful and unconcerned.

I massaged my temples in an effort to relieve a pounding stress headache. Why wasn't Deborah stressed? With the last couple days I'd lived, it seemed like everyone should be stressed. I heard the door squeak open and then *snick* shut, foretelling Walker's approach.

"I'm sorry," I said, holding my head in my hands. "I should have called, but honestly, I completely forgot that we were meeting tonight. Greta will be here any moment."

"No, I don't believe that Detective Wahl will be joining us."

My head snapped up at the silky formality in his voice. A man who was decidedly not Walker was striding toward me. The hair on the back of my neck stood at attention, and I couldn't look away. He was an exceptionally tall man dressed in Armani; no one I knew in this neighborhood wore Armani. His black dress shirt was open at the neck, so I could see a smooth hint of his throat. His thick black hair was cropped short on the sides near his face and styled longer at his crown, like Nathan's but without the spike. Most compelling were the man's strange blue eyes, their depths unfathomable. His eyes made me want to linger over his features and drown in his thoughts. I jerked my eyes away, and I suddenly noticed the harsh edge curling his lips. The man was angry, and that anger was targeted at me.

My gut curdled, but the man didn't resemble anyone in particular that I could recall. As he drew closer, however, I noticed the scar that sliced through his lip and over his chin before stopping near his carotid. I only knew one man with a scar like that, and with that realization, the rest of the man's features suddenly blended into something recognizable.

I stared at Dominic, my brain struggling between panic and confusion. My openmouthed astonishment must have amused him; even though his eyes retained the molten heat of their anger, he smiled. The scar was stiff, and prevented the left side of his lower lip from moving, but the rest of his mouth opened and spread wide, revealing the glistening points of his eyeteeth.

My gaze slid from Dominic to the document's headline plastered on my computer screen, and my stomach shriveled in unadulterated panic. He was nearly at my desk. I saved the document and clicked out of Word with two twitches of my finger on the mouse, but in that time, Dominic vaulted over my desk and stood alarmingly close to my chair. He was so unnaturally fast, my eyes couldn't process the individual movements; he was in front of my desk one moment, and the next, he was breathing down my neck.

The article was gone from the screen now, but if he could read as fast as he could move, he might have glimpsed the screen's contents before the document closed. My heart pounded sickeningly against my chest.

Very slowly, I rotated my chair to face Dominic. The edge of my seat brushed against his pants leg. I looked up. Each individual feature of his face and the set of his expression—eyes, lips, nose, and complexion—was exactly how I remembered, even the anger. But now, somehow, looking at his features as a whole, he appeared completely different, like whatever he'd been missing during our first few encounters was now present. The difference was transformative, so much so that without his scar, I might not have even recognized him. He'd always appeared emaciated despite his strength and speed, but the man standing beside me now filled out his suit quite nicely. I noticed his muscles shift beneath the fabric as he moved, and chided myself for noticing.

"Hello, Cassidy DiRocco," Dominic said, amusement slowly overtaking the anger. "Is something amiss?"

"You. I don't know. . . . I can't. . . ." I bit my lip. "I didn't recognize you at first," I admitted in a soft whisper.

"Ah," Dominic said, somehow seeming to understand. "You have only seen me at my worst: burned, malnourished, and hunting. I've never had the opportunity to feed before seeing you, so you've never had the opportunity to see my true appearance." He spread out his arms as if for my approval.

I narrowed my eyes. I'd seen him look human, but admittedly, I'd never seen him look attractive. Like someone who had achieved massive weight loss and was now unrecognizable as his former self, Dominic no longer resembled a vampire. Where his body had been emaciated and skeletal-like, his limbs now had muscles. Where his face had been gaunt, his cheeks were now full, his jawline stubbornly sculpted and boldly masculine, and I, God help me, was attracted.

I reminded myself that he had fangs and pulled myself together. "Are you trying to tell me that you attacked someone in the"—I shifted my eyes to glance at the clock on my monitor—"seven minutes between sunset and now?"

"No, I'm telling you that I fed in the seven minutes between sunset and now."

"The manner in which you feed is attacking," I hissed. "I know firsthand."

"Ask her yourself. She does not feel attacked," Dominic said calmly.

My body suddenly washed cold. "Who? Greta?"

He shook his head, but his eyes flicked to the door.

"The receptionist?" I asked, shocked. I'd just spoken to her! "Deborah?" I tensed to run to her, but before I could leverage to my feet, Dominic was behind me and bound me against the back of my chair with one arm. I struggled, but my efforts were, as usual, useless against him.

"You may ask her later," he breathed against my neck. "I have need of you now."

"Please," I said softly, desperately. "She probably can't sustain the blood loss I can and still survive. Let me go to her. Let me get help for her."

Dominic's steely arm tightened uncomfortably. "How do you know how much blood loss you can sustain?"

"She could be dying," I countered, trying a different tack. "She's just another scene you'll have to clean and camouflage."

"She is in no danger of dying, I assure you. In fact, she enjoyed herself."

"You don't know how she feels," I snapped.

"Yes, I do. I can taste it."

I paused, slightly mortified. "In her blood?"

"Yes, in her blood. In the air. Her scent. In her mind. I can feel her in every way if I choose to." He tucked his face into the back of my neck and breathed deeply. I squirmed. "Who have you been talking to, Cassidy DiRocco?"

"I'll answer your questions when you let me see for myself that Deborah is well and whole," I said, attempting to stay calm and focused even as my hair fluttered rhythmically from his breaths.

I shivered, and he made a noise, although not the same rattling I'd grown accustomed to hearing. The noise was more male than vampire.

"You will not run, scream, attempt escape, or otherwise renege on your word. You will confirm the woman's health, and you will return to this chair. Agreed?" Dominic asked.

I sighed. "Agreed."

A moment later, faster than my synapses could fire, Dominic released me and was seated in the chair across from my desk. He crossed one leg casually over the other and looped his clasped hands over one knee, at ease and waiting for my move. I stood slowly and walked to the door. Dominic looked good in his suit because he looked human, but he wasn't. He was a murdering, life-sucking animal. My hand shook as I placed it on the door's handle because I obviously needed the reminder.

The images of Monday's crime scene and the bodies from the morgue sprang through my head like a grotesque slide show. But now, as I prepared myself for the possibilities outside the office door, the bodies all had Deborah's face. In my mind's eye, her short, springy gray hair, pointed chin, and terminally accusatory expression frowned back at me from a ravaged body. Ragged slices split her legs and arms, tore through muscle, and revealed a popped socket of glistening bone. The cloying scent of rot was pungent, so even when I closed my eyes, I couldn't escape from the guilt and grief and overwhelming responsibility of her death. The stink of my negligence filled the room, and when I opened my eyes, she looked back at me with her wide, unblinking, unseeing gaze.

I swung the door open, fully panicked, my heart bursting, my lungs gasping, and Deborah looked up from her monitor, smiling.

"Do you need anything, Ms. DiRocco?" she asked, almost dreamily.

I gaped.

"Is something wrong?" She leaned forward, mouthed the word *security*, and lifted her eyebrows in question. I saw her arm shift, so it hovered near the panic button tucked under the lip of her desk.

"Not at all," I ground out with false cheer. "Did Detective Greta Wahl stop in? She was supposed to meet me tonight, too."

Deborah folded her arms on top of her desk. Her body shifted away from the panic button, and I felt a sense of doom close in around me. Deborah was safe and healthy, but I certainly wasn't. I would face Dominic alone.

"Yes, she was here a few minutes ago. Around eight o'clock."

I glanced down the empty hall. "Is she waiting for me outside?"

"I told her that you were gone for the day, as you instructed, and she left."

"As I instructed," I repeated blandly, knowing damn well I had not instructed. I had a sneaking suspicion who had, and his eyes were burning two welts in the back of my head, like a sniper's laser.

"Yes, as you instructed." An annoyed edge crept into Deborah's voice. She pursed her lips. "Honestly, hon, you don't look well. You should probably reschedule all these meetings, and call it a night."

"Actually, I was wondering how *you're* feeling."

She lifted her eyebrows, her fingers dancing eighty words a minute. "Me? Honestly?"

"Of course."

She stopped typing and frowned at me. "I've been at this damn office since seven this morning. My ex-husband's an ass, I haven't had a cigarette in over fifteen minutes, and I have a knot in my back the size of a grapefruit. Not to mention it's past eight o'clock, and I'm still here." Deborah's face was deadpan. "So it's pretty much a normal night."

"Right," I said.

Deborah returned to her keyboard.

I forced myself to step back into the office area and shut the door. I stared at the closed door, equally relieved, confused, and terrified. Deborah wasn't dead. She was whole and alive and if nothing else, physically unaffected by Dominic.

His eyes were still hot on the back of my head. I turned to meet his gaze, my hand still gripping the door's handle as if I could bolt without him catching me. He grinned knowingly and patted the seat of my chair.

I crossed the room, feeling a kinship to those on death row who'd walked their final steps. I forced myself forward toward Dominic in a silent, clenched, unwilling sort of determination.

Once I was seated, Dominic spoke. "Are you satisfied?"

"Not nearly," I muttered. "But in terms of Deborah's *physical* health, yes."

Dominic cocked his head. "Her health is good in every way."

"She doesn't remember the attack, and she thinks I gave her instructions that I never gave her," I said, pointedly. "She's not mentally well."

"We can quibble over the particulars later," Dominic said, dismissing my concerns. "Do you agree that you've confirmed the woman's health?"

"Yes," I gritted.

"Wonderful." Dominic smiled. "Who have you been talking to?"

I licked my lips. "I talk to innumerable people throughout the day. I'm a reporter. It's my job to talk."

Dominic lost his smile. "Who have you been talking to in particular about being a night blood? There are only two beings to whom you could divulge such information about yourself—vampire or fellow night blood—one of which you didn't have access to during the day and the other of which you are unlikely to have found."

I shrugged. If Walker, Nathan, and myself were any indication, perhaps night bloods weren't as rare as everyone believed.

"The man who helped you escape is a night blood," Dominic accused. His voice was barely audible, but somehow more cutting for its reduced volume.

I raised my eyebrows, struggling for a casual response. "I escaped on my own."

Dominic tutted and shook his head. "You think I didn't know the moment the man entered my coven? You think I didn't hear him pick the lock on my enclosure, or your hushed voices as you whispered to one another? You think I didn't prevent my vampires from descending on you as you fled through the tunnels?"

I swallowed, not wanting to admit that I'd suspected as much. The reporter in me itched. "So you can remain awake during the day?"

"We do not succumb to a death-like coma during the day, as much of your lore indicates, if that's what you're implying." Dominic narrowed his eyes to slits, and I realized that he hadn't appreciated my question.

"I just—"

Dominic held up a hand. "You refer to my coven as having *slaughtered* humans during their hunt. I'm not sure what word could sufficiently describe the ensuing violence should you encounter a vampire during the day. Even me. I allowed both of you to escape, and by doing so, I allowed you to live. I deserve your gratitude, not your speculation."

Leaving had been so extraordinarily easy that I'd suspected something was amiss. But I'd wanted our escape to be real. I'd wanted to believe we'd exerted a measure of control over our fate, that we weren't simply puppets in a show for the vampires' amusement.

I shook my head. We weren't even the puppets. We were the snack that the vampires munched on while enjoying the show.

Dominic leaned forward. "No?" he asked, his voice a mask of civility.

"Everything is just speculation when nothing makes sense. Why would you just allow me to leave after kidnapping me?" I snapped, anger overpowering common sense. "Did you laugh as we snuck off, tiptoeing down corridors and dodging around corners in what we thought was our silent and successful escape? Did you think we were just hilarious, the silly, weak, simple humans who thought they had outsmarted you, who thought they had beaten the odds?"

"I didn't kidnap you. If you remember correctly, I was protecting you," Dominic said. His lips pulled in a sudden curve. "Your skin smells like cinnamon."

"Excuse me?" I asked, attempting to regroup. The way he was staring at my throat was disconcerting.

He leaned over my desk, his eyes half-closed in pleasure as he inhaled. "Your skin. It smells delicious when you're angry."

I jerked away from him. "So you've said."

"No, I thought it was just your fear. Your anger and pleasure have tinges of that sharp poignancy, as well. If I were to breathe you in too deeply and too quickly, it might burn."

"Okay," I murmured, still attempting to achieve some distance, but the more I cringed back in my chair, the closer he leaned across my desk. "Your point?"

Dominic smiled widely enough to flash his long fangs. "My point is that your scent is likely the reason Neil lost his control so easily. Your skin short-circuits our self-preservation instincts, temping us to breathe you in, to bite, and to suck that burning spice deep within ourselves, despite the silver bars that may stand in our way. Night blood always has that quality, but your blood is so seasoned that its scent wafts through your pores. It's why, having tasted you, they'll continue to hunt you. They'll be relentless until they get what they want."

"You mean Kaden and his rebel vampires?"

Dominic nodded.

"Their only intent last night was to kill me," I whispered. "What else could they want? To turn me? To transform me into what you are?"

Dominic shook his head. "Only a Master can successfully transform a night blood into a vampire. Had Kaden been rational and loyal, he would've brought you directly to me upon tasting you. But the vampires in my coven who no longer want to live in secrecy no longer value anything but that ultimate goal. They want complete freedom to drink and hunt and kill at their leisure more than they want to increase our dwindling population. They would've feasted upon you until you were drained dry, night blood or not, but because you're a night blood, they would've enjoyed the taste a little more."

I swallowed. "What does any of this have to do with me? Besides the fact that Kaden and his rebels are hunting me for the taste of my blood, why do you care if they drain me or not? Why do you want me to be your night blood?"

"I need your help, Cassidy DiRocco. I must subdue Kaden and his followers before they massacre the city and expose the existence of vampires to the world. If Kaden blows our cover, Day Reapers will come to New York, and our ways of life for vampires and humans alike will never be the same again. Are you willing to assist me? Will you help me protect our city?"

Dominic asked me to help him kill vampires, protect his coven, and save New York City in the same tone that a less ambitious man might ask a woman to coffee.

"You want my help to *what?*"

"Help me subdue Kaden and his followers, Cassidy, and kill them if necessary. They're a threat to your society, the survival of my entire coven, and a threat to you personally, as well. If I'm not mistaken, you value your human life." Dominic leaned back slightly, giving me a little more physical space, but the calculation in his gaze pinned me motionless against the chair. "You're the weapon they won't expect."

"*You* want *my* help to *kill vampires*," I repeated. My brain felt like a skipping record. I could hear the words leaving his mouth, but my brain refused to progress to the next track. "I'm not . . . I can't . . ."

Dominic's gaze grew more intense as he stared. Puzzle pieces were snapping into place in his mind, and if the slow smile breaking across his face was any indication, he liked their fit very much.

I took a deep breath and started again. "I'm hopelessly ill-matched against any one of you, let alone all of you. How could you accomplish anything with me that you couldn't accomplish on your own? You took care of Kaden just fine without my help in the alley last night."

"Yes, I did take care of him last night, and that's exactly my point, Cassidy DiRocco," Dominic purred. "I wasn't alone in the alley last night. I was with you."

My name coming from his voice pulled something taut inside my mind, like someone wrapping rope around his palm in preparation for tug-of-war. I looked away, trying to dispel the feeling, but it persisted.

"I didn't help you last night," I insisted, but it was difficult to impress a point without meeting someone's eyes.

"On the contrary. Kaden is usually much stronger, but he was slow and distracted after drinking from you. They all were. You're the key to overcoming this rebellion and stopping their escalating violence before the entire city crumbles under their bloodlust."

"You don't care about this city," I scoffed. "You just don't want to be overthrown on the Leveling, and you'll use every trick in your arsenal, even little old me, to make that happen. If Kaden's powerful enough to regenerate an aorta within minutes of having it torn out, how powerful will he be at the end of the month when you lose your powers entirely? You'll be toast."

"You certainly have been talking around," he growled.

I shrugged. "Like I said, I'm a reporter. That's what I do."

Dominic was silent for a long moment. He smoothed his thumb over the grains of my desk as he mulled his next words. "You're right about my motivations. I fear a revolution in my coven. Despite my motivations, however, stopping Kaden before he furthers his hunt benefits you, as well. You'll be protecting his future victims from being slaughtered, you'll be guaranteeing your own future safety, and you'll be preventing the Day Reapers from visiting New York. Our motivations may be different, but we have the same ultimate goal. We must combine our strengths if either of us hopes to see Kaden stopped."

I shook my head slowly, unconvinced.

"You said yourself that you're hopelessly ill-matched against any of us, let alone all of us. Let me even the score. Instead of being alone and vulnerable when you next encounter Kaden, you'll be at a planned location, prepared for his attack, and you'll have me protecting you." Dominic leaned back in his chair, sure of himself and his argument. "Give me one reason we shouldn't combine our efforts against him."

"I don't trust you."

Dominic nodded. "You shouldn't, but that isn't the point. I don't trust you, either, but you need me, as I need you."

"You don't trust me?" I gaped. "Your entire plan revolves around using me as bait," I said, jabbing a thumb at my chest. "Whether I die fighting them alone or die fighting them with you, I still end up dead."

"You're merely a distraction. Once I overtake them, I'll heal any injuries you may have sustained. Your chances of survival are higher with me."

"I'm bait," I said flatly. "Even if I agreed to this, which I haven't, you're expecting a very large leap of faith on my part, and I'm not normally one to jump. After you've taken exactly what you want—Kaden is subdued, the threat to your coven is defeated, and you're once again secure as Master of your vampires—why would you bother to heal a useless little human like me?"

"You are not human," Dominic hissed succinctly. He was suddenly out of his chair and directly in front of mine, wedged between the desk and my legs. He leaned down and pressed his cheek smoothly against my cheek. "You're a night blood. I will have use of you long after Kaden and his followers are killed, I promise."

"That sounds more like a threat than reassurance," I whispered. My voice shook.

Dominic boxed me in with an elbow against each armrest. His hands grasped the back of my chair on either side of my shoulders. He pulled the chair close—the smell of warmed pine wafted down from his hovering body—and buried his face in my neck. I froze. His lips grazed over the skin behind my ear, and the hard point of his teeth scraped casually along my hairline. The core of my chest began to shake the harder I tried to remain still. I took in his scent in a slow, shallow breath, trying to let thoughts of Christmas and family and love temper the panic trembling over me.

"You fear death," he said. "You fear being maimed, but I can save you from that, Cassidy DiRocco. Trust in me, and I will give you eternity."

"First you warn me against trusting you. Now you're coaxing me to trust you. You don't know what you really want from me, but it doesn't matter because whatever it is, I don't want it," I snapped, but if he could smell my fear beneath the bravado, really, what was the point of pretending? I sighed. "I don't want eternity. I don't want anything you have to give me."

Dominic laughed suddenly. "I know exactly what I want from you. It's you, I believe, who is conflicted. You can't possibly think to win against Kaden alone."

"I won't be alone."

His body stilled. "Ah, you think that without me, you'll still have your friend, the night blood. Do you trust him, Cassidy? Do you trust him like you can't trust me?"

"He would never use me as bait for his own purposes. You saved me because you think I'm useful to you, but he saved me simply because I needed saving."

"You think he's selfless and that makes him trustworthy?"

"I can't trust someone who would risk my life for his own gain. That's not what friends do."

"But you've remained friends with him even after he used you for his gain. He used you to find my coven," Dominic said coldly.

I stared him down, but with his strange blue and white eyes and carefully veiled expression, I couldn't read anything except for my own hesitation in the reflection from his irises. Their depths didn't pull at my will this time. I jerked my eyes away and focused on the wall behind his shoulder. "You don't know what you're talking about."

"He knew you were in grave danger as you walked home from the precinct, but he allowed Kaden and the others to attack you. He anticipated it, knowing they'd recognize the taste of your blood, but he assumed they'd take you back to their Master, to me, to transform you. In normal circumstances they would have, but Walker doesn't know about the rebellion. He assumed he'd be able to track you back to the coven before you died."

I stared at him, shocked that he'd referred to Walker by name. "How do you know Walker?"

Dominic raised an eyebrow. "Ask him yourself."

I shook my head in denial. "You're wrong. He didn't know I was a night blood at the time."

"He knew enough to assume," Dominic dismissed. "You were the only one of all the witnesses I entranced who still believed the bodies had bite marks, and you were ignorant enough to let everyone know that you remembered." He tutted again, and it sparked my temper. "Oh, I'm sure he pieced the puzzle together."

I felt my anger wash over me in a bright red tsunami. "He had no way of knowing that vampires would attack me. And even if he had, Kaden would've killed me, not brought me to you. Walker would not risk my life just to find your coven!"

"Yes, he would, and he did. In any other circumstance, Kaden *would* have brought you to me. At any other time of year, my vampires *would* have brought you back to the coven to complete your transformation. Your night blood took a risk, but if it hadn't been for me, it wouldn't have paid off."

"No," I insisted. "Walker wouldn't do that."

"Why not? Because he saved you? So have I. Maybe you should acquaint yourself with the facts before deciding whom to trust. We've both used you for our own gain, but only I can guarantee your safety."

"Who will guarantee my safety from you?" I pushed back from him, scared that he was right about Walker but certain that I was right about him.

His fang sliced into my neck from my own movement. Its razor edge stung, but it wasn't pain from the cut that raised goose bumps down my arms; it was the hiss that rattled from his chest. The noise, this time, was all vampire. I felt blood drip down the side of my neck, and Dominic's slick tongue flicked over its path.

"Cassidy DiRocco," he growled roughly, "look into my eyes."

I felt the overwhelming, desperate urge to look, like my entire body ached to drown in his gaze. "No!" I screamed. "You can't—"

Dominic's mouth covered mine, muffling my screams. His lips were cold and demanding, forcing my mouth to remain open against the threat of his fangs. I struggled away from him, but he was too strong and too experienced. He wrapped an arm around the curve of my back, pulled me from the chair, and held my body immobile against the length of his with one hand. He grasped my chin roughly with the other hand, limiting my options to either shrieking ineffectively against his mouth or taking the kiss. The first was a waste of energy, and although the second was unwelcome, my mind was still my own. I would rather kiss him than look into his eyes and lose myself again, so I closed my eyes and took it.

He seemed to sense my reluctant acquiescence because the pressure of his lips lightened. I still couldn't move and I could barely breathe, but his mouth found a rhythm, an invitation that gave more than it took. A strange heat built between his cold, sleek body and mine. The heat was a pressure against my chest, urging me forward, and he must have felt its burning encouragement, too. His hands tightened roughly on my waist, and I wanted more. He might have stolen the kiss at first, but he offered more now. Unlike when he'd bitten me last night, Dominic actually invited my participation, and God help me, I responded. I kissed him back.

My lips moved against his, soft and languid at first, tentative because I'd never liked the unexpected. His left hand kept a firm hold on my chin and the other roamed over my back, moving slowly farther and farther down until his fingers slipped beneath the waistband of my pants. I felt the light brush of his touch against my hip, and instinctually, I pressed closer. He took my response as the permission it was and deepened the kiss. He angled his head to swipe his tongue against mine. I moaned into his mouth, and he pressed deeper, ruthless and untamed. I could feel my heart physically pound against my chest from need and want and heat this time instead of fear. He could probably hear it, too, and likely smelled the difference, but in this one brief, insane moment, I simply didn't care. His hands dipped into my pants to cup my ass as I shivered, feeling urgent and achy and hot and everything I hadn't felt with anyone in years. My tongue matched his movement. The kiss turned hard and feral as we collided, and I felt certain this was right because I'd always trusted my instincts.

"Ms. DiRocco, is everything all ri— Oh!"

Dominic broke the kiss. I gasped, surprised at first by the loss of the heat between us, but as my body cooled and my mind refocused, I only felt shame. I hadn't needed to meet his gaze to lose myself.

"Yes," Dominic murmured, looking up at Deborah, who was presumably standing behind me. "Everything is just fine."

"I can see that." Deborah giggled, her voice uncommonly light and schoolgirl-like.

"Deborah Rogers, please close the door on your way out," Dominic said, and the moment the words left his lips, Deborah turned on her heel, left the room, and closed the door on her way out.

I narrowed my eyes. According to Dominic, drinking my blood had weakened Kaden and his vampires, and Dominic had just tasted my blood. I had the potential to be a vampire, and what did vampires do best besides kill humans? Exert their will over others. I took a deep breath and went for broke.

"Dominic Lysander," I said with conviction, hoping that the conversation among the coven vampires last night had revealed Dominic's true full name. I commanded his name the way he always wielded mine and ordered, "Look into my eyes."

I felt an instant link between us, my mind to his. Dominic's gaze snapped down to meet mine, and I could feel his shock, horror, and rage tingle over our invisible connection. It was like a metaphysical twine connected us, but only I could pull at the string.

I grinned. "Release your hold on me, Dominic, and take a step back."

His hand dropped away from my chin, the arm around my back eased its pressure, and he shifted back one millimeter.

"Nice try. Dominic, please take five full steps backward."

He did. I could both see and feel his struggle, his desperation to break the mental straitjacket I'd forced around him. I bit my lip, terrified—now that I'd played my hand—of what he would do in retaliation once I broke my gaze.

"I'm sorry, I didn't really think this would even work," I admitted. "But while I have your undivided attention, let me just say this. I'll think about your request to help subdue Kaden. I need time to consider what's best for me, and maybe, in the meantime, you can earn my trust." *Doubtful,* I thought, but he didn't need to know that. "If I decide to help you, however, it'll be because I want to protect myself and Brooklyn from further harm. I don't want to become a vampire. I don't want you to turn me or remake me or regenerate me or whatever the hell you call it. I don't want immortality with you. Part of earning my trust will be understanding this and respecting my choice." I felt like I was talking to a lobotomized corpse, so I added, "Nod if you understand everything I've just said."

He nodded.

"Wonderful," I said on a sigh. Keeping my eyes locked on Dominic, I bent to retrieve my leather shoulder bag, stood, and edged around my desk toward the door. "I'm leaving now, and I'm asking you as a first test of trust, if you truly want my help, to please allow me to leave."

I opened the office door, stood in the open entryway, and held his captured will in my mind for a long moment. Another emotion besides surprise and anger crept from him on the mental twine between us. I'd felt the emotion before, but I couldn't identify it, as if I couldn't name it because *he* couldn't. He'd forgotten the feeling. The emotion was warm and sharp and spread from the center of his chest. It felt good, almost hopeful, but I wasn't sure if inspiring such strong feelings in him boded well for me.

"Good-bye, Dominic," I murmured.

I slammed the door between us, felt the snap of our severed connection as I bolted the door, and ran.

Chapter 7

I made it three full blocks before he attacked me. He swooped from thin air, hit my back like a semi, and pinned me up against the nearest building. My cheek scraped against the brick. I don't know how far I'd realistically expected to run, but I hadn't expected him to create a public scene. We were still out on the main drag, in full public view, and the public was certainly viewing. Several people had taken out their cell phones, and a few flashes burst. One woman in particular scooped up her kid and hustled off the street. She glanced back at Dominic as she turned the corner, murmuring into her phone. He could talk a grand talk about protecting the anonymity of his coven, but he was revealing the existence of vampires all on his own without the help of the rebel vampires.

Dominic buried his face in the hollow of my neck and breathed deeply. His chest vibrated against my back with that telltale, rattling hiss, and my body instinctively froze in caution, like a wide-eyed deer facing fast-approaching headlights. Deer at least had the option to run. The vibration brought me his scent, but instead of warmed pine and Christmas, the smell was more subtle and earthy, like grass after the rain. A warning tingle crept over my skin in a slow tide. His scent was different. His height and breadth were wrong, too. He pulled back from my neck with a snarl, and his mouth was already extending into a muzzle. His eyes glowed a luminous violet as I peered over my shoulder at him, under the darkness of his own shadow.

I shook my head in denial, but there was no denying the locks of long, auburn hair where I'd expected black hair and a short, styled cut; the smooth, unblemished curve of his soft lips; his slightly shorter, slightly bulkier stature; and the pull of his beautiful violet eyes.

"Kaden?" I asked.

He rubbed his extended muzzle and those gleaming fangs carefully over the side of my face. I was trembling, trying desperately to remain still, and in my desperation, only trembling more violently.

"Dominic beat me to you. I can smell his scent everywhere," Kaden growled.

I edged away from him, and he switched sides, rubbing his face against the back of my neck to my other cheek. I realized that he was marking me, placing his scent over Dominic's on my body.

"Was it a race?" I whispered shakily. I'd meant it as a sort of joke—although not particularly funny, considering that it *was* a race—but my voice didn't deliver.

Kaden laughed anyway. "Of a sort. He may have won, but somehow, I still landed the prize."

"Lucky you," I murmured. Kaden licked my neck. I closed my eyes against the clammy path his tongue traced.

Maybe I can control his mind, too, like Dominic's, I thought. Even as the thought passed, I realized that he would need to drink my blood to spark the connection.

He pressed me flat against the brick, and I lost my breath.

Waiting for him to drink my blood would probably be just a matter of time.

"Lucky *you*," Kaden countered. "I was wrong. Lysander's powers are certainly deteriorating, but you remember us because you're a night blood. To think, you might have been turned by a dying Master." He shook his head as if in awe of my unbelievable luck. "With me, you'll have everything: immortality and freedom. You won't ever be confined to hunt in the shadows. You won't need to contain your true nature or hide in the sewers," he growled. "You'll be born into an emerging society of predators who rule the night."

"With you?" I asked dismally. He was more psychotic than Dominic. Why did all the vampires assume that, just because I could become one of them, I actually *wanted* to be one of them?

His chest vibrated, and hollow, reptilian clicks punctuated through the growl. I leaned sideways, easing away from his muzzle. He leaned closer. The exhale of his growl was hot against my cheek. I cringed, but there was nowhere else to turn. The rattling in his chest heightened. I couldn't hear anything past it.

Kaden bit into the side of my neck, ripped out an entire mouthful of flesh, and flung it to the ground. I screamed, I must have, but I couldn't hear past his hissing, clicking growls. I couldn't feel past the pain. The unbearable pressure of his mouth clamped over my neck, and he guzzled my blood as it waterfalled over my shoulder. I kicked and fought and bucked against his hard, unyielding body. He crushed his body into mine, grinding my wrists hard into the brick above my head.

He wasn't drinking nearly as much blood as I was losing, and that pissed me off. Dominic was right. He was choosing to kill me, not out of necessity or hunger, but simply because he could.

My temper sizzled beneath my skin. I could feel the tingle of it over my whole body, through each fingertip, and blazing from my eyes. Kaden detached from my neck. He rubbed his cheek over mine, inhaling deeply, almost drunkenly, and slowly pulled away. His lips grazed my lips and the tip of his nose rubbed along the side of mine until we were forehead to forehead, staring at each other. I buried my gaze deep into his eyes—the blazing, furious anger I'd built drilled into him—and I opened my mouth to order him to step back.

Kaden's eyes widened as he felt my connection take root. "Impossible."

Headlights suddenly burst from behind, silhouetting us in spotlight. I flinched away from the unexpected brightness and lost my concentration. The connection between our minds disintegrated.

"Stop where you are," crackled a voice through a bullhorn. "Place your hands on your head, and turn around."

Kaden laughed. He cupped the unravaged side of my throat in his palm and pressed deeper into the wound at my neck. He inhaled slowly, as if he could suck the life out of me and into him through my scent alone. I tried to find that connection between us and lock into his mind again, but I couldn't think. My head spun. My vision dimmed in pulses, and I realized that in a moment, I would likely pass out and die. Night bloods were supposed to be resilient to catastrophic blood loss, but I didn't want to test Walker's theories.

"This is your last warning," the voice behind the bullhorn repeated. "Step away from the woman. Place your hands on your head."

Kaden flicked his tongue into my neck. I couldn't feel anything at first, but then a spark of searingly sharp heat burned the wound. I cringed away from him, but he held me immobile, forced my head to the side, and licked a long line over my neck to my ear. "Mmm, Cassidy," he murmured. His lips grazed my lobe. "Pardon me a moment."

Suddenly, he was gone. I crumpled to my hands and knees on the ground. Shots fired. I could just discern the faint outline of cops aiming over their car doors. Their headlights were blinding. I couldn't distinguish anyone in particular or exactly how many were firing at Kaden, but the gunfire was deafening and continuous. I shielded my eyes with my hands and blinked into the headlights. I wanted to know for certain that he was dead. I wanted to see his limp body jerk back midmotion and drop. The hand at my forehead was shaking.

Instead, a high scream burst through the gunfire. The scream cut short with a wet, meaty sound, more shots fired, and another scream pierced the air. My eyes finally began adjusting to the light. The police were aiming carefully now, more mindful of their shots to avoid hitting their fellow officers as Kaden fed. One by one, Kaden plucked an officer from behind his car, ripped out his throat, and tossed him aside for the next one, all the while undeterred by bullets. I watched, feeling horrified and sickened, as the officers fought and screamed and died for me.

I couldn't help the officers against Kaden, so I did the only thing I could do: remove myself as a potential hostage and try to survive. I crawled into the nearest alley and away from the carnage on my hands and knees. My leather shoulder bag dragged along the asphalt next to me. Kaden would probably hear it scraping, but I didn't have the strength to lift it.

My neck still felt singed from Kaden's last lick. I fingered the wound tentatively, and although I couldn't feel the pressure of my own touch, an artery wasn't squirting. Kaden's saliva must have healed the pulsing flow. I pulled my hand away from my neck and cringed at my blood-slicked palm. He might have healed the artery, but he hadn't healed the wound. I needed medical attention, and I needed it five minutes ago.

The streetlights couldn't penetrate into the center of the alley. Blinding darkness steadily closed in around me, so the sharp staccato of gunfire and the cutting pitch of the officer's shrieks from behind were my only sense of direction. Broken glass, soda cans, and bottle caps littered the asphalt. I tried to avoid anything sharp, but I was sweating and shaking and nauseous. The end of the alley was only a few hundred feet away, so I focused on my goal and forged forward over the debris.

I wondered if more officers would respond to the call to help the fallen . . . to help me, and I wondered how long Kaden would continue the bloodbath. Until sunrise? My hand crunched over something jagged, and my weight pressed it deep into my palm. I couldn't see the debris, whether it was glass or metal or stone, but no matter the material, I felt the tacky slide of blood slip between my fingers. I felt its pulsing, unrelenting, bone-ache, and it didn't matter what had caused it so much as I couldn't even see clearly enough to treat it.

I finally crawled out of the darkness on the other side of the alley. Using the side of the building as leverage, I clawed to my feet. The ground and building and sky all wobbled in and out of focus. The streetlights alternately faded and brightened as I attempted to keep my footing. I waited a moment, hoping my balance would steady and my awareness would sharpen, but I'd lost too much blood. My vision was darkening, not improving. My life was leaking away. I'd been here before—maybe not in this exact circumstance and certainly never with vampires—but I'd taken a bullet for Harroway and clung on to life long enough to survive. I could survive again. Gritting my teeth against the pain and dizziness, I pushed away from the building and stepped out of the alley.

The sky swept under me before I could take a second step. My foot never found the ground, and the night was suddenly still and quiet and calm. The building circled overhead and everything blurred into the dark night sky; I couldn't see or move or think beyond the facts that I was going to die in this disgusting alley, Kaden was likely still tearing through the line of officers, and Dominic, damn him, might have been right.

"DiRocco!"

I squinted against the glow of streetlights shining outside the alley. It took a moment, but my eyes adjusted. I groaned at the sight. Walker was jogging toward me, and I was still slumped against the brick siding where I'd passed out. He stopped at the alley, stepped into the darkness with me, and knelt by my side. The silhouette of his spiral curls and broad shoulders were haloed by the light behind him.

"Jesus Christ," Walker spat.

"We've got to stop meeting like this," I croaked. "Worse than lobby conversation."

He looked over his shoulder for a moment before facing me again. "There's a swarm out there, like bloodsucking, murdering locusts. Killing humans. Killing each other. I should've known you'd be in the thick of it. You probably caused it."

"Did not," I grunted. The buildings and ground and Walker were all spinning and swirling. Keeping my eyes open was nauseating. I closed my eyes and took a deep breath.

"Stay with me, DiRocco," Walker urged, sounding a little frantic.

I forced my eyes open and tensed to stand, but my arms weren't working properly. I couldn't leverage to my feet. People were still screaming and shouting and shrieking on the other side of the alley, and I couldn't even stand.

"How did you find me?"

"No one was at your brother's apartment, and when you didn't answer my calls, I assumed the worst." Walker shook his head at me. "I assumed right."

Gunshots fired, closer than the others, and someone let out a high, long, chilling shriek. The scream cut off abruptly and more shots fired.

"Get me out of here, Walker?" I squeaked.

"As if you even need to ask, darlin'."

He stood, leaned over me, and scooped me up from under my armpits. I doubted my legs could hold my weight, and Walker must have doubted it, too, because he gathered me to his chest, his arms tight around my waist. My body felt boneless and weak and useless. The streetlights seemed starry as they swirled and flashed across my vision, and my head lolled to the side, resting heavily on Walker's right shoulder.

"Shit!" He clamped his palm firmly over my neck.

I winced. "How bad is it? I can't really feel it anymore."

"Bad," he said tightly.

"Did you bring sushi?" I asked, trying to lighten the air between us. He didn't respond.

"I'm not having a good week. Sushi would've been nice."

Walker sighed deeply. "Your body still needed to regenerate from last night. You need stitches and you need them now before you completely bleed out."

"But I can lose more blood than most and still live, right?" I asked doubtfully. "Because I'm a night blood?"

"Sure," Walker said. "But nearly all your blood is on the pavement. You may not need as much to survive as most people, but you still need *some*."

I felt my feet drag as Walker jogged us down the sidewalk. His arms felt very secure around me, creating the illusion of warmth and safety, and my dimming mind melted deep into the feeling.

"DiRocco?"

I could hear his voice, but the reality of us running as open prey on the street was far away. My world honed down to the feeling of his steady hand around my waist, his hard shoulder against my cheek, and fresh mint.

"I'll make you crawl home if it means you won't give up, damn it."

His hand tightened on my neck, and I winced from the harsh pressure. The pain brought me back slightly.

"Ouch," I slurred.

"You've got to stay with me, DiRocco," Walker whispered against my ear. "The hospital's too far, but it's only a few more blocks to your apartment. We'll be safe there until sunrise. Vampires can't enter uninvited."

"What does that mean?" I murmured.

"Vampires can't physically enter a home without permission. They must be invited by a person within or by the home owner." Walker snorted. "They might seem invincible, and they all might think they're immortal, but silver-plated bullets, wooden stakes, and decapitation all work just fine. Nothing's immortal. They're simply long-lived and hard to kill. And none of them, not one, can enter your home without permission."

I swallowed, feeling nauseous. "Does it count if they force you to give permission?"

Walker paused. "Did you invite one of them into your apartment already?"

"Yes," I admitted. "But I have new, fortified locks on the windows."

He was quiet for a long moment.

"I didn't want to invite him," I snapped, feeling guilty and angry about feeling that way. I'd been attacked, for heaven's sake. "Dominic was controlling my mind, and there was nothing I could do about it."

I expected shock or worry or anger, but instead, his reaction seemed thoughtful—calculating, even. "Are the locks silver?"

I blinked. "No. I don't think so. My landlord installed them, and I doubt he sprang for silver locks."

"Does Dominic want to turn you?"

I chuckled. "They all want to turn me. If my choices are between my apartment and the hospital, I choose the hospital."

"All?" he asked doubtfully.

"Dominic and Kaden."

"Ah," he said. "That explains the vampire-on-vampire fighting. Normally, if a Master targets a specific night blood, other interested vampires concede because only a Master can transform the night blood."

"I'm not the reason they're fighting," I protested. "I believe Dominic. His powers are waning, and Kaden is leading an uprising against him."

"That's your first mistake. Believing a vampire."

"It's true, Kaden even said that—"

"And even if it's true, it's not our concern. We just need to hunt and kill them. Every last one," Walker said.

"Even the vampire who's trying to kill other vampires?"

"What did I just say, darlin'?" he said lightly. "Every last one."

"I'd like to see you try," purred a voice behind us.

Walker whirled around, dropped me on the concrete behind him, and yanked something long and cylindrical from his waist. I hit the ground hard on my side. The air punched out of my chest, and a rush of warmth poured over my shoulder. I reached up to touch my neck, but my hand was already gloved in blood. Whatever had cut my palm in the alley had cut deep. I felt bile clog the back of my throat.

"Keep pressure on that," Walker ordered, but he wasn't looking at me.

Walker was aiming a sawed-off shotgun at Kaden and the terrified human he held in front of him. The woman was middle-aged, in her late forties at least, with streaks of tinsel in her dirty-blond hair. Kaden held her like a shield, blocking Walker's shot. The woman's eyes were gigantic and petrified. She'd already been bitten. The tears pouring down her cheeks slid over the neat bite marks on her neck and continued down her collar in a pinkish tinge that stained the collar of her shirt.

I narrowed my eyes on those two, tiny puncture-like wounds on her neck and thought of my own gaping throat. Kaden had been considerably reserved while biting the woman compared to me.

"Walker," I murmured. "He doesn't really want her. He—"

"Pressure on your neck, DiRocco. Now."

I pressed my uninjured palm firmly into my neck, and bit back a whimper.

"I can heal her," Kaden said, nodding in my direction.

"Give me the human, and I won't shoot," Walker said calmly.

Kaden smiled. "You won't shoot anyway, not while she's in the line of fire. I'll give you this human if you give me Cassidy."

Walker didn't so much as bat an eyelash. "I'm not bluffing, and I don't bargain with vampires. You set the human aside, or I'll shoot you where you stand. And make no mistake, I've loaded silver shot."

Kaden nodded. "I'm sure you have. I wouldn't expect anything less from Bex's night blood."

"I'm not her night blood," Walker murmured.

I shifted my eyes back and forth between Walker and Kaden, and my gut tightened. Walker was dead serious. Granted, I hadn't known him long, but if this was him bluffing, I never wanted to play poker with the man. Kaden, however, was calling that bluff. The same cocky smirk he'd worn while smashing me against the building, tearing out my throat, and rubbing his scent over me was the same expression he wore now while bargaining with Walker. Kaden expected to get his way, and Walker, so help him, wasn't giving even an inch.

"Help me," the woman wheezed in a squeak. "Please, help me."

I suddenly recognized her. Without her apron, baker's hat, and sassy smile, I hadn't known her, but her voice combined with the tinsel streaks in her dirty-blonde hair finally sparked my memory. The woman Kaden was holding as a shield was none other than Greta's cousin, Jolene McCall of Jolene's Cake Designs, the woman I'd interviewed for her grand opening just two days ago.

"What are you doing here?" I asked, trying to speak clearly through the rasp in my throat.

Jolene blinked at me, recognition spreading across her features. "Ms. DiRocco?"

"Your bakery is on the other side of the borough," I insisted. She shouldn't even be in the area. But then, how did any of us land here in this moment? Did it matter why as long as we survived?

"I come this way all the time. Greta invited me for dinner," Jolene whispered. "I always bring dessert."

"Have you invited this one into your apartment?" Walker asked.

It took me a second to realize that Walker was talking to me and referring to Kaden, not Jolene. I glanced at Walker, who stared unflinching and steadily at his target.

"No," I croaked.

"It's a fair trade, one human for another, and everyone lives." Kaden said reasonably, stepping forward.

I cringed back slightly, but Walker was a rock. "If you take one more step—just one—I will shoot."

He's bluffing, I realized. He couldn't shoot Kaden with a sawed-off shotgun and not hit Jolene. He'd only temporarily wound, or perhaps only anger, Kaden while tearing Jolene to shreds with the spray. If we did trade, however, it might buy us enough time to get Jolene to safety. Walker could always come back for me; Kaden would take his time with me like he wouldn't with any other human.

"Kaden's right," I said, crawling forward. "It's a fair trade, one human for another."

"Stay back," Walker warned.

"He'll kill her," I whispered when I was even with him. "He won't kill me outright. You'll have time to come back for me."

"I'm not coming back for you," Walker said flatly.

"All right," I said, switching gears. After last night, I thought we were a team; I unquestionably would've come back for him. A small part of me was surprised, but the embers of my temper, never far from the surface, simply burned hotter with resignation. "Understood. But that doesn't mean that *I* can't—"

"I'm not coming back for you, because I'm not letting you out of my sight. We're leaving together, not separately, and not in pieces."

I crawled forward, putting myself slightly in front of Walker. "I want to take her place. I have a better chance at surviving and escaping. If we don't trade, he'll kill her now."

"I'm being exceedingly generous," Kaden growled. "I could kill both of you and simply take her, but I'm giving you a choice."

Walker laughed. "You have to give me a choice unless you want to face Bex and your final death."

"Bex is powerful, and she's a strong ally. I would never deliberately provoke your Master," Kaden admitted.

"She's not my Master," Walker said through gritted teeth. "And I'm not her night blood. I act on my own terms."

"We can both attain what we want tonight and all live." Kaden took one step closer. Jolene cringed and struggled. "Simply hear me out."

Walker pulled the trigger.

A deafening gunshot exploded from the business end of Walker's sawed-off shotgun. The ache in my throat indicated that I'd screamed, but I couldn't hear it. Kaden was a blur of movement, just as impossibly fast as Dominic, if not a pinch faster. But the spray of buckshot was massive, just as I'd anticipated; Walker never would've landed his target otherwise. The gun worked on Kaden like it worked on the quick, winged birds it was intended for: Walker was able to clip Kaden midflight. He dropped and crash-landed, motionless on the asphalt. Blood seeped in a spreading pool around his body.

Walker's hand clamped on my neck. "Pressure, DiRocco. It's not that hard a concept."

He yanked hard on my upper arm, urging me to stand, but I couldn't move. I couldn't tear my eyes from Jolene's massacred body. The last time I saw her, she'd been wearing her jaunty baker's hat and smiling coyly for Meredith's picture. She didn't even have a mouth to smile with now.

She hadn't moved like Kaden, so where only two, maybe three, pellets had managed to hit Kaden, the entire front of Jolene's body had been peppered with buckshot, ravaging her features beyond recognition. Somehow, the spray had spared the left side of her neck, the side that Kaden had bitten. The two neat holes from his fangs were still visible.

"We've got to go. The pellets are silver plated, but that'll only hold him off for so long."

"I would've taken her place," I whispered.

I could still hear her pleading with Kaden, the panicked squeak in her voice as she begged us to help her. She'd squeaked during our interview, too, from the excitement of giving us cupcakes "for the road." Meredith and I had both finished our cupcakes before even reaching the curb, they were so damn good.

I should have snagged those extra copies of the paper for Greta and asked her if Jolene liked our feature. I should have taken the time to follow up.

I couldn't stop staring at what had once been Jolene's face.

"Come on, DiRocco," Walker urged. "Don't quit on me now." He wrapped his arms around my waist and tugged me to my feet.

I slapped at him, but my movements were clumsy and weak. "You killed her!"

Walker jerked, taken aback. "I saved our asses. Now, let's *go!*"

He scooped me up, one arm under my back and the other under my knees. Holding me across his chest, he ran.

"What about her?" I gasped. My voice was becoming breathy and hollow. My anger, although fully stoked, was being fueled by fumes. "Who was there to save her ass?"

"Put pressure on your neck," Walker snapped.

"Just put me down." I struggled, but the city streetlights were whirling, tilting into complete darkness.

"We're almost at your apartment. I have a kit on me, but I won't have much time to get an IV in you before Dominic attacks. It won't take him long to contain the scene with Kaden down." Walker sighed and spoke almost to himself. "He'll know I'm with you in your apartment."

"If you take me to the hospital, instead of my apartment, you won't have to worry about him entering and attacking us. I haven't given him permission to enter the hospital like I have my apartment. We'd be safe at the hospital."

Walker pursed his lips.

"But you don't want us safe. You just want a chance to kill Dominic," I said, bitterly, hating that Dominic was right but hating that Walker was using me as bait even more.

"Of course I want you safe," Walker said, looking affronted. "What do you think the IV is for? Maybe if you had called out sick, like I suggested, you wouldn't need it now."

I blinked. "Where did you get an IV?"

Walker sighed. "I should've brought blood, too, but I didn't anticipate this. You were supposed to stay with your brother tonight. You were supposed to be safe."

"Who could have anticipated what happened tonight? You were supposed to be my backup against the monsters, not one of them," I murmured, thinking of Jolene, her lips trembling as she pleaded with us to help her. "God, she was so scared."

"Cassidy?" Walker's voice turned sharp, but all I could see was Jolene's face. "Open your eyes. We're almost at the apartment, damn it!"

The whirling streetlights winked and extinguished in a swallowing tide, abandoning me, Jolene, and her haunting pleas to complete darkness.

Chapter 8

An unendurable, relentless pain pounded through my neck. I squirmed away from the pressure, but large, steady hands held my head immobile. I was lying on my back on what felt like my own bed, but that was wrong. No one but me had ever been in my bedroom, and besides a few wishful thoughts about Walker recently, I didn't have any intention of breaking that streak. The pressure worsened until I felt strangled by the pain. I heard myself moan. I bit my lip.

"I know it hurts, but it's all right, darlin'. I'm just wrapping your neck. Can you hear me?"

"Walker?" I licked my lips. "We're at my apartment?"

"Yes," he breathed, sounding relieved. "Your neck needs stitches, but this will do for now. Dominic will be here any moment, and I still need to get that IV in you."

"You know he'll come because of me. We're not safe here."

Walker exhaled loudly, nervously. "That's the plan."

He really is using me as bait for Dominic, I thought, my heart sinking. *This is really happening.*

Something sharp suddenly dug into the bend of my elbow. I winced and jerked back.

"Fuck," Walker whispered hotly. I felt him clamp a hand around my forearm, immobilizing my arm against the bed. The sharpness suddenly stabbed even deeper. "Keep still. It's just the IV."

"You could've warned me," I muttered. My voice sounded sluggish and thready, even to me.

"I did," he said, sliding the needle out of my skin and stabbing it in again. "Shit," he breathed vehemently, wriggling the needle under my skin.

"Walker," I gasped, overwhelmed by the pain.

He withdrew the needle again. "I know. I'm sorry. Your blood pressure's too low. I can't . . . your veins ain't, well, they just ain't co-operating."

"Hospital," I whispered.

"I know. We will," Walker said, and then he stabbed me again.

I struggled not to lash out. "Just leave it," I ground out.

"Almost," he said, concentrating.

A shadow moved in the corner of my vision. I felt the hairs on my neck rise to attention and knew only one creature who made me this aware of the nuances of fear, trepidation, and undeniable heat in my body. Even though I knew who would be outside my window, I held my breath as I shifted my eyes to look. Despite all our interaction, his existence still seemed like a nightmare, but the glowing eyes and snarling face of the vampire outside my window was very much, very terrifyingly real. Dominic met my gaze and bared his teeth. Gone was the polished, handsome façade I'd interacted with earlier this evening. He wasn't even pretending to smile.

"Walker," I panted. "He's—"

"Just. One. Second," Walker whispered. He frowned in concentration, and this time, the needle slid nearly painlessly through my skin into the vein. "Got it."

Dominic slammed open the window and was inside the apartment before I could utter another word, but just as fast as Dominic blurred through the window, an explosion of machine-gun fire erupted from a mechanism on the far wall. I gaped as Dominic dropped to a complete halt in midair and crumpled on the floor in a heap.

Walker looked up from my arm, a calculating expression on his formerly boyish face. A slow, creeping smile widened his lips, not unlike the smile on the Grinch as he got his awful idea to steal Christmas, and I realized that the situation had been planned and the plan had worked.

"You planned all this," I whispered aloud. I stared at Dominic's motionless body.

"Of course. I would never deliberately put you in danger. I knew he'd fall."

I shook my head. "You set this trap for Dominic while I was passed out. You took the time to use me as bait instead of getting me help!"

"Who else would you have me call? I *am* your help." Walker ducked away from view and emerged from behind the bed a second later with a short wooden javelin, undoubtedly the stake needed to finish the job.

Jesus, I thought. *The man's going to stake a vampire through the heart in my bedroom.*

The room was still and quiet for a hushed moment, me staring nervously at Walker, Walker glaring triumphantly at Dominic, and Dominic's glassy and vacant gaze focused on my ceiling. Stake in hand, Walker knelt next to his body. Dominic was still wearing the sharp suit from earlier this evening, but now the fabric was ravaged by bullet holes. *Like Jolene,* I thought bitterly, except his blood seeped out slowly—a steady, streaming leak rather than a pulsing flow.

Walker placed the stake on Dominic's chest, over his heart.

I blinked, and Dominic's hand was suddenly wrapped around Walker's wrist. I hadn't seen him move. I hadn't even seen him flinch. One moment, Walker was preparing to stake him, and the very next moment, Dominic was restraining him with one hand.

"SHIT!" Walker shouted.

Dominic's wounds ejected the bullets and healed as we watched. Steam cracked from his skin, and I heard the metallic clatter of the bullets hit, bounce, and roll around on my hardwood floors.

Walker attempted to pull away, but Dominic's single handhold around his wrist held him immobile. "Impossible. Those are silver bullets. His wounds should heal nearly human-slow."

"Dominic is only slightly allergic to silver," I whispered, horrified.

The last bullet clattered to the floor, leaving us in suspended, breathless, pounding silence.

Dominic's eyes snapped open.

Walker struggled in earnest, attempting to break Dominic's hold. He struck out with his elbow and the flat of his hand in crushing pressure-point punches.

Dominic laughed, but it was a horrible, grating noise. "This was your plan to kill me? A spray of silver and a simple staking? I expected better. Bex has been exaggerating your reputation."

"You're just like all the rest. You think you're a god, but I've seen your kind burst into flames. I've seen you erupt into ash, and I've seen an entire body boil and melt from silver exposure. You can die," Walker snarled.

"I most certainly can, but you brought an umbrella to protect yourself against a hurricane," Dominic said coolly. "So I won't be dying tonight."

Walker adjusted his grip slightly on the stake and tensed to strike.

"Be still," Dominic intoned, staring deep into Walker's eyes.

Walker fell deep into Dominic's gaze, and his arm dropped to the side.

"Hand me the stake," Dominic said, his voice mild and soft and more dangerous than I'd ever heard.

I could see the fire in Walker's eyes, but his body obeyed without hesitation. He handed Dominic his own wooden stake.

"Thank you," Dominic said.

Dominic was suddenly a blur of speed and motion. He drove Walker backward by his neck, slammed him up against my bedroom wall, and stabbed him through the shoulder with his own stake, pinning him like an insect on display. Walker's throat made strangled, coughing noises through Dominic's choke hold, but otherwise, he didn't so much as blink.

"If I'm not mistaken," Dominic murmured, ripping the stake from Walker's shoulder and testing its weight in his hand, "I'm not the only creature in this room who can die by a stake through the heart."

Dominic tightened his grip on the stake and cocked his arm to strike.

"No!" I shouted, but my damaged throat only expelled a tight squeal. "Please don't."

His body remained poised and ready, but Dominic turned his head to stare at me. "Are you begging for his life?"

I bit my lip, unsure whether the truth or bargaining would best convince Dominic. I wasn't getting any guidance from Walker. His expression was looking increasingly like dripping paint. "Yes," I whispered, deciding on honesty. "Please don't kill him."

Dominic tilted his head slightly, looking calm and thoughtful, as if considering one lump or two. Maybe for him, the gravity of sparing someone's life wasn't particularly grave at all. A chittering buzzed from his nose with every exhale as he breathed. It sounded vaguely like the high, sharp vibration of cicadas, and I realized that he was struggling to contain the rattling in his chest. He was struggling and failing, as I failed most of the time, to control his anger. I struggled not to look away.

"You didn't beg for mine."

I frowned. "Excuse me?"

Dominic released his choke hold on Walker, turned on his heel, and strode toward me. My heart quickened. I glanced between Dominic and Walker, but Walker was still mesmerized and worse than useless, even without Dominic's direct gaze on him. He remained motionless against the wall, unblinking, unseeing, and seemingly mindless. I knew the opposite was true, that he was screaming inside, but that didn't help us now.

Dominic took his time walking to me. His skin was flawless beneath the tatters of his torn black dress shirt, healed to smooth, healthy perfection after the damage he'd sustained. Despite his body and the strength I knew he possessed, the expression on his face made my gut turn sour and tremble. His face wasn't the sculpted, jaw-dropping beauty that had visited my office just a few hours ago. Healing must have taken its toll because his mask of humanity was slipping. His cheeks were sallow. His eyes glowed from the sunken depths of overprominent cheekbones. The tips of his fangs extended out of his thinned lips even without snarling. As he approached, he did snarl, and when his lips lifted farther away from his fangs, his teeth seemed longer and more lethal.

Before he could reach the bed, an idea struck me. I took a shuddering breath against the fear, nausea, and pulsing darkness, looked into Dominic's eyes, and said, "Dominic Lysander, I revoke your invitation. You are not welcome in my apartment."

Dominic grinned. "That's the funny thing about invitations. You can revoke them all you want, but the boundaries here that protected you from me are already shattered. There's no going back."

One moment Dominic was adjacent to the bed, grinning down at me with his sharp fangs, and the next, he was straddling me, his talons clamping onto my shoulders and holding me up from the bed, centimeters from his face.

I screamed, but my voice was hoarse and weak, and it sounded more like a moan. It sounded awful and pathetic, and I hated that a noise like that came from me.

"You beg me to spare his life," Dominic growled, our noses nearly touching. I could hear the bones and muscles and tissues snapping and shifting under his skin as his jaw prepared to extend. "But you didn't beg him to spare mine."

I opened my mouth, but no sound came out. I didn't know how to respond. *Of course I didn't beg him to spare you*, I thought, but a response like that wouldn't bode well for my survival. I snapped my mouth shut.

"I have saved you as he has saved you. He has used you to bait me as I long to use you to bait Kaden, but I had the decency to ask your permission, to include you in my plans. If you're his friend, why, too, can't you be mine?"

I opened my mouth again, thinking that I knew exactly what to say this time. *You're a murderer*, I thought, but then I snapped my mouth shut again. I never actually witnessed Dominic murder anyone, but I still couldn't forget Jolene's fear-filled face or the fact that Walker had killed her.

"You seemed perfectly able to take care of yourself without my assistance," I settled on as a response. "Walker wasn't doing well on his own."

"You flee from me, leave another scene for me to prepare along with at least a hundred witnesses and over a dozen police officers to entrance, and then you watch as that boy attempts to stake me without so much as a peep from those lips of yours. And after all that, after everything you've done to slight me, you actually have the audacity to beg me for his life." Dominic shook me violently. "What have you done for me that I should consider doing this favor for you?"

Something warm oozed down my shoulder. Dominic must have torn open the wound on my neck again. Starbursts of darkness swamped my vision. "I could have taken her place," I muttered, and the entire room winked out.

The sharp, crisp scent of pine was thick on the air and brought back the memories of Christmas, the most precious days of my childhood. Mom and Dad would sip eggnog and pass gifts and take pictures, and I hadn't appreciated any of it at the time. I was appreciative of their love and their gifts, but I hadn't appreciated the simple blessing of their presence. I suppose most children don't until they're older, but Nathan and I had never been given that necessary time.

After our parents died, we let go of the formalities of Christmas traditions in favor of our careers. For better or for worse, the eggnog, gifts, pictures, and joys of the holiday died along with our parents.

Inexplicably, after five years of bare walls, leftovers, and solitude on Christmas, I suddenly had the scent of pine.

Something slick and warm was inside my neck. I winced away from it, but it pressed deeper, sliding between tendons and the grooves of torn flesh. I breathed in sharply, catching another hit of pine, and reality punctured through my memories of childhood. Dominic was on top of me. The pressure and movement of his tongue was sharp and needle-like as he healed my neck. Heat radiated in pulsing pleasure as the flesh mended, creating a strange tightrope sensation between pain and achy need.

Healing hadn't felt like this before. Although his bite had felt like an explosion of pleasure, instant and nearly unendurable, the heat from his healing had never been more than simple heat. Now, a surging wave of pleasure was arching over us, the threat of its impending crest and crash daunting.

A noise escaped my lips, a worse noise than pathetic wimpering. The noise was embarrassing and inappropriate, but I couldn't contain the overwhelming sensations brewing under my skin. I shivered and twitched and fisted the sheets in my hands, desperate to hold on to something solid as I drowned in his undertow.

Dominic placed a hand firmly on the other side of my face to immobilize my neck while he worked, and I squirmed beneath him. His shoulders were hard and ridged with beautifully smooth muscle under his torn dress shirt. I vaguely realized that I wasn't fisting the sheets but rather his shirt in my hands. I should have told him to stop, that I was healed enough to survive and would get stitches if necessary. I should have at least struggled to finish the staking that Walker had attempted. I should have done a lot of things, but instead of doing what I should, I slipped my hands through the tears of his tattered dress shirt. I scraped my nails down the smooth ridges of back muscle. I reveled in the rattling, tormented vibrations that rumbled from Dominic's chest, and the twitch of his own muscles beneath my hands.

I felt Dominic's tongue lick over the healed wound on my neck and realized that my skin was mended. He was simply licking and sucking at the scar. Something touched the back of my hand. He detached my grip from his shirt, lifted my palm to his lips, and licked over that wound until it healed, as well. I'd been so consumed by his touch that I'd forgotten the cut on my palm. I'd likely smeared blood on the sheets, his shirt, and myself, and I hadn't noticed or cared.

The sensations eventually dulled until only the faint pulse of unsatisfied, lingering desire remained. I trembled from wanting him, feeling desperate for more of his touch and ashamed for feeling that way. If I was honest with myself, if I felt past the expected emotions of shame and disgust and fear, I could admit that I wanted him, all of him, inside of me to finish what he'd started.

I took a deep, shuddering breath as he pulled away. His face was fully elongated into the muzzle he wore when he fed, his mouth coated from cheek to cheek in my blood. I felt sickened by him and by my own feelings.

"I can feel it, too," he murmured, his voice strangely civilized despite the animal-like distortion of his mouth.

I looked away. "Why did you heal me like that?"

Dominic took my chin in his hand and forced me to face him. "I will always be there to heal you."

"This was different," I said, ignoring the disturbing infinite in that sentence. "You took pleasure in healing me this time."

"Healing you is always my pleasure," Dominic said, a wide grin spreading across his animal-like features. "But I healed you the way I have always healed you. Nothing changed, except perhaps your feelings toward me. You desire me now."

"You did something different," I insisted.

"Tell yourself whatever lies allow you to face yourself in the mirror, but the truth is that I did nothing more than heal you. Whatever you felt—whatever I felt—during the healing, was entirely our own feelings."

"I don't believe you." My body was trembling. I could feel the shiver of my shoulder against the cold, unmovable stillness of his body.

He shook his head, looking vaguely disappointed. "Believe what you want. I thought you were in the business of finding and spreading truth, but maybe I was wrong."

My temper burst through my shock and doused the trembling. "My *business* is news. To keep people aware of—"

"And yet, you are not aware of your own feelings."

"I—"

Dominic placed a finger over my lips. The strength evidenced in the pressure of that single finger stopped me midbreath. "I'll leave you tonight, whole and healthy and otherwise untouched despite all you've done, if you grant me a favor."

"A favor?" I asked.

"I want you to look into my eyes, and control my mind like you did earlier tonight. Entrance me like I've entranced you."

I blinked. "Why would you want me to do that? I thought you were furious with me for controlling your mind."

"I'm delighted that you have that ability. In all my long life, I've never crossed a night blood who displayed such power. You are a wonder, Cassidy, an absolute wonder, and the more I come to know you, the more convinced I am of your purpose and of your place with me in my coven. I was only furious that you were able to use this power on me." He smirked mirthlessly, and with the extended muzzle, his mouth looked even more feral. "So think of this as a self-evaluation. Humor me, and entrance me one more time. If you can."

"And you'll simply leave afterward?" I asked doubtfully.

"I swear to you by the sun that I will leave afterward," he answered dramatically.

"And not turn, harm, or otherwise touch Walker, either."

Dominic narrowed his eyes.

"Those are my conditions. You must simply leave this apartment directly following your 'self-evaluation,'" I proposed.

"He doesn't deserve immunity from me." He studied me a moment as if considering his words before he spoke. Finally, he sighed and said, "You do realize that slapping a makeshift bandage over a serious neck wound and shooting an IV in your arm wouldn't have saved you," Dominic said, slipping the knife of doubt between my ribs quickly and deeply, all the more devastating for its truth. "He simply patched you up to survive long enough to bait me, and he put your health and safety on the line to do it."

"So you've mentioned multiple times," I bit out. "That's between him and me."

"And what is between you and me?" he asked.

Nothing I want, I thought, but I countered, "You'll earn a sliver of my trust if you keep your word."

Dominic hesitated a moment before finally nodding. "Done."

"Swear like you did last time," I insisted. "Swear by the sun."

"Smart girl," Dominic said, grinning. "I swear by the sun that I will leave tonight without having turned, harmed, or otherwise touched you or Ian Walker."

"All right." I took a deep breath, feeling as safe as I could under the circumstances.

Dominic leaned closer. I could feel the movement of his breath over my face as he spoke. "I don't want a paltry command, like 'stay where you are' this time. I want something real. Something powerful. Command me to do something I would never willingly do."

I thought for a long, quiet moment. I envisioned our few encounters: Dominic biting my neck, sucking my blood, licking my wounds, and burning himself on silver just to prove a point. It seemed to me like he'd willingly do just about anything except walk in sunlight. "Can you give me an example?"

His eyes roamed over my face and body as he thought.

"Anything involving my body isn't an option. Think of something else."

Dominic shrugged. "I would willingly do all those things anyway."

I rolled my eyes.

"Tell me to stake myself," he said.

I stared at him, not sure I'd heard him correctly. "What?"

"Command me to take this stake"—he held out the stake in his hand—"and stab myself in the heart with it."

I opened my mouth, but it took me a moment to speak. "But you'll die, won't you?"

"We shall see." Dominic smirked. "Go on. Command me. You've already sworn that you would."

I blew out a long breath. "Right."

I locked eyes with Dominic and gazed deep inside his soul. "Dominic Lysander," I said, and I felt the instant connection between our minds, as if the nerves and synapses that fired in mine were also suddenly firing in his. The last time I'd linked our minds, I could feel his shock and anger and bone fear. This time, I could only feel anticipation. "Stab yourself in the heart with the stake in your hand. Now."

My command travelled between us as fast as thought, but as usual with anything involving vampires, Dominic was faster. The moment I uttered my command, Dominic constructed a defense against it. I couldn't discern what was between us, only that our bond was blocked like it hadn't been last time.

When my command hit his defense, I could finally envision what he'd constructed: a mirror. The command reflected off the mirror protecting his mind, and without his speed or mental defenses, I couldn't defend myself against my own command any more than I could defend myself against his. The command hit me.

Both my hands reached out of their own volition, grabbed the wooden stake from Dominic's hands, and tried to plunge its tip into my own chest.

Fighting the urge to stake myself was impossible; my muscles couldn't move faster than neurological synapses, and my synapses had already staked my heart. The spear was unbelievably sharp and split my skin easier than I would have thought possible. I screamed; the pain was sudden and shocking. I couldn't believe that after everything I'd witnessed and struggled through and survived, that I would die by my own hand.

Dominic placed a hand over both of mine, stopping me from stabbing myself further. Only the tip of the stake had pierced a superficial layer of skin, so even as he held my actions at bay, my arms still strained to finish the command. Blood trickled down between my breasts and stained my already hopelessly stained silky dress shirt.

"I want you to remember this moment," Dominic said, looking utterly smug. "What you are thinking and feeling is the fate you would have given me."

"How?" Scalding tears flooded my eyes. I swallowed a sob as they burned and constricted my throat. "How did you do that? You reflected our connection."

Dominic leaned mere inches over me and licked the tears from my face. I cringed away from him.

"It's a power I've always had, but haven't put to use lately. I certainly hadn't thought to need it in defense of you," Dominic whispered. "You could see the mirror when your command reflected?"

I nodded.

"Lovely." Dominic rested his cheek against my temple and breathed in the scent of my hair. "You are simply lovely."

My arms were trembling and burning from the strain of trying to pull the stake into my heart.

"I'm going to save you from yourself, but I want your promise that you'll remember this moment and note my favorable actions when you remember it. I want you to promise me like I promised by the final certainty of sunlight," Dominic commanded. "And in return, I will never again control your mind, if you never again attempt to control mine. We will trust one another."

"Okay." I swallowed, sweating bullets from the strain in my arms. "I swear to remember this moment and your favorable actions."

Dominic raised his eyebrows. "And?"

"And?" I blinked. "I don't understand."

"I swore by the sun, my final and certain death, making my oath final and certain. You must do the same."

"Seriously," I said, trying to think past the twitching and burning in my biceps. "Something final and certain?"

He nodded.

I gritted my teeth. "I swear by the final, certain passage of time that I will remember this moment and your favorable actions."

Dominic smiled broadly, and this time, despite the blood and slight extension of his mouth, he was almost handsome by the joy that radiated from it. "Very well."

He leaned down over me, the stake like a promise between us, and kissed me. His lips were soft and sensually urging, waiting for me to respond like before. I'd have preferred that the connection between us be a fluke. I didn't want to feel the heat that sparked again, and I didn't want to enjoy the rhythm and cant of his lips and tongue. I shouldn't have angled my head to the side to deepen the kiss or felt so sizzling under his movement and weight, but I did. The heat pulsed and swirled around us in escalating momentum. Even after his lips parted from mine and he stared down at me—a deep wonder, almost fear, shining in his gaze—the heat continued to swirl and pulse.

I wondered what he had to fear. I couldn't imagine anything between us that could frighten this creature, but as I breathed heavily, both from his kiss and from keeping my own instincts to deepen and further the kiss at bay, terror washed over me. I wanted him. More deeply rooted than my instinct to live, when Dominic touched me, I unfathomably wanted more. I bit my lip to keep myself in check, and Dominic's gaze darkened.

He leaned close, his mouth against the shell of my ear. "Have a good night, my lovely Cassidy DiRocco."

Dominic flew from the bed and out the window in a blur of windswept speed, taking the spear with him. The window slammed shut behind him.

My empty fists pounded into my chest, completing the motion of spearing my heart. I fell backward, limp onto my mattress and gasping in grateful exhaustion that I had survived.

Walker blinked slowly. His gaze sharpened as his mind once again took control of his body, and he snapped back into himself.

"Son of a bitch!" Walker spat. He ran to the window and pounded his fist on the frame. The wood splintered and pieces rained over the floor, but Dominic was long gone. It had only been a moment, but with Dominic's speed, he'd likely already returned to the coven.

For all of Dominic's faults, and they were many and egregious, he obviously cared for the prosperous existence of his kind and himself. He was consistent. As much as Walker claimed that we couldn't believe the vampires, any vampire, he was making it very difficult for me to believe in him. He claimed to hunt vampires to protect humans, but the fact was that Walker ran to the window to confront Dominic rather than to the bed to check on me. He cared more about killing vampires than he did about protecting humans.

"That was much, much too close," Walker said, turning his back on the window to face me. He clamped his hand over his injured shoulder. "Are you all right?"

"I'm fine," I muttered. I was more angry at Walker than Dominic, which felt like a kind of betrayal and, like most everything lately, that made me angry.

Walker scoffed. He strode to the bed, adjusted the IV, and scanned my body for further injuries, but having been tended by Dominic, my physical condition had only improved.

"How were you able to connect with his mind?" Walker asked softly.

"Something about being a night blood that I know and you don't?" I raised my eyebrows. "I'm sure you've tried turning their mind tricks on them before."

"I have," Walker said, sounding annoyed. "And it's impossible."

I frowned. "You've never connected with a vampire's mind? Even after they drank your blood?"

"No. As far as I know, no one has."

I narrowed my eyes. "Not that you've spoken to many night bloods to know."

Walker looked away. "How deep did he let the stake pierce you?"

"Not deep."

Walker moved to unbutton the top button of my blouse.

I crossed my arms in front of myself to block him. "I'm *fine*."

"Stop being stubborn, and let me see how badly you're injured."

"No, Walker." I took a deep, fortifying breath. "I think you should leave."

"Don't push me away, Cassidy. I know you're a capable woman, but even I can't fight them and survive on my own. We need to stick together against them." He reached for my hand. "Let me help you."

I folded my hands deep under my arms and out of his reach. "I know I'm a stubborn person, but it's more than that. I *did* want your help, before you—" In my mind, Jolene's lips trembled in fear and angst and terrible hope that we could help her. I shuddered. "I just need you to leave."

"You wanted my help before I what?" he asked, looking utterly confused.

I couldn't meet his gaze. "Before you killed Jolene."

"Who did I kill?" Walker asked, looking shocked.

"The woman you killed in the alley, the one Kaden took hostage to trade for me. I knew her, Walker. Her name was Jolene McCall. She's Greta's cousin." My voice broke. "She bakes cupcakes."

Walker blinked, a sudden, hard calm clouding his expression. "I had no choice. I did what was necessary."

"What you did was completely *unnecessary*. We could have found a way to save her and still save ourselves. I told you to trade me for her. You could have used me as a distraction until she was safe. You had *choices*, Walker, and you *chose to kill her!*" I hissed, working myself into a rage as I spoke. "Just like you chose to set a trap for Dominic instead of bringing me to safety."

"We were wasting time. Kaden made his move, and I made mine. That's all there is to it."

"Wasting *time?* Who cares how *long* it took? She would have been alive!"

"We needed to get back to your apartment to prepare for Dominic before he caught us vulnerable on the street. We had an advantage here, and maybe, just maybe, we could have taken him out. Had we waited, we would have lost our advantage," Walker explained slowly, as if to the dim-witted. "I was protecting us."

"You didn't shoot Jolene to protect us from Kaden. You shot her because saving her would've taken time, time that you wanted to better use to kill Dominic," I said, beyond furious. "And it didn't even pay off. Jolene is still dead, and Dominic is still alive."

Walker crossed his arms. "Arguably, he's already dead."

"Seriously? You're going to argue semantics? Dead or not, he's more alive than Jolene," I snapped.

"Like I said, I did what was necessary," Walker said coldly. "The vampires are rampaging, unremorseful murderers, feeding from and killing humans indiscriminately, and we've got to do anything and everything to stop them. We're the only people who know they exist, Cassidy, so it's our duty to see them killed."

"But at what cost, Walker? Is killing a human justified in the name of killing a vampire?" I asked. "I don't see any difference between you killing Jolene or Kaden killing her, and I doubt she does, either. It doesn't matter who does the killing because either way she's dead."

"Killing one vampire protects all of the humans he might have killed, even if it takes one human death to accomplish it. Casualties are a part of war. It's something I've learned to live with."

"Well, I haven't." I inhaled a deep, trembling breath and turned my face to meet Walker's gaze squarely. "Did you let the vampires attack me last night so you could track us back to Dominic's coven? Did you use me as bait to finally locate where the vampires sleep beneath the city?"

"If you remember correctly, I warned you not to walk home."

"Yes, you did. You seemed to know exactly what might happen," I said softly, regretfully.

Walker stared deep into my eyes, and the sharpness of his pain made my heart bleed for him. I knew that pain intimately. He'd obviously lost someone, but I'd lost people, too. I refused to retreat from this argument because the one thing I learned from their loss was that life was fleeting, and the only people worth getting to know were people I could trust.

"I'm sorry you were attacked, Cassidy. I'll admit that I'm ecstatic we found the coven, but discovering its location was just a bonus. My priority was finding you."

"Of course it was, because if you found me, you found the coven. You used me as bait," I insisted.

He leaned closer, and I could see the muscles in his jaw flex as he clenched his teeth. "I never would have left you there."

I shook my head. "Dominic was right. The two of you are just alike."

"Excuse me?" Walker asked, suddenly, dangerously calm.

I swallowed. "You watched and waited as the vampires attacked me, so you could track me back to their coven. You let me nearly bleed to death instead of taking me to the hospital, so you could set up your vampire-trap—which failed, by the way. And your first concern after regaining power over your body was that Dominic had fled. My safety comes in second against the priority of killing Dominic. Admit it, Walker, killing vampires is more important to you than saving lives."

Walker rolled his eyes. "I kill vampires for the express purpose of saving lives."

"No, I don't think so," I whispered. "Given the choice between the two, you'd choose killing the vampire."

He placed a hand gently on my forearm since he couldn't gain access to my hands, and he rubbed his thumb slowly over my skin. "You're letting that vampire drive a wedge between us. He's manipulating us into fighting to gain the advantage."

I laughed. "He doesn't need to manipulate anything. Dominic *is* the advantage. You and I worked together tonight, and he wiped the floor with us. I doubt he's concerned that our alliance poses a threat."

"We *can* stand against them, Cassidy, but we only stand a chance if we stand together," Walker insisted. The radical in him seeped into his voice, so his tone sounded crazed with determination.

I sighed, feeling exhausted by the argument. "Listen, Walker, I'm tired and weary, and I have a lot of cleaning to do before I can go to bed. I really would like you to just leave. Please."

Walker looked around the apartment, his gaze traveling over the busted window frame, the splintered wood strewn over the floor, the pocked holes in the walls, and the buckshot and blood everywhere.

"If you think you're leavin' that bed for one minute, you're severely mistaken, darlin'." Walker said dryly. "It's my mess. I'll clean it up."

I rolled my eyes. "Walker, please, I just want—"

"Where do you keep the bleach?"

"I'm perfectly capable of cleaning my own apartment," I stated firmly. "And you're injured, too. You need to take care of that shoulder."

He stared back at me, just as resolute. "Where do you keep the bleach?"

"God, we're ridiculous," I groaned. I covered my eyes with my hands, resigned to accepting his help. "Under the kitchen sink, like everyone else in the free world."

"Was that so difficult?" he asked, already walking toward the kitchen.

"Well, it certainly wasn't easy," I grumbled, working up the nerve to detach the IV and get out of bed.

"Hey! Leave that alone," Walker chastised a moment later, walking back from the kitchen, bleach in hand. "Lie in bed, leave your IV as it is, and just rest, for Christ's sake. Is that so impossible?"

"Yes," I said, but I listened for once, my stomach roiling from tugging on the IV. I sank into the mattress, intending to simply rest like he'd directed, but my body had other plans. The moment my head hit the pillow, I could feel myself drift.

The shuffle and clatter of Walker adjusting my pots and pans roused me slightly. "Where's your mop and bucket?" he asked.

"Tall kitchen cabinet, left of the oven," I murmured, not bothering to open my eyes.

"That's where I'm looking. I'm not seeing any—oh," he said, cutting off his own sentence.

"Mmm? Is something wrong?" I asked. I forced my eyes open, but the only person in the room was Walker, and he was standing right in front of me.

"Nope, not a thing. I found it, thank you," he said.

I glanced at the cabinet ajar behind him and frowned. "You're in the wrong cabinet. I'll show you where—"

"I've got it, DiRocco," Walker insisted, catching my shoulder as I struggled to sit up. He pressed me back down into the mattress. "I'm a smart guy. I'll figure it out. *Rest.*" He reached out to touch my face, hesitated, and let his hand fall back to his side uncertainly.

I wondered what it would feel like to trust someone implicitly, for him to not only clean my apartment but join me in bed without hesitation and hold me afterward, to have his arms wrapped securely around me when I woke up for work in the morning. I almost asked him to stay, remembering the loss I'd felt when he left my apartment last night, but even as I opened my mouth, Jolene's fear-filled, hopeful expression haunted me and choked the words.

Before I could decide, Walker turned around and walked back to the cabinets. He didn't offer to stay this time, and I was too proud to ask. Feeling discontented, I closed my eyes and slipped into sleep with the sounds of running water, scrubbing, and softly muffled oaths as my lullaby.

Chapter 9

My alarm buzzed through the morning silence. I woke, disoriented for a moment because although I was sleeping on my bed with my usual quilt over me, the mattress under me was bare; the sheets were stacked on the bench of my bay window. They looked crisp and fresh and stain-free, and with that thought, the memories from last night came rushing back. I burrowed beneath the quilt with a groan, trying to find at least some reprieve from reality, but the pull and snag of the IV in the bend of my elbow sank the memories vividly and inescapably home.

The quilt was warm and smelled lightly of mint. I used their soft comfort to keep the images from last night at bay. I took a deep breath and imagined Walker tucking me in after rummaging through my cabinets for bleach and Pine-Sol. I couldn't imagine Walker mopping, but the clean shine of my hardwood floors spoke on behalf of his domestic skills.

I squinted at my apartment floor, window, and walls from under my burrowed nest in the quilt, and everything, from the crisp sheets piled on the bay window to the holes in my now Swiss cheese–like walls were clean if not whole. Walker had been very thorough, which I appreciated, although my landlord would undoubtedly reconsider renewing my lease.

I allowed myself a minute of selfish comfort before emerging from the bed. If I didn't remove myself from under the quilt now, I'd never get up. I'd already been late to work and called out once this week; Carter would have a coronary if I was late again. That thought alone gave me pause, so I concentrated on dreams of Pulitzers, carefully removed the IV without gagging, and walked shakily to the bathroom before I gave in to the compulsion to sleep in.

I cringed at my reflection in the mirror. I looked like death warmed over. Some form of masking was definitely needed before subjecting my coworkers to my appearance, but it would take more than makeup to look like myself again.

An hour later, I was washed, made up, and ready to report. I'd woken on time today, so my voice mail was blessedly empty. Nathan, however, had never returned my calls. I tried him again. His cell phone rang five times before voice mail kicked in, and I left another message, feeling dread like a knot twist through my gut.

"Yo, bro, what do you know? Nothing about me, obviously, because you never called me back. We need to talk, pronto." I massaged the frown between my brows. "Seriously, I need to see you. Call me back when you get this."

I hung up and checked a sunrise/sunset calendar online before leaving for work. The sun dipped below the horizon at 7:56 p.m. EST. I didn't know how to prepare, if any preparations could truly give me an advantage over Dominic or Kaden, but I had twelve hours, forty-two minutes, and thirty-seven seconds to plan a defense. In the meantime, I had stories to write, witnesses to squeeze, and lies to expose throughout the city that would hopefully—I crossed my fingers—not involve vampires.

I burst through the *Sun Accord* doors in my usual stride. Sometimes I could fool people into thinking I was taller and more substantial by my sheer presence, but when Carter strode out of his office with equal gusto and loomed nearly a foot and a half over me, this morning wasn't one of those times.

"DiRocco, you've got some ner—" Carter stopped dead in his tracks in front of me on his way to the watercooler. "You look like roadkill. Raccoon roadkill."

"Turning up the charm early this morning, Carter," I said snidely, although he was right. I might have been heavy-handed with the eyeliner.

I ducked around him to beeline it to my desk. I could hear his steps behind me.

"Your neighborhood's been hit rough this week, you missed the budget meeting yesterday, and frankly, you look like hell. You need a vacation."

"I'm not sure that this is the time—"

Carter followed me to my desk. "Sit. We need to talk."

Eleven hours and twenty-seven minutes until sunset, I thought, glancing at my computer as it booted. I didn't have time for a lecture from Carter. I felt like life was a ticking time bomb set on the earth's rotation. I grudgingly sat.

Carter straddled the chair across from me, turning it so that he could lean both his forearms over the backrest. The movements were too familiar. It didn't matter that he was straddling the chair instead of crossing his legs nor that he was human and not vampire; he was still a very intimidating man forcing me to sit at my own desk while he cornered me for questioning. My heart tripped a beat and then raced to catch up.

Carter is not Dominic, I thought, trying not to panic, but Carter had never talked to me at my desk before. Honestly, in the five years and six months I'd slaved for him and the *Sun Accord,* I couldn't remember a single time when he'd spoken to me about anything except work.

I cleared my throat. "I'm not sure a talk is necessary. Don't you have someone else in this office to fry?"

Carter grunted. "Normally, I'd agree with you, but normally, you don't give me this many issues."

I blinked. "I'm giving you issues?"

"Unlike everyone else working at this circus, you and Meredith have your shit together. You're a team. Your writing is engaging and accurate, her photos are enthralling, and you both make it to print on time, every time. You might make it last-minute—which I suspect is part of your master plan to kill me—but you make it, and your stories sell," Carter said, and if I wasn't mistaken, and I must be for this to come from Carter, he sounded proud.

I stared, a little taken aback by his complimentary honesty. "Oh. Thanks."

"But I don't care how many newspapers your stories sell, you're not above attending my budget meetings. I don't care what troubles you're having. You leave them at home where they belong, and you come here ready to impress me with prizewinning pieces."

"Right," I said flatly.

"That being said, I received a call from Detective Wahl last night."

"Oh?" I raised my eyebrows nonchalantly even as my heart knotted and quivered. "What did she have to say?"

"She wanted to know when we were going to print the retraction to the retraction about the Paerdegat Park case," Carter said, staring hard at me.

"We don't do retractions to our retractions," I said cautiously. "She knows that."

"Yes, I handled Detective Wahl," Carter dismissed.

Only by the herculean effort of my iron will did I resist rolling my eyes. No one "handled" Greta.

"What I want to know is, how you out of everyone, including the police who investigated the murder, Meredith who took the shots, and the paramedics who treated the victims, were the only person who saw the bite marks?"

Those damn bite marks were going to haunt me for the rest of my career. I took a moment to breathe before answering and decided to act on a time-tested motto: when in doubt, ask more questions. "Did you look at Tuesday's print again? Did you see the photo we used, the one that Meredith took and you approved?"

"I would remember if I approved that photo," Carter snapped.

"Then I must be exceptionally observant," I said simply, trying to keep the exasperation out of my voice. It wasn't Carter's fault that he'd been entranced by Dominic, but life was always a little sweeter when I could blame Carter.

He stared me down hard. "I'm not doubting your powers of observation."

I raised my eyebrows, knowing that Carter hated my flippancy even more than he hated my temper. "Than what *are* you doubting?"

He pointed a finger at my chest. "Something strange happened at Paerdegat Park because somehow, God only knows how, everyone missed crucial evidence except for you."

I shrugged. "Detective Wahl knows the bodies have bite marks."

"She does *now*, but two days ago she demanded a retraction. Now it turns out that you had it right all along."

"Just doing my job, shining light on Brooklyn's—"

"—on Brooklyn's darkest secrets. Like I haven't heard that one before."

I pursed my lips.

Carter leaned in closer. "Have you looked further into this case since then?"

I bit my lip, wondering for the second time in as many days if a lie or the truth would damn me, and everyone who knew me, more. Of course I'd researched into Paerdegat Park, especially after my article received a retraction. What reporter in their right mind wouldn't defend their article? But how could I ever confess what I'd found?

Vampires, I thought glumly. No one would believe me, and if they did, Dominic would mind-rape the belief out of them. Not even Carter deserved to be on Dominic or Kaden's radar. The only real truth in this mess was that I couldn't win, not during the day against Carter and Greta and Meredith, and certainly not at night against Dominic and Kaden.

"Well? Have you?" he demanded, leaning forward on the chair's back.

"No."

Carter glared at me. "Yes, you did. You insisted on the autopsy."

Crap. "I, er—"

"Besides that, there's no way on God's green fucking earth that you *didn't* look into the one case that you were forced to print a false retraction on. And my gut tells me that you found something you're either not willing to print or scared to print."

"You're crazy," I whispered, but my voice trembled slightly.

"Are you being threatened by one of these gangs?"

"What?" I asked, shocked.

"Greta mentioned that you dodged her last night after she offered you a ride home, the same night of the last batch of murders, which occurred down the block from your apartment, and then you come to work looking like roadkill. You're not the only one who can fit the puzzle pieces together, DiRocco."

I shook my head. "That's not what—"

"Are you being threatened or blackmailed? Is that why you won't print what you found?" Carter leaned closer. "I can get you protection. Tell me what you need, and let's expose the bastards."

I blinked slowly, unexpectedly touched that Carter would help, albeit for his journalistic benefit. But no amount of police protection would prevent Dominic and Kaden and their entire coven of vampires from coming for me.

I shook my head, resolute in my decision. "I didn't find anything. My leads ran dry." I shrugged. "I've got nothing, Carter."

Carter stared into my eyes, waiting for me to break.

I knew the trick well, having implemented it myself during many an interview. I stared back with a glare of my own, undaunted.

Eventually, Carter stood. "This isn't over. Greta's not going to let this go, and frankly, neither am I."

"You're the boss," I quipped.

Carter rolled his eyes. "Get out of here and go cover the murder on your street. Greta will undoubtedly be gunning for you, so you'd better think of a better excuse for knowing what you know than the crap you just gave me. I want you with Meredith in fifteen."

"Your budget meeting's in ten," I reminded him.

"You'd let my budget meeting get in the way of your scoop? You're not the reporter I thought you were, DiRocco."

"But you just said—"

"Get Meredith and get your ass out there. You want the *Times* getting our story?"

Carter left, and I rolled my eyes as high and long as I could with repressed frustration.

The chair in front of my desk creaked.

I snapped my eyes down, mortified for a moment at being caught mid-eye roll before I realized that the person sitting in front of my desk was only Meredith.

"Jesus." I sighed. I let my head fall forward to rest on my crossed forearms on the desk. "You just gave me a stroke."

"Good, then at least one of us can take some medical leave. We're due."

I half-laughed, half-moaned, and lifted my head to meet Meredith's gaze. "You hear about the murder we're investigating in fifteen?"

"Yes, but I—" Meredith stopped short, frowning. "You look like absolute shit."

"Yeah, I look how I feel."

Meredith shook her head. "Is this about the Paerdegat Park case, because Greta said that—"

"If I have to talk about the Paerdegat Park case one more time, *I* will murder someone," I growled.

"Fine." Meredith sighed. "Then what do you want to talk about?"

"Nothing. I don't want to talk about one blessed thing. Let's just get the scoop on this murder and get it over with."

When we reached the crime scene, I realized that I should have better prepared myself. I'd known that this murder, like all the rest, would be a faked gang war to cover the vampire attack, but I hadn't thought about how that would affect Jolene. When I saw her sprawled out on the pavement, the subject of our usual camera flashes and impartial attention, I felt sick; not necessarily nauseous, although that was there, too, but deeply sick to my core.

The side of her neck that had been pierced by Kaden's fangs was now clean and unblemished. Her body was healed, too, so that most of her skin was smooth and beautiful and perfect, not the raw, pellet-embedded, ground meat she'd been last night. Dominic had only allowed one shot to the head and three to her chest to remain.

No one would ever believe me if I told them that vampires caused this murder, despite it being true, because gangs were more believable than vampires. I'd never published anything but the truth as I'd seen it, but it wouldn't matter if I wrote about the power struggle between Dominic and Kaden. It wouldn't matter if I detailed how our city was at the mercy of an entire civilization beneath our own who hunted and fed from us and whose natural instinct to slaughter was only leashed by one vampire, a vampire whose tenacious grip was slipping.

Walker had killed Jolene to protect humans from vampires. Dominic had healed her corpse to protect vampires from humans, and I'd write a false version of her death to protect my credibility, career, and all three of our secrets because the truth wouldn't protect anything except for my pride.

I took out my pen and notepad, feeling disillusioned. Who had been there to protect Jolene from all of us?

"And you're certain that you only saw two people in the alley?" I asked. I was interviewing my fourteenth witness of the night, a Mr. Thomas Sitter. Thomas was in his late fifties and had the doughy bulk of an ex-high school lineman turned accountant. He had extremely thick glasses that pressed uncomfortable-looking dents into the sides of his face, but the eyes behind the glasses were kind and scared. I tried to be kind in return, but my patience was frayed. Everyone's account of last night's crime scene was different, which was common with eyewitness testimony, but I knew that not one testimony was accurate.

"No, I'm not sure," Thomas said, wincing as if admitting uncertainty was painful. "It was dark, so I couldn't distinguish their faces. A woman was crying and pleading for help. There was gunfire, and one of them ran back into the alley."

"Was there anyone else nearby?"

"No, not that I could see, but like I said, it was dark. I'm really not sure if someone else was there."

"But no one else came out of the alley?" I pushed.

Thomas shook his head. "There were only two people. One was shot, and the other ran. But it was so dark, Ms. DiRocco, I'm not even sure if the woman was shot or if she ran. I just couldn't tell for certain."

I sighed and crossed out Thomas's name on my list of witnesses to potentially quote. It seemed impossible, but Dominic and his coven had indeed found every witness. Granted, I had only interviewed fourteen out of the hundred or so—give or take a dozen—who may have seen the attack, but I suspected that when I did, the pattern would continue. The vampires were able to alter everyone's memory, not with the same memory, but with an enhanced account of their already existing inaccurate memory.

Eyewitness testimony was always questionable at best. Dominic was simply enhancing the inaccuracies in each person's memory, so between darkness, shadows, fear, time frame, and a million other details and distractions, everyone was unsure of when and what they had really witnessed. I still couldn't comprehend how the vampires knew whom to attack, how they were able get to everyone so quickly, or how no one found the bodies until sunrise, but having already interviewed thirteen other witnesses besides Thomas, I couldn't deny what the vampires had done. However they had accomplished it, no one remembered the truth.

"Is something wrong?" Thomas asked. He rubbed the back of his knuckles with his palm.

"Not at all. You've been extremely helpful." I offered my hand, and he stopped rubbing his to shake mine. "Thank you."

He nodded and lumbered away.

"DiRocco, do you have a moment?"

Thomas had supposedly called for an ambulance. I'd check with Dispatch to confirm his story, but I had a sneaking suspicion that a record of his call would exist to corroborate his story whether or not he'd ever dialed 911. I rubbed my eyes. There must be at least one witness that Dominic had missed. He couldn't possibly have tampered with all of them.

And what would I do with a witness, even if I found one? my conscience balked. *Quote him in my article and expose him?* I rubbed my eyes harder.

"Cassidy?"

I turned. Greta stood behind me. Her expression was stern, but when she saw my face, her expression slipped slightly. A deep crinkle etched between her eyebrows.

"Greta," I began, unsure how to navigate between the case and her loss. "I'm so sorry about Jolene."

"Where were you last night at eight p.m.?" she asked, ignoring my condolences.

"That's what I've always liked about you, G," I said, taking her cue. "You call it like you see it. But that doesn't mean that you're seeing the full picture."

"The picture you're painting is the one I'm looking at. Carter thinks that you're being blackmailed. He thinks that you solved this case and that you're backing down because of what you found."

"Carter didn't want me scooping deeper into this case, so he got exactly what he wanted. Nothing." I sighed. "I don't care what Carter thinks, anyway. What do *you* think?"

Greta crossed her arms. "I think you've finally dove deep into waters that even you can't swim through."

"I'm a shark," I said, crossing my arms, too. "I can swim through anything."

"Listen, everyone knows you're relentless. We all know what you're capable of, both in the field and professionally, and that's how I know that you know more than you're telling Carter. You solved this case, damn it, and for the first time since I've known you, the first time in your entire career I'll bet, you're not going to publish it. The people responsible for these murders aren't just sharks, they're monsters, and you can't fight them alone. Tell me what's going on, DiRocco. You can blow off Carter all you want, but I'm not letting this go until you let me help you."

I sighed. "Since when did you and Carter become such close friends?"

"Since when did you ever let a story go unwritten?"

"Since my story hit a wall. There's nothing to go on, G. My leads ran dry, I didn't solve the case, and I've got nothing to write." I tapped my recorder against my palm twice, ending the conversation. "So if you'll excuse me, I've got a story here I need to cover."

Greta's expression turned to slate. "I'm not dropping this, DiRocco. I'd prefer my answers come from you, but if you don't tell me now, I'll get them later from someone else. And by then, I can't guarantee that I'll see the picture you want me to see, let alone in the light that you want me to see it."

I could feel the burning pressure of tears behind my eyes. I swallowed and tried to breathe past the mistrust I heard in her voice. She wouldn't get answers from anyone else because no one else remembered the truth, but that wasn't the point.

"I'll ask you one last time," Greta said. Her voice was calm and deliberate and resolute. "Where were you last night?"

"If you must know," I said, just as deliberate. "I was with Walker at my apartment last night."

Greta's eyebrows rose. "Will he corroborate that?"

"Of course," I said, trying to keep my expression bland, as if men frequented my apartment regularly.

Greta waited a moment. She stared me down with the weight of her distrust and uncanny perceptiveness. I mirrored her expression, but my heart ached from the effort.

Eventually, Greta crossed her arms. "Jolene deserved better than this."

I nodded. It took me a long moment before I could set aside enough emotion to speak. "Yes, she did."

"If you're not going to talk to save your career or yourself, you should talk for Jolene and for all the other innocent bystanders caught in the cross fire. It's too late for Jolene, but we can save the next one. It's our duty to save the next one."

"If I could, I would help, but—"

Greta lifted her hand. "I know. You were with Walker last night." She shook her head, disgusted. "When you're ready to talk, you know who to call."

Greta turned on her heel and strode away from me at a hard clip. I didn't chase after her. My stomach churned into a deep knot, and I knew in the same, hard place that I knew everything, that she wasn't turning back.

* * *

I resumed my interviews, but Greta wasn't the only friend who suspected the worst of me. Meredith knew something horrible was happening. She looked askance at me a few times while she finished her shots. Unlike Greta, she didn't demand any answers. I suspected that Meredith held her peace because if she confronted me and my secrets, she'd have to confront her own, and she still hadn't come to terms with her "mugging" and foggy memory. It might have made me a worse friend, but I appreciated her blind eye for once, and in return, I held my peace, as well.

I finished the article with plenty of time to spare, feeling disheartened about my work and disgusted by my participation in both the reality of Jolene's death and the portrayal of her death to the public. Carter approved the piece with his usual gusto, unconcerned if I was having a crisis as long as my writing was on point. Meredith left for sushi after we made it to print, but I stayed behind for the second night in a row. She didn't seem surprised, and she didn't try to coax me into coming along. I think she needed her space, too.

Instead of enjoying the last few hours of daylight safety with Meredith like I should have, I stared at my monitor, trying to think of what I could have done differently last night, so Jolene might have lived. My mind was as blank as the Word document staring back at me. That damn cursor taunted me with its constant, unforgivable blinking. It killed me that I couldn't spotlight the truth for the city, and with every pulse, the cursor screamed at me, *Vampires, vampires, vampires!*

Frustrated, I did the only thing I could think to do, the only thing that I truly wanted to do even if I couldn't publish it. I clicked on the drafts folder on my desktop to start my article, "The City Beneath: Vampires Bite in the Big Apple." My fingers danced over the keys with fervor, the words and sentences and paragraphs bursting out of me like a break in a dam after having contained my secrets so tightly all day. For once in my writing career, it didn't matter if I couldn't take the glory. I had a story pressure-cooking inside of me that needed release, and it didn't matter that this article wouldn't be contending for a Pulitzer. This was more than prizes and recognition and career advancement. This was the truth.

I was just finishing the second to last paragraph when my phone rang. "Ms. DiRocco, a man is here to see you," Deborah said. Her voice scowled. "He says that he had an appointment with you yesterday, which needed to be rescheduled. Do you have time to squeeze him in now?"

I saved and closed the document midsentence, my heart pounding like a pogo stick through my throat. I checked the time, having lost track of the hours while writing about the very thing I was so terrified to confront. The computer's clock glowed an even five thirty. I still had several hours until sunset. I wiped the sweat from my forehead with the back of my hand and thought of the silver jewelry still in the box back at my apartment.

"Ms. DiRocco?"

A shuffle and a loud screech sounded outside the door.

"Cassidy?" a man shouted. The doorknob rattled.

"Sir, you cannot just pound your way in without permission," Deborah said, sounding outraged.

"Trust me, ma'am, I have permission."

I rolled my eyes and found my voice. "I know who you're referring to, Deborah. Please, allow Mr. Walker to enter."

The door suddenly opened, and Walker strode inside, carrying a plastic bag. Deborah followed close behind.

"Told ya." He winked at Deborah, and she looked scandalized.

She switched targets, dismissing Walker as insufferable, to focus on me. "If I knew your schedule more thoroughly, I would be able to screen your visitors more efficiently."

I bit back a smirk. "Don't worry, Deborah, I think you're doing a wonderful job."

"Right." She frowned. "Thank you."

Walker placed a hand on her shoulder, easing her out the door. "And *thank you* for showing me in. You've been mighty helpful."

"You're welcome," she said, frowning harder. She knew when she was being dismissed. She slammed the door behind her on the way out.

"Touchy," Walker drawled, jerking his thumb in Deborah's direction. "You get a lot of unscheduled callers?"

I shrugged. "More than usual lately. How are you?"

"I've been better," he said, sitting across from me. "I was interrogated by the police today."

"What? Why?"

"To corroborate your alibi last night."

My face heated, and the triple hit of embarrassment, shame, and exhaustion overwhelmed me. I covered my blazing face in my hands. "I'm sorry."

"Consider yourself corroborated, but the next time I spend the night, I'd like to actually remember the experience."

I glanced up, and Walker winked.

I sighed deeply, sat up in my chair, and faced him squarely. "Thank you. I appreciate you covering for me."

"It's the least I could do, after last night," he said.

I nodded. An awkward silence filled the space between us as I thought of last night and Jolene, and our fight. "What are you doing here, Walker?" I finally asked.

"Keeping my word. I promised you insider information on vampires and night bloods, didn't I?" He lifted his left leg onto his right knee and slouched in the chair.

I nodded slowly. "You also promised sushi."

He grinned. "You gonna quote me on that?"

"It's the one thing I'm good at."

He laughed. "I wouldn't go so far as to say it's the only thing you're good at, but knowing you, I came prepared." He handed me a foam container from a plastic bag.

I opened the container's lid and sighed. A neat row of California rolls gleamed next to chopsticks, a container of soy, and a pile of sliced ginger.

"So, what do you want to know?" he asked.

I shook my head, unable to look away from the little rolls. "How is any of this possible? How does a person transform from a dying, bleeding human to a nocturnal super-predator overnight?"

Walker chuckled. "The transformation is rarely an overnight process. That would be quite a speedy change and would result in a weak vampire."

I looked up from my sushi.

"Typically, a night blood transforms into a vampire over a period of three days. The vampire's blood has a regenerative, healing property, much like their saliva, which allows them to heal even egregious physical injuries almost instantaneously. When a night blood is nearly dead and their body is introduced to vampire blood, the regenerative properties in the vampire blood quickly heals them, but with more vampire blood than human blood in their system, the rapidly regenerating vampire cells spread throughout the circulatory system, into their organs and muscles to regenerate those cells, and eventually, into the brain until their DNA is completely regenerated throughout each cell in the body. You've felt the intense, focused burning of their saliva as it transformed your cells to heal, right?"

I nodded, fascinated despite myself. I'd already gone through half the California rolls.

"They say a night blood feels that sensation over their entire body during the three-day transformation. The night blood is completely incapacitated, and those who aren't protected by their makers can potentially die from other predators, sunlight, and of course, humans, whether in malice or during misguided medical care. In rare cases, the transformation is a longer process, and in these instances, Day Reapers are usually born. They are more powerful, more adept at mind control, and more dangerous than others of their kind. They usually have a talent or special ability, but of the Day Reapers I've encountered, their most commonly used talent seems to be killing other vampires."

I stared at Walker. I hadn't expected such a scientific approach to his answer. "How did this all begin? How did the first human become a vampire?"

"Classic chicken and the egg," Walker answered, smiling. "Are you a creationist or an evolutionist?"

I downed another roll and pointed my chopsticks at him. "Are you saying that we don't know where vampires came from?"

"The public doesn't know vampires *exist*. Of course we don't know where they originated. As much as I know, which ain't much, my knowledge is entirely based on either firsthand experience or the firsthand experiences of my partner. It's not like we have a night blood handbook. We don't have research to study or books to reference. We only have each other and life's lessons."

I nodded slowly, mulling everything he'd said over the sedating pinch of wasabi.

"I'm going to track and kill Dominic Lysander and his coven tomorrow at dawn."

I blinked.

"Will you join me?"

I choked. "You are going to track and kill Dominic's coven, and you want my help?"

Walker nodded, completely serious. "Like I said, all we have in this world as night bloods is each other."

I couldn't help it; I burst out laughing.

He raised his eyebrows. "I'm not kidding."

"I know. That's what makes this so funny. We can barely survive against them. How the hell are we supposed to kill them?"

Walker pursed his lips. "A stake, silver bullets, and decapitation usually does the trick. I've said it before, and I'll say it again: they're simply long-lived and hard to kill, not immortal."

I shook my head. "You pumped Dominic full of silver, and all it did was piss him off. He may as well be immortal."

He sighed. "I underestimated him. I should have moved to strike immediately after the bullets were fired. I won't make the same mistake again. I need a partner, Cassidy, like I have at home. Missions like this are dangerous with someone covering your back. It's suicide to go in alone."

"So ask your partner from home to help you," I said flatly.

Walker shook his head. "She has her own problems. I need you, Cassidy. If there's one thing I've learned in all that time with my partner, it's that I'd never survive alone."

She, I thought. His partner was a woman. I covered my face with my hands, knowing that I was probably smearing my makeup to hell and frankly not caring. I looked like hell anyway. "If my life continues on the path that it's taken this past week, I won't survive much longer anyway."

Walker pried my hands gently away from my face and held them in his own. His thumbs caressed the inside of my wrists gently. "Let me help you survive. We can kill them together before they kill you."

The movement of his thumbs warmed my body and were convincing enough without the words. I was tired and cramped and run-down and in pain, but his gestures and the warmth that spread through my body reminded me of better times when I hadn't been so completely on my own. Despite the fact that Walker wanted my help, I *needed* his help. Maybe he was right, and we could survive together.

I swallowed my doubts and met his eyes squarely. "I won't help you kill Dominic's entire coven, but the rebel vampires responsible for the recent 'gang' murders need to be stopped."

Walker smiled. "You'll help?"

"I'll think about it," I said skeptically. "What exactly is your plan?"

"If we leave at dawn, we'll arrive at the coven by noon when they're weakest. We already know where in the subway system they've nested, but we'll still need time to find the location where they rest during their day sleep."

I frowned. "Dominic had his own rooms. If each vampire has its own room where they rest, there could be a dozen rooms we'd need to find."

"Dominic has his own rooms separate from the rest of his coven because he's their Master. If his coven is anything like Bex's, each vampire will have their own room in a centralized location. So we find it, and we rig it, like I rigged your bedroom. All the vampires will be incapacitated in one shot, and then we stake each individually."

"All the rebel vampires," I clarified.

Walker nodded.

"But there's one tiny flaw in your plan that I'm not sure you've considered."

Walker raised his eyebrow. "What's that?"

"Your plan to stake Dominic in my bedroom didn't actually work," I reminded him carefully. "There will be more vampires to target this time, and we'll be trapped in the heart of their coven, not my bedroom. Do we really want to base this plan on your last attempt to stake Dominic?"

"My plan to stake Dominic didn't work because I underestimated him," Walker said. The heat of his determination stoked his voice. "That won't happen again. We'll stake the more mature vampires first, the leader of the rebels, before he heals. The rest of the vampires won't be able to heal at all until they feed, but we'll have staked them and left the coven long before then."

"What about Dominic? He's not going to let us waltz into his coven and stake his vampires."

"He won't even know we're there. Like you said, he sleeps in his own rooms separate from the rest of his coven. By the time he wakes and realizes that the rebels are eliminated, we'll already be safely back to my hotel room."

I opened my mouth and tried to respond civilly, but I couldn't help it. I laughed again. "You think he won't know we're there?"

Walker frowned. "The entire point of breaking into the coven is the element of surprise. No one will know, especially Dominic."

"We should plan on him knowing." I thought of Dominic's visit here last night, of him asking for my help against the rebel vampires, and I sighed heavily. The inevitability of this conversation felt like a crushing weight over my chest. "And I might be able to help with that."

A grin spread wide across Walker's face. He clapped his hands together and leaned in. "All right, DiRocco. Let's hear it."

I sighed. "Dominic wants help tracking and containing the rebel vampires. If I help him, I might gain access into the coven without having to sneak in, and you can infiltrate the coven under the guise of saving me again. He'll be expecting you, but instead of saving me, you set up the rigging for the rebels while I'm with Dominic."

He raised his eyebrows. "He's still playing that card?"

I frowned, confused. "What card?"

"He's gaining your sympathy, making you think that he's the 'good' vampire." Walker scoffed. "The only good vampire is a staked one."

I rolled my eyes. "I've done my research, and from what I can tell, Dominic is telling the truth about his seven-year cyclical power. He genuinely wants to put a stop to the rebellion before he loses control of his coven," I insisted.

"Right," Walker said, sounding anything but convinced.

"Look, Walker," I said, trying to keep a lid on my frustration. "I understand that you believe all vampires should be killed, but it doesn't make sense to kill Dominic. He's the one vampire keeping his coven a secret, and by doing so, he's preventing a massacre. We've seen the rebel vampires hunt. The city can't survive their massacres on a nightly basis, and Dominic is the only one keeping them in check."

Walker gazed at me with those warm, velvet brown eyes, eyes that seemed to know gentle comfort and love and undoubtedly how to seduce a woman's socks off. He said, "So help him contain the rebel vampires like he wants, distract him while I infiltrate the coven, and we'll kill them all."

Maybe women were different where he came from. "Right," I said. "Like I said, I'll think about it." I glanced at the door, dismissing him.

Walker grinned. He stood, but he strode around the desk toward me instead of toward the exit. "I don't think so."

"Is there something else you came here for?" I asked, not certain about the look in his eyes.

"There certainly is, darlin'," he said, holding out a hand.

I took it cautiously, and he helped me stand. He wrapped an arm around my waist and snapped my hips to his when I tried to sidestep him. Walker was so tall that at such close proximity, I had a very personal view of his chest.

"Walker?"

"Dominic has obviously staked his claim," he said, smirking lightly at his own pun, "But I want you to remember something when you meet him tonight."

"Dominic hasn't staked anything, claim or otherwise," I denied.

"I want you to promise *me* that you'll keep perspective," Walker said, ignoring me. "Whatever you feel for him—and believe me, I know how it feels between a Master and her night blood—it will eventually destroy you. He'll take your humanity, your blood, and eventually your life and revel in your death." Walker leaned closer with every word, bending down, so his lips brushed mine as he spoke. "But you don't need a vampire to feel something real."

"Walker, I don't—"

He kissed me.

Chapter 10

Walker's lips sealed over mine, luscious and urgent and insistent as they rocked and tasted me. My neck was craned up at an impossible angle from our height difference. I felt his arms wrap solidly around my waist, and I clutched at the smooth, strong muscles of his shoulders. His lips were hot, nearly burning compared to the cool sting of Dominic's lips, but where Dominic's kiss had scorched my soul with its intensity, Walker's kiss scorched my body. His lips left my lips tingling raw. His teeth burned a path of goose bumps over my neck with nips and licks and kisses. His wandering hands over my hips seared the sensitive skin of my lower back. I quaked under his touch, wanting and burning and wilting.

Walker's hands cupped under my thighs, and I was suddenly lifted onto my desk. His hands were everywhere—urging my chin higher, stroking my back, clamped on to the nape of my neck—and it felt so incredible that for a brief moment, I thought that Walker was right. I could feel again. I hadn't felt something real in so long, and maybe I didn't need Dominic to feel this way. Maybe I could feel again with Walker instead and keep my humanity.

Walker's hands unbuttoned my shirt to cup my breasts through my bra, and every part of me that had been screaming a resounding *Yes!*, slammed shut in a cold wash. I tore my lips away from his mouth and shook my head.

"No," I said, pulling his hands away from me when he didn't listen. "Stop. Walker, I'm serious."

He sighed heavily. "I'm moving too fast."

I nodded. That was the easiest explanation and true anyway, so I let it ride.

"I just"—he ran his hands through his hair, mussing up those golden-brown curlicues—"I hadn't expected to feel quite so much."

"Maybe there's something to being night bloods."

"Maybe," Walker said, looking doubtful.

I buttoned my shirt and sighed. "Listen, Walker, I don't want to feel anything. I—"

"That's not what your lips said a second ago."

I pursed my lips, and then relaxed them, suddenly hyper-aware of their movement. I sighed. "I said, *listen*. I resent my feelings for Dominic, and this isn't the time to begin something romantic. What I need is someone in my corner, helping me make it through the punches."

"I can be that, too. I can be whatever you need, DiRocco."

Relief doused a little of the pent-up panic that had built when he'd unbuttoned my shirt. "Thank you."

Walker's lips quirked. "Although it feels like the ideal time to start something romantic to me."

I shimmied off the desk and stood next to Walker, feeling suddenly, painfully short and more than a little embarrassed by my lack of inhibition. "How about we just handle one crisis at a time? I'll let you know how tonight goes with Dominic."

He raised his eyebrows. "Since when is starting something romantic a crisis?"

"Since kisses became weapons," I muttered over my shoulder, leaving Walker to follow as I walked toward the door.

"Since when weren't they?" he commented, close behind.

I opened the door for him and stepped aside to let him pass. "I'll see you tomorrow at dawn."

Walker stopped in the doorway, blocking my exit. "We still have over an hour until sunset. You're coming with me to my hotel room."

I crossed my arms. "Excuse me?"

"No need to get saucy, darlin'. I'm only givin' you what you need." He winked. "I've got a few weapons that you can borrow while you deal with Dominic."

I raised my eyebrows, his sawed-off shotgun coming to mind. "I don't have a gun permit."

Walker smiled. "You won't need a permit for the toys I have in mind."

Forty minutes later, I returned to my apartment laden with home-

made weapons that Walker had customized. Thanks to his prepared-
ness, I was now the proud owner of a pepper spray can filled with silver
nitrate, a miniature crossbow bracelet that shot spears from a trigger at
my wrist, a pen that clicked out a retractable stake, and silver-woven
palmed gloves.

He'd had to modify the gloves for my smaller hands. The gloves
seemed unnecessary considering that silver wasn't much of a deterrent
against Dominic, but Walker wasn't overly concerned about needing
the gloves for him. "Silver's the best defense against less powerful
vampires," he said. "You don't have to aim. You don't have to shoot.
You don't even have to reload. They're like condoms; you simply
wear them, and you're protected."

"No one likes a comedian," I commented dryly, smacking Walker
lightly with the gloves. They fit perfectly when he'd finished the al-
terations. "Like a glove," I said, wiggling my gloved fingers at him.

He snorted. "Don't quit your day job, either."

He showed me how to shoot the miniature crossbow and let me
practice before loosing me on the world. More than my poor aim, I
worried that Dominic would take the crossbow before I could shoot
him and use the stakes against me.

"Stop obsessing over Dominic," Walker chided. "He's dangerous
and certainly lethal to me, but he wants to turn you. As much as it
pains me to admit, he's probably your best protection against other
vampires tonight, and it's them you need to worry about."

I nodded. "I'll keep that in mind." I flexed my hands inside the silver gloves, admiring the fit. Finally, I worked up the nerve to meet
Walker's gaze. We were in this mission together because we were
both night bloods and the only bet this city had against vampires, but
we disagreed on too many issues for them to be left unsaid.

"Thank you for the weapons," I began.

"You're welcome, darlin'. Remember to call me when the sun rises,
so I know you're all right. I'll meet you inside the coven, and we—"

"Can the 'darlin's' for one second and listen, will you?"

Walker shut his mouth and stared at me with the undivided attention of that velvet brown gaze.

I swallowed. "I know I'm a hard-ass, but I still stand beside my
principles about Jolene. You didn't have to kill her. It's more important to save people than to kill vampires."

Walker hesitated before nodding. "That's your opinion, and I can respect that."

"But I know that's not your opinion, and I can't respect that. You're too ruthless in your quest to kill vampires, and I don't agree that the risks you've taken with people's lives, with my life, were worth the reward. It's been a while since I trusted anyone and an even longer time since I allowed myself to depend on anyone."

"I gathered as much," Walker murmured thoughtfully.

"If we're in this mission together, I need to trust you. I need you to promise me that we'll stay within the parameters of our mission, only target the rebel vampires, and not kill any humans. Are we agreed?"

"The chances of finding a human at the coven is pretty slim."

"But if one happens to be there," I emphasized, "you won't kill them. While you are on a mission with me, you will agree to weigh your options because the ends never justify the means if someone ends up dead. Those are my conditions. If you agree to them, I agree to this mission."

Walker only hesitated a fraction of a second before a smirk lit the dimple on his right cheek. "Agreed."

I held out my hand to shake on it.

Walker gripped my palm and pumped firmly before yanking me into a hug. He wrapped his arms around my back and ducked his head into the dip in my neck. "It's been a while since I could trust anyone, either," Walker admitted softly. "Thank you."

Walker's embrace was solid and secure and everything I'd imagined being held by him would feel like. I closed my eyes and let the warmth of his body soak my bruises, both the recent ones and the ones from years past that I hadn't let heal, and hoped against all odds that he could keep his word.

Sunset was minutes away. I was wearing the silver gloves and my pockets were loaded with the silver nitrate spray and retractable stake pen. I sat with my back against the far wall and waited like Walker had suggested. Dominic would undoubtedly come to me. The sky washed over red and orange and eventually darkened completely as the sun dipped below the horizon.

The oven timer clicked over to 7:56 p.m., and I propped the miniature crossbow strapped to my wrist over my bent knees, aimed at the window, and waited. I'd considered opening Mom's jewelry box for her silver crucifix like Nathan had mentioned, but after twenty minutes of staring at the box and caressing its wooden edges, I had to finally decide: open it after all these years or prepare the rest of my weapons for Dominic. I'd prepared for Dominic.

I didn't see, hear, or smell his arrival. One moment I was tense and ready and aiming at the empty air outside my window, and the next moment, Dominic was standing on its ledge. His eyes flicked to the crossbow aimed at his chest, and a slow grin spread across his face. By the looks of him, from the glow of his perfect complexion to the muscled strength beneath his leather jacket, he'd recently fed.

"May I enter?" he asked, but even muffled from the glass between us, his voice sounded just as smug as his expression.

"You know you can enter even without my permission now," I snapped.

He opened the glass and stepped gracefully through my bay window. The room flooded with the soft, sweet, lovely scent of pine. "That doesn't mean one can't be polite," he chided.

I cocked the bow. "Like last night's pleasantries?"

He raised his eyebrows. "As I recall, you attacked me first."

I opened my mouth and closed it again, hating that he was right. "Yes, we did. After everything we've been through, we naturally felt threatened."

"I'm assuming your newest weapons are a testament to that feeling," Dominic commented, pointing casually to my crossbow.

I nodded. "Why are you here, Dominic? Fighting for my life is becoming a nightly routine I'd like to break."

"I'm sorry to say that you may have to break your routine another night. I'm here to collect on your promise."

He was moving slowly closer. Although he wasn't physically walking, from one moment to the next, I could just barely discern that he was scant centimeters closer.

"Stop moving," I warned.

He raised his hands. "I haven't moved a muscle."

"You haven't moved, but you're somehow closer. Stop it, or I'll shoot."

Dominic smirked again, so smug and so infuriatingly male that I wanted to pull the trigger anyway even though he'd indeed stopped moving closer. "Very well. Now, about your promise—"

"I promised to remember your actions last night."

"My *favorable* actions, yes. I'm asking for you to remember them now as I ask you again, to please help me subdue Kaden."

"Don't you think that highlighting that your actions were favorable diminishes their charitable quality?" I asked, my voice thick with sarcasm.

He stared back at me, the inhuman qualities in him more apparent in his stillness.

"I guess not," I murmured. "All right, yes, I'll keep your favorable actions from last night in mind when you ask me."

"I'm asking you now."

I pursed my lips and felt the eerie creep of déjà vu from my conversation with Walker as I asked, "What exactly do you have planned?"

"You aren't going to make this easy for me, are you? Can't you simply trust me after my actions last night? I could have killed you, but once again, I've proven that you're far safer in my care than in anyone else's."

I opened my mouth to snap at him, but the slight twinkle in his eyes made me pause. He was teasing me. "None of this is easy for me," I said. "So I don't see why I should make it any easier for you."

Dominic's smile widened, and I realized that he didn't expect me to say yes without at least *some* coercion. In fact, saying yes outright probably would've been suspicious.

"Perhaps if you simply lower your weapon, I'll explain myself." He took a deliberate step closer.

I tightened my grip on the handle of the crossbow. "You can stay where you are. My weapon will stay pointed where it is, and you can simply explain yourself where you stand," I said, trying to remain calm while my voice cracked and quivered. His nearness made my heart beat frantically, as if my body knew on an instinctual level that he wanted the blood coursing through it.

Dominic quirked an eyebrow. "That is hardly hospitable."

"If I put my weapon down and decide later that I need it, you're too fast for me to re-aim. The weapon stays."

"You would never point such a weapon at Ian Walker," Dominic purred.

I shrugged. "I trust Walker not to harm me."

"If we're partners in this endeavor, you must trust me enough when the time comes to cease aiming at me and aim at Kaden," he pointed out.

"And if I agree to being partners, that's what I'll do, but in the meantime, the weapon stays," I insisted.

Dominic released a long-suffering sigh. To my surprise, he let me keep my weapon and my sense of security. He backed away slowly and sat on the windowsill, his hands still raised.

I nodded my appreciation and attempted to calm my heart.

He nodded back. "My plan is fairly simple. As I doubt we'll need much planning or trickery to entice Kaden to hunt you after last night, it's simply the location where he finds you that we must consider."

"Kaden is still hunting me?"

"Of course."

"What do you mean 'of course'? Maybe after last night, he'll reconsider pursuing me."

Dominic smirked. "After what happened last night, you've only fueled his hunt. Not only did you escape and injure him, he tasted you again. You've created quite the challenge for him, one that I'm sure he's anticipating very much."

I shook my head. "But more than half a dozen vampires tasted my blood. Why aren't they all hunting me?" I blanched. "Are they all hunting me?"

"No. The vampires know that you're mine, and those acting under Kaden's rebellion know that Kaden has claimed you as his. That alone should keep the rest of my coven at bay."

"Oh," I murmured, not comforted by that explanation in the least. "So what location did you have in mind?"

Dominic considered me a moment before answering. "Somewhere remote to minimize bystanders. Returning to Paerdegat Park may be a good option."

I scowled. "Why Paerdegat Park?"

"It makes sense that you'd want to visit that location for further investigation, so Kaden won't suspect a trap, and since police barriers are still present, it's more remote than most," he explained.

"I doubt I'd ever want to return to that location," I muttered.

"You might."

"I don't."

Dominic's eyes blazed. "It doesn't matter if you truly want to or not. What matters is that Kaden believes you might."

"Fine," I conceded. "So I go to Paerdegat Park for further investigation. What happens when Kaden shows up? He isn't the witty conversationalist I've found you to be."

"You let him drink your blood."

I blinked, not sure I'd heard him correctly, but his expression didn't falter. He was serious. "You want me to let him attack me."

Dominic hesitated. I could see the indecision in his eyes as he weighed his next words against what he knew I'd want to hear. Finally he said, "Yes, you must allow him to attack you. He will only be weakened after having tasted a large quantity of your blood. The more, the better, but not so much as to completely incapacitate you. I will intervene if necessary."

"If I'm at risk of dying, you'll stop him?" I clarified. I didn't want to die because we differed on the definition of "completely incapacitate."

"Yes. Unquestionably," Dominic stated. "I'll subdue him, heal you, and return to the coven."

I raised my eyebrows, surprised. "And what will I do after you've done all that?"

Dominic shrugged. "Whatever else you have planned for the night," he said simply.

"You'll let me simply . . . go on my way?" I asked carefully, thinking of Walker's plan to infiltrate the coven.

"For tonight," he said, his smirk widening.

I fought not to react to that comment. "If I go along with your plan and put myself at risk to help you regain control of your vampires, I'll want to see the fruit of my efforts. I'll want to see Kaden's death firsthand to know that the city is safe from him and his followers."

Dominic stared at me for a long, uncomfortable moment, long enough that I wondered whether he knew my ulterior motive for wanting access into the coven, before he finally whispered, "That can be arranged."

I nodded, and the rush of relief trembled through my arms. My aim wavered. "It's a decent plan but completely dependent on Kaden's motives. What if he's not interested in hunting me?"

Dominic snorted. "I have no doubt he'll hunt you tonight."

"As comforting as that is, there's another assumption I'm worried about," I said, licking my lips. "What if Kaden doesn't want to turn me after last night? What if he simply wants to hunt me to kill me, and I die before you can 'intervene'?"

"I've known Kaden for ninety-six years, and I'm certain that he wants to turn you. He wants someone strong and capable and power-ful to support his cause, as do I. He wouldn't waste you on revenge, *especially* after last night."

I glanced down at my five-foot-two, one-hundred-and-forty-pound frame of plump curves, and laughed. "Strong, capable, and powerful?"

Dominic didn't so much as crack a smile. "Vampire abilities are rooted in your blood and mind, not physical appearance. You've dis-played natural abilities without any training, as well as abilities that no other night blood in my reckoning has ever displayed. Simply put, you are astounding. I believe that the vampire who transforms you will be transforming the future of our race, and I do not intend for Kaden to be that vampire."

"Oh." I bit my lip.

Dominic cracked his knuckles. "Whether you help me or not, you'll certainly be attacked by Kaden. The only difference is whether you're attacked tonight while I'm present to intervene, or on a night of his choice while you're vulnerable. Wouldn't you rather he attack you tonight, as a part of our plan, rather than while you're unprepared and alone?"

I laughed suddenly, helplessly amused with my options. "I'd rather not be attacked at all."

Dominic's expression remained stoic. "I wasn't joking. I believe those are your only options."

"I wasn't joking, either." I sighed grudgingly. "But I think you're right."

He cocked his head to the side in a quick, fleck-like movement, similar to how birds target their prey. "You think I'm right," he said, his tone devoid of inflection. "Yet your crossbow hasn't wavered from its mark on my chest."

Dominic might be on my side for the time being, but putting up my weapon in his presence felt fundamentally wrong, like cuddling with a cobra because it promised with a hiss and a wink not to bite. My finger stroked down the trigger softly, and I gritted my teeth, trying to keep that finger steady against the frantic, pounding bass of my heart.

Dominic must have felt my tension. He spread his arms wide. "How can I trust you without a display of trust?"

"I'm trusting you with my life. My willingness to cooperate is display enough," I said, realizing that I wouldn't be able to willingly lower the crossbow. He was too close and the attacks on me had been too recent. I thought of his fingers breaking and twisting and lengthening into talons. I remembered those talons piercing through my shoulders to pin me against the wall, and I shuddered. "Once you leave, I'll meet you at Paerdegat Park, and—"

"I'll follow you to Paerdegat Park. He may be inclined to attack with bystanders nearby before you reach your destination."

I hesitated. "You think he'll attack that quickly?"

"I think he enjoys making my life difficult."

I opened my mouth to squabble over the definition of "life."

"And frankly, I've never known Kaden for his patience. He's young compared to most vampires with his abilities, and he often still feels the urgency of time from his humanity. He wants you, so he'll take you. He isn't going to bide his time."

I bit my tongue. "Fine. You'll follow me to Paerdegat Park, and you'll subdue him when he attacks me."

Dominic nodded.

"And you'll heal me if I'm injured, before you leave with Kaden," I clarified.

"Yes, of course. I won't leave you injured." Dominic stepped forward.

I jerked my crossbow to keep aim. "And under no circumstances are you to turn me into a vampire."

He raised his hands, but he continued walking toward me. "If it's in your best interest to become a vampire—"

"Being human is in my best interest," I snapped. "Don't come any closer."

"If aiming your weapon at me makes you feel protected, then by all means, keep aiming. I have something you need more than crossbows and wooden stakes and silver nitrate and anything else that boy could hope to give you."

"Dominic Lysander, stop where you stand," I snapped. The link between us opened, but Dominic reflected the command. It hit me and disintegrated, useless because I was sitting, not standing, but he continued moving toward me. "I will shoot."

He reached out to me, a casual smirk stretching his lips because he didn't believe I would shoot.

I pulled the trigger.

The mechanism actually gave some kickback, and my shoulder slammed into the wall. The wooden sliver jetted through the air faster than my eyes could track it. One moment, I felt the kickback and adrenaline spike, and the next moment, Dominic was holding the wooden sliver in his hand, its sharpened, pointed tip over his heart.

I blinked, my brain shorting out as it processed what had just happened. We were at close range, mere feet apart, and Dominic had snatched the sliver in midair before it could even puncture his skin.

He snapped the stake in half with his fingers like the sliver was a toothpick, tossed it aside, and continued walking closer.

I scrambled back, trying to reload before he reached me. Dominic was deliberately taking his time. The speed he'd just displayed was incomprehensible, yet he was walking slower than human slow, step by excruciating step when he could have easily appeared next to me faster than brain synapses could fire. I struggled with the crossbow. Walker had shown me how to reload and watched as I'd practiced, but Dominic was walking toward me now. My hands were shaking, and no matter how much I'd practiced, the arrow refused to lock.

Dominic knelt in front of me. We were almost at eye level, him on the balls of his feet and hovering slightly over me as I still struggled to hook the stake in position. He reached out. I flinched back instinctively, and my back slammed hard into the wall. A heavy blanket of damp pine scent settled thick on the air. I cringed and held my breath as his hand came closer. My heart throbbed. I felt sick and petrified and angry, so angry into the deep aching hollows in my bones, an anger that had been festering long before I'd ever had the misfortune of meeting Dominic.

He covered my hands with his icy, strong fingers, and locked the sliver in position for me.

I froze, stunned dumb and offended that he'd reloaded the crossbow. Could he still stop the stake midair at such close range? Even Master vampires must have limitations.

"Stakes and silver are effective but obviously not always sufficient weapons against us. This is why we need your blood to dampen Kaden's defenses. He's almost my equal otherwise, and if he's my equal, you certainly don't stand a chance, with or without your weapons."

He opened his hand, and in the center of his palm was a small, crystal-like vial filled with an opaque, crimson liquid I suspected was blood. The vial was about an inch long. Its cap was silver-colored with symbols etched around its surface, and it hooked on to a matching, wraith-like silver chain. The chain was piled around the vial like metallic spaghetti on his hand as he offered it to me. A faint, burning stench wafted from his palm, and I realized that the chain wasn't just silver-colored. The chain was made of actual silver.

I raised my eyebrows.

"It's a gift."

"What is it?" I asked, trying not to flinch away from his hand as he held it closer to me in offering.

"It's one swallow of my blood. If something unexpected or untoward should happen to me or to you while I'm incapacitated or unavailable, I want you to have this with you, always."

I shook my head.

"You don't want to lie alone in an alley, dying, and with your last heartbeat, regret that you didn't have a last option, a last hope at life." Dominic shot me a bland look. "At the very least, a means of healing your wounds. My blood works much in the same way as my saliva when applied directly to the wound."

I flinched, that comment about dying in an alley hitting a little too close to home after last night. "I don't want a last option," I lied. What I wanted was a *different* last option.

"You say that now because you don't need that option. Take this. When the time comes, you can choose to drink it or not, heal yourself or not, but the point is that you'll have the choice."

I opened my mouth to refuse. "I don't—"

"Wear it along with your crossbow and stakes and silver. Carry all your weapons at all times, and if you'll carry his, you must carry mine." When Dominic referenced Walker, his voice deepened to a rough, almost wet tone. The muscles in his jaw popped and stretched.

I nodded, quickly agreeing before his face completely transformed. Dominic slipped the chain over my head easily, and once around my neck, the vial fell under my shirt and rested low between my breasts. The back of Dominic's knuckles traced my collarbone as he smoothed the chain in place. My nipples tightened. I felt them stiffen against the fabric of my bra and blushed.

Dominic smiled as if he knew my body's rebellious reaction to him. With his heightened hearing and sense of smell, he probably did.

Two hours later, I was still pacing the police tape at Paerdegat Park, my nerves a wreck with each passing minute that Kaden didn't appear. Every car horn was Kaden behind me. Every rustle was Kaden approaching. Every siren was Kaden's attack. The anticipation was fraying my nerves to split threads. I took some pictures of trace evidence with my cell phone to help pass the time while I waited for Kaden to arrive: a boot imprint on a hardened patch of dirt, stained blood spatters still clinging to the grass, and bald patches in the landscape, either from the attack or simply from poor maintenance. I knelt on the inner edge of the tape to inspect a thin burger wrapper, as if it might hold crucial, case-changing evidence that everyone had missed instead of just ketchup stains.

I continued this charade investigation for a few hours, but Kaden never showed. Maybe he wasn't as interested in me as we'd all believed. Maybe he suspected the trap. In either instance, Dominic had insisted that I remain at Paerdegat Park all night. If Kaden did suspect a trap, which was likely, he was more likely to attack when I gave up the ruse and left the park. If that occurred, we'd lose home court advantage and increase our chances of incurring witnesses, also according to Dominic, so I continued the ruse even though hours of snapping pictures with my cell phone both felt and probably looked ridiculous.

I crouched next to a strip of police tape, automatically moving my hand to keep my leather shoulder bag behind my back, and I remembered for the fourth time, as if it was the first, that I'd left my bag at home. Used to its presence, I kept reaching to touch it, open it, or move it out of the way. However convenient it usually was, the bag was cumbersome. If my experience with Kaden tonight was anything like my previous experiences, I didn't want it weighing me down or getting lost, like it had in the past.

Without my bag, I tucked my phone into my pocket and continued my faux investigation. While inspecting another boot print in a long line of similar boot prints, the glow from the streetlight reflected off something in the grass. The brief flash gave me pause. Actual evidence should have been photographed, tagged, bagged, and taken to the station. If this had been any other scene, I wouldn't have given the flash much thought because Greta was thorough and competent, but since I was the only one who'd remembered the bite marks, it stood to reason that Greta could've potentially missed something else, something equally as important.

I strained to see the reflective object without crossing the police tape. My heart dropped into my gut when I recognized its shape. Heedless of the damn police tape, I ducked under the parameter and swiped the metal off the ground. *No, no, no, no,* I thought, but I couldn't speak. I stared at the initials "ND" on the silver cuff link and felt a scream sear the back of my throat.

Something slammed into my body, like being sideswiped by a silent eighteen-wheeler, and I dropped the cuff link. The impact was gut-punching, unexpected, and debilitating. I heard the crunch of my ribs snap with the hit. My feet slammed out from under me, and I hovered for a suspended moment over the grass, my ribs crushed, my breath shot, and my brain in hyper-drive.

A million thoughts crashed through my mind as I fell, mostly about work and Nathan and a little about Walker, but the most prevalent thought was of Dominic and his promise to heal me. The protection offered by the crossbow on my wrist, the retractable stake, Walker's silver-woven gloves, and Dominic's cold, silver chain was only a mirage. My head snapped back as I hit the ground. Kaden pounded me into the earth with his crushing weight and ground home the certainty that with or without my weapons, Dominic would have to keep his promise if I hoped to survive the night.

Kaden disappeared as quickly and silently as he'd appeared. I was smashed on my back in the grass like a twitching bug. The sky overhead was vast and matte black, blending with the bursts of black that speckled my vision. I tried to cope with the ache in my side, but I couldn't breathe. I could barely think.

Dominic and I should have better defined "incapacitated."

I braced myself for Kaden's return. My stomach knotted with fear and pain and trembling anticipation, but even after several minutes of tense silence, he didn't attack.

I struggled to sit up, and my ribs screamed in stabbing, white agony. Breathing hurt. Moving hurt. Remaining still hurt. I panted from the pain, but my desperate, popcorn-gasps weren't inhaling much oxygen. My head spun. I'd have to calm my breathing or risk hyperventilating, so I pushed past the pain and took slower, shallower breaths.

The vial of Dominic's blood suddenly seemed prominent against my skin, but I eased the silver nitrate spray from my pocket instead and slowly rolled onto my hands and knees. I told myself that I'd survived worse. I told myself that after tonight, I would listen to Walker and take a sick day. I told myself a lot of things, but in the end, the only thing that got me standing was to grit my teeth against the pain and stand anyway.

I took an unsteady, listing step forward, and stumbled into a jog. My legs threatened to buckle, so I stiffened my resolve and hobbled on, building a slow momentum. I was nearly at the gate when Kaden took me out again. He appeared from thin air, and before I even knew he was there, I heard the wet *pop* of my left knee shatter.

Hot, sickening pain shot through my leg. I screamed and aimed the silver spray as I fell, but Kaden reached through the spray and wrenched the can from my hand. I hit the ground hard on my side. A sharp stab tore through my ribs. I opened my mouth, intending to scream or breathe or wield another weapon, intending to do *something,* but I couldn't inhale enough to do anything. A high squeak leaked from my lungs as they tried and failed to find air. Kaden looked down at me, watching me struggle. I couldn't read his expression. His hand still holding the silver spray was burned. Welts had boiled on his charred skin, but he just stared, stoically ignoring his burns to focus on me.

My lungs finally adjusted from having the wind knocked out of them, and I screamed.

Kaden smiled a small, strange sort of smile. He watched me scream and cower from him, and his smile widened. I angled my wrist, so the crossbow was aimed even as I rocked in agony. I braced for his attack.

He disappeared suddenly, taking the silver spray with him.

I cradled my knee and continued screaming. I couldn't stop. My screams escaped in wheezing, rhythmic exhales as I tried to bear the pain. I'd lied to myself. Gritting my teeth wasn't going to help this time, and I'd never survived anything worse. Kaden was taking me out limb by limb, wearing me down like a hyena would its prey.

I reached for my cell phone tucked into the back right pocket of my jeans. Moving was excruciating. I bit my lip and tasted the warm, metallic salt of blood as I struggled. My gloved fingertips brushed the smooth plastic phone cover, and finally, my phone slipped free of my pocket.

I tore the silver-woven glove off, unlocked the screen with my thumb, and tried to calm my trembling enough to find Walker's number. Thinking past the throbbing, electric pain was impossible. I was scrolling through my contacts, their names and numbers dancing and spinning across my vision, when a shadow darted out from the darkness. One moment my thumb was hovering over the screen, and the next, it bent back at an impossible angle with a twig-like *crack*.

I shrieked.

Kaden grabbed the phone from my numb hand. I leveled my other arm to aim the wrist crossbow, and he dropped the phone to grip my forearm. I pulled the trigger. Kaden crushed the bow in his hand before the arrow could launch and ripped the entire mechanism, arrow and all, from my arm. He tossed it behind him. I stared at it, next to where my phone had landed only two arm lengths away, but it might as well have been miles.

Kaden didn't evaporate back into the shadows this time. The stench of burning flesh steamed between us, and I realized the silver glove still covering my left hand was touching his chest. He should have leapt back from the burn of silver—my hand was scorched from its heat—but his gaze honed unwaveringly on my bleeding lower lip. His violet eyes widened and turned to lust. I eased back slightly, but Kaden leaned closer. He flicked his tongue over my bottom lip to lap the blood that had beaded there—his saliva burned—and just as quickly as he appeared, he disappeared once again back into the surrounding darkness.

I lay on my back and bit my lip, trying not to scream. I screamed anyway. I couldn't move my hand. I couldn't move my leg. I couldn't do anything except scream and choke on the blood from my lip, and in that moment, I knew without a shadow of a doubt that Walker had been right about vampires. They had the ability to create a moment in which you'd agree to the transformation. Kaden was cutting me down, one bone at a time, while he waited for his real fight, the fight he was eager for with Dominic, but I would agree to just about anything to stop the pain.

"Help me," I whispered.

Nothing but the distant bustle of car horns, engines, and curses answered my plea, and I knew with grave, dismal certainty that no one would come. Dominic wouldn't come because he was waiting for Kaden to drink, and Walker wouldn't come because he was waiting for Dominic to return with me to the coven. I was going to die here tonight, alone and broken and forsaken.

A sob broke through my gasping screams, and blood from my lip spattered on the pavement in front of me. Movement shifted in the darkness, and I quieted, bracing myself for another strike from Kaden. Moments turned into minutes. I fought a sweep of unconsciousness as the darkness in my mind ebbed and flowed and begged for me to escape, but Kaden didn't strike. I'd seen his movement in the shadows ahead, but he didn't attack again.

Shivering and waiting and dipping in and out of consciousness, I lost some of the urgency I'd felt in a haze of pain. Dominic was watching all of this unfold. He was letting me struggle and scream. He was letting Kaden torture me. Turning my head slightly, I tried to see if Kaden was still watching me, too, and I choked on the blood that had pooled in my mouth. Not all of it was from my lip.

I gagged and spat out the blood, adding to the fan of blood already formed around me. That was when I noticed Kaden's movement again, a nearly invisible, frustrated pace. Sudden realization hit: my blood was tempting him. Knowing that this was a trap and knowing that Dominic was using my blood as bait, Kaden was deliberately breaking my bones, so my injuries, although debilitating, wouldn't bleed. Even just the spatter from my lip was distracting; he probably couldn't trust himself to enjoy more than a lick. If I was going to gain any sort of leverage, I needed to bleed, and I needed to bleed a lot.

The retractable stake was still tucked into my jacket pocket. I struggled to ease my body off the ground to access it, but scorching, bone-deep pain tore through my knee when I moved. After a few failed, gentle attempts, I screwed my eyes shut against any remaining sanity and plunged my hand into my pocket in a quick, tearing snatch.

I held the retractable stake in my palm, trembling and sweating and breathless. I waited a moment for the pain to wane, but if anything, the pain intensified. It focused with time, like sledgehammers pounding over my body, so I focused my mind on something else. The pen was smooth under my trembling fingertips and warmed from the body heat inside my pocket. Before I could reconsider, and before Kaden could realize my intent, I pounded on the pen's click top. The five-inch wooden stake sprang out, and I jammed its sharpened point into my forearm.

Kaden suddenly, seemingly magically, materialized over me. He sandwiched his hands roughly over mine to hold the stake in place when I would have torn it out, its thick point still embedded in my arm. A little blood welled around the stake, but nothing substantial. The pen itself kept the blood from pouring out, like a plug holding back a geyser, but with Kaden bearing down over me, I couldn't tear it from my arm.

Kaden leaned closer, and his weight drove the stake even deeper.

I groaned.

"So intelligent," he hissed. His breath was so close to my face that I could actually feel the movement of his breath as he inhaled my scent. "And so frightened, but you can survive tonight. You can survive with me."

"I'll pass," I gritted through my clenched teeth, stubborn to the end, even as my mind shrieked at me to take his offer.

Kaden's expression tightened. He leaned even closer, and the stake wedged another millimeter deeper. My body jerked involuntarily from the pain. The movement scraped my broken leg over the pavement, and I choked on a scream. Darkness pulsed at the edges of my vision.

"You've chosen a maker who won't survive the month. He won't be present to protect you through the transformation or induct you into the coven. He won't be alive to help you hunt." A low growl vibrated from his chest, rattling into the warm caramel of his voice. "You've chosen a present course that doesn't have a future in this city. Let me be your future, Cassidy. If you want to survive, you must choose me."

"I don't have to choose anything," I spat.

His cool, smooth cheek rubbed against mine, like he was scent-marking me again. I tried to move my hand, to ward him off or turn my face away, but I couldn't move. I couldn't even feel my body or focus beyond the tiny pinpoint of clarity left in my vision. He breathed in my scent, and when our eyes met, I recognized the glint in his gaze. He was turned on, but not by my body or wit. He was turned on by my agony.

I shuddered. "No one is turning me," I insisted. "Ever."

Kaden laughed. "That's where you're wrong. Once Dominic is dead, whether he's unable to complete your transformation or chooses not to, I certainly will."

I sneered. "You certainly will not."

"Who will stop me? You?" He laughed again. His lips caressed the shell of my ear as he spoke. "My dear, dear Cassidy DiRocco, you can't stop me from taking anything I want from you. And I want everything." He hissed that last sentence, and goose bumps broke out over my neck and down my spine from the cold rush of his breath.

Without warning, his hand snatched mine and lifted it into the air. His fingers caressed over my fingers. I couldn't stop shaking.

"Beautiful fingers," Kaden whispered smoothly. As if we were lovers on a picnic, he kissed each fingertip, starting with my pinkie. He took his time, nipping gently at the skin and enjoying long, smooth licks over each pad until he reached my broken, twisted thumb.

I shook my head frantically.

He looked up, so although he was talking to me, the words were obviously meant for someone else. "A shame if they all looked like this before you finally faced me. Now or nine more fingers from now, we'll have the same battle." Kaden paused as if waiting for a response. When nothing but the chilled night air and distant buzz of city life answered him, Kaden looked down at me again. He shook his head. "You're right. You don't have to choose. He's left you to me."

Kaden gripped my index finger tightly between two of his fingers, poised to snap.

"No," I managed to spit out, panicked.

The twisting pressure on my finger tightened.

"Please, d—"

A gust of incredible wind tore over us, and Kaden was suddenly gone. I stared at the night sky overhead for a baffled moment until I heard the classic sounds of scuffling and flesh pounding against flesh, sounds that I recognized as a bar brawl. I dragged myself by my elbows over the pavement and craned my neck to see what was happening, but even seeing it, I couldn't quite process the reality of it.

Dominic had attacked. For reasons I preferred not to consider, he had attacked Kaden before he drank from me, and the two of them were literally tearing each other apart. Both of their muzzles were extended. Their eyes glowed with that inhuman iridescence, and their fangs were bared as they spit and snarled and snapped like rabid animals clawing at each other's throats.

Kaden tore out Dominic's esophagus with his own fangs. A bloody, pearl-white clump of flesh soared through the air as Kaden spat it from his jaws, but before the meat and muscle even hit the ground, Dominic's throat had healed to smooth, untarnished perfection. Dominic pounded his gargoyle talons into Kaden's stomach, and jerked his hand up, obviously searching for his heart, but Kaden took another chunk out of Dominic's neck. Dominic only managed to snap a few arteries before stumbling back. He tripped over my crossbow. Kaden faltered, too, but with his heart still intact, he managed to take advantage of Dominic's imbalance. Kaden was suddenly over Dominic, ravaging his newly healed esophagus.

Dominic rolled back and bucked him off using his feet. His movement knocked my crossbow to the side, and my cell phone slid across the grass, within arm's reach. I eased toward it slowly, terrified that my movement would bring their attention, but they were too focused on their fight to notice me. They both staggered to their feet, struggling upright in spite of their devastating injuries.

A second later, they were both fully regenerated and tearing at each other again.

Dominic and Kaden were so evenly matched that it wouldn't be the stronger vampire who won. Unless one of them pulled out their clever card—which didn't seem likely as they were both more concerned with biting out chunks of the other—the vampire with the most stamina would win.

I wasn't willing to wait with my fingers crossed, hoping that Dominic would outlast Kaden. I needed to make sure of it. Taking a deep breath, I snatched my cell phone and stuffed it into my bra for safekeeping, clenched my teeth against what I was about to do, and jerked the wooden stake from my arm.

Blood gushed over my arm, my hand, and pooled around me on

the pavement. The scuffling and snarling and sounds of flesh beating on flesh stopped instantly; Kaden and Dominic halted midstrike and slowly turned away from one another to face me. I swallowed, nervous now that my blood was the focus of both their unwavering predator's gazes.

I hadn't considered that Dominic would be just as tempted as Kaden. I hoped that despite the temptation, Dominic would remember our plan and let Kaden drink. A deep, rattling growl emanated from both of them, further amplified by the contrasting reverberations of their throats. I stared back at Dominic, willing him to meet my eyes, to confirm that we were still a team. Dominic's gaze remained just as riveted on my blood as Kaden's, and I stiffened my nerve in anticipation that they might both attack.

Chapter 11

Kaden and Dominic panted from their battle, exhausted and excited. Blood dripped from their chins in thick, rope-like paths down their throats. Talon scrapes and bite wounds visibly mended themselves and healed as they stared at me. Kaden's violet eyes and Dominic's arctic thirsty gaze glowed like laser scopes, their beads focused on my arm as it pumped blood liberally across the pavement.

Kaden stepped forward and Dominic matched him, step for synchronized step, as they closed in on either side of me. I instinctively scooted away from them, but my arm buckled. My leg jarred from the movement, and I collapsed in a writhing ball on the pavement.

Dominic and Kaden became sudden blurs of speed. One moment they were midstep and walking closer, and the next, their fangs scraped over the delicate skin of my carotid and brachial arteries, their breaths hot and ravenous. I shrieked, and my heart lurched into fifth gear.

Dominic groaned with his fangs against my neck. Kaden stroked my inner arm from wrist to elbow with his fingertip. He pressed forward with his fangs, testing the elasticity of my skin before it might break under their razor pressure. I trembled from the pain and fear and cold and unspeakable sensations their fangs and claws made me feel. Goose bumps rose over my skin from Kaden's claw as it scraped over the inner elbow. My nipples tightened in anticipation.

My face flushed with shame at my body's response. I knew what was coming. I knew how I would feel when they bit me, and I couldn't help but look forward to it, anything to escape this hell.

The pressure of Kaden's fangs finally slipped smoothly into the artery like two needle-pointed knives. His bite was a slashing, sharp, unbearable pressure, and when he suckled at the wound, it didn't tug at my groin or spiral through my blood like lava, like Dominic's bite. It felt exactly like it was, a creature biting into my flesh and sucking out my blood through the wound. I could feel the warm flow of it suction from my body as he sucked. I noticed vaguely that the stab wound on my forearm had stopped gushing. It barely trickled now, and my fingertips were starting to tingle.

I grimaced and struggled away from his mouth, but Kaden only clamped his jaws tighter around my arm. He jerked my body closer to him. I felt my cell phone slip from my bra and land somewhere in the grass. I tried to find it, but Kaden gnawed at my humerus with a wild shake of his head. My vision splintered in black starbursts.

"Easy," Dominic whispered. He was kneeling on my other side, his face still buried in my neck. He lifted me from the pavement. My head lolled back, baring my neck as he gathered me to his chest. The movement was intimate and exposed, even as Kaden continued to feed from my outstretched arm. I could barely decipher Dominic's words, they were so hushed.

"I'll take it all away in a moment," Dominic said, "but I want you to remember this, like I've asked you to remember other moments. You may not want to be transformed, but transformation aside, Kaden still can't provide you with the life that I can. His bite is a painful, savage attack."

Senseless from his bloodlust, Kaden gnawed back and forth in a frenzy—tearing my skin, veins, and muscle in his jaws—before sucking deeply again. My scream cracked, and I choked on its pieces. The dark starbursts melded together into a black blanket over my vision.

"Never doubt the exclusivity of the life I'm offering you. Promise me," Dominic demanded.

I opened my mouth, but Kaden ripped at my arm, jostling my shattered knee, and my mind floated further away. My lips might have moved and I might have blinked, but I couldn't see or feel parts of my body anymore. I was dying in agony, like I'd dreaded, but at the very end there wasn't much strength for anything, not even promises.

"Promise me, *Cassidy DiRocco*."

My lips moved and my throat vibrated independent from my will. "By the final, certain passage of time," I whispered, but even I could hear the sarcasm in my tone.

Dominic didn't care about sarcasm. I'd said the words, and he struck my neck fiercely. The sharp bite of his fangs clamped into my carotid. I tried to reach out my hand to find an anchor against my own overwhelming helplessness, but even as I strained with the very last inch of myself, I felt my wrist lift only briefly before dropping weakly back onto the pavement.

Kaden must have sensed my struggle. His chest rattled deeply, and he tore out a piece of muscle in his excitement.

My body spasmed, the best defense I could manage.

Dominic reached down and squeezed my hand gently.

"Easy," he repeated in a strained, almost desperate growl against my throat.

His fingers were long and cool and strong, so very strong and un-yielding, as he wrapped them around mine. I felt the solid pressure of his grip and the tide eased slightly. I could breathe again. My lungs expanded deeply in a desperate gasp, and my heart pounded hard against my sternum to catch up.

Dominic's chest vibrated in that deep, aching rattle, identical to Kaden. He held me firmly against his chest, suspended with my neck exposed to him and his breath hot in my hairline.

"No," I gasped. If he drank, he would weaken as much as Kaden, and my suffering and risk and possibly my death would have been for nothing. "You can't. I didn't do this for noth—"

"I will not abandon you," he whispered. "But neither will I pre-tend to be a less dangerous, volatile creature than I am for your peace of mind."

I trembled, and he held me tighter.

"No." I insisted. "Please, I—"

Dominic sealed his lips around the puncture wounds on my neck and sucked a sharp, swift rush of blood into his mouth.

I arched against him, gasping. The argument that poised on my lips incinerated on my tongue as fire and spiraling need sang through my veins. My eyes rolled back and fluttered closed. My toes curled. My hips bucked, and all the pain, panic, and anger were overwhelmed by twitching waves of ebbing and flowing pleasure. It didn't matter that my shattered knee might never walk again or that my arm was a mess of exposed raw meat. My mind flooded with sizzling, throb-bing, colliding urgency, and I trembled.

The sensations waned slightly when Dominic swallowed. His suction on my neck loosened, and I could vaguely feel the tug and sharpness of Kaden at my arm. Dominic sucked another fresh mouthful of blood from my neck, and I was lost again. My hand twitched in his, but the support of Dominic's hand never wavered. His grip remained firm and unchanging whether I arched in pleasure, faded into unconsciousness, or flinched back into reality for the second it took for Dominic to suck me back into the heat of soaring, blinding bliss.

Their thirsts were insatiable. The waves of unconsciousness were becoming more frequent, and the difference between their bites was beginning to blur into a haze of numbness. I opened my mouth to protest, but nothing escaped from my lips except air. My words were lost.

Tears seeped from the corners of my eyes and slipped down my temples. Dominic released his suction on my neck suddenly, and his face hovered over mine. Blood coated his chin and dripped down his neck, but his mouth hadn't extended into a muzzle. His face was still handsome and human-like. One of my tears glistened on the side of his cheek.

"Don't leave me," he whispered, but his lips parted in a lopsided smirk. His teeth were stained with my blood. "Unless you want me to turn you now."

The fierce boil of my temper swept over me. I opened my mouth to snap something snide, but Dominic dropped me onto the ground. He disappeared into a spiraling wind and then with a final tear of ligament and flesh, Kaden disappeared, too. For a moment I stared at the sky, the same sky I'd stared at only hours ago with such different intentions for the night. The stars weren't visible in the city, but I'd always believed in our New York lights more than the lights shining from billions upon billions of miles away. I hadn't actually seen the stars in years, since childhood. The sky hadn't changed, but it certainly didn't look the same to me.

A massive pound shook the asphalt. Someone hissed and someone else growled back with that familiar, vibrating rattle. I craned my neck down and saw that Dominic's claw-like hand was buried nearly elbow-deep in Kaden's chest. With a sharp jerk of Dominic's wrist, Kaden dropped like a broken doll to the ground.

I blinked at the sight, astonished. How had Kaden weakened so drastically? Dominic hadn't resisted my blood, either. He should have been equally weakened, but he stood over a crumpled, defeated Kaden, looking more massive and powerful and dangerous than ever.

Without even a backward glance, Dominic hauled Kaden off the ground, stooped on one knee with him in his arms, and launched off the pavement into the air in a swirl of dust and stones. His blur winked out into the night, leaving the buckled pavement from the force of his launch as the only evidence of his presence. No one would suspect that just over their heads, hidden by the shadows of our own city lights and backdropped by the pitch-black sky, vampires flew overhead.

I stared at the empty space where they'd stood, not entirely surprised that he'd left me to die. Time passed, only catalogued by the faint strain of my breathing. Everything had failed. The silver nitrate spray, the crossbow, the retractable stake pen, the silver gloves, Dominic's promises, and Walker's plan had all failed, and the only thing I had left, which I'd had all along, was my stubborn refusal to let go.

My cell phone had survived the vampires' attack better than me; I could see it lying in the grass next to my shoulder where it had slipped from my bra. I only had to move my hand a few inches to touch its screen.

My finger twitched. I focused all my effort on my hand and those last few inches of movement. The twitch increased to a tremor and under what felt like an impossible, immovable weight, my hand struggled toward the phone. My fingers brushed its edge. I could see that I was touching it, but I couldn't feel it.

I swiped the screen to unlock it. The screen didn't recognize the pressure of my finger. I pressed harder and tried to stop shaking, but the blanket of starbursts still clouded my vision. I was going to die like Walker had predicted. Maybe I wasn't in an alley, but I was alone and abandoned. I couldn't see my phone and I couldn't feel the screen, but I kept swiping my finger, hoping against hope and trying against the odds that I could survive because it might be the last thing I'd ever try to do.

The *snap* of my phone unlocking startled me awake. My vision sharpened slightly, so I could see the illumination of the phone's screen at what looked like the end of a long, dark tunnel. I tapped the Call icon and tried to scroll down to *W* for Walker, but my numb, trembling fingers couldn't swipe. The phone was suddenly dialing and ringing someone else.

The call clicked through. "This better be damn good, DiRocco."

I recognized that smooth, honeyed voice. My heart ached, thinking about our last conversation. I'd been so worried about my reputation and credibility, but whether I finished and published "The City Beneath: Vampires Bite in the Big Apple" or not, my credibility was tarnished with Greta and the police department anyway. They were whose opinion actually mattered, and of course, they were the ones whose high opinion I'd lost.

"Hello?" she snapped. "The next words out of your mouth better be an apology. Better yet, skip the damn apology. I better hear the name of who's responsible for these murders or I'm hanging up."

I swallowed and tried to speak, but it was more a moan than a word. "Help."

I didn't hear anything from Greta for a long moment. When she spoke again, her tone was urgent. "How hurt are you?"

"Dying," I rasped. "I'm sorry."

"No damn apologies." Her voice seemed distant suddenly as she shouted, "She's at Paerdegat Park! Get a squad and an ambulance there stat! Cass? Are you there? Speak to me."

"Here," I murmured.

"Hang on. We tracked your cell, and we're on our way. Help is coming soon, Cass. Are you alone?"

"Yes." The light at the end of my tunnel winked out, and darkness blanketed my vision. "Alone."

"Alright," Greta said. I could hear her breathe long and deeply over the phone. Her voice was sweet again when she said, "Tell me who did this, Cass. What else can they take from you now? Don't let them get away."

I smiled at Greta's persistence, even at the end. I would have done the same. And she was right; what else could they take from me? What else did I have to lose?

"Cass? Stay with me! Who's responsible for the murders? Who attacked you?"

"Vampires," I said.

"What?" Greta whispered.

"Vampires."

I didn't hear or see Dominic's return, but I could smell it.

"The patrol car is almost there, Cass. Just hang on for a—"

I ended the call.

The scent of pine sharpened as Dominic approached. His steps were slow and deliberate as he walked through the puddle of blood around my body. After my few encounters with Kaden, I was beginning to understand Dominic's careful restraint. I imagined that the carnage probably made being in my presence irresistible, but he knelt next to me, in the puddle of my blood—I could sense the shiver of his presence—and he resisted.

I couldn't feel the pressure of his hands, but I could sense my body being moved and a distancing from the ground, like floating, as he lifted me into his arms. I couldn't feel much of anything, but the movement must have further injured my leg; my body spasmed slightly.

"Easy, Cassidy," Dominic murmured. He shifted me in his arms gently, obviously taking care not to jostle my injuries, but there were just too many to manage them all.

I choked from the sharp angle of my neck as I draped limply in his arms. My body spasmed again.

"Damn it," Dominic hissed. He shifted his elbow to better accommodate my head, and I could breathe again.

He knelt on the ground. Dust and pebbles kicked up around us, and suddenly, we were soaring. Wind rushed over me, cool and whipping. Dominic's arms were icy around me, as well, and I shivered as the wind and Dominic's body stole what little heat I had left. His arms tightened around me as I shook, but his coolness pressing closer only made me colder.

We dipped down sharply into the subway systems, curved crazily through the tunnels, and jetted into the sewer until we finally reached his rooms in the coven. Dominic slowed to a walk. His bed was set by the far wall, and the caged bedroom was positioned at the opposite end. He bypassed the cage this time and settled me gently on the bedspread. The mattress was thick and soft. My weight dipped into its downy softness, and my mind finally released from reality. It leapt to another time and place, to my first apartment with Adam where we'd shared a bed equally soft.

His smooth, handsome baby face stared down at me as his body pressed me deeper into the bed, forming a cocoon of mattress and sheets and man around me. The warm, beefy weight of Adam's muscles shifted in my arms as I nibbled up his neck to his ear. I felt him tremble from my touch. I bit his earlobe and squeezed him intimately, and he kissed me deeper into the mattress, blind to everything except our love and desperate lust, touching me until I was just as desperate as him. We'd only lived together for three months, but those first two months before my parents had died had been unimaginably beautiful.

Adam had always tasted heady and smooth, like strong coffee on a frosty morning. My eyes opened drowsily, and I realized that Adam was gone. My depression and anger and sarcasm hadn't been a part of the person he'd fallen in love with, and he hadn't loved the person I'd become after my parents' deaths. We parted, both equally heart-broken and hopeless and miserable with each other.

The love and joy and connection I'd shared with Adam had been real at the time, but I'd drifted in a tide of grief in those horrible months following the fire. By the time he'd realized how far the distance had grown between us, he hadn't stood a prayer's chance of breaching the gap. He still lived in a bright world, ripe with excitement and anticipation for the future, but I knew the truth. Adam didn't exist in the world I knew. I would never again open my eyes after a kiss, and see his smooth baby face smiling back.

Dominic was the man smiling back at me now, and he certainly did exist in the world I knew. His lips were sliced and bleeding from his own fangs.

"You came back for me," I whispered hoarsely, reality still feeling like a dream.

"I didn't want to leave you," Dominic said deeply. "But I feared that Kaden would escape if I tended to you first."

My heart skipped. "Where—"

"Shhh," Dominic murmured. "He is chained and imprisoned until his sentencing. He betrayed me. He betrayed the coven, and that is punishable by his final death. You don't need to worry about him any longer. We've succeeded, Cassidy. Thanks to you, we've won."

He leaned over me, and we were suddenly kissing. The blood oozing from the cuts on his lips flowed into my mouth. It pooled at the back of my throat. I resisted swallowing but without swallowing, I couldn't breathe. More blood poured from his mouth into mine as his lips parted and urged and nipped my lips.

I strained against him. Dominic sensed my resistance and halted my struggle with a hand on either side of my face. I tried to pull away, but the more I struggled, the more he kissed me, and the more blood poured into my mouth. I let myself choke rather than swallow. The blood spat between us as I coughed and gagged in Dominic's face.

He finally stopped kissing me.

Blood spattered over his handsome features, and he really was handsome. His face hadn't contorted into the vicious, animal-like muzzle he usually displayed when he fed. Before I'd coughed, he'd taken a moment to wash his face clean from his battle with Kaden. Now, the blood and spit I'd choked on spotted his forehead, cheeks, nose, and chin. He stared at me, unblinking after my sudden outburst, and I couldn't decipher his reaction.

"I said no," I whispered in defense. "Numerous times, I've told you that I don't want to be transformed."

Dominic blinked. "Yes, you've made that clear."

"And you knew I was choking. You deliberately held my head still, hoping I'd panic and swallow your blood rather than choke," I accused softly.

"It's usually an effective technique," he admitted.

I glared at him. "You use it often, I suppose."

Dominic shrugged. "When necessary. My night bloods have always been willing, but sometimes, the physical act of swallowing blood as a human is distasteful. My last night blood wanted to be transformed, but she rebuked my advances at the critical moment."

"Jillian?" I asked, remembering her speech about Dominic's bite.

"Jillian isn't my night blood. I adopted her into the coven after her Master met his final death. My last night blood was Sylvia." Dominic's gaze unfocused as he remembered her. "Sylvia Lamb."

"She changed her mind at the last moment, so you forced her?" I accused quietly, hoping to keep my voice neutral and not excite him with my anger.

He frowned. "She didn't change her mind. She simply refused me in the moment. I ensured that what she truly desired was accomplished."

I pursed my lips, unimpressed. "Maybe that was true for her, but I'm not Sylvia. I'm not simply refusing you in the moment. I'm refusing you entirely."

"No, you're certainly not Sylvia Lamb."

I waited in silence, unsure what else to say in response.

He smiled. I could tell that the smile was reluctant, but he smiled anyway. The smile wasn't a baring of fangs to frighten me, it wasn't a sneer of disgust, and it wasn't sardonic or derisive. Although his fangs did gleam in the candlelight, their threat wasn't his intent. He had a beautiful smile.

I smiled back, helpless not to, and asked, "Why am I not like your Sylvia Lamb?"

"In a dangerous situation, Sylvia wouldn't have questioned whether to run or stand her ground. She would have run every time. She wouldn't have chosen to willingly endure sustained, debilitating pain in the hopes of gaining a favorable result, like you have for me. Transforming into a vampire didn't change any of those qualities," Dominic said. "Her own survival was her priority, and in the end, it had unfortunately been her undoing despite my efforts to teach her otherwise."

"You expect too much from people. You expect too much from me. I'm not going through this again," I said, holding up my arm to show him my snapped thumb, but the bone was straight. I wiggled it, amazed. I checked my arm, moved my leg, and breathed air deep and heartily into my lungs, but my ribs expanded and exhaled without one twinge of pain.

Dominic grinned, looking extremely pleased with himself.

"Why did you heal me?" I asked in a hushed whisper. "If you were going to transform me anyway, why bother?"

"Your body was broken and unfit for anything besides medical attention, so I gave it the attention it needed. You still need more blood to fully recover, so if you won't accept mine, you must rest until your blood regenerates on its own. When I do transform you—"

"I don't want—"

Dominic covered my mouth with his fingers. "When I do, you'll enjoy my bite. You'll beg me to taste you. I'll give you all of me, and when you taste me, you'll be mine. Forever."

I shook my head at him.

He nodded at me, smirking.

My anger skyrocketed. "Thank you very much for healing me," I snapped. "But I'm never playing your sacrifice again. I *suffered*, Dominic."

"Our plan was a success."

"Our plan nearly killed me!"

"Only nearly," Dominic dismissed. "I've healed you. With time, the memories of pain will fade, and all that *will* remain is the advantage we gained."

"The advantage *you* gained," I reminded him.

"This was for the city, as well," Dominic growled. "You wouldn't have agreed to my plan otherwise, and I certainly didn't force you." He narrowed his eyes on me. "You've sacrificed and suffered for others in the past, and you'll sacrifice and suffer for me again if necessary." His face softened slightly. "You bear the evidence of that on your body."

His hand stroked down to caress the scar at my lower back.

I squirmed uncomfortably. "That's different."

"Why is this scar different from the others you've endured?"

"You wouldn't understand."

A rattling growl vibrated low and menacing from his chest. "Try me," Dominic rasped.

I sighed, wanting to avoid his anger, but more than that, needing to keep him distracted. Despite the wrong turn our plan had taken, I had nevertheless still infiltrated the coven, achieving my half of the plan. If Walker was going to achieve his half, I needed to keep Dominic talking while Walker entered the coven after me.

I took another deep, fortifying breath. "I was on a stakeout with Greta, er, Detective Wahl—Officer Wahl at the time—and Officer Harroway as backup. I thought it'd be a big story, the breakout for my career, but my source set me up."

Dominic nodded with grave understanding. "Betrayal is the most bitter truth to swallow."

"Wahl and Harroway had the duty to watch my back, and I had the duty to watch theirs because that's what backups do. When shots were fired at us, I literally covered Officer Harroway's back with my own." I looked away. "That kind of backup isn't something you can demand of someone. It isn't a sacrifice. It's a gift and something they would have given me had our roles been reversed. I *deserved* this scar. I'm proud of it." My voice caught as I thought of everything I'd irrevocably lost with Greta and my career tonight. "I don't expect you to understand that."

Dominic sighed. "I understand more than you know, probably more than you'd care to discover. I've endured many hardships in my time, some that have left visible scars and some that have not."

I glanced back at him, and my eyes dropped automatically to the deep groove that pulled down his lower lip. I opened my mouth to ask about his scar, as he had asked about mine, but his lips suddenly twisted. He'd caught me staring. I blushed, embarrassed, and it took me an extra moment to gather enough courage to ask the question.

"How did you get your scar?"

Dominic stroked the scar on my hip in tiny circles as he spoke. His voice was modulated, and from the pacing and cant of his story, I could tell it was one that he'd told many times over the years and had honed with each telling.

"I was very aware of my appearance, even as a night blood. Today's culture dictates that men be ruggedly handsome without seeming to know or care about their appearance, but in 1537, London society encouraged a more refined man, one who took care of his appearance and flaunted his efforts.

"My father was a skilled smith. His weapons and tools and jewelry were commissioned by royalty all across England for the quality of his work. As the eldest son, I was expected to continue my father's trade, but I was young and ambitious and unappreciative of my father's efforts to provide us with a comfortable life. I wanted more from life than comfort. I wanted riches and power, and since I'd never lived through the struggles my father had endured to simply live comfortably, I'd believed that my goals were attainable.

"Lady Elizabeth Beard commissioned my father from time to time for a variety of services, sometime jewelry, other times household items or weapons for her estate. She was a countess, the title inherited from her late husband, and although she wasn't exceedingly lovely, not like you—"

I stared at him, unimpressed by the compliment, but he continued his story without hesitation.

"—she possessed an allure beyond the color of her comely brown eyes or the lank, dullness of her hair. She was experienced and wealthy and confident in her station and in her ability to command a household. Very much like you actually, with your career," Dominic commented. "Elizabeth would have made an absolutely lovely vampire, too."

I didn't much like what he was implying with the "too," but I bit my tongue in favor of just listening. He wasn't trying to bite me or kiss me or kill me, so I didn't want to distract him.

"As a widow," he continued, "Elizabeth could travel to town unaccompanied, and after she concluded business with my father, we'd take good advantage of her new freedom. I fell in love with her and the life I envisioned as her husband.

"My father warned me against her. He knew that she'd never accept my proposal. As a talented smith, I was good enough to work for her, and as a handsome, healthy man, I was good enough to make love to her, but no matter how skilled I was in either role, he warned me that I was not good enough to marry. My father gave reasonable, hearty advice, as usual, but I was young and selfish and driven. I accused my father of being jealous, and pursued her anyway."

"What happened?" I asked, fascinated in spite of myself. "Was your father right?"

Dominic smiled warily. "I never had the opportunity to propose. My father and I suffered an accident at the forge while working on one of her commissions. She needed a new set of cutlery for the kitchens. I had begun the detailing on one of the knife's handles, and my father was tempering the butcher knife when the forge exploded. I don't know why the accident occurred. Any explanation seemed impossible at the time because my father was so scrupulous with his trade, but looking back at the accident now from a world of city codes and regulations, I can see how any number of scenarios could have contributed to the accident.

"My father was closer than me to the kiln when it exploded. I threw myself over him to shield his body from the debris, but fiery steel, like shrapnel, tore through our skin and rained over our heads along with some of the blasted rafters from the ceiling. I was able to shelter him from the aftermath, but the initial blast had maimed him. He lost an eye and most of the fingers on his right hand as well as countless superficial scars, like mine. We switched roles for a while, so he could detail the work, and I forged until he relearned his entire trade with his left hand. I'd never looked up to my father more than in those weeks following his recovery."

Dominic stopped speaking suddenly, rubbing his scarred lower lip with his thumb. I waited for him to collect his feelings, and I attempted to convince myself that his story didn't change anything. I didn't want to humanize him. I tried to harden my heart, but his story was peeling away the layers. The familiar ache for my own father tore through my gut, and for a moment, I felt a kinship with Dominic as we both mourned the lives of loved ones we'd lost.

"Well?" I croaked. I cleared my throat, so my voice sounded less harsh. "What happened with Elizabeth?"

Dominic came back to himself and sighed. "When she returned to view some of her collection, I asked for an extension. The pieces we had created had been ruined in the blast, and I couldn't work as quickly without my father; he was still recovering. She completely understood and allowed us to keep the deposit, but she needed the cutlery more quickly than we could provide it. She took the project elsewhere, and continued with their services going forward instead of ours."

"Did you ever see her again?" I asked, feeling bereft on his behalf.

He shrugged. "Yes, but only in passing. My acquaintance with her, as both her smithy and lover, had ended."

"So your father was right."

"Yes, my father was right. Elizabeth hadn't had any intentions toward me beyond what our stations dictated. I was the one with dreams and hopes and aspirations. She was comfortable with her life."

"I'm so sorry."

"No need for apologies. That was several lifetimes ago, but one always remembers his first. My existence now is much different than it was during my human life."

"Are you comfortable with your life, er, your existence now?"

"Exceedingly."

Dominic smiled, but this time, I could in no way forget the predator that he'd become. Despite the human emotions and memories he possessed, he was not currently human.

"Are *you?*" he asked.

I blinked. "Am I comfortable with my life?"

"Or existence, yes." His voice was bland, but I could tell that he was making fun of me. He cocked his head and waited for my reply.

I glanced at the room around me, at the stone walls and the silver cage that lined the far corner. I glanced at the stain where Jillian had torn out Rafe's throat and tossed it to the ground like spoiled leftovers. I looked at the doorway that eventually led to an entire coven filled with hundreds of vampires, some of which Walker expected me to find and kill in their sleep.

I laughed. "There's nothing about my life that I'm comfortable with."

"And before we met, when you were ignorant of my existence? Were you comfortable then?"

I pursed my lips. I would have loved to blame Dominic and Kaden and even Walker for disrupting my life, but my life had been disrupted long before I'd met any of them. "No," I admitted.

"Before that first stakeout, the one that you thought would be the breakout of your career? How about then?"

My throat burned. I thought I might choke on the tears rather than let them surface, but I was able to swallow them down before I spoke. "No."

"It's the scars that aren't visible that often cut the deepest."

"I don't want to talk about this," I whispered, thinking of my parents.

"Living often takes more than it gives, but I can give you something that nature intends for you to have. You were born to transform. In all my many, many years, I've learned to never turn away from the little life actually gives. Experience and knowledge has undoubtedly changed my perspective, but some things never change. I'm just as greedy and single-mindedly selfish for you as I was for Elizabeth, except now I have the means, power, and authority to take exactly what I want."

"What's stopping you?" I snapped.

"Presently, the rising sun. Until tonight," Dominic murmured.

He bent down over me, and I braced myself for his intent. I closed my eyes against his Christmas pine scent as he reached for something over the bed's edge, next to the sideboard. Nothing happened. His lips didn't grind against my lips, and his fangs didn't pierce, graze, or threaten any part of my skin. One moment I was bracing myself for his strike, and the next moment, he'd already struck, and I was still bracing myself as if the worst hadn't just happened. Dominic had wrapped nylon rope around my wrists, anchoring me to notches in the sideboard.

"Why are there anchor restraints built into your bed's sideboard?" I asked, furious.

His smile was suddenly lascivious, and I instantly regretted the question. "More often than not, I don't use them in this manner, but in a pinch, they certainly suffice."

I tugged impatiently at the restraints, and something sharp pierced the crease in my elbow.

I jerked away. Dominic had just fitted my arm with an IV. I stared at him, openmouthed.

"Ian Walker is not the only man with the resources to care for you, but I'm the man who can do so most efficiently and effectively. You'd still be in critical condition if left in his care."

Dominic picked up a syringe from the end table drawer. I realized with a mixture of respect and horror that he'd planned this. He'd planned on me being here in his bed, injured and relying on his care, and he'd prepared the necessary tools to both care for me and inca-pacitate me. He injected the contents of the syringe into the portal.

"You still need to rest and fully recover, and I must rest, as well, assured that harm will come to neither you nor my coven."

A rush of lethargy spread through my body, and I desperately struggled to focus. I recognized this weightless, unaccountably heady feeling; I'd fought through the pain of weaning off percs and eventu-ally going cold turkey during physical therapy. If I wasn't mistaken, and I was intimately positive that I wasn't, Dominic had just injected me with morphine.

"No," I whispered, equally horrified and blissful. My body wel-comed the release, while my mind raced to deny it. "What have you—"

"Be still. None of my coven will be tempted by you with narcotics in your system, and you'll finally rest." Dominic leaned over my elbow where a drop of blood had pearled from the needle, and he licked it from my skin with a flick of his tongue. He nuzzled in the curve of my elbow for a moment, and when he pulled away, his jaw had extended. I could sense his restraint as he pulled away from my skin.

Maybe it was the morphine or maybe it was my own weakness, but instead of ignoring his mutation like I'd normally have done, I ran my fingers along his jaw. Dominic froze at my touch. His breathless anticipation seemed fragile, as if he'd strike if I moved too suddenly, but I smoothed my thumb along the elongated bones and corded muscles of his jaw to the deep groove of his scar. I glided the back of my hand along the smooth skin of his cheeks and cupped the contour of his mutation in my palm until he settled into my touch.

Dominic rubbed his entire cheek against my hand, the strong ridges of his muzzle continuing to shift and elongate in my hand. Once his mouth was fully transformed, every tooth was as razor-pointed in his snout as only his eyeteeth were in his human mouth. It must have been the morphine, because even this close, I only felt partially horrified. The other part of me was, as always, full of questions.

"Why didn't you transform like this when you drank from me? How were you able to drink and still fight Kaden?" My voice was slurred and dreamy, like my head, and I remembered all over again why my rehabilitation and recovery after being shot had been so difficult. Dominic was right. Life took more than the rare instances it gave, but on morphine, I finally didn't have to care.

"I didn't drink." Dominic grazed his lips over my neck. I didn't remember him moving from my elbow. I could feel the vibration of his words against my skin and shivered. The purr of his growl was soft and satisfied, like he was enjoying my touch and scent immensely.

"Yes, you did. I remember," I argued. Although my words were combative, the sound of my voice drifted in smooth, uncaring tones. "You drank from my neck as Kaden drank from my brachial."

Dominic shook his head. "I bit you to ease your pain and to fool Kaden into believing we were pack hunting, but I never swallowed. We had a plan, if you also remember. I was your backup. Had I swallowed, it would have compromised our plan," he said, grinning. "You upheld your half of our deal, and I certainly intended to uphold mine."

Dominic pressed a soft kiss to the pulse at my neck. Even softly, I could feel the hard, lethal press of his fangs behind the feather-brush of his lips.

My breath caught. "Dominic, I—"

"The sun is approaching. Even this far below ground, I can feel its heavy, scorching weight against my body," he murmured over my skin.

"Where do you go during the day? I thought these were your rooms. Why don't you sleep here?"

"These are my rooms, but I would never leave my coven vulnerable during their day rest. I sleep with them tonight." He gave me a pointed look, and I thought of Walker's plan to slaughter them while they slept.

I blushed.

He smirked. "Sleep well, Cassidy DiRocco."

I opened my mouth to reply, but he was already gone.

Chapter 12

"This whole damsel-in-distress gig is a bad habit, DiRocco."

The slow drawl of Walker's voice penetrated the murky bog of my mind. My consciousness drifted near the surface, and I felt his hands brush the hair from my face. I grinned, my eyes still closed.

His hands trembled slightly.

"Bad habits die hard," I whispered.

"I thought that was *old* habits."

"All my old habits are bad habits." I forced my eyes open. They felt impossibly heavy. The room didn't spin exactly, but nothing around me was steady or real. It felt like a living dream, except for the solid weight and heat of Walker's hands again my skin. Walker's expression was pinched despite the lightness in his voice, and I wondered why. If he was here in the coven, it meant our plan had succeeded.

Walker was shaking his head at me.

"I'm sorry I couldn't call you at sunrise. I got a little tied up." I jerked on the restraints holding me to the bed.

"I thought I told you to keep your day job," Walker quipped back.

He pulled out a hunting knife from one of his Kevlar chest pockets and began sawing on the restraints. The swell of his muscles bulged with the effort. His thick blond brows furrowed over those killer big brown eyes as he concentrated, and I had the insane, immediate urge to kiss him. My mind flashed back to the memory of us on my desk. He'd been so warm and certain and strong, and my own issues, as usual, had stood in the way of getting what I desired.

"You really are beautiful," I murmured.

Walker's eyes snapped down to meet my gaze.

I shook my head, disappointed with myself for not taking exactly what I wanted and with life for making me this way. "This whole city's fucked up. It'd never work out, not between you and me. Not between me and anyone."

Walker leaned closer to my face, and for a fraction of a second, I thought he was going to kiss me. I froze, breathless with anticipation, and then he shone something bright in my eyes.

"Are you high?" he asked.

I cringed away from the light, but he forced my eyes open with his fingers and flashed the light back and forth as he studied each eye.

"Can't I just think that you're beautiful?" I grumbled.

"You certainly can. I hope you think about me all the time, but it's not like you to acknowledge those thoughts." He clicked off the flashlight, dousing me in blind blackness. It took a while for my eyes to recover, which was probably what he'd noticed from my dilated pupils.

"Morphine," I admitted. "What time is it?"

"Three hours past sunrise," Walker replied offhandedly. His mouth opened and closed several times before saying, "Dominic Lysander gave you an IV drip and a morphine injection?"

"I think he saw your IV last night and was inspired. He doesn't want me to go elsewhere for my medical needs." I snorted. "*Medical* needs." I laughed at my own joke.

Walker returned his attention to the restraint. "Still not funny."

"The morphine should wear out of my system in the next half hour, so enjoy the jokes while you're getting them. My mood will likely dim to its usual sour sarcasm when I'm sober again."

"I like your sour sarcasm," he replied, but there was something more to his voice than before. He looked down into my face. "I like you just as you are, Cassidy: prickly, brave, loyal, and smart as hell. Life's dished you a few lemons, and you've chopped them in half and squeezed its juice in life's eye. No one here wants to drink fucking lemonade, not Dominic, not Kaden, and especially not me. We all want *you*."

I opened my mouth to reply and just stared at him, stunned into silence for a moment by his honesty. He turned his attention back to the nylon restraint before I could think of the words.

"How long have you been tied up?" he asked.

I closed my eyes, trying to focus on actual words instead of being overwhelmed by everything his words made me feel. "How long ago was sunrise? He tied me up right before bedding for the day."

Walker shot me a look. "Sunrise was three hours ago. I just told you that."

"I know you did," I snapped. "I can't fucking think."

"There's that sourness we all know and love. The morphine must be wearing off faster than you'd anticipated."

I sighed. "I'm sorry. And speaking of apologies, I didn't get to search for the coven's resting place before he restrained me. Dominic admitted that—" *he stays with the coven during their day rest,* I thought.

"He admitted what?"

I opened my mouth and closed it again, feeling an immovable weight settle deep inside of me. I couldn't do it. I couldn't bring myself to betray Dominic with what little information I'd obtained.

"What did he admit, Cassidy?" Walker asked.

"I, er, that he wants to transform me." I sighed, and I didn't have to fake my frustration.

Walker shot me another sideways look. "We already knew that. And anyway, you distracted him enough that I was able to enter the coven, so good job. We'll find their resting place together."

The restraint around my wrist snapped. I pulled my hands to my chest and rubbed them as blood returned in a swift, tingling rush to my fingers. I could recognize that it hurt, but on morphine, I really didn't care. I rubbed the heel of my palm into my eyes, enjoying the floating, carefree sensation, and wishing it would dissipate so I could focus.

"Did you have any trouble getting into the coven?" I asked, cautiously.

Walker snorted. "Less trouble than last time," he said, stooping over my elbow. He slid the IV from my skin, and without gauze or tissues or anything remotely sterile on hand, pressed his own shirt against the puncture to stop the bleeding.

I cringed. "You're not sneaking in, Walker. The vampires know exactly who's coming in and out of the coven. Dominic can feel it."

"Did Dominic tell you that?" Walker asked.

"It makes sense that they know. They haven't survived for hundreds of years by letting people waltz in and out. Another night blood would have snuck in and killed them by now."

"I've told you before, you can't believe what Dominic tells you."

I sighed and dropped my point in favor of a more pressing issue. "Fine, you snuck in, but riddle me this. How are we going to navigate these tunnels? They're massive. We might not even find the vampires until dusk."

"We'll find them," Walker said. The conviction in his voice was strong and certain. "Their resting place will be immense. Other rooms will branch out from its center, like an open lobby."

"How many rooms will there be?" I asked, chilled to think how many vampires were beneath the city and how many we could potentially face in order to accomplish Walker's plan.

"Hundreds, to accommodate the coven as it grows. My coven back home has fifteen, but being under the city, I wouldn't be surprised to find up to fifty vampires here."

"Fifty vampires," I whispered. I envisioned them closing in around us and shivered. "How do you know what their resting place looks like or how many vampires are here?"

"Bex described it to me before I left home," Walker admitted.

I frowned. "A Master vampire gave you inside information about another coven? Why? What does she have to gain by helping a human track and kill another vampire?"

His face hardened. "What does Dominic have to gain by fighting his own to protect you? They want to turn us, DiRocco, and they'll do anything, absolutely anything, even seemingly turn on their own kind, to ensure that they get what they want. "

I blinked. "Dominic will certainly not get what he wants."

"He might," Walker whispered.

"Excuse me? I think I know my own—"

"Everyone has a pressure point that makes them willingly step over their line. Dominic is still searching for yours."

I opened my mouth and closed it before choosing my words carefully. "But you're not a vampire, so Bex is still searching for your pressure point, too."

"No, she found mine."

I narrowed my eyes. "What are you saying?"

"It's been a long time, five years and two months since Julia and I—" Walker's voice broke. He glared at me before continuing. "—I agreed to the transformation."

I opened my mouth and closed it, stunned. "But you hate vampires," I whispered.

Walker's eyes flattened. "Bex drained me, but when she should have given me her own blood to drink, she—" Walker's voice broke again. "—She didn't have the opportunity to give me her blood. After I recovered, I changed my mind about the transformation, but her failure only honed her determination to have me." Walker shook his head, his expression pinched. "But it honed my determination, too. They all need to be eliminated, Cassidy. Every last one."

"How many can you eliminate, Walker, before Bex gets over you, and it's *you* she eliminates?" I asked softly, taken aback by the vehemence in his expression.

Walker shook his head. "Vampires have long memories, and in all that time, I don't think Bex ever forgave herself for being unable to complete the transformation. Guilt and lust are powerful things, and if the one thing that Bex wanted was my consent, it's the one thing she can't get over losing. It seems the more I kill vampires, the more she feels me slipping away from that moment I was almost hers, and the more she tries to win me back. If in all this time she hasn't stopped trying to win me back, I don't think she's going to get over me anytime soon."

"Why did you agree to the transformation?" I asked carefully. "Who's Julia?"

Walker peeked at my arm from under his shirt, ignoring me. "I think you're good here. We need to start searching the tunnels before we lose more time."

Walker offered me a hand to help me down from the bed. His jaw flexed stubbornly, daring me to push the subject, but I let it pass without comment. I'd only known him for three days; what right did I have to push him if he didn't want to be pushed? I took his hands, and his fingers closed firmly around my palm as he helped me stand.

My head swam and my body felt like it was balancing on limp noodles. The floor listed from side to front to side to back, and I pressed the heel of my palm against my forehead in an attempt to ground myself. Walker took hold of my waist while I swayed. After a long moment, my head settled, and I stepped away, able to balance on my feet without his support. The floor still wobbled and dipped, like I was floating over it rather than standing on it, but at least I was standing.

"Well?" he asked.

I shook my head. "Let's just find the coven and put this entire night behind us."

"Where are your gloves and crossbow and stake? Do you still have them on you?"

"No, not that they were much help." I touched the necklace that Dominic gave me, my last weapon. "You've got weapons, right?"

Walker looked offended. "Of course."

"Then lead the way."

Walker nodded, and despite all of our setbacks, he smiled with anticipation. It wasn't much different from Dominic's smile before he bit me, as if he was getting exactly what he wanted after a very long wait.

The tunnels were damp from the underground, but I could tell by the kept walls and floor and the personalized rooms branching from the main hallways that the space was occupied. This wasn't just a place to hide during the day; the vampires had made these underground tunnels a city of their own.

The rooms branching off from the main tunnel were all living quarters with personal items and furniture. One of the doorways had two scraps of wood tied together above its entrance, like a cross. We also passed smaller rooms furnished with chairs and a stage or platform. Another was much larger than the other sitting rooms and was actually furnished with couches, pillows, end tables, and rugs.

That room gave me pause. A room like that was made for creatures who needed comfort, who enjoyed rest after a hard day and enjoyed relaxing in the company of others. It resembled a family room without the electronics, back when people gathered to talk to one another instead of to watch television. The room implied that the vampires valued more in their society than just hunting and killing. Such a room certainly fit the Armani-wearing, loquacious, well-fed version of Dominic. I couldn't imagine Dominic's true form resting in this room, with his talons and extended snout and razor-pointed teeth.

The more we searched, the more my heart ached with dread and a little panic. There were a lot of rooms, and Dominic was self-admittedly ambitious. I bit my lip, thinking about how many vampires could potentially fit in all these rooms, and if I knew anything about Dominic, and I think I was learning more than I'd ever want to know, he'd want to fill every room.

We didn't cross one vampire while we searched, a fact that didn't surprise Walker but made me a nervous wreck. They knew we were here. They probably heard our footsteps and breathing. Hell, Dominic probably heard the blood pumping though my veins, but no one confronted us. Walker reminded me that vampires were nocturnal, that they were all heavily sleeping, but despite their nocturnal nature, Dominic had refuted this myth. They could wake and function during the day, out of sunlight, if they wanted. As usual, Walker didn't want to hear what Dominic had to say, but I walked on eggshells.

Eventually, we found the coven's resting place. As I gazed at the honeycomb-like dome, I realized with a sickening, stunned drop of horror that Walker was both exactly right and horribly wrong. The resting place was a centralized location for the vampires to sleep throughout the day as Walker had expected, with bedrooms lining the walls and stacked a couple dozen stories above our heads. Unlike what Walker had expected, every room in the coven was occupied. Dominic wasn't intending to fill every room; he already had. Hundreds upon hundreds of vampires were sleeping in their beds within their honeycomb-like rooms.

"There are hundreds," I whispered, feeling equally astounded, horrified, and daunted. I took a step back, shaking my head.

Walker slid a bullet into the chamber of his sawed-off shotgun with a harsh, sliding cock.

"How do they reach the very top rooms?" I asked, needing something concrete to grasp on to. "There must be stairs from the back."

"They don't need stairs like us, Cassidy. They can jump that height."

I was fully aware of their abilities. Dominic could soar through the sky like he had an engine and wings. He'd jumped five stories to my apartment window with me in his arms. I stared at the very top rooms in the honeycombs, three times the height of my apartment building, and awe still blanketed over me.

"Jesus," I whispered.

Walker took a step forward. "We'd best get to work."

I snapped my gaze from their resting place to stare at Walker. "You're not serious," I said, surprised.

"We came here to do a job, and I'll be damned if we came all this way, came this close to killing them, and just left with our tails tucked," Walker snapped.

"This is impossible." I swept my hand through the air to encompass the metropolis behind us. "We can't distinguish the rebels from this many vampires and kill them all in a single day. There's simply too many and not enough time before sunset. We either do the job right, or we don't do it at all, and we can't possibly hope to do it right, Walker. Not today."

His expression tightened. "I'm not leaving. I came to the city to track and kill the animals responsible for the attacks at Paerdegat Park, and that's exactly what I'm doing. I've tracked them to their resting place, and I'll be damned if I'm leaving without killing them."

"Then you'll be killing them alone," I hissed. "There's too many of them, much more than you anticipated."

"Cassidy, don't—"

"We can come back another day when we're better prepared," I pleaded. "This isn't completing the job. This is suicide."

"Not if we kill them all."

Rage exploded through the haze of morphine. "That wasn't our agreement."

Walker crossed his arms. "It's an option."

"No, it's not. You'd never be able to kill the entire coven before sunset. When Dominic wakes and sees half his coven demolished, who do you think he'll come after? He'll know I'm the one who betrayed him."

"You're right." Walker stepped toward me and enveloped me gently in his embrace. His arms were warm and strong and secure as he held me, exactly like last time, and I wrapped my arms around his waist, relieved.

"I don't know what I was thinking. When Dominic wakes, you'll be his first target. You should go," Walker agreed, but it wasn't the agreement I'd anticipated.

I pushed against his chest to meet his eyes. "You're coming with me."

Walker shook his head. "Dominic will know that I helped you escape whether I leave now or later, and I'd rather take as many vampires down with me as I can. Get out of the coven and escape the city today. I've heard the country isn't a bad place to settle," he said, and he had the nerve to wink at me. "I've already told my partner about you. The first person you see, ask for Ronnie. It's a small town, and she'll be expecting you."

"What are you talking about? I'm not leaving New York City. It's my home. And I'm certainly not leaving you here tod—"

Walker tightened his grip around my body and lifted me off my feet. His lips pressed against mine, fierce at first, but as I opened my mouth to his and he swept his tongue against mine, I let myself melt into his embrace. The kiss became softer, more languid and yielding instead of taking, and for a fraction of a second, I lost time and place and all concern for everything other than this man and his lips. I touched his cheek. His hand grazed my neck to cup the back of my head. I shifted the angle of my head to kiss him more deeply, and his arm tightened around my hips.

All too soon, Walker pulled away and set my feet back on the ground. "Take care, Cassidy DiRocco."

I watched, dumbfounded and incensed as Walker turned on his heel and left me standing at the entrance of the honeycombs. He had the nerve to kiss me like that and then walk away to implement his stupid, stubborn suicide mission. I clenched my teeth as the familiar rage inside me incinerated the remaining shock. I suppose the difference between being human and vampire didn't matter; men were simply impossible.

Walker entered the first honeycomb, shotgun cocked and covering his corners when a blur of black and glowing violet eyes scorched through the darkness. A gunshot sounded. I hit the ground and took cover behind the entryway. The violet blur disappeared to avoid the bullet spray and reappeared behind Walker. He couldn't recover in time. His shotgun was ripped from his grasp and tossed aside. The vampire, having disarmed Walker, slowed to human-pace, and I could finally discern his features.

I might not have recognized him if I hadn't seen him so intimately the night before, but even then he hadn't been this beastly. Maybe during the day vampires took another form, one even more haggard than the one they displayed when they hadn't fed. Maybe without the concealing darkness, they revealed their true nature, or maybe he was just ravenous and couldn't control his form. Whatever the reason for his complete transformation, Kaden was just barely recognizable as a vampire. He'd left the form of a man in favor of a form that more closely resembled a gargoyle or bat. The glow of his violet eyes, however, was unmistakable.

Kaden stood not twenty-five meters away, alive and well and free from his imprisonment. His jaw and muzzle were extended. His nose was flattened at the front and pinched upward at its edges. His teeth were elongated past his grinning lips, the round tips of his ears had pointed, and his irises were glowing wide over the whites in one bottomless color. His hands had transformed to full claws, not just his nails, and his feet had enlarged into talon-like appendages, as well. As he closed in on Walker, his toes clicked across the stone floor. I watched in horror, but I couldn't take my eyes off Kaden because of my sick fascination with his legs. They weren't bending in the correct direction anymore. The joints had twisted, so his knees bent back instead of forward.

I scuttled behind the doorway as fast and as silently as I could manage on my hands and knees. Kaden had escaped. Either he was more powerful than Dominic had anticipated, or someone besides myself, likely a vampire from his own coven, had betrayed Dominic, too. I didn't want to leave Walker behind, but neither of us could battle against Kaden and survive. We needed help, and there was only one vampire here who I knew might save us.

I swallowed my nerve, used the wall to help me stand despite the pitch and dip of the stone beneath my feet, and I stumbled down the tunnel back toward Dominic's rooms. I only made it another few steps, however, before a silent draft of air rushed overhead and pounded into the ground in front of me. I reared back to avoid walking smack into it. My head spun from the startled movement. The floor dipped and the walls wobbled out of reach and the world suddenly spun off its axis. The ground rushed up to meet my face.

Strong hands gripped into my shoulders. They stopped my fall and twisted me around. My breath caught. Maybe I didn't need to find Dominic. Maybe I could find help right here.

"Jillian," I said, gazing at the vampire holding me.

Jillian was just barely holding on to her human form. The tips of her ears had pointed through the long locks of golden hair, the outer corners of her nose were beginning to flare, and the tip of her nose was starting to flatten. I could see the battle waging across her face as she struggled to maintain her composure. More questions than I could possibly ever utter boiled on my tongue as I witnessed the beauty struggle not to transform into the beast, but no matter the answers I needed, there was only one at the moment that mattered.

"Can you take me to Dominic?"

"Our Master doesn't take visitors during his day rest." Jillian cocked an eyebrow. "How did you escape his rooms?"

I shook my head frantically. "It's urgent. Kaden has escaped."

Jillian's gaze flattened. "You're certain?"

"Yes, of course. I saw him myself."

"What exactly did you see?"

"I saw Kaden, like a man-sized bat, in the center room of the coven," I said pointing.

I realized afterward that if she looked to corroborate my story, she would also see Walker. My heart clenched.

"You're positive, beyond a shadow of a doubt, that the being you saw was Kaden? In our most primal form, it can be difficult to differentiate—"

"I'm positive," I insisted. "Granted, I've never seen him that completely transformed, but I know what I saw. It was Kaden."

"I see," she said coolly. Jillian reached out, her arm an indecipherable blur, hooked me around the waist, and tucked me under her arm. The walls were a sudden blur around us as we flew.

I shrieked, I couldn't help it. In Dominic's arms, I'd always faced his chest, but Jillian had simply grabbed me like a sack, my front facing outward. We zipped through tunnels, dodged around light fixtures, and cut corners by running up along the walls. Each turn and jump was harrowing, made worse by the fact that everything seemed to slip past my face by mere inches.

We halted abruptly. Jillian released her hold, and my legs buckled. I crumpled to the ground on my hands and knees, catching myself on all fours before my face bit stone.

"Cassidy," Dominic murmured. "If you were anyone else, I'd be surprised to find you had escaped my rooms. Knowing you, however, I'm surprised it took you so long."

I shook my head. The stone floor swooped to switch with the ceiling, and I took a deep breath to settle my stomach. "No time to argue," I gasped. "Kaden escaped from wherever you imprisoned him. He's in the honeycomb rooms, where you take your day rest."

Dominic materialized in a crouch next to me without sound, movement, or warning. His face was inches from my face. "We have infinite time," he growled, and his words turned into the rattling hiss that raised my hackles.

He pinched my chin between his thumb and forefinger and tipped my face to meet his gaze. Dominic was still a man, unlike Kaden or the semi-transformed Jillian, but the tension in his body, the glow of his eyes, and the harshness in his expression, made me wonder how firm a grip he was keeping on his form.

His face was suddenly buried in my neck, and he inhaled deeply. "Strange that I gave you such a high dose of morphine and I can't even smell it on you anymore. How are you metabolizing it this quickly?"

I shrugged slightly. I'd have considered telling him about my last recovery with morphine and subsequent Percocet addiction, but Jillian was watching us very carefully. "How should I know why it—"

"Ian Walker may have given her a stimulant to counteract the side effects," Jillian offered.

"Do I look stimulated?" I snapped, still swaying on all fours.

Dominic stiffened. "You brought Ian Walker into my coven?"

"I didn't bring anyone anywhere. I—"

"He was about to stake Rafe when I arrived."

"If you saw Walker, than you must have seen Kaden," I hissed at Jillian. I whirled my gaze back to Dominic's face and swayed. The floor dipped and spiraled sickeningly. Dominic didn't reach out to steady me; he let me struggle as I scraped together the tatters of my strength and balance.

"Where is Ian Walker now?" Dominic asked carefully.

I swallowed and was embarrassed to hear my voice catch when I finally spoke. "The last I saw him, Kaden had him cornered in Rafe's room. I knew I couldn't fight Kaden on my own and win, so I came looking for you. Jillian found me and I—"

"I'm only asking you once, Jillian," Dominic said softly. "Where is Walker now?"

I closed my mouth slowly, unsure which one of us was suddenly on the chopping block.

"I took care of the matter," Jillian said dismissively.

Dominic stood to face her. "Elucidate."

Jillian paused, finally sensing her danger. "I didn't have a choice. He was moments from killing Rafe."

I shook my head. "He was moments from getting killed. Kaden is—"

"Kaden is where he belongs," Jillian said coldly, as if forced to lower herself to explain her thoughts and motives to a cockroach. "It must have been me you saw in true form."

"I know what I saw!" I looked between Jillian and Dominic, trying to find the words that would convince them. "We sacrificed so much to subdue him, Dominic. I bled for you. I *suffered* for you. Don't you care if he's escaped?"

"He hasn't escaped. He's due for punishment tonight," Jillian said.

"Enough," Dominic growled.

Jillian and I fell into silence.

"If Ian Walker is dead in our coven, Bex will turn against us. She won't care how much we've been through or whether or not Kaden was scheduled for punishment. She will unquestionably come to punish *us*, and we can't afford to lose her alliance."

"We could rise against her," Jillian suggested.

"Is Ian Walker dead?" Dominic asked quietly, his voice eerily calm even as his ears pointed slightly and his nose started to flatten. His control was slipping at the thought of what Bex would do to his coven. I shuddered to imagine her power if she frightened even Dominic.

I held my breath for Jillian's response.

"I don't know for certain," Jillian said.

Dominic's nose completely flattened, and his ears elongated into high points. He took a deep breath and his features retracted again. I inched back, trying to gain a slight buffer should he completely lose his grip.

"You don't know for certain?" Dominic repeated slowly.

"I prevented him from killing Rafe, but when I found *this* one had escaped"—Jillian pointed to me—"I brought her to you, as you instructed."

"Don't throw me under the bus," I growled. "I asked for Dominic the moment you found me."

"To save yourself," Jillian hissed.

"To save us all," I hissed back.

"Silence, both of you," Dominic warned again. "If you're not certain, I'll check for myself."

"Good luck finding his body," Kaden rattled from the doorway.

I only glimpsed the horror of Kaden's completely transformed, blood-slicked gargoyle features for a split second before his form streaked into the room, charging me. I screamed. Dominic disappeared, and within a blink of an eye, he reappeared in front of me, shielding my body. Kaden plowed into him, and the force of his speed smashed Dominic into the stone wall behind us.

Kaden reared over Dominic. His gleaming gargoyle claw slashed down to impale him, but Kaden was bowled over by another blur. Kaden landed a few feet away with Jillian on top of him. She reared back to strike but was much too slow, slower than both Kaden and Dominic. I could actually see the movement of her arm as it slashed through the air. Kaden tossed her aside before her blow could land, and her head snapped back into the stone. When she crumpled to the ground, her hair a rioting halo around her, she didn't get back up.

Before Kaden could recover, Dominic rushed him. He flattened Kaden on the floor, one transformed claw tight around his neck. Kaden attempted to dislodge Dominic's grip, but the more he struggled, the deeper Dominic pressed him into the stone. The ground cracked in growing spider faults around them as Kaden's struggles turned to panic, and Dominic applied more pressure.

"Who helped you escape?" Dominic growled. His voice was gravelly, like the lining of his throat had been shredded by razors.

Kaden laughed. "This coven is already mine. These vampires are already mine. You can't keep me imprisoned here when they all want me free."

"Allegiance is fickle," Dominic said, crushing Kaden deeper into the stone. "Obviously. Being Master is more than having a faction of support."

"It's not a faction when you've gained the entire coven," Kaden said, laughing. "When you die, your reign will fall to me."

Dominic laughed. "When who dies?" he asked, and he plunged his claw deep into Kaden's chest, just below his sternum. He jerked his hand up to reach Kaden's heart.

Kaden's body spasmed. He turned his head to look at Jillian, and the desperation in his human eyes made my breath catch.

I didn't even see a hint of her movement. Jillian had been an un-conscious heap in the corner, having lost her round with Kaden, and in the very next instant, her body disappeared. A sharp, deep pain im-paled through my back. I was lifted in midair, and something twisted inside me as I dangled. I coughed a spray of blood.

"Dominic," I managed to gurgle through the blood gathered in my throat, but I didn't need to say anything.

Dominic was already frozen, his hand still buried elbow-deep in Kaden's chest. He lifted his head and met my eyes, but it wasn't until his gaze flicked behind me that his expression shifted to shocked horror.

Chapter 13

"Jillian?" Dominic asked slowly, breathlessly.

Jillian's talons pierced my back between my shoulder blades, and with her incredible strength, she held me off the ground as I tried to scream and kick away from her. The movement only made me sway as I dangled. I coughed harder.

"Release Kaden," Jillian ordered. "Now."

"As your Master, I command you to set Cassidy aside, unharmed. We can still discuss this, but if you kill her, I will kill you."

"We've had enough discussion. You're unbendable," Jillian said behind me, her voice measured. "Step away from Kaden and leave him unharmed, or I'll tear out Cassidy's spine."

"You'll regret this decision, Jillian," Dominic said, his voice equally measured. I suspected that both were attempting to calm the other. "Kaden thinks he's adopting the Master's power on the Leveling, but he would be much more powerful by now if that was the case. Don't trust his delusion, Jillian. He'll never be more powerful than I. I'm still your Master."

A low, deep rattling growl vibrated through Jillian's body. Her claw imbedded inside me vibrated, too. I shrieked, coughing more blood and writhing from the sharp, needle-like pain of her claws tearing through my insides.

"I have no Master," she hissed. "You killed him, and I became my own Master."

"This is still about Desirius? I'm sorry for your pain, but if I hadn't killed him, his coven would have exposed us to the humans. I'm sorry a vampire from your own coven didn't inherit his reign, but you're my vampire now, and I—"

"The truth is here, right in front of your face, and you still don't see it. You still don't see *me*," Jillian said, laughing, but the bitterness in her voice was thick and biting. "*I* inherited Desirius's reign. Kaden isn't adopting your Master's power on the Leveling. *I am*. If you had died under the sun like you were supposed to die Sunday night, I would have already been Master and the world would know of our rightful existence."

Dominic stared at Jillian, visibly shocked. I didn't think vampires had the range of emotions to be shocked. So many times Dominic seemed more animal than human, more rabid than empathetic, but a rabid animal doesn't have expectations, and when those expectations aren't met, they don't feel betrayed. Dominic, however, looked distraught.

He shook his head. "You knew I didn't return to the coven Sunday night? And you didn't come to my aid?"

"Knew? I planned it that way."

"But I thought—"

"We know what you thought," Kaden said. A slow grin twisted his lips. "How could I overpower you on my own? I'm just barely your equal."

"I saw you," Dominic insisted, looking down at Kaden. "Just before the ambush, I saw the glow of your purple eyes."

Jillian tutted. "Of course he was there, but he wasn't alone. He was with me."

A cold, tight expression washed over Dominic's half-transformed features. He looked still and calculating, but he must have sliced something inside of Kaden, because he screamed.

Jillian twisted her hand inside of me, and I shrieked.

Dominic jerked his gaze back to us. Kaden had already recovered from whatever wound Dominic had inflicted, but I was going into shock. My teeth were chattering and my body was going numb.

Dominic narrowed his eyes to slits. "Jillian—"

"Don't worry," Kaden interrupted. His voice escaped in a painful rasp. "If Jillian kills her, I'll bring her back."

Dominic stared at him, dumbfounded. "You can't complete a transformation. Even if Jillian *has* adopted the Master's power, she can't perform a transformation until I'm dead."

"So you've been telling us for decades," Kaden spat.

"I haven't told you anything. That is simple fact." Dominic looked up, horrified. "Jillian, tell him the truth. Tell him that only a Master can transform a night blood."

"We don't know for sure that—"

"You've witnessed the horror caused by coven-turned night bloods! I pulled you from that hell! Tell him that—"

"Decide," Jillian interrupted harshly. "Step away from Kaden, and I will step away from Cassidy. Or remain where you are and kill her. Choose."

Jillian waited a moment, but Dominic hesitated, thinking on his next move. She twisted her claw a little deeper.

I gasped and twitched.

Dominic stared deep into Jillian's eyes and said, "You will release Cassidy and step away from her, now."

I held my breath, waiting to drop to the ground. Jillian's arm shook from the force of resisting the command, but the moment passed, her arm steadied, and I remained impaled on her claws.

Dominic's eyes widened.

She tore something from my body, and it landed on the ground with a wet, suctioned sound. I gasped and coughed and screamed and coughed up more blood.

Jesus, I thought, *don't let that be my spine or an organ or anything important*. As if she could have torn something out of my body that wasn't important. I laughed slightly, and coughed harder at my own twisted humor.

Dominic's chest vibrated with a loud, rattling growl. The sound grew cacophonous and vibrated throughout the entire room.

"Calm yourself, Dominic," Jillian warned. "This is simple. If you want Cassidy to live, step away from Kaden," she said coldly. "Now."

"I could tear you limb from limb before you could think to scream," Dominic growled. The room hummed with the vibrations coming from his throat.

"You could try," Jillian said blandly, "but not before I snap Cassidy's spine from her back."

"I trusted you," Dominic hissed. "Together, we've pulled this coven back from the brink of several civil wars, but now *you're* leading them against *me?*"

"It didn't have to come to this," Jillian stated, not pleading or defensive. She knew she'd crossed a line, had in fact pole-vaulted clear over it, and was unashamed. "I've warned you many times through-out the last few years that someone would rise if you didn't change along with the tide. The coven is tired of hiding our existence. We want our freedom!"

"Someone, yes, but not you." Dominic laughed, sickened. "Many times, the tide of the coven is not in the best interest of the coven. Many times, you must fight for them by straining against them. You must steer the tide in a different direction to—"

"You're wrong. The coven is sick of hunting in secret. *I* am sick of hunting in secret. We are predators, and our true place is to rule this city, not cower in hiding beneath it."

Dominic made a frustrated noise in the back of his throat. "We are predators of the *night*. We hide because we're nocturnal and vulnerable during the day. Humans may be our food after sunset, but they are our greatest risk during the day. How will you protect an entire coven when the sun rises without anonymity?"

"I've heard this speech from you many times, but it is nothing but words. I believe in you, and although I've forgiven you for killing Desirius, I can't forgive you for keeping us imprisoned here. Desirius's actions were twisted; he tortured and killed his closest and truest vampires. He tortured and nearly killed me before you saved us, but I supported his cause to free us. He was the wrong man for the right cause. I believe that you could be the right man to lead that cause, but if you refuse, then I will lead it myself."

Dominic shook his head slowly, as if the weight of her words was crushing him. "You're wrong. This will destroy our coven like it destroyed yours."

"You refuse to see an entire coven of vampires, myself included, who would stand by you no matter the cause, if only you would stand by us in this. And that's why we're here now, because you refuse to listen or change or bend for the benefit of this coven," Jillian said emphatically. "Step away from Kaden."

"Jillian Allister," Dominic intoned, and I could hear the power in his voice as he linked his mind to hers. "Place Cassidy on the ground and step away from her."

Jillian's body shook with the effort to resist his command. "Step away from Kaden, Dominic Lysander. Now."

Her own power was equally strong. I could feel their mental battle heat the air between them. Neither Dominic nor Jillian stepped away.

Jillian laughed harshly. "I'm your equal, Lysander. Step away from Kaden before we both lose what is most precious." She lifted me higher, and I felt the long, slow slide of her tongue. Her chest rattled. "I understand why you want her. She's delicious. But whether she dies now or later, it doesn't matter. The coven will sense your struggle and come to feast anyway."

The movement of her laughter was sharp inside my back. I tried to bite back a reaction, but her talons were so sharp and the pain was so overwhelming that my whimpers and moans and gasps were involuntary. I writhed, suspended in midair, and couldn't think of how to survive this. After everything I *had* survived—my parents' deaths, supporting my brother, losing Adam, the gunshot wound, and recovering from Percocet addiction—this was how I would die, caught in the crossfire of a vampire rebellion. This wasn't even my fight. My anger, that churning, unfathomable depth of seething rage that always boiled beneath the surface, erupted. I couldn't move, and I couldn't do anything to physically channel the rage, but Jillian had just ingested my blood. My rage flowed over me with the same vibrating, enflamed mental power that flowed from Dominic and Jillian.

Dominic was silent. He stared at Jillian for a long moment before shifting his gaze to me. I don't know what he saw in my eyes, if my expression had anything to do with his decision or if the potential he saw in me as his night blood overrode common sense, but he slipped his arm from Kaden's chest, stood slowly, and stepped away as Jillian had commanded.

I managed to open my mouth and uttered a low rasp. "No, don't listen—"

Jillian ripped her arm from my back and dropped me to the ground. I crumpled on my side and watched as she appeared behind Dominic, seemingly from thin air. Her claw, which she had just ripped out from inside of me, skewered through Dominic. She pounded her bloodied hand through his back and all four of her bat-like gargoyle talons punctured Dominic's chest. I looked down at my own undamaged chest, and I realized just how much she'd restrained herself while threatening me.

Could anyone, even a vampire, survive that? I thought. I winced as the next thought slammed home. *Without Dominic, would I survive?*

Kaden rose up from the stone, no worse for Dominic's wear, and faced Dominic while Jillian held him immobile. Dominic coughed, and blood spewed from his mouth. Drops clung to his lower lip. His blood was more viscous and darker than mine, perhaps because it wasn't constantly flowing through his veins.

Jillian jerked back on Dominic's head to better expose his chest, and Kaden pulled back his claw to strike.

We didn't have anything left with which to fight, but that didn't mean we couldn't survive.

"Jillian Allister," I said, and I poured every drop of rage and loathing I could summon into the syllables of her name. The moment the words left my mouth, I could feel the connection bind us. Dominic had played his cards tight to the chest as I'd suspected, so Jillian was as unprepared for me as Dominic had been that first time. She might have reflected Dominic's commands with her metal mirror, but she didn't have anything in place to deflect mine.

Her eyes widened in horrified astonishment.

Dominic jerked his gaze between Jillian and me, and I could see the instant he remembered my connection and exactly what I was capable of. "No," he whispered. "Jillian's too powerful to be entranced by you."

"Release Dominic Lysander immediately," I commanded.

Jillian's face fell slack, and as per my direct command, she released Dominic.

Dominic dropped to the stone floor, much like I had, and crumpled onto his side in a heap of black designer clothing and blood. He didn't move.

"Jillian Allister," I continued my command, "grab Kaden and lock him and yourself inside the silver cage. Now."

Kaden lunged for me in a blur of glowing violet eyes and hissing fangs, but Jillian was faster and more powerful. She rushed him before he could reach me, and they both disappeared with the force of her incredible speed. A loud *clang* sounded behind me. I jolted, but by the time I managed to turn my head, the barred door of the silver cage had already slammed shut with Jillian and Kaden locked inside.

Jillian stood silently, dumbly, waiting for her next command. Kaden raged next to her, pounding on the bars, hissing and growling and rattling the cage in a roaring tantrum. Smoke steamed from under his claws where his hand wrapped around the silver bars. He shrieked and yanked away from the cage. He stared down at his burned palms and then glared up at me, and I could see the variety of deaths he imagined for me reflected in the heat of his fury.

With Jillian and Kaden effectively detained, I turned back to Dominic. He still hadn't moved. Although I could move my legs, muscles in my back were damaged or missing, and I couldn't support myself. Everything hurt. My entire body was in screaming, chattering, unbearable agony, but I dug my elbows into the stone and dragged myself next to Dominic until my head was even with his.

I slumped next to him. I was exhausted and spent and if I admitted the truth to myself, likely dying. Dominic's eyes were open and focused on something behind me.

"Dominic," I whispered, terrified that I was too late. How would I escape the coven and survive the night without his help?

A moment of still silence passed. I held my breath, and then like a miracle, his eyes shifted to focus on me.

I exhaled in relief. "You're not dead."

"Not yet," Dominic whispered. Blood poured from his mouth when he spoke.

I winced back, but the blood spread faster than I could move. It seeped around my face as it pooled on the stone. Where it flowed over the scrapes on my cheek, I could feel the heat of it healing.

"Why aren't you healing like before, like when you were battling Kaden?" I asked. "Why aren't you recovering this time?"

"Kaden wasn't next to inherit my Master's power. Jillian is, so unlike Kaden, the wounds she inflicted are lethal." Dominic choked on more blood before catching his breath. "Without feeding, I'll die in a matter of minutes, Cassidy. My final death."

"No, you can recover from this," I insisted.

"Jillian will keep the powers she's gained thus far, and the rest of the power will die with me." Dominic continued as if I hadn't spoken. "The coven will come to either finish me, challenge Jillian, or claim Jillian as their new Master, but in any scenario, they are likely already on their way."

I blinked. "The entire coven will come here? Now?"

"Yes, and I'll be dead. You need to heal yourself as best you can with my blood and leave. You—" Dominic coughed, and although I wanted to ease back from the gore of his struggle, I needed to lean closer to hear his words. "You still have the necklace?"

"Yes, but—"

"Take it, and use the blood I'm hemorrhaging for yourself. I wish I had more time. You would have been—"

More coughs racked his body. I waited for him to gather his composure and continue, but he couldn't stop coughing this time. Blood poured in a steady flow from his chest wound, hemorrhaging in a strange, thick viscosity that seeped instead of pumped onto the floor around us. My skin burned from its healing as it soaked into the superficial slices and nicks on my arms and legs.

The other vampires were approaching. Their growling rattles and the clicks of their talons scraping against stone grew cacophonous as they closed in. I opened the vial of blood still hanging from my neck and stared at the shining crimson liquid inside, reluctant to pour it on my injuries. With the coven approaching, the healing properties of Dominic's blood would only prolong the inevitable.

"Do you hear them?" Kaden hissed from across the room, echoing my thoughts. "Go ahead. Use his blood to heal, and see how far you can run, little one." Kaden laughed.

I shifted my gaze back to Dominic. His coughing fit was starting to subside, but so were his breaths and bleeding and movement. He was dying, and even with his blood, without him, I wouldn't survive. I needed him. I hated not being able to save myself, but I'd always believed in facts. And the fact was that I would not survive the next five minutes without Dominic Lysander.

I twisted the lid off the vial and poured Dominic's blood down my back to heal as much of myself as possible. The heat of its healing scalded my wounds, and I felt some of the strength return to muscles as they regenerated. But it wasn't enough. It wasn't nearly enough considering the extent of my injuries, but I didn't need to heal completely to survive.

I smashed the empty vial on the stone floor and sliced my wrist open with the jagged edge of the broken glass. Blood welled from the wound. I massaged it to gain a steady flow and held my wrist over Dominic's mouth, streaming the blood down his throat.

Watching my blood flow from my wrist into his mouth made me nauseous and woozy. Black starbursts dotted my vision. I closed my eyes and focused on the chill of the stone floor beneath my cheek to ground myself. A minute passed, and Dominic still remained unconscious. I bit my lip. The vampires were approaching, hundreds of vampires who would release Jillian and Kaden and feast on me. I could order Jillian to protect me, but there was an entire coven of vampires against only one of her. I bit my lip harder, feeling desperation, like the approaching vampires, closing in from all sides.

"Dominic," I whispered. I scooted closer to him, ignoring the tacky cling of blood suctioning my skin to the stone floor, until my body spooned the side of his. "Your coven is coming. This is your chance. You are the only one who can save them from Jillian and Kaden. You are the only one who can save me."

The vibrations of the coven's approach shook the floor beneath us. I flexed my wrist over his mouth to increase its flow, and blood poured into his mouth.

He didn't stir.

"You said that life often takes more than it gives, but you were born to lead this coven, Dominic. Life gave you this coven and this opportunity to prove to them that you are their rightful Master. You are greedy and single-mindedly selfish, as I recall, and you have the means, power, and authority to take exactly what you want. Isn't that what you said to me?" I leaned even closer, so my lips pressed against the shell of his ear. "But I've never been one to believe in words. You want me? You want to lead this coven? Prove it. Dominic Lysander, I dare you to heal stronger with my blood, survive this, and fucking prove it! Take back what is yours!"

I'd meant my words as a taunt or pep talk, but between our shared blood and my command, our minds connected. I felt the frayed thread of his will stiffen with resolve as my words shot through his defenses and into his brain. His eyes snapped open. They glowed a luminescent blue, and he stared at me with inhuman stillness, like his thoughts were a language that I couldn't comprehend.

His hand suddenly clamped around my wrist with crushing force. He pressed my hand to his mouth, bit into my wrist, tore my veins open, and guzzled my blood.

"Dominic," I whispered, unsure if I should command him to stop, and if I did, trying to think of a phrase that wouldn't endanger me if he reflected it.

Before I could decide what to do, Dominic rolled on top of me. His weight pressed my butchered back hard into the stone. My wound sizzled as it suctioned into the puddle of his blood and began to heal. I screamed. I struggled against him and the burning snap of pain, but Dominic pushed my head to the side and sank his fangs deep into my neck.

The pain was sharp and immediate and tore away my breath. His lips clamped on the wound to suck my blood, but instead of the pain turning to exquisite pleasure, like it had before, it just felt like horrible, aching, throbbing pain.

I pushed at Dominic's shoulder and yanked hard on his hair in a final, desperate attempt to gain his attention, but my efforts were weak and he was astronomically strong. Eventually, even that movement was too much for my body, and I felt my arms drop away from him. My knuckles scraped against stone as they fell limply to the ground.

His fangs sank in deeper. He tore my neck open a little bit wider, and I heard a noise escape from me. I felt myself twitch in pain. The attack lasted mere seconds, but he was efficient and experienced and ruthless. Mere seconds was all the time he needed to drain the rest of my blood. I couldn't move. I couldn't feel. My mind drifted, and I saw everything as if from above, hovering over our bodies and watching from the rafters.

Hundreds of vampires entered the room and flanked around us. Dominic was holding me with an arm under my back and my neck clamped in his mouth, but as his coven approached, he dropped my neck to growl at the coven, like a dog will drop its bone to protect it from being taken.

I fell limply to the floor underneath him. My neck was bent at a harsh angle. The wound was still pumping blood and spilling in a creeping circle around us to mix with his, but Dominic didn't notice my neck or the blood; he growled at the enclosing vampires. The noise began as the same low growl that I'd heard rattle from all their throats, but the noise quickly expanded, vibrating through the room in a terrifying, encompassing, awesome cacophony that shook my roots.

Most of the vampires shrank back, instantly recognizing Dominic as their rightful Master and bending to him. Some fought the compulsion for a moment or two, testing whether he was still strong enough and powerful enough to lead and protect the coven, but the majority of those vampires succumbed to Dominic after a moment, as well. They bowed their heads, hunched in on themselves, and backed away from the room in supplication.

A little over a dozen vampires stepped forward through the cacophony and stood in front of us in a tight semicircle, refusing to supplicate, denying Dominic as their Master. The rebels. They were all fully transformed into the gargoyle, beast-like version of themselves. Their eyes glowed brightly in the dim room and seemed to glow more luminescent as they growled back. Their own growls mixed into an equally awesome and compelling rattle. Together, theirs were almost as moving as Dominic's, but Dominic didn't flinch. He hovered over my body, spread himself over me in a strangely protective stance, and stood against them.

The first rebel attacked from his left. Dominic let the vampire approach from the crowd, but once separated, he met the attack. Dominic's movements were faster than Kaden and Jillian, faster than I could comprehend. I couldn't even track his exact movements, only their devastating effects.

Dominic's hand blurred through the air, and the vampire's chest exploded in a spray of blood. Their eyes met, and even impaled by Dominic's arm, the vampire didn't bow down. Holding his gaze, Dominic twisted his wrist while still inside his chest, and the vampire's knees buckled. He crumpled to the ground, twitching and gasping.

Another rebel attacked, and a third and fourth, until a swarm swelled from the hallway, charged into the room, and crashed into Dominic. Dominic, however, crashed right back, and the faster and stronger they swarmed, the more powerfully he stood against their undertow until a ring of incapacitated vampires was strewn at his feet.

One of the vampires inched closer to me while Dominic fought. I felt myself trying to open my mouth, to warn Dominic, but I couldn't form the words. Nothing was left inside of me that could speak or move. Dominic was distracted by three other vampires, and I couldn't do anything but watch my own death approach from the sidelines.

The approaching vampire knelt beside me, and I recognized the burns across his face from my last visit to the coven. He was Neil, the young vampire who had singed himself on the silver bars trying to attack me. Neil gazed at me with his starving otherworldly eyes. My head was still bent backward where Dominic had dropped me, baring my esophagus like an offering. Neil rubbed his nose over the front of my neck and released a restrained, pain-filled exhale against my blood-soaked, clammy-cold skin.

Dominic froze for a fraction of a heartbeat, recognizing the movement and noise and intention behind it. Without further thought or hesitation, Dominic lashed out at the vampires currently fighting him with his long, lethal talons. He ripped out all three of their throats with one swipe of his hand. Blood sprayed in an arching wave, and their spines gleamed through the blood and hanging tissue.

Dominic was beside me before the three vampires hit the ground. I could feel the rush of his movement whip over my face as he flew, collided with Neil, and smashed him on his back into the ground next to me. Neil struggled and whipped at Dominic with his talons, but Dominic dodged his movements easily, punched his hand into Neil's stomach, and jerked up into his chest cavity. Neil screamed, but Dominic didn't even flinch. He twisted his wrist nearly elbow-deep despite Neil's squealing pleas.

"No," Neil hissed, his voice keening. A shocked, affronted expression lit his face as he stared at Dominic. "You can't. You're not my Mast—"

Dominic tore out Neil's heart.

Deep red, nearly black, ropes of blood stretched from the gaping wound in Neil's chest to his heart raised aloft in Dominic's hand. The blood ropes broke after a moment and dripped in long strands from the heart, down Dominic's blood-soaked hand, and to the stone floor.

Neil struggled for a frantic, ineffective moment, attempting to snatch his heart from Dominic, but Dominic restrained his efforts with one hand and held the heart out of reach with the other. Neil's movements became lethargic and strained. His body jerked involuntarily. His eyes glazed and his lax, unseeing expression dropped to the side to face me.

Neil's gargoyle-like features weren't any less horrifying in repose, but his expression was still human-like enough to chill my heart. Neil had felt betrayal and fear and uncertainty at the very end, but he'd also looked desperate to recover his heart. I had a horrible, sneaking suspicion that if someone were to shove the heart back into its chest cavity, Neil could still potentially recover.

The hundreds of surrounding vampires shrieked, and a low rattle hummed through the room. The few whose throats had been slashed were healing quickly, and although bloody, their throats were formed enough to function again. They bore their fangs, and joined in the vibrating growl that spread through the coven. They shrieked and chittered like the frantic dissonance of insects.

I would have covered my ears if I could still move. I watched them form a tight semicircle around us, becoming a united force of will and power and strength. Even the majority who had initially shrunk back from Dominic were swept up in the current. Rage and solidarity infused them with courage, and they joined in the attack.

Dominic sheltered me under the protection of his body, lifted Neil's heart high over his head, and belted out a blasting roar that shook the very foundation of the coven. From one heartbeat to the next, Dominic transformed from his human-like vampire form to the gargoyle-like version. Gone were his captivating blue eyes, replaced by glassy, black shark eyes. His fangs elongated, his ears pointed, his nose flattened, his forehead thickened, and his muzzle extended until he barely resembled himself. This massive, rabid, lethal creature crouched over my body, protecting me and claiming me as his in front of his entire coven. To cross me was to cross him. And no one would dare cross him.

Every single vampire, including the dozen rebels who had stood firm against his rule, were knocked back by the force of Dominic's roar. They stumbled to regain their footing, hissing frantically to each other, but they reluctantly kept their distance.

Holding his crouched stance over me, Dominic met each of their eyes. He growled, and the noises that escaped his throat were like aftershocks to the initial blast. The vampires continued to stumble back, some unwillingly and others in complete submission, but not one could withstand the force of his power.

Dominic held the heart a little higher. "Anyone else?" he asked, and his voice scraped through his throat with a very inhuman, gravelly growl.

The vampires each averted their gazes. Even Kaden bowed his head, quelled without Jillian's lead. I doubt Jillian would have bowed her head. She might have been the only vampire in the coven with the ability to overthrow Dominic, but she was still staring limply at the wall, waiting for my next command.

"Anyone else?" Dominic repeated.

The vampires shrank further into shadow, hunched in on themselves from the weight of Dominic's voice. No one rose against him. Even if they still wanted to, and it looked as if a few were straining against the will that Dominic imposed on them, not one vampire was strong enough to act. Their mouths trembled and their fingers locked into fists and some of them even looked to Jillian for guidance or action, but they couldn't defy him.

"I want all of you to remember this moment," Dominic said, and his voice was harsh, like a cheese grater against my temple. I felt its grazing, and I wasn't even the target of his command. The surrounding vampires hunched further in on themselves and shuddered. "I am your Master. Even as the Leveling approaches, I continue to safeguard this coven at my own peril. Some of you would rather use our temporary weakness for your own gain instead of pooling resources to strengthen us. Even against these adversaries, against vampires I trusted with my life, I still fight for you.

"I want you to remember this moment because should another rebellion rise, although my own strength may appear to decrease, I will not be vulnerable to anyone else's rule; I have resources to counter such an attack. Should another rebellion rise, I will be less inclined to forgive."

Dominic threw Neil's body and his heart to the ground at their feet. A few vampires from the crowd carefully scooped up his remains and quickly disappeared into the hallway. The remaining vampires slowly exited. They eased out of the room without turning their backs or relaxing their guard, and once they reached the hallway, they fled in a blur of speed.

Dominic held his pose over me. He was powerful and massive and it wasn't just his gargoyle form that gave him that weight, although it certainly helped. The strength of his will and mind and body became one leading force that was irrefutable. His growls urged the last remaining rebels from the room. I could see him with my own eyes—the drowning sharpness of his midnight gaze and the immense strength in his arms and body over me was spellbinding, like the beauty and uncertainty of encountering a tiger—but I could also see both of us from above, from my vantage on the rafters.

I felt myself slip further away, my spirit dampened by the force of his power. My view from above was becoming the more predominant one. I couldn't feel or move or breathe, although I could smell a faint freshness, like the content comfort of coming home.

Dominic didn't break his gaze or retreat from his protective stance over me, but I think he could feel my passing. I think it troubled him. He brushed the pad of his thumb against my bare shoulder. The comfort of his touch, of a wild animal's concern and protective possession over me, brought me back slightly. My vision from the rafters receded, and I could feel the dull pounding of my injuries as if from behind a thick cushion.

From my strange double vision, I watched Dominic's back muscles tense and his lip curl back in a grim snarl. He had expected me to stir from his touch. He had expected me to moan or respond, but I suppose even a night blood's capacity for blood loss had its limits. I'd reached mine.

When the last vampire departed, Dominic gathered me in his arms and held my body against his chest. I couldn't move to wrap my arms around him or support my head, so my arms and neck arched back, still grazing the floor as he lifted my back. Blood from his bite leaked over my jaw and behind my ear. This close, I could feel the vibration of the rattle in his chest before sound emerged from his throat.

"I can taste the thready squeeze and contraction of your heart, Cassidy DiRocco," he murmured against my neck. The whisper of his breath caressed my skin when he spoke my name. "You are mine, and I don't care if it takes an eternity to receive your forgiveness. At least you'll be alive for me to receive it."

No, I thought, not liking where his thoughts were leading. *Find a better solution or let me die, damn it! I don't want to be a vampire.*

But I couldn't respond aloud, so my opinion went unspoken and unheeded.

Dominic pressed closer, rubbing his cheek along my cheek. "Thank you for saving me and for helping me keep my coven." He laughed slightly, and the human vibrations of his laughter coming from the depths of his gargoyle throat were deep and rattling, like his growl but without the intent. "Thank you for having my back."

Dominic shifted my body, so my head was supported by the bend of his arm. He lifted his right arm to his mouth and tore open the veins at his wrist with his own fangs. Blood poured over his forearm. He stared at me, then at his arm, and back at me for a moment, undecided, and I wondered if he was having second thoughts about keeping me. He hesitated with his arm raised, the blood dripping over his entire hand, wrist, and lower arm in a thick crimson glove. I braced myself for him to drip the blood into my mouth, but part of me, a denied, unheard part that crept out unexpectedly from the darker shadows of my heart, braced herself for him to change his mind.

Dominic's arm finally lowered, but not to my mouth as I'd expected. He wrapped his arm under my back, so his dripping, blood-gloved hand grazed the wound I'd sustained from Jillian. The wound hadn't completely healed even after using the vial or being soaked in the puddle of his blood. It was too deep, and his blood hadn't reached the more extensive, debilitating injuries inside.

I couldn't feel the pressure of his fingers against the torn skin, but I could feel the burn of his blood mingling with mine. It began as a dull tingling on the skin around the wound and quickly escalated to a deep, unrelenting inferno.

The pressure of his hand became unbearable. My body twitched.

"Yes," he breathed. His own voice sounded strained. "Come back to me, Cassidy."

His cheek grazed over my skin until our noses slid against one another, and he stared at me from inches away with his solid, midnight, gargoyle eyes. I didn't feel the pull of his gaze capturing mine, but I felt a different kind of pull, a hypnotism that had nothing and everything to do with his strength of will.

He breached the mere centimeters of air and breath and anticipation between us and pressed his lips firmly against mine. My entire being rushed back into my own body. In a single blink, the double vision was gone; I could taste and breathe and hear and want again, but I could also feel.

The pressure of his lips was overwhelming, but not nearly enough to wash away the pain completely, like his bite. I understood why he'd chosen to kiss me—my body couldn't sustain further blood loss—but my injuries coupled with the burning of his healing blood was anguish. I shrieked and writhed against him, desperate to find an escape. Dominic kept a steady pressure on my lips, nipping and licking and sucking and moving in the rhythmic motion that curled my toes. Although distracting, his kiss was like a Band-Aid for a torn limb. It couldn't staunch the blood. It couldn't salve the burn. It could only serve as a temporary, makeshift solution that would eventually succumb to the very injury it was attempting to maintain.

"I know this hurts," Dominic whispered against my lips, his tone calm and deliberate. "Find something to anchor your mind, and just breathe."

His hand slipped inside my back, deep into the wound to heal the torn muscle and flesh and organs from the inside. My breath caught, and I couldn't think beyond the twitching writhe of agony.

"You can survive this," Dominic growled, throwing my own words back at me. "Do you hear me, Cassidy? You have survived worse and have lived to bear the scars of others' betrayals. You'll live to bear this one, too."

I tried to breathe with his hand inside of me and choked instead. His fingers caressed a muscle inside my back, places that fingers should never touch, and as he shifted his hand to caress an adjacent muscle, it burned even hotter.

"How did it feel when you realized that your source had betrayed you all those years ago? How did it feel when the first bullet was fired, and you realized that you'd placed your friends at risk, friends who'd trusted you and were willing to put themselves at risk on your judgment? And your judgment had been so terribly wrong. They would die because you were wrong," Dominic said harshly, pressing deeper into my back. "Can you still taste the bitterness through to your core? Does it still rot inside of you and taint your judgment of others? Who can you trust when you can't even trust yourself?"

I finally managed to squeeze in a breath, but it wasn't enough. It wasn't nearly enough.

"Is that why you have such a crisis justifying why, despite your better self, you actually trust me?"

I felt the steady, constant anger that always boiled below the surface rise up and ground me. I knew what Dominic was trying to do, as I had done for him, and it was working. I could feel my mind shifting from the insanity of unrelenting pain to a more focused state of mind, but the pain was too much even for my temper. My vision spotted and dimmed in ebbing flashes.

Dominic continued to speak. I could see his lips moving, but I couldn't hear him anymore. The black holes swiftly expanded and melded together into one inky sheet across my eyes until the inferno across my back, the pressure of his demanding lips, and the comfort of his arms cradling my body faded into nothing.

Chapter 14

Living was sucking the life out of me. Loved ones died. Physical injuries felt like death, and emotional wounds felt like physical ones. People I'd known and trusted and confided in had betrayed me, and if I didn't check myself when my wants interfered with my morals, I might betray them. It wasn't until I was at risk of losing it that life even seemed worth having. These days, I'd been at risk of losing it more often than most, proving without a doubt, despite grief and addiction and heartache, that I wasn't ready to let go.

Someone was holding my hand. The person's fingers fit loosely between mine. An achy stab shot through my midsection, and I tightened my grip, trying to anchor myself. The pain was fleeting and disappeared almost as soon as it came, but I embraced it. I was still in pain. I was still weak and achy and recovering.

I was still human.

The hand squeezed back. "Cassidy? Are you awake, babe?" Meredith asked.

Feeling returned in ebbing waves. Although he hadn't turned me, Dominic hadn't finished healing my body, either. The pain was dull and becoming constant. I took a deep breath to manage it, the familiarity of recovery bearing over me. I never wanted to experience that again, but I'd lived. For now, that was enough.

"Can you please do *something* to make her more comfortable? This is ridiculous. She's obviously in pain," Meredith snapped.

"We must moderate her dosage until she regains consciousness, ma'am," a deep voice responded calmly, and by the patient deliberation of the voice, I'd guess this had been explained several times to Meredith already.

"She's in pain," Meredith repeated, just as deliberate. "She needs more."

"I'm fine." I forced my eyes open, and indeed, Meredith was next to my bed, holding my hand, and about to burst into tears. My voice was hoarse and scratchy. I cleared my throat. "It's all right, Meredith."

"Oh," she breathed, turning back to me. "Cassidy." Meredith sandwiched my hand in both of hers before whipping back around to face the nurse. The movement made my bed dip slightly. "More meds. Now."

"No, I said I'm fine, and I meant it." I winced as pain lanced through my back at the bed's movement.

Meredith pursed her lips. "You're the furthest thing from *fine*."

I shook my head. "Where's Walker? Is he—" I swallowed uncertainly. Dominic could hide his death so thoroughly that I'd never know the truth. "How's Walker doing?"

"Just rest, and I'm sure—"

"I need to know how he's doing, Meredith, I—"

"What you need is—"

"What the woman needs is to use her breath answering my questions, not wasting her energy fighting with you," Detective Wahl interrupted.

I glanced across the room, and Greta winked.

"Give her his damn note, not that it divulges anything. The bastard knew I'd read it," Greta muttered.

"Note?" I croaked.

"Questions?" Meredith squeaked. "What kind of questions? She solved your entire investigation for you. How many more questions could you possibly—"

"There are always questions, but they'll all keep for today. I'm content to see you still breathing, DiRocco. For now." Greta pushed away from the wall and walked along the opposite side of my bed across from Meredith. She leaned in close, so only I could hear her whisper. "And to have the *vampires* behind bars," Greta murmured. "Thank you for the tip. Brilliant."

I raised my eyebrows. "But there are still questions, after everything I risked for you?" I asked, trying to act like I knew what the hell she was talking about. God only knew what cover Dominic had fabricated for the police and press.

Greta squeezed my hand. "Don't push my patience, DiRocco. You just crawled back into my good graces."

"But pushing your patience is one of the few things I'm good at."

Greta pulled away to lock her gaze with mine, and I knew that she was having a hard time swallowing the bullshit story Dominic had fed everyone. She was mollified from having solved the case, but she was still searching for answers. And apparently, she expected those answers from me.

"Take care tonight. We can talk more tomorrow," Greta said.

I nodded. "You mentioned a note from Walker?"

Greta sighed. "Walker left without even a good-bye, without waiting until you were stable. He's not worth your worry."

Meredith stared at Greta, looking scandalized. "He saved her."

"That's debatable."

"Be that as it may, I'd like my note, thank you." My heart fluttered.

Meredith glanced at the beeping monitors. "Maybe the note can wait."

I stared at Meredith until she caved. With a heaving sigh, she opened the bedside table's drawer and pulled out a smooth, white envelope. She opened it for me, unfolded the letter, and handed it over. For a moment, I couldn't even read it. I just stared at his signature, amazed.

I never would've left without saying good-bye, but a job is
waiting for me back home. You know what a Master pain in
the ass bosses can be. I'm so sorry to leave your bedside. I
doubt the city will need my tracking expertise again
anytime soon since the "animal attacks" were just punks
with claw knuckles, but you're more than welcome to write
a feature on the world's best environmentalist. It could be
your Pulitzer, so don't wait too long to begin your research.

D. Walker

I stared at his signature, and an enormous, suffocating weight lifted from my chest. Walker was alive. He wasn't here and he was facing the wrath of his own Master, but he was alive. Not to mention he'd left me a note, a beautifully informative note. I felt a smile spread across my face even as tears dripped over my cheeks and pooled beneath my chin.

"Cassidy, babe? You okay?" Meredith whispered.

I swiped at the tears with my fingers, and to my embarrassment, they were trembling. "I'm just relieved. I thought maybe"—I cleared my throat—"I couldn't bear the thought that he might have—"

"That he left without saying good-bye?" Greta finished for me. She snorted.

I nodded, letting Greta live with her own conclusion.

"It sounds like he regretted leaving. You two really hit it off this week," Greta said.

I shrugged.

"It's good to have that kind of friend, someone who's dependable and loyal." Greta began, and I could tell she was steering the conversation in a particular direction. "Walker found you pretty quickly at the scene, faster even than my squad car."

Ah, I thought, *there it is.* Greta didn't believe Walker either. "Walker found me? I only remember calling you."

"You managed to call Walker, as well," Greta admitted. "We think you were trying to call him back when you hit my number instead."

"Oh," I said, trying not to sound too pleased. As usual, Dominic had taken care of the evidence. "Then it makes sense that he found me so quickly, if I called him first."

"Right." Greta pursed her lips, obviously not convinced. She produced something from the inside pocket of her blazer and placed it on the bedside table.

I stared, dumbfounded. "My phone!"

"Don't say I never did anything for you," She said grudgingly, and then suddenly stepped aside. "I'll see you tomorrow, DiRocco."

"I'm not sure yet, but I might be calling out sick tomorrow," I said sarcastically.

"Of that I have no doubt, but I'll have tons of questions for you by then," She said, her tone wary, but she smiled on her way out. "And this time, I'll bring the recorder."

I grimaced. "It's a date."

Meredith and I waited until Greta shut the hospital room door behind her before speaking.

"She's not happy with Walker," Meredith stated flatly.

I snorted. "You said it yourself. He saved me."

She nodded. "Obviously, but Greta's asking questions like he didn't, and she's particularly pissed that Walker skipped town before she could 'interrogate his ass.' That's a direct quote."

"He didn't skip town," I said, shaking the letter at her. "Duty called."

"Right, like Greta cares if the man has a career." Meredith shook her head.

I smiled. "Speaking of difficult men, have you called Nathan? I'm sure he's freaking out by now if you haven't." I reached for my phone, clean now of blood and dirt and all evidence of my encounter with Kaden. Clean now of all evidence of any sort if Greta had anything to do with it. I frowned at my phone, wondering about the voice mails and texts Greta might have snooped through.

"Who do you need me to call?" Meredith asked.

"My brother, Nathan." I frowned harder, looking at two measly missed calls, neither from Nathan. "If you didn't yet, someone must have. He hasn't called or texted me once, the bum."

Meredith didn't say anything. I glanced up from my phone, about to complain about uncaring, ungrateful brothers, but her expression killed the words before they passed my lips.

"Your brother," she repeated.

"Yeah," I said carefully. "We were supposed to meet up yesterday. Considering the stories I've been covering lately, I thought he'd be worried about me." I looked down at my phone. "Although now, I'm not so sure he cares at all."

"Ok. I'll call your brother," Meredith said. "Nathan, is it?" She was agreeing with me, but it didn't sound like agreement. It sounded like appeasement.

I blinked. "You're kidding, right? Of course, Nathan. My hair. My height. My eyes. Nose ring. Basically a funnier, more pleasant and compassionate, male version of me?"

Meredith stared at me.

"You've known my brother just as long as you've known me," I said, dumbfounded.

"Sure," she said. She stood from the bed. "I'll be right back, Cassidy. I could really use some coffee after the day I've had. Do you need anything?"

I shook my head, watching her watch me with very careful consideration.

She squeezed my hand firmly. "I'll be right back."

Meredith left the room, and dread tightened through my stomach, aching worse than the real pain of my physical injuries. I could only think of one scenario in which Meredith would suffer from memory loss, and only one creature who could possibly confirm my suspicion. Although Meredith's scrambled memory was worrisome of its own accord—I wondered how much a memory could be altered before permanent brain damage incurred—a worse question haunted the rest of my evening: Why would the memory of my brother be the memory in need of alteration?

I keyed up the contacts on my phone, scrolled down to the D's, and called Nathan myself. I thought of all the grievances I'd blast at him as the phone began to ring—skipping our meeting, ignoring my calls, sending Greta to my office after sunset, not caring that I was in the hospital—and as his phone continued to ring, I thought of the most important words I needed to say, the words I'd been too scared to voice earlier: *I'm a night blood, vampires exist, and we're going to survive this together.*

But his phone just kept ringing.

As the evening darkened, the hospital settled into the drones and beeps of quiet hours, and Dominic, as usual, didn't disappoint. The sun had just dipped below the horizon, and shards of sunlight still pierced the sky with red and orange hues when the window curtain fluttered. I couldn't see him. From the angle of the window and the position of my bed, I could only see the sky outside, and not one inch of him had crossed the threshold.

"I thought you had permission to enter, permission that couldn't be revoked," I said to the window.

Silence answered me.

I sighed. "I saw the curtain flutter, Dominic. I know you're there."

"I can only enter your apartment," Dominic admitted. I could hear the grumble of grudging frustration in his voice. "Public places are accessible to me, but this is your room as assigned by your chart. You must invite me before I may enter."

I swallowed. "You didn't turn me. When you had the opportunity, you chose to let me live as a human. Why?"

"I will not explain myself to you while clinging to the side of a building in plain sight," Dominic said stubbornly. "My actions speak for me. If I still haven't earned a modicum of your trust, there's nothing I can say to assuage your doubts. Will you invite me of your own free will, or must I convince a nurse to allow my entrance? Either way I will enter your room, but after all we've survived together, I'd say that such games are beneath us."

I hesitated to agree. Despite what was probably my better judgment, I wanted to let him enter. He hadn't turned me when he'd had the chance, and frankly, I needed answers. On a sigh, I breathed, "Dominic Lysander, you may enter this room."

I blinked, and he was at my bedside. He stared down at me with those otherworldly, luminous blue eyes that reflected the moonlight like a fractured mirror. He was once again the perfect, polished designer version of himself. Gone was any evidence of gargoyle features, savagery, and blood. His hair was immaculately cut, faded on the sides, and styled in a deliberate tousle. His clothes were once again high fashion, fit to his form, and sleek. He looked like trouble, a different sort of trouble than he truly was, but even posh and polished, you couldn't take the predator out of the beast by pinning a bow to its collar.

I lifted my hand and gestured at him to answer to my question. "Well?"

"They haven't given you a sufficient dosage of medication," Dominic said, frowning.

"They gave me exactly the amount necessary," I snapped. "Besides, you haven't even looked at my chart; how do you know how much medicine they did or didn't give me?"

"I know a great deal. Your blood smells delicious. Not as sweet as usual, but not as bitter as it should smell if you were properly medicated." Dominic narrowed his eyes. "You need rest. Night bloods don't heal as quickly while in pain."

"I'll heal just fine," I gritted, having already received this exact lecture from my doctor and several nurses, and also feeling disturbed by the fact that he could smell the sweetness in my blood. "What I need is answers, which I can't ask while drugged into oblivion. Medication wouldn't even be in question if you'd healed me completely," I muttered.

"You think I deliberately left you injured?" he asked. A low vibration hummed through his voice. "When have I ever left you in any condition other than whole and healthy after being in my care?"

I opened my mouth.

Dominic continued before I could respond. "You called Greta. She knew you were severely injured, police had already investigated the scene, and you were declared a missing person. They had already gathered samples of your blood. Although I may have been able to convince everyone that you hadn't called, that the blood wasn't yours, and given you a credible alibi for the twenty-four hours you were missing, Detective Wahl would"—Dominic mulled over his words a moment—"complicate the matter."

"She doesn't know about vampires. She's not a night blood."

"Of course not," Dominic scoffed. "But she doesn't quite believe my version of events, either. In order to convince her, I couldn't change what she already believed. I could only capitalize on it." Dominic leveled his gaze on mine. "You told her vampires were responsible for the murders."

I opened my mouth and closed it, at a loss.

"Yes, I knew about that," he added smugly. "I know everything."

I rolled my eyes.

"So I planted evidence to corroborate her suspicion that a gang, now referred to as vamps, are responsible."

I blinked. "But they aren't. You can't just blame innocent people for crimes that your coven—"

"I can do exactly as I want, and they are in no way innocent. The gang is responsible for other murders. They should have been incarcerated long ago. After I regained control of the coven, I healed you and Ian, and I convinced him of my plan. He brought you to the ER to convince Greta, and I took care of everyone else."

"You healed Walker?" I asked, shocked.

"How else could he have survived?" Dominic said, frowning. He looked offended. "Unless you wanted me to turn you, this was my only option."

"No, I appreciate that you didn't turn me. And I thank you," I said evenly. "But I thought, if given the opportunity, you would anyway."

"Yes," Dominic hissed with an elongated *s*. "I could have healed you completely and erased all memory of you from the humans." Dominic snorted. "Your Ian would've been a problem, of course."

I frowned. "What does Ian, er, Walker have to do with anything?"

"He would have retained the memory of you, and been a, how to put it delicately"—a grin spread across his face as he deliberated—"a permanent pain in my ass."

"Walker's a pain in your ass anyway," I countered. "Why didn't you turn me?"

Dominic rubbed the back of his neck with his palm, and the helplessness of his frustration seemed a very human gesture. "Did you want to be turned?"

"No, but I didn't think my willingness mattered to you," I whispered.

"It didn't, nor should it. I am Master of my coven, and should we need or want more vampires, it's my right to change whom I desire," Dominic said haughtily. "But then, Jillian never wanted to be a member of my coven, and I adopted her as my own anyway." He sighed. "She seemed loyal and steadfast, but she obviously had her own agenda."

I nodded. "What will happen to her and Kaden and their followers?"

Dominic's expression tightened. "Jillian and Kaden are being punished for their crimes against the coven as I see fit. The rebels have once again accepted me as Master, but as my powers wane, it may only be a matter of time before another decides that he or she is capable of overthrowing my rule." He inched closer, his gaze unwavering. "I need someone who will fight my battles by my side, someone who will be my eyes and ears and strength during the day, and I will unequivocally be hers during the night." He met my eyes and smiled a genuine, friendly, lovely smile, knowing that I would love his next words. "I need backup."

I was helpless not to smile back. "I am very good backup."

Dominic nodded, his smile widening to expose his fangs. "Yes, you are. And that is exactly why I did not turn you. You risked your life to save mine. You chose to heal me instead of yourself during a moment in which I never expected such selflessness. And I thank you."

I could feel the heat of my blush to the root of my hairline. I cleared my throat.

"Although we must discuss the fact that you broke your promise."

I leaned my ear closer to him, pretending that I hadn't heard him. "Excuse me?"

"You promised me that you would never again use mind control against me. You swore by the constant and certain passage of time."

My anger was swift and boiling. "You were dying, and I commanded you to heal! If one command should be excluded from that promise, that would be it! You—"

Dominic laughed. "God, your anger is delicious. I am merely, how do you say, kidding."

I blinked, thrown by the genuine pleasure in his laughter. "Oh."

"You saved us. I am not quibbling with that. After my experience with Jillian, however, more imperative than becoming a member of my coven, I feel it imperative that you *want* to become a member of my coven. When I turn you, I'll already have your loyalty from the start."

I tapped my index finger against the mattress, mulling his words. "I'll agree to be your backup and loyally work toward the best interests of your coven if you'll agree to loyally work toward the best interests of this city."

Dominic nodded deeply.

"But understand right now from the start that I do not and never will want to be turned. I'll consider you turning me a violation of our agreement. I will never be your backup as a vampire, even after having been your backup as a human." I was so adamant that my voice shook at the end.

"Night blood," he countered.

"What?"

"You will never be my backup as a vampire, even after having been my backup as a *night blood*."

"Semantics," I snapped. "You understand what I'm saying."

He tried to mask it, but I could see Dominic smelling the air. His expression darkened and tightened and a very low, nearly imperceptible growl rumbled from his chest. I realized that he could smell the scent of my mounting anger, and he liked it. He liked it a lot.

"This isn't a game," I whispered

"This is all a game," he said hoarsely. "You just haven't moved any of your pieces."

"I thought such games were beneath us," I mocked, trying to temper my anger. He was right. I'd been bombarded by attacks this entire week and only reacting to them. Even my one plan to infiltrate the coven was for Walker, and we'd all barely survived.

Dominic reached out and smoothed his thumb down the side of my neck. He closed his eyes for a moment, his fingertips resting against my pulse, and I tried to keep my breath steady. I felt my heart spike despite my efforts, and Dominic groaned.

"Some games are worth playing," he said, and the timbre of his voice was once again under control. "And I have a move for you."

I lifted my eyebrows.

"As I understand, Walker has extended you an invitation to visit him at his home in the country."

I nodded, not sure where he could possibly be going with this conversation, but positive I wouldn't like it one bit.

"You should visit him."

I blinked. "I should?"

"Yes. He is deeply involved with his Master there, and she will no doubt question our alliance after yesterday's events. You must represent yourself as exactly what you are to me, a night blood who has willingly agreed to help the Master of your city. You must present me in the best possible light, prove that my alliance with her has not dwindled, and display your anticipation of being turned."

My temper erupted. "I am *not* anticipating being turn—"

Dominic covered my mouth with his hand and rolled his eyes on a sigh. "I know. I understand your position on the matter perfectly, but that is the role you will play. She will see in you the exact person she is trying to create in Walker, and she will come to me in peace to understand how such a feat was accomplished rather than in war."

Understanding dawned and my temper alleviated slightly. "You want me to soften her image of you."

"Yes. Walker was gravely injured in my coven. Although I healed his injuries, Bex will undoubtedly consider this a break in our alliance. Her coven is smaller, but she is older and more powerful than me when I'm at full strength. As the Leveling approaches, I grow weaker every day. With my coven threatening rebellion, I'm sure another coup will rise before the month's end; the last thing we need is a vampire like Bex to compound the issue."

I frowned. "Would she attempt to usurp the coven from you?"

"I believe her main focus for many years now has been Walker. If she believes that course has run dry, I don't know where her motives may refocus, but I'm certain that I don't want them focused on me or my coven. Since she won't allow me to mend our bond in person without declaring war between us, you must go in my stead."

I had planned to visit Walker anyway, so Dominic's plans would only expedite my own. "All right. Agreed, but I have a request of my own."

Dominic nodded. "Of course, *partner*," he said on a grin. "I wouldn't expect anything less."

I pursed my lips, unsure how to proceed. "Could a member of your coven have turned a night blood into a vampire without you knowing it?"

"Absolutely not. Despite what Jillian and Kaden claim, only a Master's blood has the strength to sustain the night blood through the change." Dominic's eyes narrowed. "Why do you ask? Is there another vampire who has approached you?" Dominic growled.

I shook my head, not wanting to fight about Kaden. I had other concerns. "You also mentioned that had you turned me into a vampire, you could erase my human life. What did you mean by that?"

Dominic pursed his lips. "No one would remember that you existed, except of course other night bloods."

I covered my face with my hands, suddenly exhausted and sickened.

"What do these questions have to do with your request?" Dominic asked. He seemed truly baffled.

"I think I—" I began, but my voice broke. I swallowed and started again. "I think I need your help to find my brother. I think he might have been a night blood."

Dominic nodded. "Considering you're a night blood, that is most certainly the case of any sibling. But why would you need my help finding him? Wouldn't a simple call suffice?" Dominic asked dryly. "Or do you want to bring me along as proof when you break the big, bad news to him?"

I swallowed again, attempting to speak calmly through the emotion clogging my throat. "No, I think he knew more about vampires than either of us wanted to admit. And I don't think he's a night blood anymore." My voice broke again on a sob. I clenched my hands into tight, impenetrable fists to pull myself together and speak past the grief. "Dominic, I need your help to find Nathan because I think he might be dead. Or worse, I think he might be a vampire."

Loved THE CITY BENEATH?
Keep reading for a sneak peek at SWEET LAST DROP,
the next book in Melody Johnson's thrilling Night Blood series
Available Fall 2015

"I can't wait to see you, darlin'," Walker said, at least once per conversation during the multiple phone calls we'd enjoyed daily for three weeks. I would have found his consistency and regularity toward someone else nauseating, but between all the *darlin'*s and *ma'am*s, we shared an indelible bond that went beyond incorrigible flirtation. Meredith assured me that I owed it to myself to discover how deep that bond could grow, but I remained skeptical of both him and my feelings for him. We'd only been in the same place for one week. How well could I legitimately come to know a person in one week? But when I looked back at the week we'd shared and survived, I swallowed my doubts.

"Pu-lease, you say that to all the girls," I said to him. My tone was deliberately sarcastic, but I was glad we were over the phone; he'd know by my ridiculous smile that I was just as excited to finally see him, too. "You forget that I've seen you in action."

"You certainly have." Walker's voice deepened salaciously, and I was reminded of that one night in my office. He'd lifted me onto my desk, and his strong hands had touched me in places I'd never thought I could feel again.

I swallowed. "My point is that this is a business trip. Carter finally approved the piece on crime fluctuation—"

"That I encouraged you to write," Walker interrupted.

I rolled my eyes. "—and as one of my primary sources, you and I will—"

"Be spending hours upon hours alone together."

"For interviews on your experiences and discussions on crime rates and—"

"I have an experience I'd like to discuss: how delicious your body felt against mine."

I sighed heavily. "You're killing me."

Walker laughed. "Good."

"I really am writing this story, Walker, despite your ulterior motives for inviting me to your home."

"You like my ulterior motives. The most grievous crime at the moment is how long it took for Carter to approve your damn story. I miss you, DiRocco."

I swallowed again and forced myself to say the words because they were true. "I miss you, too."

And now, after three weeks of battling with Carter, avoiding Greta's stink-eyed interrogation, bracing against Dominic's creeping advances, and swallowing my festering doubts about Nathan, I had finally arrived in Erin, New York, early this afternoon for what should have been a vacation from all those demons back in the city. Walker was just as blond and tall and capable as I remembered. A month apart hadn't changed the aching thrill I'd felt at seeing him or the warmth of his giant-like hands as they spanned across my back in hello at the bus terminal. I tried keeping my thoughts grounded in the real purpose of my visit to Erin, New York, to make Bex's acquaintance and forge an alliance for Dominic, but an entire month on the phone had somehow only strengthened my physical feelings for Walker.

Less than twenty-four hours into our reunion, however, and Walker and I weren't putting the moves on either my career or each other. He'd barely had time to give me a proper tour of the town before we were once again, as I'd remembered all too well from his last visit into the city, staring at a body.

Her name was Lydia Bowser, and she was last seen by her grandmother, leaving the farm for a walk before dinner. According to her grandmother and Walker's detailed notes, she'd loved the last moments of daylight, when the sun had already dipped below the horizon but its rays still lit the sky with a dim, burning glow. I raised my eyebrows at the description, both from its nostalgia and its telling time frame. Foul play after dark only meant one thing.

Melody Johnson graduated magna cum laude from Lycoming College with her B.A. in creative writing and psychology. While still earning her degree, she worked as an editing intern for Wahida Clark at Wahida Clark Presents Publishing. She was a copyeditor for several novels now in print, including *Cheetah* by Missy Jackson; *Trust No Man II* by Cash; and *Karma with a Vengeance* by Tash Hawthorne. Currently, she's a client relationship coordinator and copywriter for Internet Inspirations, Inc. An active member in Romance Writers of America (RWA), Melody has attended many conferences to hone her craft, including NJ RWA "Put Your Heart in a Book" conference, GA RWA "Moonlight & Magnolias" conference, and GLVWG "The Write Stuff" conference. When she isn't working or writing, Melody can be found hiking the many woodsy trails in her Pocono, Pennsylvania, hometown or sunning and swimming at the beach.